Supper with the Borgias

by Richard Jones

THE THREE SUITORS

SUPPER WITH THE BORGIAS

Supper with the Borgias

A Novel by

RICHARD JONES

These days of disinheritance, we feast
On human heads . . .
           On these we live,
No longer on the ancient cake of seed,
The almond and deep fruit. This bitter meat
Sustains us . . .
           Who, then, are they, seated here?
Is the table a mirror in which they sit and look?
Are they men eating reflections of themselves?

WALLACE STEVENS : *'Cuisine Bourgeoise'*

An Atlantic Monthly Press Book

LITTLE, BROWN AND COMPANY   BOSTON   TORONTO

LIBRARY OF CONGRESS CATALOG CARD NO. 69–12635

FIRST AMERICAN EDITION

Published in England under the title
THE TOY CRUSADERS

The author wishes to thank Alfred A. Knopf, Inc., for permission to quote from "Cuisine Bourgeoise", one of the poems in *Parts of a World* by Wallace Stevens, copyright 1942 by Wallace Stevens.

For my wife

ATLANTIC–LITTLE, BROWN BOOKS
ARE PUBLISHED BY
LITTLE, BROWN AND COMPANY
IN ASSOCIATION WITH
THE ATLANTIC MONTHLY PRESS

PRINTED IN THE UNITED STATES OF AMERICA

Part One

In the hours between the setting of the crescent moon and daybreak, the deck passengers, talking and smoking through the last reaches of the journey, were the first to see Mount Atthis rising slowly on the eastern horizon. It rose in a dark mass against the sapphire sky and the white tangle of the stars. The summer, just officially ended, lingered in the still air and held the sea in its power. As far as the eye could see, the waters of the Mediterranean were stretched out like a silk screen, and brimmed, without motion, the harbours where mercantile civilisation had had one of its first homes. Under such a night, moving to such a shore, it was natural to assume divine purpose working through the lives of men, and to find, in the night-skies, a mask of the numinous. This was the night and the coast of the early Christian fathers, who subsumed in notions of rebirth and redemption earlier cults, at once more mystical and orgiastic, and some of the earliest dialogues between man and his creator. At any moment, a light not of this world might glitter like a cosmic sparkler at forty-five degrees to the calm sea, and the destinies of all those on board the liner be changed for ever.

There were lights certainly – from cars moving up and down the mountain roads behind Baida, from heavy traffic on the coast, and from the blue and white Pharos at the harbour mouth, which lit the bay with regular sweeps of light. At that hour, this was the only welcome for the ship. Welcome back! it seemed to say: *Soyez le bienvenu! Ahlan wa sahlan!* Welcome! The piers of the harbour received the liner after her voyage from Marseilles, and she came to rest under a promontory crowded with pastel-coloured buildings, some in the arcaded Turkish fashion, some four-square and many storeyed in the international modern style. Once the engines were off, the sounds suggestive of North Africa and Western Asia, the muezzins and the cockcrows, carried offshore and evoked palm-trees, domes, and women with water-jugs on their heads.

Nothing could have been more prosaic than the near landscape of warehouses, customs-sheds and cranes, and the only thing which distinguished the Baida skyline from the European ports was its unfamiliar scale and emphasis. A minaret was counterbalanced by an Italianate campanile, a Turkish *khan* by a French railway station; festoons of telephone wires united the whole. Under the pressure to make a hundred-per-cent profit, Baida could permit itself the contradictions which might be fatal elsewhere; and because of this commercial pressure, this town of very ancient foundation, with its roots in Phoenicia, Greece, Rome, Byzantium and Arabia, gives up its essence slowly and confusingly.

In terms of trade and manners, it is sworn to both east and west. It names itself The Gateway of the Orient, the bridge between two worlds, but it is anchored finally in neither. Like shot silk, its colours depend on the viewpoint and the light. On certain days the French provincial imprint is strongest, and the Orient is little more than a cultivated, exotic element, as in the paintings of Delacroix. It needs only a wedding procession or a Muslim feast to change all this, as the crowds take the city back into Arabia and leave the Crusader churches that have become mosques, and the nightclubs with their unreal nostalgia for Paris and New York, as so much imported irrelevance. To make up for its inability to commit itself, Baida involves the newcomer in its colour, gaiety and vitality; and even its business streets give out an implied promise. After a time it becomes clear that the promise will not be fulfilled, because the town lacks all sense of responsibility. Like a host who opens his door to all comers, the port smiles for everyone – and establishes a personal standing with nobody. Because of this, nothing can be depended on or taken for granted. The dove of heaven is always about to descend, but the serpent is coiled around the tree waiting for the dove to alight.

RHODA and Neville, the brother and sister named after characters in the novel which pleased their mother in her last days of pregnancy, were on the deck with the first light. The water in the harbour was still and clear; beyond the breakwaters the Mediterranean was shot with different shades of blue. Overhead the azure sky deepened and gradually absorbed all but the white bars of the liner's Greek flag. It was the morning of 21 September.

The harbour gates had not opened, the customs men were not expected until six o'clock and so no one could go ashore. The brother and sister had the promenades to themselves, where they could watch the apricot dawn behind the mountains and sniff the early morning. It was a process of re-rooting. Windows and doors which had been shut during their three months in England were reopened, and they felt they were in business again as human beings. They were free to be contradictory and spontaneous, in sensual rapport with themselves and the world around them. They were complex people, and they needed Baida's complexity. They were people with a sense of the distant past – inherited from their father – and they needed the suggestibility of that coast.

Rhoda spoke for them both when she said the voyage had renewed her: 'I immediately feel so well. Everything I do is right for me. It's really a sort of ecstasy. Why, in God's name, do we ever go back to London? There's nothing for either of us there. We don't fit in. We never have.'

They carried with them, like a hair-shirt, their vision of the London they detested and the sensation, on arriving at London airport, that they had reached the end of the track, but there was one shadow over her return: her husband, known to herself and Neville as The Consort. Shortly before she left for England she had been sleeping apart from him, and the great debate for herself and her brother, all the way back, was whether Rhoda and The Consort would re-establish normal marital relations.

Rhoda looked tragic. 'The idea of congress with The Consort doesn't appeal to me vastly. At this moment, nothing could be further from my calculations. Of course, so much depends on the mood of the moment. If he stirs himself to meet us, instead of just sending his driver, I may feel touched, and everything will come right. I might want him madly as soon as I see him. On the other hand, I may not. You see how it is with us. The Consort just hasn't got any conversation. When we're not going to parties or eating out or driving around or making love, there's nothing to say. A marriage is on the right lines when a couple can find something to chat about all day. Marriage is chit-chat. It's nothing if it's not a long conversation. I mean, as soon as you meet you've got hundreds of small things to say to one another. You get rid of all your doubts and contradictions. And the other one understands perfectly what's a temporary mood and what's part of the permanent drift. I tried to explain this to The Duchess, and she didn't understand. She said I married him on the rebound, and that was what people got. I think she's going to take The Consort's side.'

'Rubbish. The Duchess is here to rest and relax. She won't interfere.'

Rhoda turned this over, and then agreed that The Duchess – their stepmother – was in a 'melting mood' and had been ever since they left London. On the boat she had been docile, easily amused, impressed by the scenery and the people. In short, she had behaved exactly as they knew she could not be expected to behave for long.

The Duchess joined them shortly, dressed for going ashore. She had her sun-glasses on, a green scarf tied over her green straw 'fun-hat', bought in Genoa, and the matching straw hand-bag dangled from her plump wrist. Between the dark lenses, the scarf, an escape of hair and the low sun-hat, all that could be seen of her face were two deep lines either side of her mouth, a flattish little nose and bunched-up lips picked out with lipstick. She had plump arms, like the more cosy kind of village postmistress and, as became a former semi-imperial lady from Cairo, a vast sense of her own worth. Although she was short and plumpish, with thick, unfashionable ankles, there was nothing short about her aura. By holding her head back, by piling a high hat on her head and by letting everyone know that she was not to be trifled with, she imposed a seven-foot-tall quality.

9

Neville was the first to kiss her lightly on both cheeks: 'You look splendid, Duchess. Ready for anything.'

The Duchess kissed Rhoda: 'The best night's rest since we joined the boat. I can see how much good this trip is doing me. I'm completely unwound.' She joined them for a turn on the deck. As she put her arm around their waists – they were not much taller than she was – she thanked them for being so good to her.

Rhoda and Neville were impressed by their stepmother, even when she riled them. Her enthusiasm was admirable; and her opinions, often crusty and sharp, made her, at her best, good company. They could see what their dead father – her second husband – had liked in her, and this was important for their relationship. Her first husband, the distinguished Anglo-Egyptian official, was known to the brother and sister as The Provider. Among the Things Provided were The Duchess's jewels, what she called her 'small but perfect' house near fishing water in Herefordshire, and keen social values.

3

THE dock gates opened and people drifted in. The Consort – to everyone's surprise – turned up with his driver. He waved from the quay below: 'Bless you! Lovely to see you!' They talked in half-shouts over the side of the ship – the customs men were still expected – and Rhoda, suddenly remembering her own diplomatic passport, tried to advance their disembarkation. She bustled along to the ship's officers, who told her nothing could be done until the ship had been cleared. She began to raise her voice in a high-handed, British way, which did not help, and the men hardly bothered to hide their amusement. They knew her better than she knew herself. During her time on the liner they had observed the child-like absorption in the role of the minute, which some people took for eccentricity; and they knew that, at that instant, she was being an embassy wife, prepared to slap everyone across his face with her C.D. passport. The more she shouted, the more they delighted to thwart her. It was no go. She retired, baffled, back to the promenade rail where Neville and The Duchess were ticking off The Consort's points. They decided he had a good, superior sort of presence but dressed in a 'common way'. The Duchess made Neville laugh until the pupils of his cold little eyes danced and were shot with light, when she said that nobody ought to wear suède shoes before six o'clock in the morning. 'But why not, Duchess?'

Rhoda knew exactly what The Duchess meant. 'They look so *intimate* at this time of the morning. Wicked, importuning shoes.'

'And nobody wears a moustache like that any more. It dates him so much. It makes him look older than he is.'

'In fact, nobody is English in the way The Consort is English any more.'

'How clever you are, Neville.' The Duchess was genuinely impressed. 'That's the whole matter in a nutshell.'

Meanwhile, the poor Consort stood below them in a position of disadvantage, and his grey Prince of Wales check suit, his expensive brown suède shoes, his ash-blond handlebar moustache, his sweet smile and his soft, ineffective hands were nothing. He waved up to them as much as to say, 'There can't be anything more that's fit for us to shout across the heads of the crowd, so can we please wait until we meet before we say another word?'

The Duchess looked at Rhoda in wonder: 'But you can't have a single thing in common. Why are you bothering to go back to him?'

Rhoda became mystical – her way of playing for time – but Neville had the harsh answer: 'Because there's no one except The Consort who can offer her a comfortable life here at this moment.'

Rhoda agreed: 'I can't think of anyone who gives me just what The Consort does. I really am free, more or less, to go and come as I please.'

'But that's all wrong! Marriage isn't like living together in a station waiting-room, with a quick sandwich in between trains. He's not a man. It's disgusting to be so apathetic about . . . about . . . one's wife. I mean, a man's got to show a bit of sinew sometimes.'

like his, marriage is a haven of refuge where he can doze his

'The fires of life are low in The Consort. For a tired soul life away, and wake up from time to time to ask for an ice-cold lager and place a bet on the two-thirty.'

Rhoda was most displeased, even though Neville was merely quoting back at her things she had said in the past: 'Please don't talk about my marriage like that. Please!' She paused for emphasis. 'Certain things are sacred.'

'Come off it!'

'I'm serious.'

Neville stood back and did a hasty version of a hornpipe while singing the old music hall song with which he had teased his sister since childhood:

> 'Rhoda, Rhoda, ran a pagoda!
> Selling teas and ices and soda!
> The milkman never leaves his can
> In the little pagoda Rhoda ran.'

At that moment, Rhoda was taking her marriage seriously – she ignored him. 'I say, isn't that Paul Brophy?'

They waved, and the man waved back, as he joined The Consort.

'So that's your chum, Paul.' The Duchess had never seen him before. 'He's what I call decent-looking.'

Rhoda blew Paul a kiss. 'He's a frightfully good Arabist.'

Neville picked her up: 'All your acquaintances are "frightfully good Arabists" if they can count up to ten in Arabic, which is about all Paul can do.'

'What a silly lie. You know quite well he's lived in Tunisia and Algeria for years and nearly went over to Islam.'

The Duchess thought this excessive.

Rhoda disagreed: 'His point of view is perfectly clear: you'll never understand the Arab world until you know the Koran.'

'But he can still only count to ten.'

'That's a lie. Why do you want to cut him down? He does marvels in his office with a mixed staff of Egyptians, Baidanis and Lebanese, who all adore him!'

Neville laughed cynically: 'Arabs never adore Englishmen. That's an old romantic lie dreamed up by stupid people who thought there was a "special relationship".'

'Well, they'll eat out of his hand.'

'They won't. They distrust all Englishmen as hypocrites. And double-dyed ones, too.'

The Duchess was struck by Brophy's appearance: 'He towers over everybody. A really splendid young man.' Even The Consort seemed diminished at Brophy's side. The Duchess wanted to know what his firm was.

'MEDOC.'

'Isn't that a table wine?'

'Middle East Documentary Centre. He's got a plum job. It's under UNESCO.'

'You get everything mixed up, Rhoda. It was started by the French before the war in order to correlate information about economic developments, especially oil and uranium; it was helped by Gulbenkian and Rockefeller grants – and now it's fallen into British hands. It's a purely commercial undertaking.'

The Duchess thought any man with Rockefeller and Gulbenkian behind him must be a success. 'What does the centre do?'

'What its title implies. It documents the Middle East, which in this case takes in North Africa, this place, Ethiopia, Somalia and Pakistan. God knows why.'

'Yes, but what for?'

'God knows. It's an academic thing and is addressed to academics. Isn't that enough?'

Rhoda, determined that justice should be done to Brophy, protested: 'You make everything absurd. And it's not. It's a most valuable service, and there's a possibility that the local university may take it over.'

'But is it worth doing? I mean . . . producing sheets of facts and figures which tired tycoons and dim researchers flick through. Can't help but be dull. Masses of figures and tabulations. Grim Arab specialists working out percentages and foretelling growth. Would bore me to tears.'

The Duchess asked about Brophy's wife. Rhoda shook her head.

Brophy knew they were talking about him and raised a hand stiffly from time to time, like a little boy playing soldiers. He was ill-at-ease with The Consort and moved from one large foot to the other and kept running thick fingers through an untidy thatch – very Cambridge – as he talked. He looked uneasily over the swarming crowd around him, waiting for liberation from his companion.

From afar, The Duchess was impressed by him because he gave the impression of being a man of character and sinew – in contrast to The Consort, who tended to bend about like a plastic rod. Neville was jealous of the good impression his friend had made. 'He's rather a tenebrous creature, really. His soul is full of unswept corners. I'd like to know what makes him tick.'

4

WHEN, eventually, the customs men came aboard, there was a further delay, so that the travellers and The Consort and Brophy went into a saloon to wait, and The Duchess observed that if the officials wore less comic opera uniform and put more thought into their work they would be able to leave more quickly.

The Consort, who was silently holding the hands of his wife, looked up in surprise: 'But they're really most efficient and helpful.'

'You've been here too long, my lad.'

The Consort accepted The Duchess's opinion without comment. In any case, he was gazing into his wife's eyes, speechless with devotion. They sat back from the crowd, lost to the world, like Dido and Aeneas in the Purcell opera, while Rhoda debated whether she wanted her husband or not, at the same time thinking, 'Our non-conversation is beginning.' She was pleased to see him, although unsure whether she was any less detached. The great question – what was there to like about him except his salary and his perks of office? – remained unanswered.

Their hand-holding ('ridiculous pair!') irritated The Duchess, and the exclamation marks gathered around her head like a porcupine's quills. She turned to Neville and Brophy with a deliberate gesture, and they walked off together.

Brophy towered over them like a giant with two children, and half bent his neck to speak to them. He had a faded, apologetic manner, not at all what The Duchess had expected; and, observed at close quarters, his face was – as Neville had suggested – tenebrous and pouchy. He was very dark, with lifeless eyes and with thick, prominent, rather out-rolled lips. He looked like a physicist or a mathematician – intellectual without being perceptive. All the same, he had a certain self-importance and began asking The Duchess about her Herefordshire neighbours in the conventional English way. To cut the probing and social prancing short, Neville said: 'Paul's mother is one of the Mortimers.' He twinkled wickedly. 'On his paternal grandmother's side he's a Fitzpierpoint, so only the Brophy is plebeian.'

Brophy looked at Neville in surprise but was too slow to think of a suitable reply. The Duchess understood his dilemma: 'I'm very proud of my forebears; and I'm sure you're no exception, Mr Brophy.'

Brophy was suddenly enchanted by her understanding and smiled gratefully, showing a lot of teeth and gum. There was no doubt he was a defenceless man.

To make talk, Rhoda asked whether The Consort had seen much of Brophy. The Consort, without releasing his wife's hands or altering for an instant his hieratic position, said it was rumoured Brophy was a queer.

'Does that matter?'

'I don't care. They say he lets it influence his judgement.'

'In what way?'

'At work. Promotes unsuitable people and goes to unsuitable lengths about the wrong kind.'

'He has his *mignons*, you mean.'

The Consort looked vague, completely uninterested. 'So they say. They say similar things about anyone these days. They've probably said them about me.'

Rhoda disengaged one hand in order to tuck her hair under her hat. 'Yes, I'd certainly want to be more definite before I passed comment or allowed it to influence me.' She formally replaced her hand in the hands of her husband, who still sat staring at her moonily with every hair of his huge moustache appeased and relaxed.

'Don't mention this to The Duchess. She's got a thing about homosexuals.'

The Consort, never a fan, observed that The Duchess probably had 'things' about a good many subjects. He was not involved. Then he suddenly shook his head like a water-dog rising from the river. 'Darling, you look more lovely than ever.'

'Sweet of you.' She gave him a provocative glance with her absurd, half-closed eyes and decided she wanted him. 'So sweet of you.'

5

THE CONSORT invited Brophy back to his house for breakfast, and the party arrived there about half-past seven.

The old Ottoman house was in a distinguished residential backwater, only a stone's throw from the banking district. It stood alone in its own grounds, on its own eminence and approached by a flight of elegant stairs.

The servants were leaning over the balustrade, looking down the hilly, shady street, and, as soon as they saw the cars, they ran: *'Ahlan, Madame. Ahlan wa sahlan!'* The servants loved Rhoda. She was simple and generous with them, and rarely noticed their pilferings. The heavy gates creaked open, more shouting and joy, and then Rhoda began the climb towards the house under overflowing heads of jasmine and bougainvillaea. At the first turning of the stairs was the bust of the old warrior, the house's tutelary spirit, engarlanded with variegated ivy. At the stairhead, a huge urn overflowed with geraniums. It formed the end of a balustrade entwined with white jasmine. Behind the balustrade was the breakfast-table.

An old man, who padded around every morning in his baggy trousers while he swabbed down the terrace and watered the garden, came forward with a bunch of gladiolus: *'Ahlan wa sahlan, Madame!'* Rhoda gasped with appreciation and pleasure. Everyone cried *'Ahlan wa sahlan!'* and clapped: a moment of pure goodwill. Through the brilliant spikes of gladiolus Rhoda saw the black-and-white tiled terrace, the slender white ironwork chairs and table, the roses in the middle of the table and, beyond, the drama of the city skyline – skyscrapers and old houses white in the sun, pigeons rising and falling from rooftop cotes, a boat moving in a clear curve across the still bay and, behind and over all, the blue-green mountains, lightly tipped with morning cloud towards Sittaya. 'Why does one go away?' Rhoda smiled at her household. 'I'll tell you. For the sheer pleasure of coming back.' She handed the flowers to a servant and passed into the house.

Brophy sat down near the table with The Consort and, while they drank orange juice, heard the women in the house pursuing Rhoda with cries of '*Ahlan*'. Brophy was fascinated by her. When she talked or moved or made a strange movement with her head it was like watching a film of, say, 1932 or 1933.

6

THAT evening, The Consort threw a party for the new arrivals, and about forty people turned up. A buffet was laid out where the breakfast-table had been and a bar set up in the poetic little garden at the side of the house.

The Duchess was solemnly introduced to all the guests. She was at her worst because, under her panache and white hair arranged like a *pièce montée*, she was not sure people found her attractive. To compensate for uncertainty she spoke more forcibly than was needed about trivial things.

'Such a pleasure,' she was saying at one point, 'to have servants around you again. My dear, I tried to get a gardener for my little place near Hereford, and, do you know, they wanted every penny of eight pounds a week?'

The American girl looked vague: 'How much is that in dollars?'

'About twenty-four!' The Duchess replied dramatically.

'You mean to say you can get a full-time gardener for twenty-four dollars a week!' The American girl was aghast. 'Why, I'd be ashamed to employ a boy of fifteen at that salary a week. I really would. I mean to say, what can a family man *do* with twenty-four dollars a week, even in England?'

'It's the going wage.'

'You call that a wage? My, you English people have some feudal ideas. I spend that much every month on cigarettes, movies and drink.'

'I think it would go rather further in Herefordshire.' The Duchess pulled down the shutters on the conversation and half turned aside with her drink, as though dismissing the girl.

7

NEVILLE waited until this moment before rushing into the American girl's arms.

'Fay!'

'Neville!'

'Fay, darling!'

They both burst out laughing, although the girl was afraid of Neville's tongue and never knew where she stood with him. Neville led her to one of the white chairs. 'Who in God's name is that haughty-looking old woman who pays slave wages back in England, Europe?'

Neville placed a finger on the girl's orange lips. 'Hush, child, that's my stepmother, the woman my father married for companionship and intellectual stimulus four years ago.'

'Why didn't you tell me? I might have got really rude, or something.'

His eyes flashed with wicked, inner joys: 'I heard you! It served her damned well right.' He drew closer. 'I want you this evening. I'm famished. A long voyage without anyone on board one could be sweet on.'

The girl pulled a wry mouth: 'Didn't you find anyone in England, Europe, who'd have you? You're becoming a social problem. Dashing about making up to all the unmarried secretaries, and not so much as whispering of honourable intentions. You've got to get this resolved, Neville.'

'But Fay . . . you're so adorable, so tantalising.'

'You don't mean it.' She said this, but she took him half-seriously. 'I've already told you that you're not going to possess my body. No one is. My mind is made up.'

'You're getting older, Fay. Time is passing for both of us.'

'Hey! Speak for yourself. I'm very happy as I am.'

Fay began telling Neville how difficult it would be for them to save their friendship, 'which I really do value,' if they became lovers. 'I've seen these local *affaires*. They last a movie show and a party, and that's that.'

Neville raised his eyes in mock horror. 'Fay, listen to me. Please listen. Dearest child, hasn't anyone told you? That's all so old-fashioned. It dates you like my brother-in-law's moustache. People don't have those attitudes any more. Assume we sleep together. Assume we make love madly, passionately, and in the morning we decided it was all a mistake. So what? We'd still have the memory of that physical pleasure between us, wouldn't we? And whenever I looked at you, there'd be that warm light in my eye, and whenever you looked at me there'd be that warm light in yours. That's all life is for. Just turning on the warm light in other people's eyes.'

'Please. Please. Neville. It doesn't make sense to me. This place is full of people with warm eyes, all looking for people in the same state. No, Neville, for me it's a change to have the other.'

'How exciting for you.' Then, ruthlessly: 'How can you keep so West Orange and virginal, when all those lovely warm eyes are lit up for you everywhere?'

'Arab men repel me.'

'Well, I'm not Arab.'

'Maybe, but in your mental attitudes you are. I always feel I'm dealing with an Oriental when I speak to you.'

Neville had never heard this before and was fascinated: 'What makes you say that?'

'Everyone thinks so, Neville. All your attitudes are oriental.'

He pressed her to be more explicit, but Fay (repeating someone else's remark) had nothing to add.

'If being oriental means taking happiness when it comes, then I'm oriental.'

'You certainly are, Neville. You get a big bang out of life.'
She added this in case she'd offended him in some way.

Neville felt no mercy for her: 'I think men repel you.' He
pretended to sulk.

'Now, Neville, that's bitchy. What's more, it's untrue. You
keep saying it to torture me, and I don't think it's funny.'

Neville sighed again and felt the teasing had gone on long
enough. 'Let me get you a drink.' He brought her another glass
of *vin rosé*, then ditched her and went back to the buffet table.
He put on his elegant new half-moon glasses in order to
examine the spread more thoroughly.

8

NEVILLE was the only member of his family who ate the local
food from choice, and The Consort, a liberal host with an aristo-
cratic sense of responsibility towards his guests, had provided
abundantly. Among the open plates of cold meats and European salads were *kibbeh* (in lozenges), stuffed vine-leaves, deep
bowls of *tabbouleh*, oval platters of fish and rice and several
small round local slipware dishes of Egyptian beans and *homos*,
the chickpea paste, set down wherever there was a spare place.

Neville began working from one end of the table and, absorbed in his discoveries, nearly tripped over The Duchess,
moving in the opposite direction. She whistled when she saw
the pile on his plate: 'How do you keep so slim and neat? You
eat like a gannet!' She was resentment itself, as she showed
him her own plate, with its hardboiled egg and a bit of cos
lettuce.

'I didn't know you were on a diet.'

'Oh,' – more aggrieved than ever – 'I'm not. There's nothing
fit to eat.'

She reminded him that in ten years in Cairo she had never
allowed Arabic food at her table. A grilled chicken, perhaps,
or a shashlik, but all the whipped-up oily things – never! To
work out her irritation with Fay she became upstage about

Arabic food in general—'So fattening and indigestible!' – and took a mere spoon-tip of *tabbouleh* to prove her point. 'The women sit around like fat hens eating those honey-and-nut cakes until you can hardly see their lips for grease. Too disgusting for words.'

'But why should it upset you? If they like honey cakes and get fat – so what? It's no good getting unhappy about it.'

'*I'm* not unhappy.'

'Oh, come off it, darling, it makes you very unhappy. Let things be as they are – the facts are always wrong, people are always illogical. The times are always out of joint, but you must learn to be happy. This is the east, and happiness *must* fall out of the skies, or it will never come.'

'These finicky, twizzled-up things to eat! Nothing to do with happiness at all. We always served two good rounds of meat: cold beef and cold ham for the non-Mohammedans – something substantial you could cut, with lots of salads. *That* was my idea of a cold collation.'

Neville shrugged.

'It's the usual thing now to serve local-style buffets if you have Baidani guests. The people – and the food – are too rich to be ignored. You can't spit on the Baidanis as you spat on the Egyptians.'

'And people are so rude. Who is that dreadful American girl with a mouth like a split tangerine? I could have killed her cheerfully.'

'You let Fay get under your skin?' Neville picked up a table-napkin before moving away with his haul. 'She's a professor at the local American Girls' College.'

9

KATHERINE THOMSON, resplendent in purple and deep pink, was holding on to Rhoda's arm and laughing with the pleasure of seeing the brother and sister again. 'That gorgeous tea-set you brought me!' She released Rhoda, kissed Neville and walked into the garden with him, complaining about an earlier reception at the Kuwaiti Embassy. 'They've gone dry again and, although their fruit juices are *packed* with vitamins and goodness, give me a drop of the hard stuff. Do you know, Margot was there cheerfully emptying her own gin into her juice? You know – those small totty bottles you buy on planes – she'd brought them in her hand-bag.'

Neville and Katherine sat down. 'You're looking ravishing!' It was his usual kind of exaggerated compliment, which she now knew how to take.

'Now tell me all about London. What's going on? What did you get up to?'

Neville told her those things that were of interest, and she told him where people were bathing, what they were saying, eating and drinking, who had given parties of note, who was new, and who had gone away. Katherine Thomson had adopted the inflexions and values of the brother and sister in addition to her own. As she and her husband had found their living, if not their pleasure, in the east, they were permanent residents, who observed and documented those on short contracts with an expert and socially aware eye. They knew almost everyone and knew when and how to discard acquaintances, an essential gift. A local contracting firm paid Thomson far more than he would have earned at home, and success had made them a little arrogant – at all events, they were the ones who bestowed patronage and enjoyed putting new people in their places. As with Neville and Rhoda, theirs was the snobbery of connections, intelligence and general switched-on-ness; unlike the brother and sister, for whom snobbery was an end in itself, the Thomsons cultivated it to give their life the social form it lacked. Underneath the social blandness they were serious people, hard-headed and involved in events. For this reason, Baida bored them – the boredom coming in waves – and deprived them of chances to get the best out of themselves. Richard Thomson would have dabbled in local politics, written to the press, expressed not always entirely predictable opinions; in Baida the delicately balanced political background meant that all involvement was forbidden, and, in a society where corruption was the norm, the big joke, they looked on and pretended to be amused. They tried hard to put down roots. They took Arabic and French lessons, they cultivated local acquaintances, and, supreme test of good faith, they bought themselves a country retreat. They wore themselves out travelling back and forth to the mountains, and eventually had to sell because no one cared to drive so far for a visit. In looking for somewhere nearer town, Katherine had heard of a villa in Ain-al-Nabi. Should they go up there the next day, taking a picnic lunch? Neville agreed, and Katherine included Rhoda in her invitation.

'She's already booked up like the new tart.'

'Then let's take your stepmother off her hands.'

'Rhoda would like that.'

'How are things? I didn't have a chance to ask her.'

'Just at present she and The Consort are holding hands all the time. They've hardly unclasped since we got here.'

'Hope it lasts. The trouble with Rhoda is that she goes off people so quickly.'

'Luckily The Consort has the patience of Job. He's always there.'

10

BACK and forth went the conversational tennis-ball in the high, artificial voices people at parties use when they imagine wit and sophistication are called for. They were half-laughing all the time, but more at their own cleverness. This was part of Neville's effect on people. He gave off self-confidence and a sort of dry mental crackle which made people hesitate to make banal remarks to him; he pinned down bulbous conversations with a flash of his wicked little eyes. In the pursuit of a funny phrase or image almost anything could be said. It was because of this that Katherine enjoyed his company, while her husband – who was slower – found it tiresome. For Richard Thomson, Neville was one of his wife's clever friends. He tolerated him because they made her happy and, as there was no suggestion that she and Neville were lovers, the friendship throve. Thomson could not even dimly imagine that a woman married to him could find any charm in a Neville.

And London, Katherine asked with an expatriate's intensity: How was London?'

Neville thought it was awful: 'Everybody was bothered about taxes and rents and rates. No one seemed to have any money. I really looked forward to coming back here where it flows a bit more freely. No one gave any decent parties, and the one or two I went to were full of envious, petty people gobbling up one another's reputations as fast as they could.'

'But you said you enjoyed the theatre.'

'I soon get bored. Those West End voices soon pall. The London theatre forms a distinct caste divorced from the rest of the people. I got the impression people went to the theatre to see people living in a way they no longer know how to live themselves, don't you agree, Duchess?' He turned towards his stepmother who had joined them.

'Everything you say is so clever I merely say, "Hear, Hear." '

'Let me introduce you.' The two women smiled and nodded. 'As I was saying,' Neville went on, 'the London theatre is some simulacrum of life for people who aren't doing anything very interesting any more.'

'Oh, come! In Herefordshire we never stop our good works and whatnot.'

'Herefordshire isn't London. The people there spend the best years of their lives in bus queues.'

'You make it sound dreadful.'

'Don't you think it's silly to be nostalgic for London, Duchess?'

'People must be allowed to hanker after what they like.' She smiled at Katherine, who was the first person she had met at the party of whom she wholeheartedly approved. She liked the way she picked up her gold clasp-bag and readjusted the folds of her dress and walked demurely – and not without self-consciousness – across the room to meet someone her husband wanted her to know.

Later: 'My God, what a marvellous-looking girl. What a thoroughbred.'

'You'd never think she had a boy of thirteen would you?'

'People seem to stay young in this climate.' The Duchess looked bemused; she had taken Katherine to be about twenty-seven.

PAUL BROPHY, who had been to an embassy reception, arrived, as usual, late and the worse for wear. During this period he was drinking a good deal by himself and falling asleep in odd corners. Sometimes – although that day was not one – he looked as though he had not washed or shaved for days. He joined a conversation around the writer, Albert Hijjazi, and appeared to follow every word that was said.

As a servant passed with the drinks, Brophy helped himself to two whiskies, drank off one at a gulp and began to sip the second calmly. The damage was done. His sentences grew longer and meaningless, like German phrases cut off from their verbs. He drank a third whisky, and then – without warning – he was no longer present: his enormous length was stretched out on the floor in a corner of the room, fast asleep.

No one, as the saying is, turned a hair. Those who happened to be near merely suggested someone find a cushion for his head. The Consort, always the perfect host, found one and arranged Brophy more comfortably. The smudged, unhappy face contrasted strikingly with the deep red cushion. The conversation crackled on.

The Duchess was shocked, and Brophy slid down to the bottom of the league in her estimation. People came to stare at the sleeping drunk and those who had never seen Brophy before – but knew of him by name – found it vaguely troubling that a man in his position could so lack dignity and self-preservation that he could lie in a corner of a crowded room showing the two small pennies of hard wear on the soles of his enormous ill-brushed shoes.

The local guests found the spectacle peculiarly satisfying. Underneath their diplomatic silence they hated such behaviour, and yet it pleased them, because it was the way they expected most Europeans to behave. To an international *entrepôt* like Baida, the European connection was essential – had been for centuries – and the Christians especially believed they had more in common with Europe than with Africa or Asia; but, it had to be confessed, long experience of their European friends had taught them to accept one thing: that underneath the technological efficiency and the business drive lurked the old Frankish nature – absence of inner balance, the residue of the gross habits of less polished times; and they were always waiting for this Frankish licence to show itself.

Despite an almost Levantine love of display – which sent most Baida women to cocktail parties tinkling like chandeliers – the Baidanis were hard on themselves, careful in public and deeply concerned for their good name. They had a core of good mountain common sense and when they came to European parties they ate and drank carefully if well, carefully observed their fellow-guests and waited for the European Old Adam to reveal himself. What usually happened was that an American or European woman would disgrace herself by drinking a little too much and talking too loudly – or even being ill – and generally behaving like a *charmoutah* (most western women were suspected of being so, in any case).

Brophy was exceptional. For a man in his position to stretch out on the floor and sleep in front of a fairly distinguished gathering was another proof that Europeans have no *savoir faire* or real sense of the fitness of things. So much, in the Arab world, depends on the instinct for self-preservation. No one gives himself to another whether in politics or love; no one abandons a position of strength out of pity or altruism. Four hundred years of Turkish suzerainty had taught them that a sleeping man is a defenceless man, and a defenceless man invites trouble.

They carefully crossed the room to stare at the sleeping Brophy, saw the mark of defeat on his face and the doom he was creating for himself, metaphorically spat on him and retreated. He was a tree about to be felled; the fatal white cross was painted on his brow.

The only person who might have saved Brophy from himself that evening was Neville, but he was far too busy meeting new people – he was a tremendous social climber and name-dropper – to be bothered about Brophy. There was, too, one important distinction: whereas Brophy regarded Neville as his friend, joined by acquaintance since schooldays, Neville did not have a similar feeling for Brophy. Certainly, he found Brophy more interesting since he had become head of MEDOC, but he felt no more for him than before, largely because Neville, as a

26

sensualist and *farceur*, had no real feeling for anyone. Brophy was too slow for Neville, too uselessly conscientious. While Neville had expressed an opinion and was off over the hills and dales showing a clean pair of heels to those who disagreed, Brophy was still struggling through the marshlands at the foot of the hill, slogging away to find something that no longer mattered. He was even too slow and, in a way, too trusting, to realise that Neville laughed at him.

12

THE party went on until nearly ten o'clock, and then people began to leave, kissing Rhoda with all the enthusiasm that comes from repletion: 'Lovely to have you back with us again, dear!' '*Merci pour tout, chère Rouda. Je vous attends chez moi samedi soir.*' '*Je vous remercie infiniment, chère madame, pour une si agréable soirée. Ne nous quittez pas encore, je vous en prie.*'

Rhoda received their homage like little Clara in the Land of Toys. Where else could she play the queen except here? Who would kiss her hand and flatter her in London, where people could leave parties without even saying good-bye to their hostess? Where could such social success be achieved so effortlessly?

'*Je vous assure, monsieur, que c'est tellement agréable d'être parmi vous de nouveau. C'est mon pays ici. Je suis baidani en tout sauf le passeport!*'

The Mercedes, the Jaguars, the Chevrolets began to move away, and within minutes the house and garden emptied, and the family and its intimates were left: Rhoda and The Consort, The Duchess, Neville, Katherine and Richard Thomson, the sleeping Brophy and John Macrae, The Consort's new deputy, who had arrived in town about three weeks before.

They went into the garden, leaving Brophy asleep on the floor. The fairy lights in the stone pines were put out, and the terrace was lit by the light from the ottoman windows of the

27

main room. The lights of the mountain resorts glittered like huge constellations along the horizon, outshining even the endless depths of the night.

Thomson – all businessman, all tough drive and sound, hard-headed judgements – thought Brophy 'a bloody fool' to imagine that a man in his position could get away with such behaviour.

'MEDOC means something. People are always looking for something to destroy here. He's offering himself as a sacrifice. Why don't you speak to him, Neville? To get a reputation as a drunk and a queer in less than six months must be a damned record.'

Neville shrugged.

Katherine sighed: 'He comes to parties, falls into a gloom, or expresses wildly controversial opinions which upset people – and then spends the next day writing notes of apology. I can't make him out.'

'He's that crank, Commander Brophy's son.' (Only Thomson remembered the case of the Commander, who was interned in 1940 because of his extreme right-wing opinions.)

The Duchess agreed that such a father was 'tiresome' – a favourite word – but no man could blame his father for everything. 'He's had all the blessings of his class: jolly good education in a good school and Cambridge, and a further period in America, he was telling me; so what do such people want. Oh, no! There's no doubt that, in the old days in Cairo, a person like that would have got a couple of warnings and been packed off home if he went on being an ass.'

The others listened doubtfully. Richard Thomson, who was usually fair-minded and saw the main point – could not see how the comparison with Egypt could be maintained. Although Britain, along with the great powers, had guaranteed the international status of Baida, the city and its environs had never been a colony or a protectorate. 'My impression is that the British don't mean very much here; we've never registered as a people. The Spanish, the Italians, the French, yes.'

Somebody pointed out that the resident British community in the city was never less than about five thousand, so the inhabitants had ample opportunity to observe them.

'It's not the same. The French and Americans have this old relationship with the local Christians. We don't. Generally speaking, the Baidanis have difficulty in distinguishing us from

28

the Americans or the Germans; we slip between two stools.'

The Consort twirled his moustache with a lissom hand: 'But what you were saying just now, Duchess, about English people behaving themselves: the truth is, they didn't. The old colonies were full of blackguards and drunkards and misfits and what-have-you. They gave us a stinking bad name, and yet they inspired the legend that all English people were somehow characters: violent, red-blooded people, bristling with strange opinions and unspeakable courage. Now, when foreigners go to London and see lines on lines of regimented people in the tubes they come to the conclusion that the British are decadent. They've been used to something far more gutsy and eccentric.'

'What nonsense! In Cairo in the old days there was a most interesting collection of people who could get into any society with distinction: scholars and gentlemen.'

Neville said deliberately, softly: 'That was hardly true, was it?'

'How can you talk? You weren't there.'

'But we were. You forget we were there as children when Father was digging at Tell Manar.'

The Duchess ignored him: 'The summers in Alexandria were more elegant than Nice, in my opinion. Everybody was there. You could travel on the old tramways and hardly see a native.'

Everybody understood that The Duchess, because she had been put out, was talking like a caricature of herself. They sipped their drinks, and looked up at the huge sky and the spangled hillsides, where the mountain resorts were still enjoying the full season.

Into this sudden silence stepped the dishevelled Brophy. He was trying to walk with a sort of military precision and erectness (as though, by keeping the cheeks of his behind together, he held a penny in position). He extended his hand in a stiff gesture of conciliation towards Rhoda and half bowed from a great height. 'I can't ever explain,' – speaking through the twitchings of his stiff cheeks and lips – 'how disgracefully I've behaved. I can't expect you to forgive me.'

Rhoda looked vague. 'We were going to leave you asleep there all night. You were obviously dog-tired.'

No one else made any gesture to him. Stuck in the centre of

general dislike, Brophy again half bowed from stiff hips. 'I ask all of you for your indulgence and forgiveness.'

He walked stiffly from one to the other, shaking hands. Yes, he said, he was leaving. The Consort threw his car-key to Neville; it was easier to drive Brophy home than worry about him.

Brophy left, and the others tore him to pieces. John Macrae – who was new to the self-congratulation and self-satisfaction of such gatherings, listened fascinated – and eventually over-stayed his welcome and left in confusion (and vexed with him-self). He reacted strongly to the whiff of insincerity, like brim-stone, which such a social occasion gave off, and was perplexed that such people could command respect.

Rhoda had not been impressed and dismissed him as a gauche Scots hobbledehoy. The Consort said the man was put out at being sent off to the Gulf, adding, 'I suppose I should have gone, but as Rhoda's just back it seemed a trip one could well afford to miss.'

Thomson wondered why people disliked the Gulf. 'People there are so hospitable – parties every evening, whisky like water. And your Macrae should be at home – Scots are thicker on the roster there than in Edinburgh.'

Rhoda hated Scots people – 'so boring and self-satisfied'. The Consort raised an eyebrow: 'I always thought your grand-father would have been the Plaidmore of Scrife if he hadn't been diddled by a wicked lawyer.'

'Oh, some such. All that bores me to tears.'

13

BROPHY looked contrite as Neville ticked him off. 'The family doesn't care a damn what you do; but, with so many people milling about, it was hellish indiscreet. Don't put weapons in people's hands. There are so many people who envy you and would like to see you come a cropper. Not because you are *you*, but because you've got somewhere.'

'You could be right.'

'I know I'm right.'

There was a pause. 'Was I very bad? Did I make a scene before going out?'

'Not at all. One minute you were telling Albert Hijjazi just what was wrong with the modern movement in Arabic literature – and next thing The Consort was putting a pillow under your head.'

'I must write to him.' This was said desperately, as though writing cured everything. 'You're sure that's all that happened? You're not being nice to me? Not trying to make me feel less bad?'

'Why should I? That's the truth. I won't repeat the nasty comments made . . .'

'Oh!' Brophy was all hostility. 'What were people saying?'

'Just that it was a bad thing for a person in your position to make an exhibition of yourself.'

For a moment Brophy hated Neville. It took an effort to realise that Neville was doing his best to help him. He began to whine. 'Things have gone badly at the office recently. They say I'm furtive and suspicious and don't know how to be frank or delegate authority. I can't hit it off with the people who matter.'

Neville was fascinated. He switched off the car engine – giving a sign that the conversation might be prolonged. Just a shade too eagerly, he asked, 'Is it still Doris Parslow?'

'Of course. She's the instigator. She's more or less lined up the top four people against me. Everything I do is criticised. If this goes on, I won't have any faith left in myself.'

'But she's subordinate to you. Crush the bitch.'

'You try it. It's not easy. In the first place, I don't want to. In the second, she's a good person.'

'This academic fairness!' Neville spat with contempt. 'She's a bitch, let's face it. She's got this thing about Shamseddine having the job. You'll never make the slightest impression so long as you stand in his way.'

Brophy rubbed his cheek thoughtfully.

'Look, Paul, tread warily. I'm warning you. Every little thing will be held against you. This evening: someone is bound to go back and tell her that you were cold and paralytic on the floor.'

Brophy sniffed, stifling another weak wave of hatred for

Neville. 'It's more complicated than you know. Come round tomorrow and have lunch. We can talk.'

'Can't. Going on a picnic with The Duchess and Katherine.'

'Another time, then. I've got a little offer for you. It might appeal if you feel free to take on an assignment.'

'For what?'

'MEDOC, of course.'

'Since when have you been a source of patronage?' Envy and incredulity were equally balanced.

'All part of the job. The assignment involves a trip round North Africa. Does it appeal?'

'Need I answer?'

'Good. Come in the day after tomorrow.'

Brophy left the car and disappeared in the wide glass doors of his apartment house. Neville waited a moment before going off. A trip round North Africa? The man had his uses.

14

NEVILLE was restless, ready for adventure. His thesis on the evolution of western ideas about Islam was to all intents and purposes finished. He lingered over the work as an excuse to stay on in his sister's house and in Baida. This period of study was being financed by the money left by his father – it might last four or five years. Before it went he would have found a job; something new and interesting would have turned up. Neville drove slowly along the Corniche towards Azurah, where the restaurant terraces were still crowded with people looking out over the sea.

Walking along, tingling with diamond-sharp exhilaration, Neville felt immensely at home, free to observe things around him, free to pass judgements from a position of superiority. Then, in the same way as a bird takes a strange object into focus, Neville marked down a youth loitering near the line of cars parked outside a café. He had all the casual furtiveness of a sneak-thief, and Neville, with the fire in his blood restored by the clear air, was ready to run across and drive him away. But the youth started to stroll slowly towards Neville and, drawing nearer, wished him good evening in English with a strong American flavour.

'*Marhaba! Kifak?*'

The sneak-thief turned prostitute smiled brilliantly: 'You speak very good Arabic, sir!'

'I used two words. I speak Arabic like a Damascus donkey!'

'You are trying to make fun of me. You speak Arabic very well.'

The youth lounged against the sea-wall alongside Neville, and, as an atmosphere of good humour had been established, Neville asked him what he was doing. The youth asked the same question back. 'Sniffing the breezes,' was Neville's reply; and the youth said he was doing the same thing. They looked at one another, half-smiling, and the youth sighed provocatively.

When Neville asked him how much he wanted, the youth shook his head in an owlish way, as though he had not understood. Neville repeated his question without haste or irritation. The youth looked at him reflectively a moment, and then said, 'Twenty-five.' Neville waved him away, as though he had been buying oranges. 'Too much. Fifteen.'

'What, with a room and hot water? Never.'

Neville laughed at the faked-up anger, the creature's pretence at honest brokering. 'What the hell do we want a hotel for? I've got a car here. We can go off somewhere. Where? Tibatram, maybe.'

'Too far.' The youth looked offended. 'Twenty-five or nothing.'

'Fifteen.'

'Twenty-five.'

Neville walked away, and the youth followed him and brought his price down to twenty and, without further discussion, got into the car with Neville. He sat in a corner and looked at Neville resentfully. He had noted Neville's directness, light-heartedness, hard bargaining and complete absence of strain. These were typically Baidani; they sprang from a belief that selling oneself was not necessarily a bad thing. The Europeans and Americans of the youth's experience made false moves, were apologetic. 'You're an Arab,' the youth said, at length.

'I'm from Portugal.'

'That's why you speak Arabic so well.'

'Of course. You're clever, aren't you?'

The youth's naïve conceit was touched. 'Not clever, sir. But I knew you spoke Arabic too well to be a student.'

The youth was of a kind to appeal to Neville, who had an oriental indifference as to the direction of his sexual interests: thick-set, ambiguous (like himself), but all touched with a certain countrified grossness. He admired The Consort's car and had ambitions to own a similar one of his own, run a taxi business and earn money on the side fucking tourists.

'It takes all manner of men to make a crowd,' was all Neville said.

They had left the city behind and were driving towards the open beaches. Between the houses and apartment blocks they glimpsed the Mediterranean. The youth asked whether Neville had a house at Tibatram. Yes, Neville said, right on the beach. The youth was indignant and wanted things in style in a hotel. Neville merely made himself more comfortable in his seat and drove on.

'What's your name?'

'Hassan.'

'Where from?'

'Here.'

'But you have an Elhabi accent.' The youth was dumbfounded and, so intense is the devotion of the average Arab to his native village, deeply moved. To recognise an Elhabi accent meant that Neville had been there, and to have seen Elhabi was to love it – thus the youth's reasoning; and he burst out into a song of praise for his native town – its waters, its cafés, its food. Perhaps, he suggested, he and Neville would go there one day and have a meal together. The youth had been in Elhabi the Sunday before and had eaten grilled chicken and smoked a *narghilé*. It had been perfect. Did Neville like a hubble-bubble? Neville was never sure. He liked the mystique of the thing; the silent satisfaction on the faces of the smokers, the feeling of stillness and perfection, but otherwise not. Other people's pleasures gave him more satisfaction than his own. The youth could not understand this; he enjoyed everything that came his way.

'What's your job?'

'This.'

'Good God. You can't do very well.' Neville meant: There are so many doing the same thing; but spared the youth's feelings.

'I used to work for a travel agency.' The youth was put out by Neville's cold, matter-of-fact manner and his inquisitiveness, like a bird darting into a bush for fruit. 'My father thinks I am still there. Every week he asks me for money to help rebuild our house. He is very poor.'

'And he still thinks you're at the agency?'

'I think so.'

Neville thought otherwise, but again kept his opinion to himself. All he said was, 'I hope your father keeps well.'

'*Al Hamdullilah,*' the youth replied, and Neville repeated the phrase after him, in the approved way.

Like most other prostitutes, Hassan had no idea how to please, and there was never, for a moment, a suggestion of surrender. In fact he was wondering how he would be able to nick something from the car on their return journey, and he was determined not to give anything except the bare minimum that the encounter demanded. He objected to a proposal to make love on a blanket on the beach by the light of the crescent moon over the sea, and pointed to the flotsam and jetsam everywhere. He looked pettish and disgusted. Neville spread out the blanket, all the same, and the youth eventually sat down and began to smoke in a hangdog sort of way. Neville, with the authority of the buyer, asked him sharply when he was going to take his trousers off. The youth was genuinely perplexed. 'No, sir. I have you.'

'No you don't. I fuck you.'

'Never. I always fuck the tourists.'

'I'm not a tourist. Did you think that's what I wanted you to do?'

'It's what they want. Those tourists.'

'I tell you I'm not a tourist.'

'You're a diplomat. You've got special plaques on your car.'

Neville was displeased by the idea of involving his brother-in-law in the affair and said the car was borrowed. The youth now disliked Neville, and said, 'You say you're not a tourist, not a diplomat, and yet you speak such good Arabic; you must be a spy. Most foreigners in Baida are spies.'

35

Neville was sufficiently in command of himself to laugh. 'I might be a spy if someone paid me enough. I'm now working as a teacher.'

'At a university in Portugal.'

'Of course.'

'But you aren't from Portugal. The number on the car is from Germany.'

'Of course it's not.'

'You're a German.'

'I look like a German, don't I, with my black hair and dark face?'

'You are half-and-half. Half-German, half-Arab.'

'You're more clever than you know. My mother is German.'

'You see. I understand.' Yet, the youth felt he was being made fun of, held cheap, so that when Neville asked to see him, he refused.

All this time, the youth's indifference was total, and it would continue, Neville knew, until the moment when he believed he had Neville in a position of utter dependence and willing to do anything to reach the necessary climax. This, after all, was not so much love-making as a fight to the finish. For a moment, Neville's control almost slipped when he flopped down by the youth's side and, in – what in the west would have passed for a gesture of tenderness, endearment – tried to pull the youth towards him. In a flash, the youth grabbed Neville and hissed at him, 'Let me fuck you. I will make you very, very happy.'

Neville retrieved his balance, but not before the youth had given him a light blow to the chest, and, 'I'll have you whether you want me to or not,' he said. The threat left Neville un-moved – though slightly-built, he was no weakling – but the youth's duplicity stung him. He pushed him aside, and, when the youth attempted to pursue his advantage, Neville grabbed one of his hands and locked it behind his back. Hassan showed genuine amazement, rather like a giant challenged by a gnat, and then grinned: 'Is this supposed to make me afraid? I could kill you with my thumb – like a cockroach.'

'But not without a struggle, *habibi*!' All the same, Neville released the hand and got up: 'We'd better go home.'

'You don't want me to fuck you?'

'Never.'

36

'O.K.' The youth zipped up his trousers, and then stopped and turned his head quickly. Both he and Neville were aware that two men were hurrying towards them across the dunes. One of them was saying, 'What are these people doing here? What is there for us?'

Hassan fled. Generations of bunkers gave, as they say, wings to his feet; while Neville, too startled to know what he was doing, sat down on the blanket. As the men drew nearer, his self-possession returned: '*Tfaddalu*. Be good enough to sit with me and enjoy the night, if it please you.'

The men stopped, sniffing the situation like dogs. Then they came forward, mumbling greetings and peering down at Neville. They recognised the special, charmed quality about him, that special certainty which protected him like a halo. One asked where the youth had gone.

Neville knew he had the two men in their places, so replied with a heartlessness that is almost a form of humour: 'God keep him happy, but away! He is a *charmout* and ran off before I could have him.'

'And you had paid him?'

'Of course not.'

'*Al Hamdullilah*. God be praised.' The idea of a bad bargain was appalling.

'Yes, my friends. We were still arguing which way we were going to pray, and, because of an argument over *hadeth*, we had almost decided not to take the prayer mat out tonight.'

The men slapped their knees and sat down on the blanket beside him. Neville could see them peering at him curiously. His intonation had given him away as a foreigner. They asked him about it, and, without thinking, Neville said his mother was half-Egyptian, but he did not specify what his father was. The men murmured appreciatively. 'By God, by the name of God,' one said, 'if I spoke American as you speak Arabic I would have one of the best agencies for cars in town.'

They wanted to know where he lived, what he did, whether there was a 'Madame' – meaning a wife – and children. Neville ad-libbed gloriously, and all this was far more satisfying for them than the truth, because to that kind of men only the incredible is true. One asked him what he thought of some pro-Egyptian local politician. Neville thought nothing of him, but carefully altered his opinion when he replied.

'He is our leader,' the sturdier man said. *'Zaimna.'* He let the information soak in: 'He and Abdel Nasser are like brothers,' and then, because he assumed Neville was also an admirer of the Egyptian leader, added: 'Nasser was the first man to tell the Americans to drink water from the Mediterranean. And he will destroy Israel. So long as he leads the Arabs, people will listen to us.'

Neville impressed the men by recalling his one meeting with *al Rais.* 'My father was a great friend of Egypt, and when he was alive – God rest his soul – he took me to Cairo, and we had an audience of President Nasser.'

'Your father was a great man!'

'Al Rais knew my father loved Egypt. He was a man who looked for the treasures of the past.'

'Now that he is dead,' the sturdier, more intelligent of the two asked, 'who looks after your Mamma?'

'My mamma died before him.'

They murmured sympathetically, and then the simpler one said, 'I think you must be very rich.'

'Wait until you see me in the daylight before you lend me a taxi fare.'

As Arabs, with a feeling for the magical power of words, the men were deeply impressed by Neville's quickness and verbal dexterity. They praised him one to another, and then the simpler one asked where Neville's 'Madame' was.

'I told you, I'm not married. Are you?'

'Of course.'

The intelligent one laughed: 'He's been marrying for twenty years and trying for a son. All he gets are daughters, who eat up his money like locusts.'

'When I get a son I will stop,' the other replied meekly.

'I will do it for him one day to put him at rest. I will give him and his wife twenty sons.'

'He must have a prick like iron,' Neville said sarcastically.

'Mittel haddid!' the sprightly one replied, with a note of wonder that Neville could have known anything so intimate – and so true – about his person. 'Believe me, my brother, when I was in Persia, I went to the girls in Abadan, and they said they had never felt such a piece of man inside them. Never such pleasure! And you know what Persian women are like.'

'They have cunts like ovens,' was Neville's reply. 'They burn and drain you. They never have enough.'

'*Quss mittel furn!*' they repeated in wonder; and the phrase, the implied experience, gave Neville a new dimension in their eyes. It was agreed that Persian women were better than local ones – who were all *charmyt* and wanted nothing but money. Even the Egyptians were better. They liked to be pleasured for hours at a time.

'They like it like a baby likes its *massassa*,' was Neville's comment. The word for 'comforter' was an odd, homely word for a semi-foreigner to use; both men laughed.

'We are the comforter for the women,' the brighter one agreed. 'If the women do not have our comforter they are unhappy. And when they get plenty of it, they are very, very happy. Too much. They sing like birds. Their arses grow fat, their lips get full. They like to make their husbands nice things to eat. They know we are men, and they are women.'

'Thank God that it is so.'

'Thank God,' the two men said. They went on to discuss the circumcision of women in Egypt (a brutal, dreadful subject that always made Neville squirm). This, they explained, was why Egyptian women needed prolonged stimulation.

15

THE father of the daughters went away to relieve himself in the sea, and the other leaned towards Neville: 'I will be your friend. We can go to your house.'

Neville caught his breath. 'You want to fuck?'

'Always.'

'But where?'

The man suggested they leave in Neville's car, drop the third man at his home and then go on to Neville's place or go somewhere in Neville's car. This was agreed. They shook hands, and the man said his name was Iskander.

Neville asked whether the men spent much time in pursuit

of night-visitors. Iskander gave a spanning-an-octave gesture with his hands. '*Shway, shway.* When we want to amuse ourselves we come down here to see what's going on. You know, just when people have begun their pleasure we see if we can help. Sometimes the man gives us money to keep away; sometimes we like the woman. Last year, we caught Izzat Halami's son here with a Spanish artiste. She wanted him to fight us, but he paid us to let us do a man's work with her, so that they could both leave in safety. Then he wanted me to have him, too; but I was too tired – and I despised him too much. She slapped his face, and he began to cry: "*Ya ummi! Ya ummi.*" I told him, "Don't worry, little boy. You'll get home to your mamma." By the name of God, if I had a son like that I'd shoot him with my own hands. Izzat Halami is someone. He has a lot of power.'

Neville listened dispassionately, trying to decide how much of the story was true: 'Aren't you afraid of offending someone as powerful as Halami? After all, he was in the cabinet not so long ago.'

Iskander spat: 'Halami is nobody in my world. I've got my *darrah*. He's got his *darrah*, so there's nobody wants to touch me – unless he wants us to touch him.' He touched his hippocket where, it was understood, there was a revolver. When the other man returned, Neville asked how much money they would want from him. Neither had anything to say; it was a form of embarrassment. Iskander was reassuring: 'You are my friend. That is different. Perhaps you can lend me twenty pounds.'

Neville handed over the Baidani pounds, which he knew he would never see again. As the price of that incredible encounter which satisfied him as nothing had done for years, it was cheap. The air had restored the fire to his blood; he knew the kind of relief he needed; and having sexual relations with the man who had set out to rob him satisfied every one of his darker instincts: the encounter of a lifetime, an intoxicating mixture of danger, violence and sexual pleasure. The father of the daughters also wanted a loan from Neville: 'What about *baksheesh* for me? *Donnez-moi un joli cadeau.*'

Iskander pushed him aside. 'Get away, you *charmout*. This man is my friend. Do you take money as though you were an old beggar hobbling from door to door? Get into the car so that we can take you home to sleep.'

The other was not put down. 'But *you've* had a present, and you've put it in your pocket; and you want me to go home without anything.'

'Do I have to tell you to go to sleep twice?' The whiner backed away and was ordered into the car. Iskander got into the seat beside Neville, and something possessive in his manner made the other man jealous. He knew Iskander had entered into a winning relationship with Neville and that this excluded him. 'We'll take the man without a present home first,' Iskander said largely, putting his arm comfortably along the top of the seat. 'We will take him back to his daughters.' Near the city, Iskander practically ordered the man out of the car, treating him with contempt. The man complained he had a long way to walk. Iskander called him a rag, and asked him if he wanted to be feathered like a fowl? The ditched man came around to Neville's window, cringing and degenerate in his thin tartan shirt: *'Un tout petit cadeau, monsieur.'*

Iskander suddenly began to bawl at the man, who retorted, 'One of my daughters has a skin complaint.'

'Peel it off, then. Yesterday, she was dying of a disease of the heart. Today it's her skin. One thing is sure: she'll end up a *charmoutah* like her father.' With this final insult, Iskander ordered Neville to drive off.

'You're very hard on him.'

Iskander spat out of the window and looked aggrieved and long-suffering. 'I have to fuck the man! Unless I fuck him he cannot have pleasure. That is why he has daughters; he'll never have a son. He'll have a miserable old age, with ten ugly daughters around him, all unmarried, to shame him to the grave. He'll live to wish he'd never seen the door of his mother's womb.' Iskander shook his head in wonderment at the follies of the world and the hard way it treated him.

Neville joined him in heartless laughter at the third man's expense. 'I think he knew we were going to do something.'

'Maalum. Of course he knew. He would have liked to come with us to watch.' Iskander gave his brigand's laugh and smoothed his bushy moustache; there was a corpulence about his manner, as though it were waiting for him to put on another couple of stone. 'He's a person without luck. I don't know why I bother with him.'

Having dismissed the other, Iskander pinched Neville's

cheek and proposed they go into a nearby lane, a dingy track between pinewoods, rubbish-dumps and shabby apartments. Neville was afraid to commit himself in such surroundings; but Iskander insisted, and he had Neville like a woman in the back of the car. In receiving the fiery Iskander, Neville's pleasure was largely in the mind, in the idea of the adventure itself: an overpowering pleasure in submission to a thug – the man who had originally set out to rob him – was the sex-play of opposites, who find common language only in the enjoyment of the body. For the more intelligent, who enjoys disgraceful abandon, the whole mind is involved in the action of over-coming barriers within itself. The absence of tenderness, of endearments, rounded off the experience. Neville understood that this kind of encounter might occur at any hour of the day for Iskander, with man, woman or child. The appetite was not channelled or confined; its satisfaction was as mindless and heartless as eating an apple.

This, Neville had always understood, was the sort of sensuality that withers Europeans, whose souls or guilty consciences drag along after the delights of the body, spreading corruption and disorder. A man like Iskander, with a consciousness attuned only to the body, feeds himself on his own prowess: the fuck becomes a thing in itself, a moment of isolated contact and pleasure which justifies his vision of himself as a man. It is enough for him that he does and gives pleasure in the doing; no contract of any kind is implied. Neville understood this point of view perfectly. He believed the heartlessness of the libertine is tolerable only when it has a hard, eighteenth-century glitter. He admitted heartlessness in himself and did not object to it in others. This was why he arranged to meet Iskander again. He recognised a blood-brother.

To cement their coming together he drove Iskander back to his native village in the lower hills, and they discussed the pleasures of the body. Like Neville, Iskander preferred women, although pleasure with a man could be more intense. For the greatest pleasure he chose girls in their early teens – and offered to introduce Neville to the right places.

The village was silent when they got there, but a light was burning on the verandah of Iskander's house. He wanted to show Neville his terraces and offer him coffee, but Neville refused.

NEVILLE was happier than he had been for a long time. In all his years – ever since his adventures began in adolescence – he had known nothing to equal the value of the night's events in terms of sensual pleasure and the even more intense pleasure of the thing relived in his mind. The perfection of this thing snatched from the edge of danger and disaster, with comedy and village humour thrown in, satisfied his conceit. Surely, he thought to himself as he speeded downhill, surely, this is the way to enjoy oneself. Before he reached the city outskirts, he had decided it was time to find his own place to live.

Back in The Consort's splendid house all the rooms were filled with early morning; the dim, comfortable acres of the house held only sleeping people. Neville, alone, overcharged and superexcited, could not sleep and went out on the balcony to smoke. He was very close, at that moment, to the dawn-grey world around him, very close to it and yet aware of an impending separation. He was overwhelmed by nostalgia for the place he was in, although partly sure that something of the place would always remain within him. The nostalgia arose from the satisfaction of the physical urge to know every-thing, to taste everything once, the pleasure of knowing that one has spent oneself in acquiring new knowledge of oneself. He had gorged himself with this knowledge, and he was proud.

Time and time again, after one of his adventures, Neville marvelled that the European mind had need to clothe the physical exchange with fictitious exhalations of the soul. Mak-ing love to someone out of duty or propinquity, because of marriage or some long-standing commitment, was – for Neville, at least – a form of death. The clean exchanges of people profoundly excited by the other were infinitely less sapping – must be, he thought, having never entered into any relation-ship long enough for staleness to begin or goodwill to end.

Neville looked towards the mountains, where the first signs of dawn were appearing. Up there, Iskander was asleep, un-concerned by the slightest notion of romantic love and unaware of the secret tensions and triumphs of Calvin's children, who can never have the freedom of their own bodies. Neville knew that a relationship could exist between him and Iskander. The man might bleed him white yet call him a friend and, so lightly does life sit on such people, make considerable sacrifices for him.

The dawn of 22 September: about four o'clock, the muezzins began chanting to the empty streets and the thousands of lights still burning from the night. The Pharos and the airport lights along the coast were still flashing. At that time of day before the first bakeries open and the first reveilles sound from the barracks, Baida is a spacious city, ample, a place of endless possibilities. The first apricot light behind the mountains showed up the outlying detail: the summer palaces and radio-masts to the west, the minarets to the north; and, near at hand, the slapdash but purposive confusion of a Mediterranean Hong Kong that has to live by its wits and expects the tocsin to sound hourly. In the moment between the two lights was all the exhilaration of living in a foreign place, where even the movement of the first car could not be taken for granted.

Underneath the balcony stretched the paved terrace, with chairs and flowers arranged for the events of the next day. There were still no heads at the windows of neighbouring buildings, and no vendor was moving in the streets: autumnal dawn on the coast and silence and peace everywhere.

Thus within less than twenty-four hours of his return to Baida, Neville Lorimer de Vries had begun his secret life, as well as returning into the superficial and essentially suburban social life and routines of the local foreign community.

17

JUST after Neville fell asleep, The Duchess got up and went off in search of a lavatory. While fumbling at strange doors she ran into The Consort, splendid in a bright orange-and-red silk dressing-gown. He invited her (and at once regretted doing so) to join him and Rhoda at early-morning tea.

The Consort and Rhoda rose early, no matter how late they

went to bed, and made up their sleep in the afternoons. Rhoda was already sitting at a small table near the french doors, which were wide open on to the verandah. The young woman, stirring her tea and looking vaguely beautiful in her whimsical, old-fashioned way, was engulfed in a diaphanous dressing-gown. Behind her was the pearly charm of the morning and the diminishing perspectives of the coastline to the north of the city, the mountain mass still half-hidden by a pale grey mistiness up to about two thousand feet, and then breaking free into radiance, so that the villages and convents, perched here and there as strategy had dictated, seemed ready to explode into whiteness and life.

Yes, there were mornings like that: like some Bonnard interior come to life. Nothing would be missing from the morning stillness of the distant mountains to the morning stillness of the woman, sexually appeased, stirring her tea in an elegant cup. Between the foreground figure, quite tender and dreamy, and the superb open view of the outside world were sprays of blue jasmine, hanging down from the verandah and nodding in the slow breeze.

What no painting could give, all the same, were the sounds from the streets below. The first vendors were moving around; some with panniers on their arms or heads, some pushing the handcarts on which fruits and vegetables were arranged in prodigal artistry. *'Battikh'* a voice came from the street below. 'Melons like honey.' The fish-vendor's cry was more raucous: *'Taza sammak!* Fresh fish: fish newly come from the sea!' The first women leaning over balconies were letting down baskets on ropes for the vendors to fill.

Yes, there were mornings like that, and for The Duchess moving across the room towards the blue open doors, this one was an echo of another life, of earlier mornings in Cairo. *'Sabbah al yasmin!'* Rhoda lifted up her face from the contemplation of her cup. 'May your morning be scented with jasmine!' Even that, too, recalled the Nile valley.

They both agreed this was the best time of the day, and The Duchess thought it a shame to waste it.

'I bet my darling brother's still asleep. He still hadn't come in when I went to bed.'

'Where did he go?'

'Oh, he sometimes drives off up the mountains.' Rhoda, un-

45

involved in her brother's movements, was pouring out tea. The Duchess sniffed. She was 'deeply offended by Neville'. He and the 'orange-mouthed American girl' had treated her abominably the night before, and she would never go out with Neville again until he apologised. This meant that the trip that day with Katherine Thomson was off.

Rhoda was bewildered. Neville was often casual, even brusque, when people seemed slow or deliberately tiresome, but never discourteous. The Duchess was not convinced: 'He can be exceedingly rude, I assure you. He and that odious girl laughed at me. And Neville was rude to me at the buffet.'

'You mean he jostled you for the eats?'

The Duchess was not taking the matter lightly. Neville, she said, had cut her short with his 'intolerable, glassy manner' and left her alone among strangers. No one had been so rude to her since the old Bloomsbury days, when everyone had had an insufferable superiority and bounce. 'He even accused me of spitting on the Egyptians.'

The Consort heard this as he came in. 'Who did? You did? You spit at the Egyptians? Duchess! Why, everyone knows you were besotted about them.'

He had mistaken her tone of voice, but quickly became more sympathetic when she repeated Neville's exact words. 'Imagine such a thing! Me! And I always had more Egyptians among my friends than English.'

The Consort sipped his tea and thought she was taking Neville too seriously. 'You ought to know he says anything that pops into his head, if he thinks it sounds clever or good. You can watch his new attitudes developing.'

The Duchess, ignoring Rhoda's stone eyes, asked how.

'Oh, someone will mention – let's say for the sake of the argument, shall we? – plums. Yes, plums. Dear old Neville – who has never given a moment's thought to them – hears someone say plums are an aphrodisiac in Crete – any silly little phrase. Abracadabra, lo and behold, sure enough Neville will go around at the next party offering plums. 'Have a Cretan love-potion. Guaranteed to give new life to an old-age pensioner." It's become one of his little tropes. Astonishing how he can adapt things to his own uses. Take up other people's experiences as his own. He's got this phenomenal instinct for what he's going to find useful.' He caught his wife's black eyes and added hastily, 'I admire him enormously, although not even his best friend could say he had a heart. He's as clever as they're made – and twice as cold. My advice to you, m'dear, is this: never take the little blighter too seriously.'

The Consort hit Neville far more savagely than anything The Duchess had said, and she was taken aback. She reminded The Consort that she had known Neville for years, and he might well be everything The Consort said he was, but he was not normally rude.

Rhoda, still gazing balefully at her husband, agreed that Neville was not a person to offend people deliberately: 'All the same, I'll tell him as soon as he gets up. And you must go on the trip. You can't disappoint Katherine.'

The Duchess was firm: 'Never. Not until Neville apologises. I don't want to put myself at his mercy again. I was left almost *entirely* alone, the *entire* evening.'

'If anyone's to blame, it's ourselves.' The Consort dusted his moustache. 'We'd no idea you weren't enjoying yourself.'

Half-mollified, The Duchess eventually wandered back to her own room along the verandah. She hummed with the satisfaction of the born troublemaker.

'How tiresome The Duchess can be,' Rhoda was saying. 'Neville couldn't spend the whole evening with her. The Duchess made a bore of herself with silly chatter about servants and wages.'

The Consort said people should try to understand her point of view: 'She's a bit uprooted at the moment, and she's a lonely person: a very lonely person.'

'She's got to learn to make herself acceptable to people. She was determined not to enjoy herself. The buffet vexed her, and she looked down her nose because there wasn't a single ambassador present – nobody whose name she'd care to drop afterwards. I told her plainly, "These are our friends. Everyone's here because they amuse us." She clearly thought it faintly improper.'

The Consort was surprised: 'Is she such a snob?'

'She's a priceless snob. When she saw the people at the party were not impressed by her she turned the whole thing into a tragic experience, and now she won't enjoy anything.'

Rhoda put her cup down. 'And I was mad at the way both of you picked on Neville. He's not half as rude to The Duchess as he might be. She's always dropping hints that he's wasting his time and ought to be more serious and ought to husband the money he inherited. Secretly she's mad that we got anything at all.'

The Consort thought it would be a good idea to get Neville to speak to her.

'Of course. He will. If that makes her feel any better. You made it worse by making out Neville to be an utterly silly person. It was completely unfair. We all know his first interest is himself – he makes no bones about it – and he can't tolerate fools; but to suggest he picks up ideas like a magpie! Really! You can't know him very well. I won't let you and The Duchess criticise him. Do it when I'm not here, but never in front of me. I thought you enjoyed having Neville with us.'

'I certainly do. Have I ever said otherwise? But he does pick up attitudes and phrases if he thinks they're interesting or amusing.'

'So do I! I'm always being told I play-act. If Neville does the same, it's because it's in the blood. We're an explosive mixture – Plaidmore and de Vries. You ought to know.'

The Consort put up a limp white hand. 'O.K. We'll agree you're both alike. Let the matter drop. An argument on the first morning together. I refuse to be drawn into your squabbles.'

The use of the word 'squabbles' made Rhoda even crosser. 'We just don't use the same vocabulary. It's better not to talk.' The notion that she and her brother squabbled with The Duchess angered her. Their whole relationship was built on the premise that it was provincial and nineteenth-century not to get on with stepmothers.

18

THE trip to Ain-al-Nabi was put off unexpectedly. Richard Thomson's brother, Maxwell, on his way from the Far East to London, was to fly in with forty-eight hours to kill. Katherine Thomson invited The Duchess to accompany her to the airport

and then return with the traveller to the Thomsons' summer
home in the hills. Neville was still asleep, so did not enter into
the arrangement, and, to the great relief of Rhoda, The
Duchess went off.

19

WHILE shaving, The Consort decided there were too many
people in the house, too many soprano voices, too many people
ready to make him a stranger on his own territory. Ever since
the three travellers arrived – in fact, ever since he saw them
together on the liner – he had wondered whether he had not
been too generous in having both Neville and The Duchess
as winter guests. Now that he knew tensions had arisen between two of the invading army, he was more than ever sure
he had made a mistake. On the whole, women bored him –
the way their minds worked was entirely alien to him – and
quarrelling women were worse than a crateload of time-
bombs.

The Consort was a mixture of delicacy and philistinism. It
was hard to interest him in a serious subject – he was incapable
of abstract thought – and ideas without a practical purpose
in view baffled him. The free play of association which formed
the basis of the average social conversation was unknown, and
the small events of life held no charm for him. His happiness
rarely depended on other people, so he tended to form opinions
about them with the same coolness a dealer brings to the judg-
ing of store cattle. He had real affection for only a few, and –
his bookmakerish 'm'dear' notwithstanding – he discounted
personal relations in work and private life.

Yet he could be touched. A letter from The Duchess, for
example, complaining that her first winter without Rhoda's
father was hard to bear, had moved him; and, almost without
thinking, he said The Duchess must spend the next winter
with them. Rhoda had doubts and – this was the irony – she
invited The Duchess because The Consort insisted.

49

The Consort assumed Neville would not return. In his view, a year's reading in the local libraries was ample; he imagined Neville wanted to get on with his own life. He was disappointed when Rhoda spoke of his return as a foregone conclusion. He said nothing, sulked and called Neville 'a little tick' under his breath. The Consort did not mind Neville's being a paying guest in his house – although his privileges were of a kind no weekly rent could pay for; nor did he object to Neville's friends 'swilling my booze and eating my nosh' (to use The Consort's own elegant phrase) but he did object to his hold over Rhoda. He dominated her, and eight times out of ten in any argument between them – politics, behaviour, small arrangements – Neville and Rhoda were together. The Consort expected Neville to be neutral and to respect the marriage.

If friendship is a perilous thing, so is living in other people's houses, especially when the husband believes the guests not only come between him and his wife but accept everything as their right: a splendid house, servants, comfortable circumstances.

Worse than this, though, was the uncomfortable feeling that The Duchess and Neville knew as much about him as Rhoda. Their eyes all held knowledge of him: he was a shared experience. It made him furious that people should refuse to respect the husband-wife relationship. Yet, because Neville and The Duchess were Rhoda's relations, he could not stop himself being good to them. He made kindly gestures to them – such as inviting The Duchess to early-morning tea – but because of his resentment, regretted his action the next moment. He carried over his hidden ill-will into the office and took his sense of injustice out on John Macrae, even calling him a 'bloody, rugger-playing Red!' to a colleague.

20

The plane from Singapore was late, and the two women went into the airport restaurant to drink iced water and coffee. The Duchess, flopped out by the heat and humidity, sat down in the watery light of the restaurant, where curtains shut out the glare of the sun on the tarmac but could not keep out the whine and rumble of jets. She was feeling sorry for herself and thought letting her home for the winter had been a mistake.

'You're jolly well going to love it here!'

The Duchess was unconvinced.

'But why not?'

'Because I'm not the person to share the lives of clever, heartless young people. We don't speak the same language.'

'You mean Rhoda and Neville?'

'Oh, I know they're brilliantly clever – especially Neville with his flair for languages, his elegance and his knowledge of this and that . . . but as you get older you distrust cleverness. You look for other things.'

'Such as?'

'Loyalty. Probity. Humanity.'

'Oh, Mrs de Vries! Neville has all these things. The most devastatingly honest person, with real heart!'

The Duchess edged her lipstick with a small handkerchief. 'Really? Heartless little brute. Always ready for fun at someone else's expense.'

Katherine was scandalised: 'Never! He's the most loyal, patient friend. So is Rhoda. I'd be lost without them.'

It was true. Katherine's friendship with Neville and Rhoda had a vividness and body which no other had. This was partly due to the underlying danger. The brother and sister were brighter than Katherine and much less tolerant of stupidity. In loving her, they also protected her from their own ruthlessness. She was good for them, too, because, as a being too good-hearted and beautiful for them to savage, she brought out their latent kindness. Rhoda and Neville enjoyed Katherine as a work of art they were still creating.

Katherine knew this. Neville's devilishly clever little eyes had vampirised her months before and had also told her plainly he was capable of anything; yet this 'anything' would be made amusing with self-mockery and endless good humour. What finally charmed her was that Neville 'respected' her: he never made a false move. He had understood that Katherine was not looking for adventures but wanted the sort of education in taste and values which Neville and his sister could give. And so Neville became guardian angel, wicked elder brother and worldly friend, and she enjoyed a close acquaintance with him. No one appreciated more his sharply-defined contours and textures. Physically there was no spare flesh on him, and his mind was the same – everything he had was of immediate use. Katherine Thomson thought he was exceptional, and he and Rhoda were the people she – if not her husband – had most enjoyed meeting in all her time abroad. How could The Duchess have failed to understand this?

'Of course, the trouble began when they were children. They had all their own way. Their father was too busy, and their mother was a complete ninny. They grew up anyhow and fed one another's conceit in the most extraordinary way. All he does is marvellous and vice versa. Now she's let him get his oar into everything. I don't think there's anything Neville doesn't know about her marriage. Believe me, you'd be astounded if you knew just how much they feel free to discuss.'

'Really?'

'My dear, the marriage will never work so long as Neville's around. He comes between them. With Rhoda, Neville comes first every time. The poor old husband and breadwinner comes a poor second.'

From this point Katherine was undermined by the simple fact that The Duchess said things which Katherine herself had secretly thought.

'Don't you find Neville and Rhoda too close? I mean, it's absurd the way they carry on.' (Katherine's mouth was dry; she was speechless.) 'They're altogether too close. It's unhealthy.' The Duchess leaned closer and said the brother and sister were too fond of one another. Not lovers, perhaps, but emotionally involved.

'Do you really think so?'

'My dear, it stands out a mile.'

'Is it such a bad thing?'

'It must be. When two people are wrapped up in each other as Rhoda and Neville are, it must be bad for those who are around them.' The Duchess touched Katherine's arm – a gesture which appeared to make them blood-sisters in scandal – and drew her once more into the orbit of secrets: 'Rhoda even talks about the physical side of her marriage with Neville. She's shameless. Shameless.'

'Oh, no!' Katherine drew back. 'That can't be true.'

'I've been cooped up on a boat with them for days on end. It was the *one* subject of conversation.'

Curiosity overcame discretion: 'But what could they say?'

The Duchess wrinkled up her face as though swallowing bitter aloes. 'Don't let's discuss it.'

At that moment a baby from a nearby table fell near Katherine and began shrieking. Its *fortissimo* broke The Duchess's spell.

'But you're saying lies. Mrs de Vries, I can't believe it.' Katherine covered her face with her hands, shamelessly ham-acting. 'It's not right to say such things. I shall never repeat them.'

The Duchess saw through her play-acting: 'My dear, Rhoda wouldn't mind what you repeated. She's completely shameless – just like her brother. I've already told her what I've told you.'

Katherine Thomson hardly seemed to be hearing. 'You mean you told her all this?'

'Why not?'

'It's all so personal!'

A goose, thought The Duchess, and a beautiful, middle-class one, too. 'We talk personally from time to time, you know. We're that kind of family.'

Katherine saw she was being made fun of – her theatrical gestures of shock and dissociation dismissed as juvenile. 'I don't understand you.'

'I told Rhoda she was wrong to have Neville back for a second year. I said he divided her loyalties, and the husband suffered. She thought I was talking nonsense, and yet she knew I was right. She knows well enough, and at the same time she doesn't want to know. It's a mental trick she has.'

'I can't believe Neville would deliberately come between his sister and her husband.'

'But I don't think so either! Neville's got used to his sister's devotion and can't live without it. He wants a nice home where he can return after sunbathing and flirting with the girls at the Beach Club. If the husband is mug enough to provide the home, well and good.'

Katherine Thomson refused to be drawn further. 'The idea had never struck me, I must confess.' And, because this was untrue, she lost her nerve and rose hastily, saying she would make enquiries about the plane. She was running away from the hard ungenerous eyes of The Duchess, which were ready to make her confess things about her friends – doubts, sudden intuitions, errors of judgement – that humiliated her. Her friendship with the brother and sister was the most important commitment she had at that time. She liked their understanding of one another and the way they somehow created a space on the seat between them for herself. They amused her, they kept her on her toes.

Back in the restaurant: 'You've been a bit shocked, I think, by what I've said.'

'Well, a bit surprised, you know?' Katherine attempted to smile.

'I didn't think you'd take things so much to heart.'

Katherine Thomson gaped: 'I don't know anybody who wouldn't. Don't you see that Rhoda and Neville are my best friends here? They're young, gay, amusing. And we've got the same interests, the same outlook on life. One has to speak as one finds – you know? And Neville's been a good friend to me. Nothing too much trouble for him. Marvellous in every way.'

The Duchess agreed that Katherine had to be fair.

'No, I'm not being fair. I'm being truthful. To say anything less would be untruthful. A lie.'

'His instincts are *never* generous. All that counts is Number One: Master Neville. The rest are comic turns in a private circus – to be laughed at or used. The way he talks about his so-called best friend, that drunken degenerate Paul Brophy! He was unwilling for anyone to say a good word about him.'

Katherine Thomson's shock turned to resentment. What did Mrs de Vries hope to gain by being so vicious? It was pointless; and yet The Duchess had not finished: 'They're really amoral. Don't know the meaning of ordinary, decent behaviour.'

'I'm sorry, I don't agree.'

The two women stared at one another and then, as the plane was announced, walked downstairs into the main hall. Neither spoke, and The Duchess did not accompany Katherine to the customs hall. Katherine remained uncertain, perplexed, sickened. She could not forgive herself for even listening to Mrs de

54

Vries. She felt guilty about her part in the conversation; she felt she must have encouraged The Duchess, even by silence; and this was the last thing she wanted to do. She might be simple-hearted, even socially naïve (as anyone might guess from her round, schoolgirl handwriting with its big vowels and self-important squiggle) but she was loyal to those she liked.

She left The Duchess walking around the central concourse, easing the pain in an arthritic hip. The life about her seemed formless, distasteful. She hated the placid lifeless women in black – some still veiled – waiting to be shipped away like so much baggage to Kuwait; she hated the pushing and screaming children. Somehow, in that new, post-oil boom world she was out of place – ignored – and it made her furious. She was cross with herself for speaking out of turn about her stepchildren to Katherine Thomson; she knew her mistake, without being able to help herself. She stopped, prepared to turn. The man who had been mooching around her suddenly spoke. 'You want a porter.' Taken by surprise, The Duchess reacted sharply. 'Leave me alone. Go away!' She put all her rage and frustration into the words. The man fell back, more astonished than hurt. He stood still. They looked at one another. 'Will you please go away. *Imshi!* How these people stick and pester you!' The man smiled at the aspect of God's truth she presented, but did not move. 'Trying it on!' The Duchess stopped to look back at him indignantly. 'They're all the same.'

As she turned, she saw Katherine Thomson coming towards her with a tall rawboned man in tow, hung with camera equipment and wearing a light summer hat with a gaudy band. She stopped and waited for them.

21

FOR Maxwell Thomson, The Duchess summed up everything he had run away from at home: a short, plumpish woman with thick legs and irascible, rather British, feet; even the

55

dimples in her plump, cook's arms – normally so endearing – looked put out. 'At last! So you've come!' Then, for good, irrational measure as the young man held out his hand, 'Anyone would take you for an American.'

It was not meant as a compliment, but Maxwell Thomson laughed. He had outpaced The Duchess's world years ago, bouncing from success to success with the single-mindedness of the man who has made up his mind that living in England was a pleasure for other people. Ever since graduating from Manchester University he had worked abroad and acquired the classless, stateless, free air of those who are more familiar with other countries than their own. He had his life taped; he expected other people to be in the same situation.

He at once criticised his brother and sister-in-law for going up into the mountains for the summer when an air-conditioner would have saved them the trouble. Trailing back and forth every day – what was the point of it? Katherine accepted *estivage* in the mountains as a local custom.

'Only because it's the done thing. And what a bore driving up and down this road all the time.' He was dogmatic; he was sure – absolutely sure – she and his brother hated driving up and down.

'You are funny, Max. We don't mind at all. I like the way the landscape opens out behind the bay, the ships, the mountains.'

'Not *every* day.'

'Until the end of the month.'

'All unnecessary in these days.'

'How tiresome he is.' The Duchess in the back of the car could contain herself no longer. '*It's the done thing.* There's no one left in town during the hot months.'

'A lot of fuss and inconvenience when an air-conditioner would do the trick.'

The Duchess believed air-conditioning was unhealthy. It damaged the membranes of the throat and nose.

'An old wives' tale.'

'Well, it's true.'

'Anyway . . . let's forget it, shall we, and enjoy the view . . . ?' Maxwell looked back; and beyond The Duchess in her all-secluding sun-glasses he saw the sweep of pastel-shaded skyscrapers and belts of pinewood with the Mediterranean's smooth waters beyond and the September blue sky over all. It was noon, and the country houses, roofed in the Marseilles tiles so detested by Miss Freya Stark, were partially shuttered against the heat. Families lolled on gaudy sofas, and children leaned over balustrades, watching the traffic screech by. The poetry of the ascent, through groves of umbrella pines and over open shoulders of the hillside, with wide views behind, was spoiled by the Arab indifference to detail. Every other house had an unfinished floor or wing, with cement rods sticking into the air like clusters of pipecleaners. At almost every bend of the road were ill-constructed shacks selling Coca-Cola and ice-cream, with an accompanying rash of metal advert plaques and empty cartons. The refuse – bottles, papers, boxes – filled the storm-drains alongside the road. Even in Jaufa, one of the most elegant hill resorts, the hotels in the pinewoods were joined together by garlands and trails of rubbish.

The Thomsons had an apartment in a stone-built house which stood at the point where orchards and pinewoods met, and looked south-east across a steep ravine to Athoum, where Saudi and Kuwaiti cars flashed in the sun. The house was cool, but not much more so than on the coast, and Maxwell, standing on the balcony listening to the insects scratching away in the trees, said that, apart from the view, the long journey had hardly been worth the effort. He said it to tease Katherine, but she was vexed. As a conventional girl she disliked things she took for granted to be questioned, even though he was saying things she secretly believed to be true. The boredom and heat of the mountain resorts have to be experienced to be believed – 'Capitals of Ennui,' the French-language paper called them. The boredom was more intense because everyone knew everyone else was afflicted. Nothing would happen until the sun began to go down – and even then it would be nothing more than small domestic detail: the families would assemble on the balconies for coffee and cards, and everyone, from grandmother to toddler, would sit back and watch the night fall and the mountainsides break into light under the serene sky.

After the midday meal they all had a siesta (like everyone else), and rose in time for coffee and ice-cream (like everyone else), and yawned and felt dissatisfied at the way another afternoon had been gobbled up by sleep (like everyone else), and felt that peculiar anguish which British people know when they

57

indulge in siestas – a sense of narrowing possibilities, of life cut before the spool has reached half-way.

Gradually the anguish passed, constructive thinking became possible. Maxwell appeared in a clean shirt, his hair slicked flat by the shower, and organised his brother and his wife in a corner, near a wall covered with roses, and snapped them at the moment when the setting sun made everyone's skins a rich, golden colour. He caught The Duchess, still flopped out in her green linen, sitting on a striped sofa holding a Japanese fan, while the Thomsons' Siamese cat washed its paws beside her.

Beyond their balcony, beyond the Provençal-red roofs and pine-trees of the village, the day was ending in huge sweeps of colour and different textures of light and shadow over the Mediterranean. The night was announced by the sudden winking of the Pharos down below; yet light still lingered on the mountain slopes about Jaufa: Mount Atthis was an enthralling golden-mauve colour. Against the backcloth of the mountain, villas and monasteries gleamed a whitish-purple and then disappeared into the gathering night.

One by one and string by string the town lights came on. Athoum, so close as the crow flies across the ravine and so far away by car, began to flower with light from the long, graceful chains of street-lamps in undeveloped quarters to the huge hotels which glowed, floodlit, against the pale mauve sky. Two red aircraft beacons on the mountain crest above the resorts lit up, and an incredible tenderness came down from the skies with the ingliding planes, whose lights flashed like constellations briefly across the panorama.

The terraces around the house had withdrawn into the night – become mysterious night-woods, where only insects scratched away. Down below, Baida had become a vast jewelhouse of lights and neon colours, twinkling, coruscating brilliantly, and inviting the hand to lean over the balcony to pick up handfuls of treasure before the wall of humidity came in from the sea. Yet the city was a good twelve kilometres away and over eight hundred metres below. On the balcony all was calm and reposeful, as though the consciousness of the world, in shedding an outer skin of self-defence and prickliness, had become one with the beauty of the night.

22

THE evening brought up The Consort, Rhoda and Neville to fetch The Duchess. Paul Brophy, who had attached himself, came last through the garden gate. 'That young chap's adopted your family,' Richard Thomson said to The Duchess. 'If I'd behaved as he did I'd have stayed away for a short time.'

'He probably doesn't remember.' The Duchess stood up to wait for the new arrivals.

Katherine Thomson watched her to see how she would behave with the stepchildren she had so maligned. She noted Neville speaking to her and leading her, almost at once, into a corner; there was urgency in his low voice. Neville was being as charming as he knew how, and The Duchess, who listened gravely, nodded and gave him one of her rare, intimate smiles and patted his cheek: he was forgiven. Katherine breathed freely again; she might have been involved. The Duchess then joined Rhoda on the striped settee.

The Consort asked if he might hear the latest B.B.C. bulletin; a minister was planning a visit to the area. Maxwell Thomson almost split at the sides with vexation that anyone could care what a British minister did. 'There's not a single statesman at home. Not one. And the parties are so much alike you can hardly put a pin between them.'

The Consort, who claimed he was a Liberal who would rather vote Tory than let the Socialists get in, crisped a little at the tone. 'That saves you the bother of voting, then.'

'Sure. I wouldn't vote for one of the blighters. Democracy's clapped out. What we want is a benevolent technocrats' dictatorship – something like the Gaullist régime in France. We'll never have anything worthwhile at home any more.'

'What nonsense!' The Duchess spilled her drink in her irritation. 'Why is everybody so anti-British? Rhoda and Neville are always saying life at home is dull, and no one's got any money – and it's not true. They just know the wrong people.'

Maxwell Thomson laughed: 'And as soon as I leave England I seem to meet all the right ones.'

Richard Thomson tried to smooth things over: 'Well, Max, how nice for you you don't have to live among the British any more. All the same, remember they're your fellow-country-men.'

'They're not. I'm stateless. The whole tissue of British values – the self-consciousness, the class-consciousness, the bent little people in charge – is foreign to me. The place is run by a fumbling bunch of quacks.'

'Rubbish! I wish I had a Union Jack to wave at you!' The Duchess looked ready to rush at him.

'Well, that's my opinion. Nothing works there any more. Trains are as often late as they're to time; London's jammed up with traffic; the people are so dim you feel they'll swallow almost anything . . .' He was interrupted by a general shout. He had a thing about Britain, they said. He was passing through a phase, like pimples or blushing. Maxwell showed no rancour. He merely insisted that as soon as he returned to London he felt unwell – unnerved by the anxious, half-impotent feeling in the air. Everyone trotted out favourite views, and in the middle of the excitement Maxwell went off to bed.

'Air travelling is awfully exhausting!' Katherine spoke in her most worldly way, and Paul Brophy, sitting on a sofa (drinking and being inscrutable) agreed with her. 'A vastly over-rated form of transport.' He blinked at the others.

'You're dressed to kill tonight.'

'I went to a reception at the Soviet Embassy.'

Neville could not stand Brophy when he put on airs; to watch him preening himself on his connections with the communists infuriated him. This was Brophy's weakness: never being able to resist a social engagement, and then talking about his exalted contacts.

The Consort wondered how the Russians could pursue an anti-religious policy and yet have so many friends in Islamic countries.

'Oh, not so many as all that,' Richard Thomson said, and from this they went on to talk about Islam's attitudes to the non-Islamic world. Here The Duchess came into her own and said what a mistake the Islamic religion had been: 'It's contributed nothing and held everyone back.'

In the ordinary way there was no one there who had any very strong feelings about religion, except Brophy for whom religious observances were bound up with some childhood obligation to believe; but The Duchess brought the argument

60

down to everyday levels, where everyone could count her misconceptions. She believed Islam forbade men to speak kindly to women; she believed it was wrong to ask a Muslim about the health of his family; she swore that Muslim children were brought up to recite a verse from the Koran giving them the right to cheat and kill Christians. On her own premises, it was only through sheer good luck she had not been killed, raped and pillaged, in whatever order.

Neville pointed out that she was denying the evidence of her own senses. Everywhere around her people were saying nice things to women and generally making a great fuss of them. To which The Duchess replied: 'European women get different treatment.'

Rhoda objected: 'Darling, we're exactly the same. Go to the snack-bars and cafés near the university, where the students and poets meet, and you'll see the young people of the new generation talking politics and looking soulfully into one another's eyes just as they do in Oxford or Paris. Given half a chance, the young men whisper sweet nothings into the girls' ears just as they do at home.'

'They despise women. They think we have no soul.'

'That could be. At the same time, women command a great deal of love and respect. We know many Arab families – don't we, Neville? – where the mother is the pivot; and we've known many men emotionally attached to their mothers until late in life. Muslims may believe women have no souls, but they cherish and respect us, too, if we behave properly.'

The Duchess waved this away. The men were only interested in one thing.

'Like European men, then! But, Duchess darling, believe me, I feel safer wandering around the *souks* looking for old furniture than I do walking downtown in the evening. The really unpleasant incidents always happen in the tourist district.'

'That's because it's a hybrid, semi-Americanised, semi-Europeanised, semi-Christian district – it's a mishmash of corrupt values.'

'That may well be, Neville, but I've never yet heard any woman say she felt happier in Muslim areas. I'd rather die than walk out in one at night – even at my age.'

Nothing could shake The Duchess's conviction that Islam was incorrigibly hostile to anything that was not of its own kind. Neville reminded her of the verse in the Koran which, in effect, calls on Muslims to look favourably on Christians. Paul Brophy had the text word for word: 'You will surely find that those nearest to us in affection are those believers who say, We are Christians.'

The Consort whistled ironically: 'Haj Brophy must be going to Islam.'

Brophy flushed: 'A little basic knowledge of the people you live and work among is always useful, don't you agree?'

'Carry on! Carry on! I couldn't agree more.' The Consort was amiable offhandedness itself. 'All the same, I believe that for every dictum in the Koran there's an antidote three pages later.'

The Duchess had heard this, too – which accounted, she said, for the gap between what Muslims read and did. 'They talk about giving alms to the poor, yet all the rich people in Egypt hadn't enough conscience to put in a thimble.'

'They were probably Christians. Before Nasser came to power, the Copts, the Lebanese Christians, the Greek Orthodox and the Italian Catholics had Egypt in their grasp. They battened on the poor Egyptians like leeches.'

'Oh, Neville! How you exaggerate.'

'They did, Duchess.'

Richard Thomson thought the non-Muslims had made Egypt, and the place had gone downhill since the foreign elements were expelled.

Paul Brophy blinked like a cat: 'Egypt will survive.'

Neville and Rhoda let the others argue and agreed that The Duchess was tiresome. 'To think she's lived in the Arab world for years and goes around with all her misconceptions fluttering around her head like old flags.'

'All shot to pieces, darling, but still flying.'

'The idea that Arab men are told not to be nice to women.' The absurdity of it! They began to laugh until they cried. 'They can't stop being the opposite!'

Yet The Duchess, side by side with her misconceptions, had an instinctive feeling for Islam's poetry. She never tired of the muezzin calling the offices of the day, and she got Paul Brophy to write out a transliteration of the call to prayer, so that she might follow it. 'God is most great. I testify that there is no god but God. I testify that Muhammed is God's apostle. Come to prayer. Come to security. God is most great.'

Brophy said each phrase is repeated at least once, and she might find confusion in the way a muezzin distorted certain sounds and lingered over others in the interests of the beauty of the chant. In addition, the morning call has a special reminder that 'prayer is better than sleep'.

'Oh, please keep to the main outline. Don't give me variations.'

'Oh, Duchess darling, don't be so testy! Paul is trying to explain to you that, if you listen to the dawn call to prayer, there'll be this little extra piece.'

'I see.' She looked a monument to stupidity and irritation. 'You mean the dawn call is different from the others? That's the one I'm most interested in.'

'That's what Paul was saying.'

Paul Brophy liked her interest. 'If more people tried to understand, tried to see things as they are, not as they might be, people would get more out of their stay here. It would be happier for everyone.'

'But, Paul, m'dear, what is there to be happier about? I thought most people were happy as things are.'

'I mean, people wouldn't say offensive and untrue things about the Arabs if they understood something about their history and about Islam.'

'Look here, me old beauty' – and when The Consort put on his racing tipster voice everyone knew a jab was coming – 'Let's get this straight. Say what you like about the Arabs – and it can be as vile as you like – yet it'll still be true.'

'Oh, balls!' Rhoda flushed with rage at her husband's manner and opinions.

'You know the old Tommy's verse?

"Don't let's be beastly to the A-rabs.
Don't let's be horrid to the wogs.
The Queen has sent instructions
To avoid all kinds of ructions;
We mustn't call the sons of bitches dogs!"'

No one laughed; Rhoda asked ironically if The Consort meant to be funny. 'Not funny. Just a bit of Anglo-Arab folklore.'

'Anglo-Arab folklore?'

63

'It's the real British attitude – whether you like it or not.'

'Balls!' (The Duchess winced a second time.) 'It's as bad as The Duchess saying every Arab tortures his wife.'

'People talk too much about the Arabs and miss the reality under their noses.' Neville threw away his cigarette with impatience. 'If only people would try to learn the language, or better still if they'd only assume that because they can't speak it they must be missing most of the flavour of local life. Imagine how we'd react to an Arab speaking no English, living an artificial life on the cocktail and canapé circuit in Belgravia, living in a flat no English person can afford, with wall-to-wall carpets, central heating, mirrors from ceiling to floor, with armfuls of roses even in winter and an ormolu table worth a couple of thousand quid to hold the visiting cards: I say imagine how we'd react if such a man laid down the law about the English – and even told people what English people think and feel.'

The Duchess did not see his point.

'I'm drawing a comparison between the way we live and the way we feel free to pass comments on the life around us.'

'*We're* not correspondents.'

'The correspondents are worse. They sit writing their articles in the bars of the plush hotels.'

'That's rot, too.' The Consort drew in a deep breath.

'I wish you could discuss things in an adult way, darling.' Rhoda said she liked people able to savour ideas and experiences like fruit. 'We aren't obliged to be violently involved in everything we discuss.'

The Thomsons understood that in the futile argument between the brother, the sister and The Consort something else was at stake. All were saying things for effect: Rhoda and Neville to irritate The Consort, The Consort to get his own back on the people who were exploiting him, including Paul Brophy.

Paul Brophy had found paper and pencil and, while writing out the transliteration for The Duchess, let himself be drawn into the family tussle: 'It's self-evident that if you like something you get more out of it than otherwise.'

'And it's also self-evident that the people who like the Arabs are mostly cranks or queers. So where does *that* get you?'

'*La illaha illallah wa Muhammad rasulallah,*' Brophy half-spoke to himself, as he wrote slowly, and gave no sign of having heard The Consort's remark. The others heard. They saw Rhoda's face turn white, pinched.

'Oh, you bloody Englishman.'

The Duchess leaned towards Brophy: 'You'll write it big enough for me, won't you? My eyes aren't what they were.'

Brophy finished off the transliteration and, still half-absorbed by his printing, said: 'The Polish Ambassador said a clever thing at the reception this evening. He said West German foreign policy has always suffered from the same ailment: it jumps on an express train five minutes before disaster.'

23

WHILE helping Katherine to make coffee, Rhoda complained about The Consort's attitudes and manners: 'He's got that dreadful English public school philistinism and malice. He's got a down on Neville at the moment, and Paul Brophy got the backlash. I ought to walk out on him. Yes, I shall never respect myself until I get away from him.' Katherine's attempts to calm her were only partially successful; she reminded Rhoda how depressed she got at having to live in England. 'That's just it, darling. I stick with him for the foreign travel. It's a fine basis for a marriage, isn't it?'

Katherine had nothing to say.

Just before The Duchess was driven home, she took Katherine aside and apologised for having given the impression of being over-critical of her stepchildren. 'They're dear things in many ways – good and bad points like the rest of us – but I went too far. It was a lapse of taste and I apologise.'

Katherine was relieved and grateful. She kissed The Duchess fervently and her world clicked back into place. The effect was hallucinatory: she knew how The Duchess felt about her stepchildren, but she had also had a glimpse of The Duchess's ability to be big and contrite. She warmed towards the old lady and was pleased she would accompany them to the ruins at Helisson the next day. Her husband was less pleased and gave a solemn warning against getting too involved.

'As you know well enough, a little of them goes a long way with me. They're all a bit over-theatrical, and they get you worked up for the sheer pleasure of it. I can see where the trouble lies. I wouldn't like to have your brother living with us and referring to me as The Consort, like a joke – and having that creep Brophy trailing around sopping up the liquor and never inviting people back.'

'Hospitality isn't cutlet for cutlet, is it?'

'Here it is. You've got to be damned good value for money before you can go around eating and drinking as much as Brophy does without drying up your welcome.' He laughed. 'Why look at me like that? If you can't face the truth . . .'

'But it's different when you're a single person. I mean, there's always room for an extra place.'

'O.K. Once. Twice. Maybe three times. But all the bloody time? No. Rhoda must face up to it – her man's got a point.'

Indifferent to the residents, the cockerels of Jaufa were crowing here and there, as though announcing dawn, disturbed by the luminous night. Low in the western sky, the moon – filling out from its first Islamic crescent – floated down like a curled feather towards a mass of pearl-tinted clouds. Near at hand, the water-tanks, the fruit-trees, the flower-pots seemed spellbound in the nostalgic afterlight; while, a couple of terraces away, a banker and his family were listening to music which seemed to have been conjured out of the night itself.

The still morning, breaking over the mountains, was at first apricot-coloured, then old gold, before merging into the pearl grey of sea and mountains. Jasmine, hibiscus, bougainvillaea and frangipani glittered under windows, hung over the mellow walls and balconies of the old city; and, in time, from hundreds of open windows came the tuning signal of Radio Baida, followed by the gay, French-provincial station signal and the husky woman announcer: *'Huna Medina-al-Baida, al izza'at al gumhuriyyah al Baidaniyah . . .'*

24

THEY set off with their passports for Helisson at about eight o'clock with Katherine at the wheel. They drove against the morning rush-hour traffic taking business people into the city, against the gaudy village buses, laden with people and goods, and the huge transporter lorries, sky-high with melons and boxes of apples, grinding painfully downhill with every cylinder backfiring. They passed through Khadra – and glimpsed the white MEDOC building in its bower of olive-trees – and Hezrayah, the nearest thing to Beverly Hills in the Arab world: a millionaires' suburb in every known style of architecture. At Athoum they ran into a gigantic traffic-jam – seven cars had collided near the station – and a friendly traffic policeman advised them to take a coffee while they waited. Katherine flicked the car into a vacant space at the side of the road and led them into a nearby restaurant. The din by this time was unbearable: every driver in sight had his fist on his klaxon, and the balconies were filled with townsfolk enjoying the diversion and calling out to one another. 'Uncivilised bastards!' Maxwell took the noise as a personal insult. They passed through the restaurant, where the radio was relaying western pop from the British forces station in Cyprus, to the terrace behind, and sat down in the shade of a poplar grove.

Pressed lemons with ice, coffees, ice-cream and lemon-tea were served at a table under a blue-and-white umbrella, where the chairs were arranged for the view down towards the sea. 'You see the charm of the life here . . . always an excuse to have refreshments . . . nearly always somewhere pleasant to have them . . .' As Katherine spoke, the poplars rustled, the water tinkled into a tank in the garden below. 'And it's always like this – something unforeseen every moment. Life is really spontaneous – you know? We seem to create it hour by hour. Maxwell turning up like that – a day out – an excursion. It's very pleasant. Somehow one can't get this kind of pleasure at home. Things are too painfully arranged, too laboriously worked at.'

'It's my happiness out of the skies,' Neville said. 'If it's not caught like this it's nothing.' He went off into a daydream, while the other three discussed the family sitting nearby. Maxwell had been impressed by the chic of the daughters – and by their dissatisfied faces. 'They want things to happen.'

'They're waiting for marriage. Then they'll be free to do as they please.' Katherine saw nothing out of the ordinary in the family, which had seemed a typical middle-class group, good-looking and well turned out. Maxwell noticed that they had stopped speaking French and were trying out their English.

Katherine smiled: 'That's because they've heard us talking in English. They're real parrots.'

'Then say something in Arabic to fox them.'

'Me? I've been taking lessons for years, but I can't *talk* it!'

Neville listened, while the other three debated the need for Arabic, and Katherine said she had never seen the need for it until she knew Rhoda and Neville – 'Then I saw how much more they got out of their lives here, how much closer they were to their Arab friends. It struck me I'd been silly not to try. But it's difficult, believe me.'

Neville passed the Arabic menu towards her: 'Let me test you.' She read the bill of fare easily; he was impressed. All the same, he wished he were a hundred miles away from people discussing the characteristics and foibles of another race, piling generalisation on generalisation until they no longer saw what was under their noses; it was the failure to react to a natural, human situation that astonished him: 'You know, it's a marvellous language; it gives me more pleasure to use it than any other. It has a directness and honesty that English has lost. It has no false sense of shame; I can't quite explain it. One can say things elegantly in Arabic that would sound dreadful in European languages.'

Shut in the car with the three others, Neville felt he could not breathe. Maxwell's empty bombast, The Duchess's gentility and Katherine's English-miss manner at one go were too much for him; he was homesick for his own kind, for the concrete, practical Arab spirit, with its basic need to be assured about family relationships and whether one was looking after one's mother and its moments of understanding and fire. He had seen the expression in the eyes of the elegant girls in the restaurant – the awareness, the moment of honesty, quickly hidden, but lingering in the dissatisfied mouths, the droop of the neck. It was the fire which consumed a person such as

Iskander – a person capable of despicable, unmentionable things – and gave a sort of innocence to him. The fire was everywhere, subtly transforming the simplest occasion into something memorable, alive.

'You're very silent, Neville.' The Duchess nudged him with her elbow. 'A penny for your thoughts.'

'I was thinking that down there a saint is buried. Can you see the little white dome in the trees?'

They reached the frontier, bought visas and began the slow descent into the Helissonic plain. A last glimpse northwards to the outrider ranges of Mount Atthis, green with pines and enlivened by the pink roofs of villas, before the rocks shut them in, and the plain – that astonishing corridor of abundance between golden-puce and barren mountains – opened before them. 'Look, there. The old granary of the Byzantine Empire!' For a moment, Katherine's pleasure lit up the old guidebook cliché, and the plain's lines of poplars, vineyards, fields of harvested corn, water-channels, and plots of maize and pumpkins, were something she had created. Although Katherine warned Maxwell that photographs of the view rarely succeed, he insisted on taking the chance.

The Duchess and Katherine stood together, looking down at the dappled chequerboard below them, while Neville held some of Maxwell's expensive Japanese equipment. Then, as so often happens there, a sensation of perfect happiness came down on them. The plain below withheld its essence from the camera, but the lyrical impulse it inspired (it is, all said and done, one of the great human landscapes) was overwhelming. In each of them was the knowledge that they had fulfilled an old obligation to themselves, in the everyday phrase 'they had broken a dream'. The dream had foretold this experience of the beauty and fullness of the earth; and it had come – without warning – out of the landscape and the late September day. Happiness comes down this way in the east and creates its own moment of awareness. For a short period, the movement of their lives was held up, and the completed fragment of perfection revealed to them. Time would tick by, the sensation of abundance and rest pass away, but the knowledge of perfection would remain. In experiencing it, and in recalling it, they would feel themselves to be perfect, too.

Half-past two: they were seated in a shady garden eating

grilled chicken and staring at a huge bowl of grapes. They had visited Helisson, been defeated by the guides and curio shops, and decided the temples should be visited in the rain. Exhausted, the visitors took refuge in the restaurant and sat at the edge of a pool watching the fish wink a languorous fin from time to time. Their table was set at the edge of a large expanse of greensward, on which the first golden poplar leaves had fallen: it was a slumbrous afternoon.

Neville was telling Katherine that he had decided to find a flat of his own, when a large American car drew up the other side of the pool, and four people got out.

Neville recognised them. 'Look: Paul Brophy's torturers!'

They all turned and saw a tall heavily-built man, a typical Baidani middle-class woman with plump feet overflowing small, high-heeled shoes, a girl of about fourteen and a hag-gard European woman, who walked strangely like a jerky puppet, hidden behind the huge sun-glasses that were popular that year. The woman waved; Katherine and Neville waved back.

'Dot Parslow and Shamseddine!' Neville grimaced. 'I wonder what they're plotting over here.'

The newcomers walked along the other side of the stream to the bridge and entered the garden. Two such groups of people, meeting by chance at such a place at the quiet end of the season attracted one another irresistibly. Before anyone could think up defensive phrases about 'just going' or 'only staying a minute more', Shamseddine had ordered coffees all round, an Arabic ice-cream for his beautiful daughter and was paying court to The Duchess.

Shamseddine was as tall as Maxwell Thomson, heavily built, and with the large, apparently gormless head of what the ignor-ant tend to think of as the Egyptians. He had remarkable eyes, observant, globular, rather over-liquid – his dominating fea-ture. These same eyes were all that was left of the gazelle-eyed youth, all soul, all full-lipped emptiness, all plum-ripe dedica-tion, in the photographs, taken at Alexandria, of himself and his wife at the time of their wedding. He laughed easily, in a fat-boy way, showing sophisticated teeth, well-laced with gold. He exuded bonhomie; he had bounce and energy. When serious or gloomy, his mouth sagged and brooded on the hard-ness of life, and his eyes grew mournful, as though at the realisation that all man's effort revolved around the demands of the ever-open hole below: Shamseddine was a glutton.

He ordered a plate of nut-and-honey pastries, and, as everyone else was too replete, he finished off the lot himself. The Duchess was charmed by him, and his English, she said, was a pleasure to listen to. He was delighted by her compliment and said his father, a Lebanese born in Palestine but brought up in Egypt, had insisted on his having an English education. Four visits to England had greatly charmed him. And what especially? asked The Duchess.

It was hard for him to say, since he was a devotee of English literature. Of course, he had liked Stratford-on-Avon and Oxford and Cambridge; but his old English teacher in Alexandria, Mr Mountford, had introduced him to other writers and had recommended other visits. He mentioned Keats House in Hampstead and a car trip with Mr Mountford – who had retired to Worcester – into the Kilvert country. The Duchess opened her mouth wide. 'That's where I live!' she managed to blurt out.

'Then I envy you, my dear.'

With pathetic intensity, as though exiled for years, The Duchess described her house with its discreet additions and its fields by the water.

'And do you have a ha-ha?'

'A ha-ha?'

'Mrs de Vries, don't tell me you don't know what a ha-ha is!'

'Yes, I know . . . a sort of defensive depression around paddocks or between the park and the garden. No, I don't have one. But imagine your knowing the word!'

'I first saw it in Jane Austen. It amused me. I've never forgotten it. I like to ask English people if they have a ha-ha and get a lot of pleasure explaining what it is. Only people of breeding know the word.'

The Duchess tittered ecstatically (having been found not wanting): 'It's quite out of use now. It's not really fair to judge.' Of course, she was thrilled by the compliment, thrilled.

He went on to talk of Henry Vaughan – a writer The Duchess had never looked at.

'Oh, but, my dear, you must. I will lend him to you. "The Evening Shower": it's my own experience of that country. I understood how it is that we Arabs always have our vision of God as something burning "in the white forenoon and in the burning noon" and you in England see Him in the strange half-lights.'

The Duchess clapped her dimpled hands with their elegant red nails together in a sort of prayer before the man's understanding: 'I want you and your wife to come to stay with me for the *whole* of your next visit to England. You'll really appreciate my little place.'

'We shall be delighted to.' Shamseddine's eyes were liquid with pleasure.

'I really do mean that. I take to people. I've lived in Cairo for years. I know when people are my friends. If I never see you again from now until the day you turn up on my doorstep: come to see me. We're already on the level where the ordinary palavers of friendship – what Mark Twain calls the folderols – don't matter.'

Now it was Shamseddine's moment of emotion and elation, and he took The Duchess's hand and kissed it lightly – and all this, as it were, sideways to the startled people around: 'That I promise you.'

Shamseddine's success with The Duchess irritated Neville. He had always understood that the man knew how to get round European women of a certain age. He found Shamseddine repellent in every way. He hated the overlarge head with its full, deeply cleft upper lip, its sloping brow ending in black, crinkly hair, and the – to Neville – ingratiating and ignoble smile, with its hint of Egyptian bisexuality.

Mrs Shamseddine continued her bright, brittle conversation with Katherine and kept wiping her slightly pockmarked cheeks with Kleenex tissues, as though by using a western product the gesture was less offensive. The daughter, after eating her ice-cream, wandered away to look at the postcard kiosk.

Maxwell, left to show his cameras to Mrs Parslow, asked whether she was Australian. She gave her great, gawky laugh: ' 'Course I am. A genu-ine Sydneysider. I wonder how you guessed?' She laughed loudly at her own joke, and Maxwell did not need to tell her that he had seen many other Australian women like her in the Far East – wives of bankers and business-men – with lined, sun-scorched faces and sun-dried hair, so tufty and dyed such an odd colour as to look like fuzz on a doll; and well-dressed without ever suggesting taste: women who drank hard and laughed loud, and had always been tomboys and were ending life as real guys.

'But you've been out here a long time.'

'My husband was in the Australian Army. Then he got a job in the Persian oil-fields, and we stooged around, and I ended up here. You've seen the place; do you blaim me?'

'Not really. You probably feel the same about Australia as I feel about England.'

'I've got no connections in the U.K. I go for leave about every four years. The people give me the creeps – they've had all the stuffing knocked out of them. They don't mean a thing. You ought to see the staff we get sent out from London.' She waved her hand in a gesture of contempt. 'We've got one of them on our hands at present. Don't start me on that. I never knew such drop-outs existed.' She dropped her voice. 'What's wrong with them all there? They don't seem to be able to respect themselves any more.'

At that, Maxwell was well-launched.

Meanwhile, Mrs Shamseddine talked non-stop about *la rentrée des classes* and the difficulty of finding school places. Then, when she thought people looked bored, she tried to include Neville in the talk by saying: 'I understand your friend Paul Brophy is going home shortly. He's had a very short tour. I'm sorry. I liked him. He's the tallest man I ever saw.' The others looked perplexed. 'Yes, he's going. My husband told me.'

Shamseddine laid a hand on The Duchess's arm and called across to his wife: 'What are you saying? You misunderstood me, my dear.' He tried to overcome his agitation. 'It was only a possibility.'

'Oh, please, my dear,' Mrs Shamseddine enjoyed chaffing her husband in public, as she had seen western women doing. 'Please will you make up your mind? You distinctly told me he was going home. There was no "if" and "but" about it.' She laughed shrilly, and there was nothing more anyone could say.

Katherine turned to Neville: 'Paul never mentioned this to you, did he?'

'Never.' Neville looked at Mrs Parslow and guessed by the ghastly expression on her face – the attempt to be unconcerned – that Mrs Shamseddine had uncovered a piece of underhand work. The chill reminded Shamseddine – who had been as expansive as a sunflower – that it was time to go.

'Oh, these men!' Mrs Shamseddine seemed the only person unaware she had put her foot in it. 'They change their minds like children. They fidget. They must be on the move.' She laughed shrilly again.

Shamseddine's anxiety to get away almost spoiled the good impression he had made. He smiled brightly, he promised much, he kissed hands, his black-and-white shoes twinkled and moved about in agitation as he shifted from one foot to the other; but the fatal impression remained – he was bundling his wife away. Mrs Shamseddine was determined to do the correct thing. She shook hands all round and arranged to see The Duchess again.

Doris Parslow called out, 'See you!' in a way reminiscent of travellers calling from a moving train. 'Let's get together some time.' Before anyone could name a date (an unlikely event) she had tottered jerkily away.

The question was simple: What had gone wrong? Had Mrs Shamseddine given away a secret move against Brophy? The Duchess was appalled they had jumped to conclusions so quickly. (She was still under the spell of Shamseddine's liquid promising eyes.) She was very wise. People had become infected with the current mania for seeing plots and stratagems everywhere.

Neville did not bother to argue, but told Katherine Thomson he would warn Brophy the next day, when they lunched together. While The Duchess bought postcards at the nearby stall, Katherine asked why Shamseddine and Mrs Parslow should want to destroy Brophy. Neville was not sure; but thought the reason was probably banal. He smiled at Katherine: 'We'll never know. We'll ask questions and talk about it, but we'll never know. The hate was there waiting for an object; after a time, Mrs Parslow found an excuse. They say she wants Shamseddine to have Brophy's position – God knows if it's true. She trails around with Shamseddine and his family like some gawky country cousin, but she doesn't really love him – or them. She'll go around for the laughs, as they say, and for the companionship. Mrs Shamseddine loathes and resents her. I never realised this until a do last spring when Mrs Shamseddine – we were talking about family life – said she thought it

74

a scandal that elderly people in western countries lived alone
and had no one to cherish them as they did in the Arab World.
I remember her saying "I'd be ashamed if our old people had
to go abroad and work in offices like Mrs Parslow and live in a
big flat by herself, without anyone to care whether you lived or
died. European women must be very different from us if they
can enjoy such a life." She went on about "lonely old people
like Mrs Parslow" although there isn't so much difference in
their ages. Pure bitchery. A hatchet job.'

25

MAXWELL enjoyed the trip, but found The Duchess heavy
going. He told Neville he wanted to spend his last evening on
the town, and they ended up, after midnight, in one of the
dimly-lit drinking-places in the cinema district with the English words 'Red and Gold Bar' in neon over the door. By cutting down the lighting to a single spotlight over the bar and
by installing a couple of indirect lights on the walls, an atmosphere of mystery and *intimité* had been created at the expense
of comfort and good sense.

They ordered beers, and Maxwell looked around in a dissatisfied way. The pleasures of Baida were coarse and trumpery
after the subtleties of Hong Kong, and he thought it had been
an expensive evening and a poor one. They had done the usual
tour of night-spots and cafés, looking for the offbeat, and had
found the same beers, the same pop-songs in the juke-boxes
and the same absence of real charm or atmosphere. The 'Red
and Gold Bar' was the last port of call; they had reached the
end of the road.

As the bar-girl handed over the beers, they both realised by
her stiff, doubtful manner that she was English. The spotlight
gave her bare arms a greenish-white tint, without detracting
from the general effect of physical grandeur. Neville was spellbound: 'A noble creature,' was his verdict. 'A creature to be
worked on.'

The girl first filed her nails and then read a magazine – there were no other customers – and looked across at them once or twice doubtfully. Her pale blue eyes, offset by kohl, seemed troubled by the bar's silence and the men watching her from the half-shadows. She arranged the bodice of her green satin, strapless dress which, in a normal light, would have set off her red hair well.

Maxwell popped a couple of coins in the juke-box and invited the girl to choose her numbers. She chose Maya Casabianca – who was all the rage that year – and the hit tune from 'Hello, Dolly!', a taste she had brought with her from England. The music attracted the door-boy, a mournful youth in an absurdly braided uniform, whose duties were to help drunken people up the steps into the street and blow three blasts on his whistle for the *shurti* if a customer grew unpleasant. Neville beckoned to him. Was the girl for sale? The boy gave the Turkish negative. But when she finished? 'What she does after four o'clock is her own business, but, by the name of God, if my sister worked in a bar, I would call her a prostitute. Why should an English girl be different?'

'Why, indeed!' Neville was amused by the boy's mournful, old-fashioned manner, like a sawn-off schoolmaster. He translated for Maxwell. 'It's his way of saying she does. She must do! These girls get shipped here for it.'

'Some of them are respectable.'

'Some, maybe.' Neville was scornful. 'An exception here and there. They all pretend, of course.'

The boy had been listening solemnly without understanding. 'If she won't come, I will come with you.' The offer was squarely, innocently put. Neville's manner was absent. 'Another time. Tonight I want to get my teeth into that meat.' He indicated the girl with his head. 'Come, boy, you must have heard what she asks. Tell me and I'll give you a present.' He held out a couple of notes – about five shillings – and the boy hissed a figure, adding, 'but more for Americans.' 'Fair enough.' Neville handed over the money and leaned back on his chair. 'Yah! I'm already there,' he said to Maxwell. 'It's a long time since I've wanted anyone so much.'

They wandered over to the bar. The girl put her magazine away and looked up doubtfully. 'Have a cigarette?' Maxwell opened a box of Benson and Hedges bought on the plane. The

76

girl lit up with surprising amateurishness. 'I smoke one or two a day or when I'm in company.' Neville was thrilled by the lower middle-class 'in company', with its flavour of lace curtains and contrived gentility. For him that was façade: 'They are here to fuck. They fuck for money. Why do they pretend?' Bar girls sometimes claimed they were doing the work to be near a boy-friend working in the oilfields; sometimes they claimed to be friends of the owner's family and suggested that the women of the family received them. At all events, they usually felt obliged to explain themselves; the red-haired girl said she had met the bar-owner in London and 'knew he was O.K.' She told her fellow-countrymen how careful she had to be, how strict the owner was, how soon the girls who went off the rails got the push.

'You must get hundreds of offers.'

'Any girl does. You've got to be a boss-eyed, one-legged, bearded wonder in this place before they leave you alone. You do. Honestly. You do. And then there's probably someone kinky who likes it all mixed up.' She giggled. 'What am I saying? You oughtn't to hear such things.'

Maxwell was appalled by her; the mixture of defensiveness and lewdness reminded him of all that he loathed at home. He had to catch a plane at five o'clock, so wanted to get away. The girl agreed to meet Neville at four o'clock, when the bar closed, so the two men left to find a taxi. Maxwell was disgusted by Neville falling for such a 'coarse bitch' and recommended a visit to Hong Kong for the real thing. Waiting for a taxi in the street, the door-boy came up and tugged at Neville's coat: 'You want me?' Neville, vexed by Maxwell's contempt, turned on the boy viciously. Mistaking his anger for frustration, the boy held on. 'How old are you?' 'Sixteen.' 'Where do you live?' 'With my family.' All the Arab mournfulness was in the face, all the precocious knowledge of its market value. Neville – without thinking – said, 'We'll go to my house one day, but not now.' The boy changed at once. His eyes narrowed: 'Fifty pounds!' Neville's momentary sympathy, even pity, for the depressed youth vanished. 'You ask fifty pounds, and for one-fifty I get all that meat down there.' – Pointing back to the bar – 'My boy, when people get fish for nothing the price of lemons comes down.' 'Forty!' The boy pursued them miserably to the taxi and forgot to open the door. He was still lowering his price as they drove off. Maxwell was nauseated and disgruntled, and added the Arabs to his list of *bêtes noires*. 'These people are really the scum of the earth. How can you bear to live here? Whining, bad service, extortion – the lot. Never anything graceful or refined; and then to have to import a Soho redhead to attract customers. Christ Almighty.' He shut his eyes in disgust and slumped back into the car seat.

When Neville returned at four o'clock, the boy had still not found a buyer, and his price had come down to twenty-five. Neville waved him away; but he persisted. As Neville was opening the door of the taxi for his woman, the boy hissed, 'Twenty for you.' The girl thought he wanted a tip. 'Give him something. He earns practically nothing.' 'Never.' So she leaned across and handed the boy a pound. 'He'll do anything I ask him.'

On the way to her flat, Neville began to ask questions. 'Now then, Mr Busybody, don't you try to worm no secrets out of me. How do I know you're not a spy?' She giggled again. 'There's spies everywhere in this place.' She refused to let him kiss her, having learned that wise people do not commit themselves in public. At the end of the journey, she walked into her building quickly while Neville paid off the taxi. She complained because he dawdled upstairs reading the graffiti on the wall. The Arabs, he explained, are a literary people with a vast literature. They live for the spoken and written word, and their graffiti have a humour of their own. 'Fuck the owner of this building,' was one; and underneath was written: 'Do not. Done so. Disappointing.' Then, on the wall near the girl's door was, 'An English prostitute lives here,' which was shocking. 'Why don't you clean your walls?' he asked her. 'Why should I? The children do it. You can't stop them.' Later, Neville took her kitchen sponge and wiped the wall and, on the greyish smear he had created, drew a left hand of Fatima to ward off the evil eye. The girl thought he was 'screwy' and said so. 'Screwy' was her favourite word; it suited every other situation and person she met.

Inside the little flat, with the door locked, she bounced across to Neville and gave him a swingeing kiss. 'And now a cup of tea.' As she waited for the kettle to boil, she complained about the liquid gas everyone was obliged to use; it was smelly and slow. Then she looked at herself in a mirror over the sink and ran a hand through her hair; she was indistinguishable from any girl at home receiving a friend for supper, and Neville, leaning on the doorpost of the kitchen, knew she was looking forward to going to bed with him. After they had drunk tea and were in bed, Neville also realised that fucking was her only complete means of communication. She might not have Chinese refinement, Neville thought, but she certainly knew how to give a man pleasure. She did so with an abandon, a suggestion of self-destruction, which made him question her. She opened her eyes and giggled: 'I get like that sometimes. My girl-friends used to tell me I'd better be careful. That's the way to get into trouble. I've known lots of girls who got themselves worked up over a man – you know, can't have enough of him – and they want him to finish off inside and they haven't taken precautions – and bob's your flippin' uncle.'

'People not taking precautions nowadays? People must be mad.'

'Some girls like the risk. Deep down every girl wants a baby.'

'Well, Christ, I don't.' He was shocked, profoundly shocked.

She touched his mouth. 'We're women. We want children. We can't help it. You like a man very much and think it would be nice to have his children; you give him everything you can. You can't help it. It's natural. That's when you let him go too far.'

Neville was staggered. She laughed at him: 'Have I taught you something? Well, live and learn.'

'Do you think you might go overboard for me?'

She weighed him up. 'I could do. I can tell you like doing it. And it's clean. Not like some of the locals.'

'Perhaps you'll marry an Arab.'

'Don't be daft. Who'd want me in this place after it got around that I worked in a bar. Even if the men are pushing sixty – almost too old to cut the mustard – they still want their brides from school – like my boss who's still waiting for Miss Right at forty-six.'

'Does he pester you?'

'You kidding? Lucky for me the other girl – she was off duty tonight – does for him. She doesn't mind getting a load of Trex on top of her. Hey! Watch it! What am I saying.' She looked at him severely. 'You should stop me when I say things like that. Just say, "Marjorie, please don't forget yourself".' Neville laughed. 'No, honest. They're strange people. They can make you feel wonderful. Be generous, spend a fortune on you. Treat you like a queen. And then spoil it all with a remark which shows they can't respect you or take you seriously. You know it by the way they touch you. They hate you, in a way. They'll try their luck that you'll let them do something a bit disgusting that they like, and then, instead of being grateful, they'll insult you.' He was eager for her to tell more. She hung back a little, secretly shocked by his interest. At last she said, 'Oh, they like to get up to all sorts of tricks. Some of them bring their boy-friends along, and we have a threesome.' He wanted to know more, but she dismissed everything as 'vicious little tricks': 'They bothered me at first but now I don't care. The whole thing's a game to them. Quite simple for *them*, in some ways; but I can't understand them. They're really all twisted up inside. Someone told me it was because they'd been shut off from women for centuries and looked on them as lower than dirt – almost like cows. They can only respect a man. You know what I mean? Their mental love is for their own kind. Women are just to be used and degraded – yes, I mean that. So they try to combine both. That's how I look on it. I could really tell you some things.'

'Well, go on. Do so.'

'Realleh! Neville darling!!!! I don't think you're quite, quite naice to know. Asking a girl questions like that. Watch it, old chap. There's a limit, you know.'

She giggled again and Neville winced: 'Why do you make that silly noise? It spoils you.'

'That's what my mother always said. She used to say, "Laugh refined." I said, "How?" and she told me to keep my mouth shut when I laughed. Like this . . . see what I mean? . . . what a damned silly sound I make, like steam escaping from an espresso machine. Isn't it just?' She shrieked with amusement. 'So I said to hell with that and for ever. It's not me. Now, I just let meself go and hope for the best. If you don't like it wear ear-plugs.'

'You're a nut-case.' Neville put his hand under her bottom and pinched it. Her shriek of anguish, her 'AHOUOW!' was ferocious and uninhibited. 'You'll do. Where are you from?'

'Ramsgate. You been there?'

'Nope. But if they make creatures like you there I'll go there next summer.'

She took him seriously: 'They're very strict there, you know.'

'Rubbish. I bet they're not.'

'They are. They wouldn't speak to you in our road if you didn't do the right thing.'

'Thank God you're here.'

'You really are a bit screwy, aren't you?'

'Does it matter?'

She lifted herself on one elbow. 'I've been thinking: you're not particularly good-looking or witty, but there's something about you that's a bit fascinating. Give me your hand and I'll see the sort of person you are.' He held up his free hand and she peered into it carefully. 'You're really a sexy little stoat, aren't you? There's only one thing that counts for you: having a good time. And that means one thing. What am I saying? No, serious, now, you're a level-headed person, really. Quite clever. You see things clearly and you don't let sentiment stand in your way. You get a lot out of life, and, in your own way, you put a lot into what you're doing. You'll always have money. No difficulty there at all. You're just lucky. I think you're going to have several interesting offers – one of them very soon. You won't refuse it. You may do. Yes, you really are a lucky person. You'll get away with murder. You're very impatient at times, aren't you? You see things clearly while other people are still bothering about trifles. You never lose sight of the main chance. Never seen such a clear headline. Really terrific. Now let me see the other hand – the one that shows what you're making of your life.'

'Afterwards, afterwards.'

In the mid-morning, a little tousled, a little haggard, Neville telephoned his sister from a nearby shop. She was completely uninterested in his movements. 'But come home soon. The Consort and I have been having sharp words. He's bitching because I buy too many books. Accusing me of snobbery – all I wanted was the right titles on the coffee-tables. Bloody cheek. He thinks everyone is as ignorant as himself. Sometimes that man frightens me. There's something bottomless in his viciousness. He'll do something terrible to me one day.'

Neville sighed and hung up. He was tired, and even more tired of his sister's marriage rituals.

'What did she say?' Hello Dolly! looked up from pouring hot water on the coffee-powder. Neville waved his sister away wearily. Her household, with The Duchess and The Consort, nauseated him. As human beings they were lies.

The girl was in splendid trim, but warned him that he would have to go away while she got some sleep. She had bathed, newly brushed and combed her hair, which shimmered in a plate-like arrangement, held in place by a green Alice band. 'Cheers!' She bumped his coffee cup. He bumped back. She took a gulp and said, 'One of these days I'm going to give up sex.' Bemused, still thinking of his sister, Neville looked up, 'Why, don't you enjoy it?'

'You think I'm a cold fish? No, I enjoy it too much. Too flippin' much. It'll ruin my health. That's what they all say.'

The way she held her coffee-cup, and her Lucille Ball expression, made him laugh until the lights returned to his cold little black eyes. 'What a quaking bog of superstition you are!'

'Quaking bog yourself, mate.' She nearly winded him with a poke into his stomach – her little white fist taking him by surprise. For a moment he could have killed her. 'I suppose you know that hurt.'

'Was supposed to.' She took another gulp of coffee and gave her maniacal laugh. He looked at her over the coffee-cup with a murderer's cold calculation – the look of a man seeking the most subtle way to his ends.

Part Two

1

Paul Brophy's Diary:

> *24 September*
> *0930: Maître Germanos re sacking of Ahmed*
> *1030: John Macrae from British Embassy*
> *1330: Neville: lunch*

Like most offices in Baida, MEDOC opened its doors for business early, and by half-past seven the parking lot among the olive-trees was full of employees' cars. The working day lasted until half-past one; by two the building was empty, closed. MEDOC set great store on punctuality. In the land of *'Boukrah bil mishmish'*, the English administration insisted on timetables honourably fulfilled in a way they rarely are at home; and Brophy, as the head of the office, was expected to give a lead in this respect. Although he longed to arrive on time and to present a glittering intelligence to the first arrivals, he was nearly always late. Sometimes he was very late. Once every fortnight or so, he would arrive before the Kurdish cleaning-women had finished and would then sit at his desk with the door open so that everyone could see the miracle. He even permitted himself a virtuous scowl, so that people who kept good time nineteen days out of twenty were rewarded with a stabbing glance if they happened to be five minutes late. All this was shameless play-acting which everyone but Brophy saw through: one of the reasons why his chief assistants could not take him seriously and why they resented him. They took this more as an example of British hypocrisy than as evidence of Brophy's immaturity.

That day he arrived at ten past eight, passed gloomily into his office, and wondered what he was being so tense and dramatic about. On his desk, stuck into the blotting-pad, was an account from a London oriental bookseller. It was open for all to see – with a red reminder sticker in the middle of it. Attached to the bill was a note: 'Opened in error', signed 'D.P.'

He blushed; folded the bill away, and sat down at a side-table where he kept a typewriter. He wrote the following memo:

FROM: *The Director.*
To: *The Business Secretary.*
SUBJECT: *Opening of Mail.*

I have been disturbed to see that, once again, private mail addressed to the director has been opened 'in error'. While it is understood that such mistakes can occur once, or even twice, it becomes a matter of concern that they should happen with weekly regularity. It suggests that greater care should be taken. In future, too, would the person who opens mail 'in error' please replace the contents in the envelope; or, if the envelope has been thrown away, in another one? In this way, the contents can remain, to a certain degree, at least, private. Although it is neither here nor there that I owe £15, it would be preferable that the whole office did not know.

A messenger took the letter to 'D.P.' – Mrs Parslow – and within minutes she bounced into Brophy's room – mouth working, tears gushing from her mournful eyes – to challenge his suggestion that she tampered with the mail. The whole thing had been a genuine error. The mail, that day, as it happened, had been opened by Salima and she, as it happened (etc. etc.) had then, as it happened (etc. etc.) gone into his room without seeing her for, as it happened, she was (etc. etc.); and wouldn't it be better if he got his facts right before making dirty hints and accusations? Brophy tried to reply curtly and meaningfully but waffled. This was because Mrs Parslow vampirised him; she had only to look at him with her mournful, all-knowing eyes, for his assurance to vanish.

'You must remember, Paul,' – as in most public organisations, all the hatred in MEDOC was on first-name terms – 'You must remember that neither Salima nor I are paid to sort out private mail. If anything we do offends you, the cure is in your own hands. Why not get your mail addressed to your flat?'

Any other man would have said, '*You* get your mail addressed here. Most foreigners here get their mail *via* an office box number for quicker delivery, so why make so much fuss?' but Brophy lacked this brisk ungallantry. However nasty Mrs Parslow was to him – and she was becoming more so – she knew instinctively that Paul Brophy would, in the end, be too gentlemanly, or too weak, to give her the come-uppance she needed. Brophy believed – in his ignorance of women – that Mrs Parslow was in some sort of menopausal difficulty, and he relied on her sense of fair play. This merely encouraged her. She paralysed him because she knew his kind; he blustered but he also cringed before her. Even when he stood up, he looked ineffective and caught out, and when she went away he could only sit down and feel foolish. Mrs Parslow, aflame with embattled virtue, told Salima that if Mr Brophy had been a man he would have apologised for his memo.

The issue was still open. Brophy tapped out another memo, although more urgent things were on hand, and it was delivered as Mrs Parslow was drinking her first Turkish coffee.

FROM: *The Director*
To: *The Business Secretary*
SUBJECT: *Incoming Mail and Personal Letters.*
Henceforward, all letters, whether for the office or for private individuals, will be brought to the Director. He will divide private mail from that addressed to the institute. The personal letters will then be delivered by messenger and the office mail taken to Mrs D. Parslow for attention.

Mrs Parslow's cup clashed on the saucer and before Salima could say 'Oh!' Mrs Parslow and the memo were inside Shamseddine's office, and Maître Germanos, a mild-mannered little lawyer, who looked like a Spanish poet of the School of '98, had been nearly knocked over. Shamseddine read the memo and exchanged exasperation with Mrs Parslow. Their daily hymn of hate against Brophy became an oratorio. Shamseddine put on his coat – a sure sign of battle. He read the memo again. 'And what happens when he's away? Do we sit looking at the letters until he comes in?'

Maître Germanos was long and tedious on the Ahmed case – justifying his fee by complicating a simple issue – and Shamseddine had to sit around for his chance to see Brophy. When he did so, his head of anger was no less.

'Ah,' – Brophy tried his inscrutable smile – 'you want to attack me because of the memo. Well, let me speak first. Mrs Parslow has got to learn who is boss here.'

Shamseddine laid the memo on the desk. 'Paul, I ask you: is this the work of a man fit to rule an organisation like MEDOC? Read it again. Every word is steeped in pettiness, paltriness, pifflingness. The effect of this unreasonable and stupid document is to make me lose faith in your judgement.'

Brophy looked ahead, working his thick lips into little purses, like a virgin in raffish company.

'Paul: we cannot run an office on these lines. What happens to the mail when you're late?'

'Am I late?' Brophy's eyelids fluttered uncertainly.

'Yes, sir! You are usually late. This morning, you were forty minutes late.' Shamseddine consulted his diary. 'I've kept a check, and there's only one day in the last fourteen when you were here before me. And one day you didn't turn up until ten o'clock.'

'The day my friends arrived from England.'

Shamseddine knew this (the office driver was a mate of his) and grunted agreement. The main point remained: Brophy was so unreliable that the work of the office would be disrupted. The office could not wait for Brophy to decide to come in. 'There could be a letter from my own mother announcing my father's last illness, and yet I should have to wait until you arrived. Paul, I ask you: is this sensible?'

Brophy did not answer the question directly; he repeated his own ideas, and the argument moved on parallel lines. At last, as Shamseddine's spittle began to fly, Brophy sat quite still. He blinked like a fuddled man – white, taut and miserable – and then Macrae breezed in, unannounced.

Brophy presented the two men. Another incompetent schemer, was Macrae's summing up of Shamseddine, and he nodded curtly. He did not offer his hand, and this upset Shamseddine, who felt cheapened as a human being. Humiliated and angry, he went back to his room to tap out a letter to Dr Armstrong in London. He was about fifteen minutes behind Mrs Parslow, who had already sent Brophy's memo to the boss, along with an appeal that he should come out to Baida at once and take Brophy back with him. 'The man gets more dictatorial every day. He has put everyone's back up with his high-handed methods.' Shamseddine took two pages to give the whole story – his English being more literary – and ended up: 'If you say this is the behaviour of a sane man, I must beg to differ.'

2

MACRAE sat down opposite Brophy and accepted a coffee. The two men were poles apart: Brophy was sallow, compressed, blurred; Macrae, red-browed, freckled, rather pop-eyed, his collar open and his tie yanked aside to let his bullneck breathe. Brophy was not disposed to talk; Macrae crackled with indignation against his boss and the embassy in general.

He belonged aggressively to that class of people which, he believed, had been called on to save all those things which middle-class ineptness had imperilled, including Britain's position in the Middle East. In Macrae's view, Britain was more threatened by its decadent ruling class, which had allowed events to overcome it, than it was by any foreign power. Like Maxwell Thomson, he was anti-English, anti-home, anti the entrenched order. Unlike Thomson, who had escaped from what he thought of as the English suffocation by going abroad and finding his own level among international technologists – he was deeply involved in the muddled British machine, and his life was affected by attitudes he despised. Thus, his hatred was more personal, for he believed himself in mortal combat with entrenched privilege. He had one weakness: he never recognised a fellow spirit. He might say, 'You're dead right!' – a favourite phrase – but it did not mean any alliance. His only relationship was with The Enemy – the people who had held on to power and no longer offered leadership, the people who had faltered their way through the first half of the twentieth century and had gone to sleep in the second.

To reduce the decline of British world power to such black-and-white terms suggested that Macrae was stupid. This was misleading. Macrae, as he was not slow to tell people, had had to work far harder than a middle-class person to make the grade. He had achieved this by battling through competitive examinations and generally bringing more energy and intellect to bear at any given point than, say, The Consort. Inevitably, the comparison was with the man above him, who, according to Macrae, had had life offered him on a golden plate with an arm-rest for easier eating.

Within a few weeks Macrae had turned the wretched Consort into a cartoonist's symbol of all he detested. The Consort might be a figure of fun to his wife and her brother, a joke to his equals and a pain to his superiors; to Macrae he was a personal threat: a menace to his values and a patronising so-and-so, to boot.

The Consort knew his man, too, and treated Macrae with a deliberate offhandedness. When he stopped thinking of him as a rugger-playing Red he thought of him as That Bloody Scots Pusher. The Consort disliked, even distrusted, Macrae's enthusiasm, his awkward questions and his half-obvious disapproval. Enthusiasm ill-became anyone, in The Consort's eyes; in a subordinate it was irritating; but enthusiasm in a subordinate of Macrae's stamp and background was intolerable. That rawness! That fresh-from-home look! Those Doric vowels! The man was anathema!

The relationship started on a level of mutual contempt and jelled into hatred over a specific point of disagreement within the first few days.

Macrae was married, with one young child. As a besotted father and passionate husband, he wanted his family to join him as soon as possible. On the very day they flew out from London, The Consort announced that Macrae would have to go to the Persian Gulf. As a great concession, it was agreed that Macrae could have a week or so with his family before going, but no more. Macrae was put out, but really 'blew his top' when told The Consort should have visited the Gulf weeks before, and had dillied and dallied deliberately, awaiting his new deputy's arrival. Macrae complained. The Consort, very stiff and cold, said: 'You aren't being very co-operative, are you?'

Macrae was still finding his way, so said no more, but he nourished his grudge with Scottish fervour. He tried to read up the Gulf background and found The Consort had 'mislaid' certain files, including back numbers of the MEDOC digest. Macrae complained again, and The Consort suggested he should speak to Paul Brophy since he had recently visited Bahrain and Dubai, and read the MEDOC back files at the same time.

Macrae did not get on well with Brophy. As a working-class imperialist, Macrae did not ask himself whether the British presence in the Persian Gulf was a good thing; he was merely there to save it. He was puzzled, out of his depth, to find himself led by Brophy's middle-class liberal paths into a maundering discussion on continued British involvement. Brophy had hated what he saw of the British role in the Gulf, but was prevented by his position from saying so openly. His reports had been full of disconcerting questions and a marked half-heartedness towards official attitudes. He failed to see that Britain had any clear purpose in staying in the area, and thought it had been rash to spend three times more there on military matters than on civil development.

Macrae's attitude was clear: 'It will all end one day. Everyone knows *that*. In the meantime, we've got our responsibilities, and I'm involved. Asking hypothetical questions won't get me anywhere. I want to do my little tour, write my little report and get back to the bosom of my little family.' For him the trip was a clash between duty and domestic cosiness.

Brophy had misjudged him, having thought any man who was so vocal and radical would have a general framework of protest or doubt to his thinking. With a peculiar twitch of his mouth Brophy observed that Macrae was lucky to keep his eyes blinkered. 'Interesting to see if you feel the same when you get back.'

'Are there things there that aren't what they should be?' Macrae meant: 'Is some dowdy, snobby, pansy Englishman making a balls-up of things?'

Brophy smiled mysteriously. 'I wouldn't want you to get an impression I said things aren't right. We have our own peculiar institutions which – well, they make you think a little.'

The smile was entirely derogatory, yet the words hedged. Macrae put the man down as another middle-class muddler whom, he, Macrae, would eventually have to save from himself. He disliked waffle. If something was wrong, it was a man's duty to speak out. To hint at dark things and refuse to be explicit was the sort of spinsterish behaviour to be expected from a faded middle-class thing like Brophy; and part of the middle-class inability to come to terms with the modern world (another of the large generalisations Macrae specialised in).

Macrae knew Brophy was part of the Rhoda–Neville–The Consort caravan, and used him as a listening-post. 'I can tell you this bloody trip makes me as sore as hell. Master Handlebar should have gone there months ago, but preferred to wait for the new sucker from home to do his dirty work. Come a nice little trip to the fleshpots of Teheran or Istanbul, and Master Handlebar will be off like a shot.'

Really? Brophy tried to show by his expression – he had the habit of reacting by a little grimace, but a pursing of the mouth or a slight upward turn of the eyes – that Macrae was out of bounds.

'He's a perfect specimen of his class. Lord Handlebar belongs to the Big Middle-Class Club which A. L. Rowse talks about. He's got all the assumptions and that effortless belief in his own superiority which makes foreigners think the British must be mad.'

Brophy smiled mysteriously again. 'Am I following you? He's always quite normal when I meet him socially.'

'He's always got it, man! That sense of communing with higher forces directly, unlike poor old hoi-bloody-polloi, who've got to go through the ordinary processes.'

'*I* always find him easy to get along with.'

'Actually,' – and here Macrae deliberately went out of his way to be offensive – 'I sometimes wonder when Lord Handlebar and his wife are together which one patronises the other. They've both got an outsize bump of superiority. Unreal bloody pair! When they're around there isn't a pinky's worth of place for down-to-earth people.'

'I get along with them very well. You're the only one who can't.'

'Oh, come off it. Who can get along with them? He's just an English prig – but she's the great cosmopolitan lady – and the bloody end of the line: all airs and graces – as though everything she thinks must be right because she thought it. They're a right pair. I don't know which I feel the more sorry for. Actually, I think I've got a soft spot for her because her man's a shiftless, good-for-nothing bastard, who doesn't know his backside from his brain, except he uses the first more.'

'You mean he uses his backside more than his brain?' Brophy gave a wintry little moue, that might have been sarcasm.

'Just that!'

'Thank you. I wanted to be sure I understood.'

'He's the blasted limit. "M'dear boy, don't let's argue about small point." Small points! He meant I was making a fuss about leaving the family a few days after they arrive in a strange country. Och, he makes me bloody sick.' Macrae was getting down to his subject. He opened a new packet of cigarettes and offered one to Brophy. 'You know, I've noticed that whenever I go abroad there's always a certain type of English person at the centre of things making a balls-up. Yet they're always marvellously arrogant, with this good opinion of themselves.' He paused for effect. 'And when you get to know them there's damn-all there but family connections. They move around calling everyone by their first names and think they own the show.'

Brophy thought this inevitable when people had lived for some time in a place. Macrae would be in the same position once he'd put down roots.

'Oh, sure! It's easy enough here to get friends with an entertainment allowance. You can soon get all the heaviest drinkers in the house. The question is whether these friends are worth having. Lord Handlebar goes about me-dearing people and saying "Bless you!" at every verse-end, but it doesn't stop him doing everything to put a spoke in m'wheel. He says yes-yes to your face but pours poison on your ideas when your back is turned. He's just a double-faced Englishman. His two great phrases are, "Well, that let's me out," or "That's a good let-out."'

Macrae turned his jibes at Neville – 'a slick, slippery little customer, if you ask me. A dead cool operator.'

At this, Brophy stood up. 'I've known him for over fifteen years. That aspect of him has never struck me. He has a sharp tongue and a cruel one, but when you know him better you'll see other things.'

Brophy suggested Macrae should go with him to the library and shut him in with the files. Eventually, about quarter-past eleven, Brophy began dealing with the proofs.

'The search for a magic formula,' he read, 'to unite the Arabs: King Feisal is the latest leader to make the attempt, although he proposes to approach the problem within the wider context of Islam.'

Later, he grimaced as he came to: 'I was impressed by his presence and stature . . . the lean, shrewd face of wisdom and austerity – the tall, spare figure in flowing robes.'

Why did people write such things, and why did MEDOC feel it had to publish them?

3

BROPHY said as much to Neville as they sat on the balcony of his own flat drinking whisky and soda. Inside the flat, an uninspiring countrywoman prepared a meal.

'God! – I hate that kind of writing,' Neville said. ' "I departed into the desert-scented evening" – the sort of rubbish which is tacked on to a listless reappraisal of Arab nationalism. It means nothing.'

Brophy agreed. He thought the real difficulty for English people face to face with Arab nationalism was that, on the whole, they had no real understanding of nationalism. A country which has not been invaded for a thousand years cannot imagine what it is like to feel its nature threatened by an alien culture. Neville agreed and instanced the unreality of talking politics to his brother-in-law's colleagues from the Embassy. Surrounded by people who ate, talked, breathed and dreamed politics, those 'rather low-toned British Embassy people' thought politics meant working up a 'tepid preference' for either the Labour Party or the Conservatives, and imagined that returning 'nice people' – perhaps Liberals – to the local council was its essence.

'And then,' Neville went on, 'the British role in the Middle

East has been so particularly dirty. For thirty years we tried to do the impossible: to provide the Jews with a national home and supervise a predominantly Arab country for the League of Nations. And now everything revolves around the cynical oil bonanza.'

'A bit extreme, aren't you?' Brophy's mouth worked like a soiled debutante's; and yet this was the sort of critical attitude he had been working towards in his chat with Macrae. Brophy needed to be contrary.

Neville had long ago seen through British pretensions and said so: 'Oh, come off it, Paul. Just what do the British stand for any more? When you're there in England you appreciate the fair play, the social justice which you don't get here, and nobody's starving; but on the other hand, what does it all add up to in the larger context?'

Brophy blinked like a cat, playing for time, trying to find something contrary to say. 'I don't disagree. I'm not sure I entirely agree, all the same. Can you talk of what Britain stands for in such slap-dash terms?'

He helped himself to another whisky and sat back.

'Granted!' Neville drained his glass ostentatiously in the hope that Brophy would notice. 'But you can't offer me a better definition.'

'I don't quite see what you want.'

'Oh, God! Everything's so dull – politics at home gets wetter every day.'

Brophy blinked and sipped his whisky. He ignored Neville's empty glass.

'You say British politics is dull. What about the situation in the Soviet Union or West Germany? In both countries, politics is drained of interest. I mean, if the only thing you look for in politics *is* interest. Of course, I know public affairs are interesting . . . but . . .' he grimaced. 'Well, if you know what I mean.'

'Of course I don't. You don't know what you mean yourself.'

Brophy looked seraphic: 'Yes, I've been caught flannelling again.'

Neville hardened his mind to his splotchy, ungenerous, contrary friend: 'I always understood you were like myself. Basically, if the world were divided into two camps you would be with the democratic left.'

94

'Suppose so . . . Don't think I've ever gone as far as you . . . Democratic left sounds rather too splendid.'

'It's what the Labour Party is. Few things could be less splendid than that. It's composed of groups of people basically committed to social justice as an end in itself . . . some want to move on to a revolution of taste and feeling . . . Some even want to renovate society from its roots.'

'Very few.' Brophy seemed scandalised. At least, he gave Neville an odd look, but this might simply have been a cover-up for his helping himself to a third drink. Neville's face changed.

'Oh, I suppose you'd like another, too.'

'Another what?'

'Another whisky.'

'No. Thank you.' Neville determined never to invite Brophy to his sister's parties again.

There was a certain slyness about Brophy. 'I don't think I offered you one last time.'

'Since you're counting,' Neville was beyond caring what he thought – 'let's make it quite clear that that's your third, and this is my first and *last*. Anyone would think we were in Pinner, where one has to decide whether to have a second drink or pay the school fees to time.'

Still irritated and rubbed the wrong way, Neville went into the dining-room, where the unpromising woman had set out a meal on an ugly, glass-topped table. She had made an omelette, over-cooked into leatheriness, and a country-style salad of tomatoes and cucumbers, swimming chunkily in vinegar and oil. Next to a plate containing two pieces of Arabic bread was a small bowl of *homos*. At the far end of the table were the later courses: a bunch of grapes and a selection of Aleppo cheeses, which taste like fire and brimstone and look like old dogs' crots. In the middle of the table was a pitcher of iced water. Brophy frowned, went across to a locked cupboard and brought out a half-finished bottle of cheap wine – it was selling at that time for about half-a-crown a litre – and sniffed it. He offered it, as an afterthought, to Neville.

Neville smiled ironically at the serving-woman standing at the door. She was wiping her large, brown hands on her apron and half-bowing, as though in apology – her inborn Arab sense of abundance outraged by the mean snack Brophy had ordered.

Poor as she was, she would have lost face had she placed such scrimping fare before a guest.

Neville's resentment almost choked him. He thought of Brophy drinking his brother-in-law's whisky and eating his food, and took the meal as an insult to his sister. He showed his vexation by taking only a dab of *homos*, a spoonful of the wishy-washy salad, a couple of grapes; after the first sip he left the peppery wine in his glass and drank iced water.

As they returned to the balcony Neville carefully refrained from making any remark about the meal. He sat quite still, waiting for the promised coffee and liqueurs, and pretended to be absorbed in the spacious seascape. The Turkish coffee was excellent, and Neville congratulated the woman, who took this as forgiveness for the meal. Brophy walked out with a pretentious silver tray full of liqueur bottles. Neville accepted a Grand Marnier; Brophy served himself an enormous Remy Martin and then carefully corked the bottles and carried them away. As Brophy was 'out of cigarettes' and had only one cigar, Neville had to provide his own.

Brophy was no fool. Knowing Neville was furious about the meal, he made an excuse, saying the woman's powers were limited. Neville looked unconvinced. 'I've never met an Arab countrywoman yet who couldn't produce a damned good meal. You've picked one in a million.'

'Anyway, I think I've got a solution for the problem. I've sent for my old manservant from Tunisia. He's a properly trained person, who knows how to wait at table and that sort of thing.'

Before Neville could stop himself he had flashed out: 'Well, I hope you give him enough to eat!'

Brophy looked displeased. 'That's a funny sort of remark to make. I suppose you think I'm showing off.'

'Quite the opposite.'

'I merely mentioned this to see what your reaction would be to my having a manservant. I thought he might be misinterpreted.'

This mysterious remark caused Neville to look at Brophy sharply. Was it merely absurd, or a joke in questionable taste? Brophy and Neville had never spoken frankly to the other about their private lives, since both, curiously enough, suspected the other of tenebrous activities. It was the great unspoken thing between them. Neither would have condemned the other; but neither would have wanted the other to know. It was an unconscious form of rivalry: the need to have power over the other, by knowing something the other wanted kept secret.

'But why? What grounds can there be for misinterpretation?'

Brophy did not say what was really on his mind. 'Oh, people think a manservant is showing off. Everybody's got maids – or a woman who "does" daily – but houseboys and butlers are only for the really well-to-do.'

'You're not poor, are you? Doesn't the office give you an allowance to cover all that?'

Brophy did not say yes or no, but made a swaying gesture with his head, which could have meant anything, and smiled in a cautiously pleased way. He liked Neville to know he was elevated enough to get an executive's allowance for gracious living, but he had no intention of going into detail.

'It's not important. I don't entertain much. All the same, it's pleasant to have someone you can rely on.'

'You say he looked after you in Tunis?'

Brophy nodded and smiled like someone with pleasant secrets. Neville looked at him coldly. He hated Brophy's immature conceit and would not give him a chance to show off any more. He did not even ask – as he had long meant to – what exactly Brophy had done in Tunis. It was understood he had represented a London insurance company: a front for something more interesting probably.

Brophy finished his cognac, and there was a pause. Neville tried to think of something to say, but his disgust and contempt for Brophy prevented him. He looked at his watch and said he wanted to go swimming.

'Don't go yet. You came here to hear my offer.' Brophy looked at Neville in perplexity. 'You're still interested, aren't you?'

'Oh, that!' Neville smiled with difficulty. In his irritation he'd overlooked the main reason for his visit.

'Wait a moment.' Brophy rose, crossed the balcony quickly and went indoors. Neville went on sipping his Grand Marnier, looked at the clock on his silk socks and wondered how he would recompose his soul to listen to Brophy's offer. He heard the lavatory flushed and then – a moment of suspended belief

— the guggle-guggle of liquid and the clink of a glass stopper.

Brophy returned. He blinked. His face showed nothing at all. He set down a pad and pencil on the table. He leaned back in his chair and asked Neville what he proposed to do. Neville said his immediate concern was to find a small flat, finish his doctorate, and then ask himself whether he had come to the end of his foreign experience or whether he wanted to make his life abroad.

'You mean a job?'

'It depends.'

Neville had made an application to the local American college but was unlikely to succeed because of the university's personnel policy. He had also toyed with the idea of getting a job with the British Council, since the money was fairly good. He wanted a job in Baida for the time being.

'Then I may be able to interest you in a job with MEDOC!'

This was the big moment, but Neville lay back in his chair. He was very still. 'Such as?'

'Well, it's not executive like mine.' A pause. 'It means some responsibility and travelling.'

Neville's neutral expression hid a world of loathing for Brophy's grand manner. 'That's vague enough. You want me to blot your notes for you?'

Eventually, like a building emerging out of a mist, Brophy was able to sketch in the sort of job he had in mind for Neville and the reasons why Neville was being asked: the most important was his fluent Arabic. That he understood and appreciated the Arabs, and could write grammatically, were also counted.

Brophy then went into a long rhapsody about MEDOC.

Neville was hardly to recognise this as a warmed-up version of the MEDOC Song of Praise which Brophy's boss, the ubiquitous Dr Armstrong, had composed for delivery at international seminars. It went something like this: Every day, and from the most unusual sources, proof was coming in that MEDOC's pioneering work in statistics and long-term prognostication about business life in North Africa and the Middle East was meeting a long-felt want. Owing to wise management and keen editing, MEDOC was producing better and more perceptive documentation than any other firm in the Arab Affairs Industry. Every organisation that meant anything subscribed to its private service, and its background knowledge was used, though unacknowledged, in all serious journals of opinion.

Brophy interrupted himself to go into the flat, and Neville presumed he helped himself to another drink, because he came out wiping his lips. The clink of the stopper and the glug-glug of the liquid had been drowned by the whining of an airliner. Brophy handed out a small brochure – promotional material drawn up by a firm of consultants in London. On the inside cover was an impressive list of public bodies subscribing to the MEDOC reports and papers.

Inside, too, was a photograph of Dr Armstrong, seated at a tycoon's desk about to sign, by the drama of the picture, someone's death warrant.

Neville commented on the patriarchal figure – the huge beard, the beringed fingers. 'Oh, yes, he's a striking figure. Not very tall, but with powerful shoulders and this leonine head. It doesn't mean very much.' Brophy stopped himself. 'I oughtn't to say that.'

'You mean, no one could look so Big Wheel as *he* looks.'

'He reminds me of Beaverbrook, in some way. He was born in Canada, although brought up in England, and I can't take anyone seriously who still has a Canadian accent after forty or even fifty years out of the country.'

'For God's sake, how old is he?'

'No one knows. Probably over seventy.'

'Isn't it time he retired?'

'This isn't an ordinary sort of organisation. He's retired from his university post, but he's got some advisory job, which I never fathomed. You know him, of course?'

Neville had met him at a party some time before.

'What did you think of him?'

'I got on with him very well. He's a charming sort of person. It was my impression. Would he approve of my appointment?'

Brophy did not reply – he had a habit of suddenly dropping out of the conversation.

'Of course,' – and here he suppressed a burp – 'you'd have to sign the Official Secrets Act.'

'Are you signing me on as a spy?'

Brophy's flutter of self-importance modified. 'Hardly. I can only tell you if you're genuinely interested.'

'We seem to be discussing the matter arse-first. Tell me what the job is. If I can do it, I will.'

'When could you begin?'

'In about a month.'

'Perfect!' Brophy suppressed another burp.

'For Christ's sake, what is it?'

'Yes,' – as though the whole thing were an afterthought and a bore – 'Well, we've now decided to issue special monthly supplements on individual countries, coming round to each country or sub-region once a year. We kick off with the three Maghreb states – Morocco, Algeria and Tunisia – so I'll want you to make a swinging trip there and do a report of about five thousand words. The next one will be devoted to the Arabian peninsular – with special reference to the Trucial States, Oman and so on. You'll need to go there, too.'

'Good God! Everyone's going to the Gulf these days. British experts must be thicker than sand there.'

'It's the next trouble-spot.' Brophy might have been handing out a piece of classified information.

For his North African trip, Neville was to get £350, and would be allowed a generous expenses allowance and all air-fares and transport. A subsidised six-week tour of North Africa and the Persian Gulf! He accepted with enthusiasm. Brophy smiled paternally. He then asked whether he'd like to help in between times in the MEDOC office.

'There's far too much work for me. Fred tells me I must delegate more. I tend to get bogged down in detail and don't have enough time to see the institute in its broad outline.'

Neville listened grittily to the Brophy waffle and asked about the local staff. Weren't they well trained?

'There isn't a single person there I can really trust. I've tried to get Fred to do something about this, but he moves so slowly. He's terribly vague. He likes to keep everyone in suspense. This is part gamesmanship, part sheer forgetfulness. The principle seems to be that you forget everything but your own main chance. He's got international connections now – twenty years in the same job—'

'He must be making a packet.'

'I'd say he's touching about £10,000 a year, including expenses.'

Neville sat up.

'Well, he's got this advisory post, which must bring him in about £4,000 a year; his emoluments from MEDOC are in the region of £3,000, and then he's got his broadcasts, his articles and his books, and almost unlimited expenses when he travels.'

'Does his wife get expenses, too, when she travels?'

Brophy smiled strangely: 'Not legally.'

'You mean he fiddles a bit?'

'I ought not to say that.' Brophy's mouth twitched with a knowing, slanderous smile.

'You can't make hints like that unless you have something to go on.'

Brophy grinned broadly; his eyes disappeared behind his cheekbones. 'Forget what I said. I sometimes . . . put . . . well . . .' He burped, and made this an excuse to go indoors, on the pretext of taking a digestive tablet. This time, Neville heard the liquid and the glass stopper distinctly.

'Tell me, Paul, does Armstrong know you're taking me on?'

Brophy sat down abruptly and looked grand. 'I hope I'm allowed some latitude in such matters. I'm paid to be head of this office, and it's my duty to hire local staff. Fred knows I need an editorial assistant, and as a great believer in personal contacts he'll be delighted it's you. That's Fred's failing, really. If a matter can't be discussed over a lunch at MEDOC's expense it isn't worth bothering about.'

'The institute must charge the earth for its services if it can support all this affluence.' Neville said this in the hope of getting something more out of Brophy. 'Usually, research organisations of this kind are run on a shoestring.'

'Well, I can tell you: we receive a subsidy – quite a generous one – from H.M.G.'

'Ah . . . hence Official Secrets Act!'

'Of course. All our directors are nominated by the government. I'm surprised your brother-in-law never told you this. It's fairly generally known among the embassy people.'

'He never says anything about his work. Anyway, tell me more about the directors. Who are they?'

Brophy named them, only to dismiss them as ciphers. Dr Armstrong had all the power. 'They get a thousand guineas a year each from a secret Foreign Office fund and meet once a quarter in London – usually in the Waldorf in Aldwych. They eat toast and tea, get their cheques from Fred and accept everything he says. There's only one thing' – Brophy had become serious again – 'even though you sign the Official Secrets Act, never refer to the matter in front of Fred. He thinks it's bad form – gets quite upstage, like a Gaiety girl turned Debrett.'

Behind his Mongol cheeks, Brophy was having a joke at the expense of his boss, and he appreciated Neville's round laughter. 'Oh, yes, Fred is a split personality. When you see him with his white silk shirts, his elegant lightweight suits, shoes well polished, himself always rosy, well-dined, well-travelled, all toilet-water and fresh linen, you think this must be a really high-powered man. Once you get close, a picture of utter confusion emerges. No organisation powers, no method at all, and a capacity to use other people ruthlessly. I like him – of course – he's been good to me, but I know he would never think of me if I really got in his way.' Brophy also hinted at certain currents within the organisation, certain relationships from the past, which he did not understand.

'I suppose you'll take over from Fred eventually.'

Brophy tried to hide his pleasure at the suggestion. 'It has been understood; but we never mention it. Most things about MEDOC are "understood".' Reacting to Neville's strange expression, Brophy added, as an afterthought: 'There isn't anything underhand about us. Nothing to be ashamed of. There's no risk to you anywhere. It all boils down to a sense of discretion. It's much simpler in fact than on paper.'

'The local staff must be curious. They must ask questions?'

'They don't ask *me*, at any rate.' A twitch of fuddled annoyance reminded Neville that Brophy took himself seriously.

'Shamseddine, for instance?'

'Oh *him*. I've been trying to teach Michel his place ever since I've come. I'll succeed if Dot Parslow doesn't undermine me.'

'She knows everything?'

'Of course. She's been in on the game for years. It makes her partiality for Michel all the more strange – an Arab could never run the outfit. I can't understand why she doesn't see this and stop trying to undermine my authority.'

'You ought to stop her. Report her to Armstrong.'

'I have done. It doesn't do any good. In many ways, he prefers to believe her than me. She knows things before I do very often. They're always swapping letters.'

This reminded Neville of the restaurant incident, and he repeated Mrs Shamseddine's remark and the effect it had had. Brophy's eyes were narrow slits of suspicion and pain. 'You misunderstood her – or she's got a garbled version of the story. Fred wanted me to go back to London for consultations, but I refused. I asked him what we had to say that couldn't wait until his next visit. It was an oblique way of making him come out into the open with a criticism of my work. He has never answered the letter, so the trip is off so far as I'm concerned.'

'What a bloody odd way to run things.'

'It's a running battle. The other morning' – Brophy had no sense of time – 'Shamseddine produced a diary in which he had written down all the times of my arrival at work for the past fortnight.'

'Christ! I wouldn't put up with that! Why the devil don't you lash out at them?'

Brophy looked vague and blinked. He blinked again and looked vague. He wanted to change the subject.

'I told you, didn't I, that I was sending for my old manservant from Tunis?'

'Yes, you did.'

'He's an old friend. I think of him as more than just a houseboy. He's very dear to me.'

Neville thought he understood. 'Well, in that case, I'm not so sure it's a good plan. You're too exposed here – surrounded by envious people.'

Brophy's head sank on his chest. 'I hate envious people. Little people who long to strike but fear to. Dreary little nothings without the courage to live . . . to be themselves. What do I care what they think? I have nothing but contempt for them and their thoughts. "Nothing that common women ponder on, if you are worth my hope," ' he intoned in his most patrician manner. ' "The proud furies each with her torch on high!" '

Neville hardly knew what to make of him and waited for some elucidation. None was forthcoming, for Brophy had fallen asleep, and his regular breathing kept time with the afternoon breeze which slapped the awning overhead.

4

NEVILLE went into the apartment, and the housekeeper came out of the kitchen.

'I am leaving. My friend is asleep.' He looked around and saw a decanter containing an amber-coloured liquid through the half-open door of a buffet. A used glass was alongside.

'By the name of God, Mister Bol is always falling asleep. Sometimes when I come in the morning he is asleep on the sofa with his clothes on. Why doesn't his wife come from England to look after him?'

'He is unmarried.'

She knew, of course; she was fishing for information. 'He has told me someone is coming to look after him next month.' She looked knowing. 'A friend. I said, as Effendi wishes. I have many other offers. But when he said friend I wondered if he meant his wife.'

'Why should he? No, it won't be his wife . . .' Neville's phrase petered out – or would it be? The woman noticed his moment of doubt. Her eyes moved strangely – with irony? Amusement? Neville was unsure. 'Perhaps God will send him an Arab wife.'

'Pray God, indeed.' The woman bowed her head again like a serving woman. 'Pray God. There are many beautiful girls here of good family.'

She went to the far end of the balcony to watch Neville leave the building, then removed the empty coffee-cups and the glasses and went back into the kitchen. Because she had nothing else to do, and the day dragged like a funeral – and she lived from one sensation to the next – she rang the concierge's wife to tell her the guest had gone and that her boss was in another drunken sleep. It never ceased to amaze the woman that her employer faded out with such ease, leaving everything unguarded. The silence of the apartment, with only the flap-slap of the awning and the billowing curtains and the white young man lying full length on a chair, oppressed her. She went back into the kitchen and turned on the transistor radio. Yet she could not forget him, and returned again to stare down the long cool room to the open glass doors and the balcony where Brophy slept.

The balcony and the room were in the shadow of the blue-and-white awning. Outside this cool foreground everything was blue, shimmering – the sky, the sea, the late afternoon heat. The woman wandered away vacantly – then went up to the roof, where Brophy's shirts and pants were bleaching in the sun. She held up her arm against the landscape of white walls, which beat back the glare and heat at her. She returned with relief to the cool rooms below, where the white terylene curtains billowed out in the five o'clock breeze from the sea.

5

RHODA was as proud of Neville's new job as any woman of her knight returning from the wars. She wanted to keep him with her and, knowing his money was limited, welcomed any subsidy of their – to her – charmed life together. She was sure Paul Brophy had made the offer out of friendship for them and admiration for herself, and said so. Neville, who never grew dim-eyed over people (even those who helped him) cut her short: 'If he hadn't come up with something positive after his ghastly, penny-pinching meal I'd have asked you never to have him here again.'

Rhoda thought Neville set friendship at a sordid level.

'Now, look here, Rhoda. Friendship means striking the right note well and truly. I like people with a cutting edge – no time at all for dim people. If any friend of mine doesn't know that I enjoy a good meal, then he's dim and shouldn't be a friend at all. By any standards, that meal was an insult.'

'Well, he came up trumps in the end. I'll invite him to lunch one day when The Consort's out. The Consort's beastly to him.'

'I'll leave the coast clear for you. You deserve that pleasure.'

'Sarky! I know Paul's got a soft spot for me but I know I'm safe with him. Several people have told me he's queer.'

Neville thought her remark common. 'It's worthy of Doris Parslow. I'm surprised at you.'

'It was a friend of Doris Parslow's who told me first. She said Paul has sent to Tunis for an old boy friend to come to look after him.'

'How do people know?'

'Shouldn't they know?'

'I suppose Paul told them himself. He trotted out the subject today as though I were the first person he'd mentioned it to.'

Rhoda was indifferent. Things got known whether people talked or not; she did not find it shocking that Doris Parslow should put out a scandalous story about Paul before the Tunisian had turned up. 'In fact, I think she said he got MEDOC's travel agents to arrange the passage.'

Brophy's absence of commonsense hit Neville like cold water. 'Do you know something: that man won't be here this time next year. Why? There are too many dice loaded against him, and the most dangerous enemy he has is himself. He won't face up to the fact that this Parslow woman and her cronies are out to get him.'

'Why are English people so nasty? They delight in being mean and cruel. Do you know that The Consort told me this morning that I was a poseur and a fake intellectual?'

Neville raised his eyebrows.

'I was reading Diehl's book about the Byzantine empresses, and he said I was only reading it to show off. I said, "But the book reads just like a novel." And then he attacked me for the books I bought yesterday. He was dreadfully insulting and silly, and I told him to shut up or we'd move to separate rooms. Anyway, he wouldn't shut up, so I'll take up the spare room tonight. I can't bear him near me another moment.'

If Neville showed no interest it was not because he was indifferent to his sister's marital troubles: it was merely that this was the third or fourth time she and her husband had divided at nights. Neville was not sure whether they parted for the pleasure of reunion – so that they had a honeymoon every few months – or whether they came together for the pleasure of separation.

'And you're in trouble, too, my boy. Listen: where did you get to last night? The Duchess was curious this morning when you didn't turn up and no one could find you.'

Neville laughed loudly. 'Couldn't she guess?'

'When you're The Duchess you don't guess. You have forebodings.'

'I'm not going to tell her.'

'But you'll tell me. Maxwell said he left you drinking in a bar with some ravishing Titian-haired hostess.'

'Actually, she was fun. A sort of strong-arm girl from Ramsgate. She tells fascinating stories about working the strip-clubs in Manchester and getting the willies because the audience was so grey.'

Rhoda's mouth had parted slightly with pleasure. 'A stripper's own view of things! Oh, that's priceless. I must meet her.'

'Would it be quite the thing for an Embassy wife to meet an *animatrice*?'

'Why not?'

'Well . . .'

'Oh,' – as the light broke – 'would this have been a sort of *petite aventure*?'

'Well, what do you think?'

They looked at one another and laughed. Rhoda understood. *'Tu as des vilaines mœurs, mon frère. C'est fort heureux que je te comprenne.'*

She was unruffled by his confession – if this was the right word. It was the most natural thing in the world that Neville should have an *aventure* with a hostess, and equally natural that he should tell her about it. In a sense, it was the chit-chat, the conversation, missing from her own marriage. This was not to say, all the same, that she would have welcomed a similar confession from The Consort; on the other hand, as proof of some sort of human relationship, some dim, human lighting-up she might have welcomed it.

Rhoda wanted to know more about the Manchester strip-clubs and Neville recalled the girl as an English exotic – a sort of Kentish Pre-Raphaelite girl with a 'gawky folk-humour'.

'You mean, like that Elizabeth Siddall, who was taken up by Rossetti? They say she was perfection until she opened her mouth. You *must* bring her here! I know she's just the sort of girl to cheer up our parties. We need someone to replace that slashy-mouthed Fay and her Baptist homespun. There was a young woman I met at Josiane's whose husband is at the American Embassy, and I decided they'll be our resident

Americans this year. So you're never going to see Fay again, in any case. I hope Paul Brophy's Tunisian will be equally amusing. I don't want anybody over forty-five – except The Duchess – and we can't get rid of her – unless she takes up with Mrs Shamseddine in a big way. My dear! They are already on telephone-call terms.'

'Fuck The Duchess,' – it was Neville's last word – 'I wish she could get a big, fatal dig in the ribs from the Ramsgate girl!'

Yes, Rhoda said, such a girl was exactly what they needed to get a new outlook, and, privately, she thought such a girl was exactly the sort of person her brother ought to go to bed with. 'Yes, *do* bring her up to see me – but when The Consort is away. You can take me down to the bar one evening.'

Neville could not understand why his sister should fuss so about the girl. Neville was sure that to take Rhoda to the Red and Gold Bar was hardly the thing, for he believed in the value of appearances; and his good sense told him it was unwise for his sister to try to recreate a hostess's menagerie such as might find favour in parts of West London. He backed out of any promise to take Rhoda to the bar.

'Oh, please, I'd love to see this place where she works, where you met her. She sounds such a character. It all seems so right for this year.'

'What a silly phrase. You can't change your behaviour according to the season. Really, darling, you take up some silly postures.'

He was perplexed by her – and incredibly tired. His adventures of the last couple of days and the short nights had left him frazzled, so that when The Duchess came in from a visit to the cinema at midnight and asked suspiciously where Neville was, Rhoda was able to say quite calmly that he'd been in bed since half-past eight. Even this did not please The Duchess. 'Oh, after recommending a film so wholeheartedly I think he might have waited up to discuss it with me.'

The Consort and Rhoda exchanged glances, and the absurdity of The Duchess re-created a bond between them, so that bedtime found Rhoda once more in the Bonnard bedroom.

The Consort was displeased about Neville's temporary berth at MEDOC: 'Something fishy about that place. Nobody stays for long, apart from Mrs Parslow and her clique. Tell him not to get involved.'

At breakfast the next day, The Consort was unusually eloquent. 'There's something vicious there. The bloke who runs it – Armstrong – can't get people to stay, and I feel he doesn't want them to. The Embassy has been concerned about it for some time, but nothing's done. Nobody knows what to do with the bloody lot. From what I hear the best thing would be to pour some kettles of boiling water on them – as you do with cockroaches.'

Neville explained his overseas commitments.

The Consort was relieved. 'So long as you're out of the office you'll do O.K. Seriously. It's not a place I'd want anyone of mine to get involved in. It's not quite the thing, if you get me.'

The Consort had a shrewd idea of what was going on there and, moreover, thought the position an inferior one. He felt demeaned that his brother-in-law was getting mixed up with such a crowd.

6

BROPHY was never to know, despite Neville's warning, that Mrs Shamseddine's indiscretion had saved his career at MEDOC – at least for the rest of that winter. Both Mrs Parslow and Shamseddine wrote in haste to the boss in London, reporting Madame's bloomer and suggesting that any recall be postponed.

Until then the plot had been going quite well. Weekly letters from Dot Parslow and Shamseddine had convinced Professor Armstrong that somewhere or other there was a 'situation'. Armstrong, without getting in touch with Brophy to ask whether the things reported to him were true, decided to call Brophy back to London (on the grounds that he needed someone to act as deputy), while, in typical Armstrong fashion, he worked out the next move.

He took advantage of Mrs Shamseddine's gaffe to write long

letters to Mrs Parslow in which he said he was not recalling Paul Brophy but was going to give them 'a last chance to get on with him'. The letter ignored the whole tissue of plotting that had gone before and might have been written by an innocent party. Dot Parslow was furious; so was Shamseddine. Neither of them carried a torch for Armstrong, and their hatred for his methods had, for some years, been directed at the most vulnerable person – Armstrong's deputy in Beirut. Armstrong knew this, but had not been able to take the strong action against them he would have liked. Both Mrs Parslow and Shamseddine had got Armstrong out of situations which only his own ineptness could devise, so that the flowers of their friendship had turned into a wreath around Armstrong's plans for modernising MEDOC and getting greater personal control of its day-to-day workings.

Mrs Parslow and Shamseddine did virtually what they pleased, and, although Armstrong tried to pretend he initiated all the moves, his self-deception only increased the contempt in which Mrs Parslow and Shamseddine held him. They marvelled such a man held such a post. 'In a normal, competitive society he would be running a watermelon stall,' Shamseddine said. 'In a proper business, he would have been found out years ago,' was Mrs Parslow's verdict.

They hated him, they despised him, but they used his name whenever it suited them. He was the person who was likely to be hurt, appalled, broken-hearted, upset, by any show of independence at MEDOC. Both Shamseddine and Mrs Parslow tried to create an image of Dr Frederick Armstrong as the soul of probity and good sense, yet, whenever they caught him at his waffling, they wrinkled their noses in disgust; they spat at the picture on the wall, figuratively speaking. They believed that, like themselves, he was in the business for the pickings; there were successive layers of gravy on his chin. Whatever had happened, *he* had not gone without.

7

To the surprise of both Shamseddine and Mrs Parslow, Armstrong approved the appointment of Neville de Vries as an editorial assistant, and Neville went off to Rabat. Later he was appointed on a part-time basis to help read proofs and edit reports at an especially favourable salary. Neville owed everything to Brophy's patronage, but this did not make him in any especial way loyal to Brophy, whom he had decided lacked *hadh* – good luck – the essential quality of leadership among tribes in the Arabian peninsula.

While Neville was away in October, Brophy's Tunisian turned up, and Rhoda told him in one of her short, enigmatic letters that 'Paul did not seem very pleased by the new arrangements. The servant cramps his style.' Neville was in Casablanca when he received this letter, and laughed knowingly. Rhoda also reported that The Duchess had been to Athens for a couple of weeks. There had been a touching get-together at the boat to see her off and a party at the bar; at which they had bumped again into the Shamseddines and Mrs Shamseddine's sister, Victoria, who was an old Cairene acquaintance. Mrs Shamseddine was now preparing a party for The Duchess's return, so that Victoria Ghanem could get together some more of the old Cairo crowd, who were now all refugees, more or less, from Nasserist expropriations.

8

WHEN Neville got back to Rhoda's, much was changed. The Consort had been called back to London for urgent consultations, and Rhoda had decided to throw the welcome home party at her house. With The Consort away, she felt free, and the guests she assembled ignored almost totally the Embassy crowd: they were the people she and Neville had met in

Baida, with their new resident Americans, the resident Raving Beauty (Katherine Thomson) and the resident intellectuals. When Neville saw the guest list he saw how far his sister had gone in freeing herself from outworn commitments since her return: out of thirty-five people only seven were British.

That was an evening of surprises. The first came early on before the guests arrived. Neville went out on the verandah to catch up with the news in old copies of the airmail *Times*. He held a tumbler of Scotch and water, and was draining the last drops off the ice as Brophy arrived. He turned and saw Brophy and his sister coming towards him, arm-in-arm, like old cronies, almost like a married couple. Their pleasure at being together made Neville jealous; he noted resentfully how pleasure and acceptance had altered Brophy – his eyes had disengaged themselves from their protective cheekbones.

'Oh, Neville, Paul's got his new flat. MEDOC have approved the extra rent. It's a marvellous place, like a dream. You know, Paul, it's just as well the office approved, because I could see you'd set your heart on the place. We'll be able to go ahead with the new material for the chairs.'

Neville loathed chit-chat about furnishings and materials and lost interest. Rhoda went on to talk about the balcony which ran around the apartment like a deck, and the rooftop garden, which could be replanted and made attractive. Brophy paid Rhoda the compliment of wanting his terrace to have the 'civilised' appearance of her own; he visualised his place looking as Rhoda's terrace had looked that morning when she, Neville and The Duchess arrived from Europe: the blue, white and red flowers, the purple bougainvillaea, falling over the walls, linking the world outside and the house interior; and the white furniture laid with the pink cloth and the breakfast dishes. Already, only a couple of months later, that morning seemed like a golden age.

'Good; now let's all have a drink before the others come. And then tomorrow we'll go around to the apartment as arranged.' Rhoda took her diary out. 'I'll be there about four o'clock. We can have a cup of tea in the Patisserie.' That was another afternoon successfully filled in. That, also, was Neville's first surprise and a disagreeable one.

His second was to see how matey The Duchess had become

with the Shamseddines, especially with the sister Victoria.
Victoria was completely Europeanised. She spoke English,
French, Italian, Spanish and Turkish – but Arabic? *Yok!* This
was the old mercantile class which had had its teeth into Egypt
since the 1860s and had been evicted with ill-gotten gains
by the revolutionaries in the 1950s. The cliché 'disgustingly
rich' had been made for her and her husband, who was back
in Baida directing a bank, several subsidiary investment com-
panies and, to use American terminology, 'real estate'. There
was nothing he would not sink money into, provided it yielded
ten per cent. They were living in the old Christian quarter, in
the top half of a mansion. Every time they went in and out,
their progress down wide, marble stairs was overlooked by
gilded, heroic figures holding electric flambeaux; every time
they sat down to dine, the table was decorated with a silver
centrepiece which had once been used by the Empress Eugénie
on her visit to Egypt in the 1860s. They had a Sudanese major
domo and three other servants. In brief, they were the sort of
old friends The Duchess felt it was particularly suitable to
remember and re-establish contact with.

The arrival of the two sisters was like the ball scene in
Cinderella. Both were plump, both good-looking in the vivid,
clearly defined Lebanese-Egyptian way, with heavy feet thrust
into shoes of the latest fashion and inconsequence; both had
just been to their hairdresser to get their hair whirled into
shape. Their milky white necks glittered with the Ghanem
jewels – Victoria had lent a necklace to her sister – and Victoria
Ghanem wore a mink jacket, although it was a balmy November evening. When they took their coats off, there was another
layer of brilliance and conspicuous consumption underneath.
Victoria Ghanem was in deep red silk, with a fancy bodice
held together with a huge diamond claw. She removed her
gloves to show about four rings; her wrist-watch was of gold
and diamonds. To complete the effect, she carried a tooled
leather case holding a silver lorgnette, which she flung open
from time to time, to look at a flower arrangement, or at
Rhoda's opal cluster, which had come down to her from a
great-grandmother.

Mrs Shamseddine was in café-au-lait lace, which had been
built over an infrastructure of whalebone and elastic. An indiscreet giggle, an uncontrolled sneeze or a cough, would have

burst the whole thing. As it was, she was obliged to balance on one buttock when she sat down. Because she was in company she wiped her face with a small lace handkerchief, carried in a Chinese silk evening bag. Her jewellery was not as spectacular as her sister's Egyptian spoils; she redressed the balance by having at least three gold teeth.

The two sisters sat either side of The Duchess in a corner. '*Ah, ma chère,*' Victoria Ghanem kept saying, '*comme nous étions heureux en Egypte. Si on avait su ce que la vie nous reservait comme surprise. Ce Nasser – il a tout pris!*' And as she said this she made a gesture with both hands, and about two thousand pounds' worth of jewellery winked in agreement. Mrs Shamseddine, whose name was Alexandra, nodded in violent agreement, even though her husband was a Nasserite sympathiser, and added: '*C'était dégoûtant. Immonde.*'

Mr Ghanem, a benign, exquisite little man, like a faded photograph with sepia blots here and there, saluted all the women. He had perfectly manicured hands, with the nails slightly lacquered, and was The Duchess's idea of what a retired diplomat ought to be like.

The *ancien régime*, as Neville put it, kept together. Shamseddine joined them and complimented The Duchess on looking so well after her Greek visit.

'Thank you, Michel!' The Duchess replied.

Michel! Neville had another surprise. While he was eavesdropping, a servant came up and asked him to take a telephone call. A voice said, '*Allo! C'est toi, Paul?*' Neville revealed himself, and the voice immediately said in bad English that he was Paul Brophy's friend and wanted to speak with him. Curious, Neville asked, 'Who shall I say it is?'

'Pierre.'

Neville knew no one called Pierre, and, without thinking, announced the name to Brophy, who was drinking whisky with Sophie Azberzhian and Rhoda. Brophy was flummoxed: 'How the devil did he know I was here?' Pierre, they were to discover, was the Tunisian servant.

Brophy walked across to the telephone. A pinched conversation followed. Neville asked Brophy whether all was well. Brophy blinked like an owl in daylight. 'He may ring later. It would be better if you said I've left.'

Twenty minutes later, Pierre rang again. Could he speak 'wiz Mr Broffi?' Neville said he'd gone. The reply was unforeseen: *'Il se cache de moi. Dites-lui, Monsieur, qu'il est menteur, et je sais qu'il est menteur.'*

A less malicious person might have refused to pass on such a message; but not Neville. Brophy winced. 'What can you think of it all?'

'I should think it's time to give him a month's wages and the sack. Why should he keep pestering you?'

Brophy was plainly hunted. 'I made a mistake. It's a complex situation.' He thought a moment and then walked back to Sophie Azberzhian, talking about her scholarship. 'Off *cohwress*, there will neverr be a careerr forr me herrre. It means if I have success I shall have to stay in Europe or America et *pourtant j'adore mon beau pays.*'

Ah, they encouraged her, since she was such a lovely girl as well as talented, she might find a place in films in Rome. She was determined to suffer. 'For us Armenians, Baida is another home. Our real one is closed to us. Baida is our tender mother.'

Brophy nodded distractedly.

'And I want to devote my whole life to my arrt. Maybe, it will be possible in two or three generations . . .'

Brophy nodded stupidly, like a wound-up toy: a cover-up for his own thoughts of the imported incubus, who was at that moment, he had said, walking around the flat with a knife waiting to finish them both off. He rose abruptly and left the singer in mid-phrase. He had to talk to Neville. 'Will you come back with me to the flat this evening? I'm afraid things will happen which might be regretted.'

'Such as?'

'The boy – he – tends to get a bit the worse for wear and bangs the furniture about.'

'Good God, you're mad to keep him. Why don't you get rid of him?'

'I may have to. He may force me to send him back.'

'Now. Do it now. He's a menace.'

'He knows his job.' Brophy's prissy voice tried to neutralise the situation, but Neville knew the drums were beating a totally different message in the background. He agreed to go. Brophy pressed his arm – a rare gesture for him. 'I'm in a sticky patch at the moment. God knows why I get into these messes.'

'It's your mad, impulsive personality!' Neville tried a joke, but it misfired.

'I hope you don't really think that. I'd hate to be thought impulsive.'

God, what a drip! Neville moved away and they left for Brophy's flat together an hour or so later; and this was the start of Neville's third surprise.

Neville's previous visit had been on 24 September for the inadequate meal, when the flat had been a place of billowing curtains and coolness – a friendly, welcoming place on a humid day, a place of repose and stillness. Returning to the flat at night was a different experience – the carpets had been relaid for what, in Baida, passes for winter, and the windows were closed. As they stood in the hall while Brophy fumbled about for a switch – the bulb of the main light was broken – Neville had the disagreeable impression of someone malevolent hidden in the darkness. The walls were hung with unhappiness and ill-will. The light went on. The impression of horror and menace passed.

Brophy blinked in the new light and looked around uncertainly. He moved on gingerly into the main living-room and lit another lamp on the balcony, near the bar. Neville followed uncertainly, noting the half-open doors on either side and expecting, from one moment to the next, someone to hurl himself at them.

Trying hard to sound natural, Brophy told Neville to make himself comfortable on the balcony sofa, while he went into the kitchen for ice. Neville picked up a magazine on the wicker table and flicked through it, his ears straining, his eyes darting about. He heard the refrigerator door slam and the tinkle of ice in a container. Still no sign of the Tunisian.

'Where is he?' asked Neville.

'Asleep, I suppose.' Brophy was not convinced, since he kept looking towards the living-room.

They sat together under the solitary balcony light all alone on the face of the tall apartment block, drinking whisky, which Brophy – under the pressure of events – served with a prodigal and quaking hand. The situation demanded an explanation. Neville expected it and, as Brophy drank on, he felt obliged to give it. 'It's been a mistake, my having him here.'

'In what way?'

The servant was an embarrassment. He drank, he was rebellious and he wanted Brophy to pay for him to study medicine. Neville saw no problem. A person imported as a servant had no right to expect superior treatment; if he failed to see this he must be sent home. Brophy hinted at an unspecified obligation to the man's family, to his parents – and, in some dim way, to the man himself.

'You know what it's like in Tunisia. About one person in four is unemployed, and his family think I offer him a chance of advancement. He's got no education but what he's picked up here and there: good French, shaky English. He's had to make his own way.'

Brophy went on to talk of the Tunisian, sometimes calling him Bahige, sometimes Pierre, as though he had been the hero of a folk saga, so that Neville felt that for Brophy the movement of the Tunisian's life from barefoot street urchin to manservant had an epic quality. It was the sentimentalising of the poor by a man who had never known want; and it bored Neville. Would Brophy have had the same glutinous admiration for, say, a Scottish miner's son who rose to be head of a big concern? Neville doubted it.

Clearly, what had upset Brophy about the Tunisian was his refusal to remain the unsophisticated village boy. In the two years since they had last seen one another, the Tunisian had changed. As a realist, he had no time for Brophy's mystique of desperation; he wanted to get on; he wanted a diploma; he took himself seriously. He was no longer grateful to Brophy for rescuing him from poverty but resentful that Brophy did not give him more generous help. He complained that Brophy had only bought him a fourth-class ticket to Baida, that he refused to take him out to meet his friends, that he tried to edge him out of his life. Brophy was disconcerted by the way the Tunisian had aged, looked at him with the cool eyes of an equal and embarrassed him by the chronic over-development of his semi-education.

Brophy – grown self-indulgent on the subservience of the MEDOC junior staff, found Bahige cheeky. He was shocked and embarrassed because Bahige refused to sleep in the servant's room off the kitchen and took up his quarters in the guest room. He shared Brophy's bathroom, he helped himself to his whisky, and had turned the relation of master and servant into – whatever its basis – a *ménage*.

Neville listened patiently but with increasing disgust. 'But why do you put up with him? He sounds a bore.'

'He's so defenceless!'

'You mean, the wild child of nature in the big city?'

'In a way. In a way, I feel responsible for him.'

'Yet he has no other relationship than that of servant?'

Brophy looked guilty: 'No. Why should there be?'

'No reason at all; but no one will believe you.'

'You don't think so.'

'I know they won't.'

Brophy looked hunted, bit his lip and said nothing.

Neville did not believe Brophy and shared his disbelief with his sister the next morning as they took their coffee together.

'It's as plain as my nose they never were boss and servant. It worked well enough in Tunis. Here it's less successful because the man's older and the question of exact status is important. Paul insists on describing the man as his servant or, alternatively, as his cook. The man won't hear of it. He tells people who call on the phone that he's Brophy's secretary or chauffeur, according to the whim of the minute – and all this is crazily embarrassing for Paul. He tells me he's desperately trying to pass off the whole thing as some foible, some *folie de grandeur* on the man's part, but, of course, he knows people are talking.'

'Then why doesn't he send him home?'

'That's the question. I suppose that's what will happen, because so far he hasn't got a work permit for him. When he came he was granted a week's *permis de séjour*, and that's run out. The man's now an illegal immigrant. If the authorities found out they could dish Paul, too.'

'What a mess! I wish he'd told me these things. I'm sure The Consort could arrange something.'

Neville shook his head. Brophy would never ask The Consort for help. 'But, go on, Neville. Did you actually see the man?'

'Not really. After we'd sat there some time, and Brophy was mumbling on in his usual sottish way, a voice cried out from one of the bedrooms *"Qu'est-ce que tu racontes à mon sujet?"* Dead silence. Brophy jumped up as though he were going to draw a revolver – it's that funny way he has of holding his hands. The voice went on: *"Assez de blagues, Paul. Dis à ton ami de foutre le camp. Laisse-moi dormir en paix!"* Brophy went over to the open door and asked whether the man wanted a drink. He got an absolutely filthy remark in return and a torrent of abuse about Paul's sly behaviour and all the rest – going out and leaving him alone a prisoner in the flat – the whole lot. So I thought I'd better get up and go. I asked Paul whether he thought the man would carry out his threat to knife him, and he just put his hand over his face and looked desperate. As I came away, I looked up at the balcony and I saw that the man had got up and was looking down at me – he one end of the balcony and Brophy the other.'

'But it's very serious. Paul is open to blackmail – God knows what. He must be in torment.' A pause. 'Why didn't he mention this to me?'

'Probably he can't talk about it to a woman.'

'Because of the queer relationship?'

'Of course.'

'You're sure it's queer?'

'But what else?'

Rhoda sighed, looked gloomy. 'Everybody says so, of course. I know myself – well, I just don't feel there's any danger in him. Do you think – in the ordinary way – it matters?'

Neville was surprised by the question. 'It doesn't matter to *us*, because we don't care. It matters a good deal to Paul's position. People are vicious about such behaviour. And I can't say I admire the way Paul goes on. It's limp and unclean. Everybody's unhappy. Nobody's getting anything out of it. And Paul's such a mess. Half of him thinks it's fascinating to be talked about.'

'God, darling. You *are* cruel!'

'Well, let's be honest. Brophy brings the worst out in me.'

'He's so good to you. He told me it was a relief to have one person in the organisation he could trust. You can't let him down.'

'He says one thing to you and another to me. I know he's been good to me. I've had a marvellous tour thanks to him. At the same time I loathe everything that's ineffective and bumbling. He's a bumbler. Who but a bumbler would compromise his position here with his cook? He's such a fool. Such a muddled, silly person; and in the Arab world he'll come off worst. This is a primitive society, like a chicken run, where every bird pecks at the sick fowl. By Arab standards he deserves all he's going to get. He's asking for trouble, and it will come to him. He's got no *hadh*. Defending him is a waste of time.'

'But, he's got such good qualities. Real taste and finesse. Real judgement.'

'Sorry, darling, he can't have. Only a fool would have brought that man from Tunis, and only a treble fool would keep him on. As I came home this evening I knew that I should have to finish with his organisation. I'll do this trip to the Gulf and perhaps the one to Ethiopia, but I won't stay after that. I've worked it out, and as far as I can see Brophy will last until about next April or May. After that, he's a goner. He'll have to be recalled in disgrace.'

Rhoda had rarely known her brother so passionate, so sure of himself, and when he added, 'It's asking for bad luck to stick to such a person!' she stopped sipping her coffee and held the cup slightly away from a mouth which had formed a round O of astonishment.

Part Three

1

IT was easy to be Dr Armstrong for the simple reason that, in his own eyes, he never made a mistake and was never guilty of poor judgement. Things went wrong from time to time, but only because of other people's ineptness or bad faith, or because someone had not lived up to the high ideals Dr Armstrong had for him. When he discussed Paul Brophy's conduct with the directors of the institute in London it was always as though the original appointment had been forced on him by a higher authority.

'I'm beginning to ask myself,' he would say, 'whether he *is* really fitted for the responsibilities of the post. He's got a crowd of hysterical people to handle, and he's not being very subtle about it.'

The directors nodded sagely and shuffled in to tea, where Dr Armstrong, well briefed by his regular letters from Mrs Parslow and Shamseddine, would hint that Brophy, caring more for the fruits of office than the work, put too much stress on car allowances, travelling expenses and the need for suitably impressive apartments. There were suggestions that Brophy was an empire-builder with *folie de grandeur* – this was said with Armstrong's fellow-feeling for an egoist – and the criticism moved on to the sublime doubt: 'To our great disappointment, he has not turned out to be the man we thought he was.'

The others nodded, too little involved in the affair to realise that Brophy was Armstrong's creature. If they sighed it was because staffing problems at the institute were an old worry. When Armstrong suggested that it might be better for Brophy not to finish his contract, they nodded equably.

Armstrong, under strong pressure from Mrs Parslow and Shamseddine, wanted to finish off the Brophy affair quickly.

The longer it dragged on, the more letters were exchanged, the greater the evidence of base collusion with his senior people. Armstrong shared one illusion with his doomed second-in-command: that he could appeal to Mrs Parslow's sense of fair play. When her complaints continued to arrive, he grew angry and, to reassert his authority, wrote the stern letters telling her and Shamseddine to get along with Brophy. He enjoyed putting the two firmly in their places; he eased the burden – intolerable to one with a Jehovah complex – of being in cahoots with the unspeakable. He enjoyed reasserting his authority and decided he would continue doing so when he visited the institute in December. He would begin with Brophy. He would make a direct attack – ask him whether he was unable to have relations with women and, if not, why he should give other people this impression? He would ask him why he took so few pains to inspire confidence in the senior members of the staff and why, if he could not hold his liquor, he drank so much. By speaking brutally he hoped to get Brophy to admit everything and so clear the way for his departure. No one, Dr Armstrong was inclined to think, seriously objected to homosexual behaviour, but it made an excellent excuse for breaking a man. After seeing Brophy (and even if he beat him down to a confession), he would take Shamseddine aside and ask him what right he had not only to make imputations against a man's integrity but to write unproven, scurrilous things about the person whom he, Armstrong, had appointed as head of the Baida office. He would treat Shamseddine like the sordid professional Palestinian he was; there were years of insubordination and cheek to square off. Finally, there was Mrs Parslow, who had to be handled with more care. He intended to get her mellow with Johnnie Walker and go on from there.

These interviews, these questions and these assertions of authority would be part of a holding operation and would be useless unless Brophy could be got out of the place before a really dangerous scandal broke. Dr Armstrong set Easter as the date by which Brophy must be back in London. In so far as he was capable of drawing up a clear-cut plan of campaign, this was what he proposed:

(*a*) Brophy withdrawn to London on a temporary basis with

suggestions of bigger things ahead; his vanity and ambition untouched.

(b) A replacement? Someone who would find out whatever Brophy's darker secrets were.

(c) This 'X' might find things out but decide not to interfere and leave the scandal undisturbed – who would put pressure on this 'X' to speak? This 'X' would have to be made to speak in order to clear his own good name of any suggestion of collusion.

(d) If this 'X' did not make an unfavourable report on Brophy; what happened? But he *must*. Everything depended on this, so that Brophy would be arraigned, told he had betrayed a heavy trust, etc., etc.

(e) Brophy would be given the chance to resign – a favourable settlement – perhaps money for the rest of his contract – *but he would be OUT*!

(f) Appointment of another man?

By this plan Armstrong imagined he would maintain his image and avoid the damaging imputation of having conspired against his own deputy. Armstrong aimed at being a Jehovah in the modern style: a Panurge by consensus and political persuasion. In the end, everything boiled down to politics.

There remained the personal relationship between himself and Brophy, which dated for some time before Brophy was taken on by MEDOC. Armstrong's admiration for the younger man had been of the kind which great men bestow on those who are useful to them, no more: the kind of patronising goodwill which implied that Brophy could never be as good as Armstrong, but was near the top of the second division. It was the exact spacing needed for the man who was good enough to be given responsibility but could never be considered as Armstrong's successor. Brophy was well-connected, well-educated, a first-rate Arabic scholar and what, in the old days, might have been called a gentleman. Armstrong had been genuinely appalled to hear how he fell asleep on the floor at parties, was unpunctual, wrote stupid memos, behaved in a waffly way, could be needlessly authoritarian, and refused, on principle, to discuss office affairs with his closest associates. The arrival of the Tunisian had frightened Armstrong; he saw at once the false position Brophy had made for himself;

it proved what Shamseddine and Mrs Parslow had been saying all along, that Brophy had no judgement.

2

MRS PARSLOW wrote about this time, asking whether it had been decided to raise the wages of all junior and menial employees from December the first. She enclosed a Brophy memo asking her to work out a 12½ per cent rise above the local minimum wage. Was she to act on Brophy's instructions?

Armstrong had received a copy of this memo and had been reminded that, at one time, he had thought of putting the lower-paid staff on a new wages scale, but had never got round to it. MEDOC paid its unskilled staff the minimum legal wage; when the government decreed an increase, MEDOC paid up – but not until. The senior men, the academic specialists, were treated well, even handsomely; and, of course, in the way of things, the well-paid cared nothing about the hardships of the less fortunate.

Brophy was the first British member of the staff to take up the matter and found no one, British or Arab, to back him. This did not prevent his writing the memo to Mrs Parslow and an accompanying letter to Armstrong showing the extent of his concern that a British institution should pay a young married man – he instanced a case – less than an errand boy got in London, when the cost of living was the same.

Armstrong's reply accepted the principle of change in the salaries structure but added the important rider that timing was the great thing. He advised Brophy to hold his hand until he came out in December. In the meantime, Mrs Parslow could prepare an outline scheme.

This was part of Armstrong's Jehovah-game. He wanted to be in the office when the increases were announced and to be seen to be the prime mover in the matter. He would have liked to arrive one day in the office, assemble the staff and hand out little envelopes, and, as the staff enthused over their new-

125

found wealth, he would explain that he, Armstrong, had been moved by their plight, had felt for them as a father for his children. The underpaid messengers, drivers, and library assistants – about fifteen all told – would look at him reverently. There would be tears of gratitude and devotion; there would be tears in his eyes, too; and for an hour – for, maybe, ninety minutes – the shopworn platitudes about Anglo-Arab friendship would be true. How he enjoyed the scene. How often it went through his mind. How vexed he was when Brophy gave every sign of getting in on his act.

In a second letter to Brophy – for Parslow warned him that an immediate increase was under discussion – Armstrong restated the position.

When you are dealing with Arabs you have to pay strict attention to timing. Their reasoning is not like ours. They think if they pay now why did they not pay us a year before? They will want more. I accept that, as manager, it is your business to discuss the salaries and conditions of work of all the employees and I am grateful that you have prepared a scheme of general upgrading for junior personnel. As you know, I have always had the welfare of the staff at heart, and what contributes to their happiness contributes to mine. All the same, I must make this point clear: I think the first of January would be a good date to start any new payments and would give the accounts department [i.e., Mrs Parslow] time to work out the scheme properly.

Brophy was not impressed by Armstrong's reasoning – what was a difference of twenty-eight days, when the salaries ought to have been increased years before? Brophy saw no especial Arab illogic in asking this question and, in irritation with Mrs Parslow for her delaying tactics and Armstrong for his ill-disguised play-acting, ordered the salaries for the lower-paid to be increased from November the first; accordingly the increases were paid at the end of the month. As the lower-paid workers' pay was not subject to negotiation, in the ordinary way, there was no consultation. News of the proposed increase leaked out before the end of the month, but no one believed the rumours. The increases on 30 November had all the charm of a golden shower.

3

DECEMBER 1: a black day for Brophy's enemies, as messengers and menials walked about with shining faces and, hands on heart, swore that Mr Brophy was of the incandescent Host. Mrs Parslow, totting up the month's accounts, prayed Dr Armstrong would not have kittens. The senior Arab staff, out-raged by their juniors' good fortune, hated to see Brophy basking in their approval; they hated this proof of his author-ity. They were angry because the ill-informed juniors thought Brophy had paid the money out of his own pocket, and one of the library-assistants told Shamseddine that Mr Broffi was a friend of all the Arabs! Shamseddine bent down over his papers. '*Aywah!* And so can all of us be when we give away other people's money.'

The resentment, the nastiness, of the senior people was more than counterbalanced by the gratitude of the ill-paid. That afternoon, after work had finished, they solemnly invited Bro-phy to drink a whisky with them in a simple café on the main road.

It was an innocent, touching affair. Brophy was served a whisky on the café's only chromium-plated salver, while all the others solemnly drank his health in Pepsi or orange juice. The cry was raised: 'Mr Broffi for President!' and he was cheered and acclaimed: a spontaneous gesture of affection never before given to anyone in MEDOC. Not even the great Dr Armstrong had been able to raise a cheer.

It was only minutes, of course, before news of this homage reached Shamseddine and Mrs Parslow. Brophy's behaviour – they claimed – humiliated them, and MEDOC had lost face because its boss was seen in a roadside café drinking whisky with the ragtag and bobtail and enjoying a sort of junior fan-club triumph.

It was, perhaps, foolish of Brophy to allow the staff to identify him so completely with the rises in salary, but the incident did not warrant the lurid accounts which reached Dr Armstrong. The fact that all those present were under twenty-five, and one or two of them handsome adolescents growing their first mous-taches, was not overlooked in the Shamseddine–Parslow letters;

and the charge that somehow had been levelled against Brophy ever since his arrival – that he showed more than a professional interest in his younger staff – was filled out and revived. In Mrs Parslow's mind, the celebration became a carnival of unspeakable pleasures. Brophy's popularity with the younger staff became for her, from that time on, inseparable from her instinct about his perversion, and she was to refer to the celebration again and again.

The news of the rises was an unpleasant blow for Dr Armstrong on the eve of his departure – and his reaction was the same as Shamseddine's – 'easy enough to buy popularity on other people's money'. He wrote to Brophy briskly, and although he could not criticise the principle of the salary increases he criticised the timing. It was a vague letter, shot through with ill-will and displeasure. He could not be known to be against the increases, since this would have undone years of careful building up of himself as the father-figure of the organisation, as the all-merciful one who, with regular chats about school fees and doctors' bills, kept up-to-date with his senior men's private lives, and whose smile could be seen whenever the clouds parted: a dear old man beyond the mountains stroking his beard that trailed out into the Milky Way and encircled the cosmos.

Brophy, who could never resist an occasion to type a note, answered: 'Dear Fred, Briefly: the salary increases were sorely overdue and sorely needed. To keep people at that level waiting for two months was cruel. I only wish the increases could have been greater. I have been greatly moved by the gratitude the men and boys have shown. Yours, Paul.'

Had Brophy only added some small untruth such as 'The men and boys are deeply grateful to you' – thus bringing Armstrong into the act (if only at the final curtain), the old man's displeasure might have been less – but Brophy never thought of such a thing, and Armstrong's displeasure was increased.

4

Dr Armstrong left London on 10 December accompanied by his distinguished wife and a distinguished woman friend – they were to spend Christmas in the Holy Land. In Baida they stayed at the Maximilian Hotel, and the three of them drove in an Embassy car the next day to the university, where Dr Armstrong delivered a long-billed lecture on British foreign policy since 1945. The lecture – the last of the university's autumn cultural events – was packed to the door. *L'Aurore* paid Armstrong the compliment of sending along one of its clever women-journalists for an interview, and his lecture was printed in the paper's week-end review.

After the lecture, there was a supper at the Ambassador's private house, at which *tout* Baida was present, among them Brophy, The Consort and Rhoda. It was a great success; but, when Rhoda returned home, the chief thing she could remember was that someone had been playing Mahler in a flat overlooking the Ambassador's house, and while waiting for the car at his gates she had been haunted by the martial rhythms, the trumpets and celestial alpine cowbells: it had made a weird impression on her in the beautiful winter night.

For The Consort it had been different. He used the new meeting with Armstrong as an excuse to sneer at MEDOC. 'What a very purposeful little man your boss is,' he said to Neville. 'He got the golden carpet treatment all right. There were ambassadors falling over themselves to meet him,' – an ironic exaggeration – 'and ambassadors' ladies ready to risk their reputations for a touch of his hand. He strode through it all like a little Canuck Caesar.' The Consort, who usually had little feeling for character, had been taken by Armstrong. He thought the man was a sham who was getting away with a big act. As such he admired him in the way an upper-class Englishman relishes a wide boy once he is alerted to the dangers. For The Consort the great Dr Armstrong belonged to a special category of absurd people: he was the man who employed a clever little tick like Neville (who was having whom?), and he was the man who had assembled MEDOC from nothing – for what?

Neville was not sufficiently involved in MEDOC to find anything personal in The Consort's remarks, although interested to see how well-informed he was about things that went on there, as when he continued, 'What a dreary collection of people you work with in that organisation! There's Shamseddine suffering like hell because he's not an Englishman and hates England and has got to work for an English organisation. Then there's old Doris Parslow, who smoulders on because Armstrong won't tell her how big her bonus will be when she retires. And she was on the phone to the Ambassador's secretary wondering why Brophy had been invited to the supper and not herself. Had she done anything wrong? Was there something against her? And there was Brophy, looking more lost than ever, not sure whether to follow the Big Man around like a dog or arm his grisly women! And he's all heated up, too, because the Big Man won't formally announce him as his successor. The whole operation is an example of futility – but, my God! how people burn themselves up over nothing. Like actors in a cheap play.'

The Duchess thought it reasonable enough, since people were attached to their careers.

'Christ, Duchess, that's not a *career* in MEDOC: it's a knacker's yard. It's a very third-rate and questionable organisation, run – as we dairy farmers say – by flying herds. No one stays there long. They get a glimpse of the intrigue and bugger off as fast as they can. And Neville will join them if he's as sharp as I think he is – won't you, old chap?'

Neville laughed easily: 'MEDOC makes you more eloquent than anything else I've ever known.' Rhoda looked at her husband with the eyes of the basilisk itself, blasting by its breath and look. In this case The Consort's slight tipsiness was the antidote for the fatal stare.

5

ALL the same, he agreed to give a luncheon for the Great Man and his women, and about fifteen people turned up, including, of course, Paul Brophy, who had still not had the chance to have a private word with his boss about things in general. Rhoda made a special effort, since Dr Armstrong was Neville's boss and the servants thought God and his mothers were arriving.

Afterwards they discussed his appearance. Rhoda thought he was a small-scale Chesterton. He had not, of course, the Chestertonian humour or massiveness, but he had that set of the head.

'Your father adored Chesterton,' The Duchess said. 'Chesterton was awfully nice to him over something or other.'

'You mean father knew Chesterton?' Rhoda looked at The Duchess in surprise.

'Of course.'

'Father must have been very young at the time,' said Neville.

'Even if he was in rompers – which he was not – it wouldn't have stopped his knowing and admiring Chesterton.'

'We were talking about Dr Armstrong's appearance,' Rhoda said.

'And I'm objecting to the odious, glassy way Neville takes me up on everything,' The Duchess cried.

Anyway, after a pause in which they exchanged burning glances and wounded, they were back to Dr Armstrong's appearance. He was every inch the great man. He had a hairline like Lloyd George's. Surely, that was unintentional? No one would want to imitate that Welsh twister deliberately? Or would they? The Duchess found much of the intellectual dandy in the way he held up his hand while waiting for the right word, the exact word, to drop into his head; and the way he held his head, carefully listening, taking in everything, balancing what was said: surely this was the sign of a remarkable man? And the way he stroked his beard!

In the general admiration for Dr Armstrong, his two horse-faced women were almost overlooked – they were happy all the same – and went off to Jerusalem the next day to start a tour of archaeological sites while waiting for the great man to join them for the Christmas festivities.

6

IN one of his more forthright moments, Brophy had mocked Dr Armstrong's belief that if a matter could not be discussed over a lunch at MEDOC's expense it could not be worth bothering about; he would have smiled on the wrong side of his face had he known his boss planned a series of meals at which Brophy was to be the main dish: a series of last suppers: *la cena à la chaine*. The dinners, suppers and evenings in nightclubs which marked Dr Armstrong's Middle East tours were famous; and the first of the series began with Brophy at the Copacabana. After a drink at the bar, they went out into the sunshine on the seaside terrace, where the heat of an English July was offset by the noble white cap of snow on Mount Atthis. The winter landscape around Baida has great beauty: distances have a greater clarity than in summer, the mountains are not 'volatilised' by humidity. Despite the heat and the brilliant light the seashore was almost deserted – a couple of foreign tourists swimming, but no water-skiers.

'Have you been up to the snow yet?'

Brophy shook his head. Winter sports bored him and, in any case, the early snow was not much use.

'It always falls in the first week of December,' Armstrong replied with some irritation. 'I saw some cars with skis on the top. You ought to take an interest in outdoor things more. You look as pallid as though you lived in London.'

Armstrong followed this lordly pronouncement by moving dramatically into the sun and turned his face towards it as though showing Brophy how to get a tan. Brophy was too self-conscious to do likewise and sat, uncomfortable and alone, twiddling his glass in the shade of the umbrella. He had never known Armstrong make so critical and personal a remark. He nursed it like a wound. Still with his eyes shut, Armstrong asked how Neville de Vries was getting on.

'Well, you see his stuff. I think it's first-rate. He's got a good, clear brain.'

'I didn't say otherwise. I meant – how is he getting on with the staff? Dot Parslow, Michel, Laurence and the others?'

'They like him.'

Armstrong deliberately opened his eyes and moved towards the table: 'I think you've made heavy weather of your relationship with them haven't you?'

Before Brophy could answer, the waiter arrived with the *moules marinière*. 'More of the stock!' Dr Armstrong said. '*Encore du potage!*' He drew up again to the table and changed his glasses. He peered expertly at the dishes before him. 'Perfect! Really perfect!' There was real Canadian warmth in the r's. The waiter, unused to British enthusiasm over food, smiled.

'Yes, Paul, there's got to be some determination on all your parts to get on. We can't go on like this.'

Brophy, who had flushed at the first attack, was still an unusual, uncomfortable red. 'Do you blame me for the tension?'

'In a way, I do. I confess, I do.'

'I'm sorry. I feel I haven't had any respect or support since I've been here.'

'Respect and support have to be gained. They don't go with the job.'

'I felt they resented me as a newcomer. They'd have resented whoever came in my place – as they apparently resented my predecessors.'

It was a point well put for once. Armstrong grunted and went on eating. He ignored this aspect and went back to the tablets of the law: 'You see, I think you misunderstood your position. You aren't here to be the high-handed boss. You are here to lead a group of intelligent people who are doing a skilled and useful task. You ought to consult more often; advance together in your work and spend less time shut up in your own room and own thoughts.'

At last Brophy got it out: 'It looks as though Dot Parslow has been writing to you more often than I thought.'

'She has made her points.'

'I wish you'd send on her remarks to me so that I can comment on them. I don't accept her criticisms for a moment.'

Brophy had stopped eating. He watched his boss attack his shellfish like a seasick man watching an immune traveller eating. His world was spinning.

'It can't go on, Paul. I intend to speak severely to Dot Parslow and Michel. I'm telling you all that it's *your duty to get on.*

That's all it is. I'm fed up with the endless wrangles over nothing. I'm a busy man, and I look to you to take the burden off my shoulders, not add to it.'

'You know, it's the last thing I want to do.'

'What is?'

Crushed by the irritable tone of voice, Brophy said meekly: 'Why, to add to your burdens.'

'Well, that's something—'

'Yet I take decisions – the wages, for instance—'

'You mean the recent upgrading?'

'Yes—'

'It was badly timed.'

'It was overdue.'

'Are you arguing with me?'

'Please forgive me – I'm not arguing with you – I'm telling you that people on such low salaries cannot be kept waiting for their money.'

'You sound as though you were the only person who knew what was what.'

'I'm sorry. You seem determined to misunderstand everything I say.'

Dr Armstrong wiped his mouth with his napkin and looked around for the waiter. 'Some more white wine, *minfadlak*!'

Starting to shake with indignation and irritation he turned on Brophy: 'Half a bottle is never enough for two.' The tone of his voice told Armstrong he was being unfair, especially since little could be served by crushing Brophy on small points.

'If you'd rather I left, Fred, I'll do so. I don't want to spoil your meal.'

'Don't be absurd. Who wants you to go?'

The wine waiter came with a full bottle of Pouilly-Fuissé. 'Fill up both!' Dr Armstrong watched the wine rise in the glasses with an angry intensity. 'That's better. You never gain anything by being cheese-paring,' he said to Brophy. 'The things of this world are to be enjoyed.' He might have added: 'Especially when MEDOC is paying!'

Brophy was too miserable to make any gesture of good health as his boss lifted his glass. It was his suggestion they only had half a bottle. He had meant to show a fine sense of economy.

'Listen, Paul, you've got to get it into your head that I'm annoyed with you because you've let the side down. When I appointed you to this job – and there were people, I may say, who warned me that you were unsuitable' – Brophy winced – 'I thought you knew what the score was. When you get your kind of money – the sort of money about five per cent of the population are getting in Britain, if that – I expect a certain standard. I gave you permission to take this new flat – about three thousand Baidani pounds above the orig-inally agreed rent – and I gave you the benefit of a large entertainment allowance, and I expect you to do something with it. I must say I'm shocked you haven't laid on a single gathering for me. I expect it. I want to meet people – I have to meet people – and I expected you to do something about getting in people to meet me. You can't leave everything to the British Embassy!'

This attack caught Brophy on the wrong foot. He blinked, but before he could begin Dr Armstrong went on.

'No, wait a minute. It doesn't only arise out of my visit. Everywhere I've been since my arrival I've heard people say they never see you, that you've never given a party or a cocktail. I know an intellectual like you finds the whole cocktail circuit boring, but in that case you shouldn't have accepted a senior public post. People expect you to cut a figure – to be someone – and all they see of you is you drinking more than is good for you in other people's parties. It's not fair to us, Paul. And I want you to mend your ways.'

'Well, I had intended inviting you and some close friends for a dinner when you could fit it in.'

'Good! I'm glad to hear it! I'd begun to think you had something to hide.'

Brophy's smile was ghastly: 'What should I have to hide?'

'I don't know. But when people never see the inside of your flat or the taste of your food they begin to think there's some-thing odd there, even before you invite an old friend from Tunis!'

All Armstrong's blows were masterly. They came straight from years of talking to inferiors at university boards and at inquests on bad examination results; they were based on the notion that illusions are poison, and no one, if he has anything in him, is killed by the truth.

The waiter brought chicken grilled with oil and garlic. Brophy was near to tears. He turned away as he was being served.

'Do you think there is anything strange about having an old friend from Tunis to look after me? I call him a friend although he is, of course, my servant. I won't be frightened off from standing by him for fear of what people say.'

'Well, Paul, you know your own business best, but people are talking. Somehow or other – God knows why – a man of your age – and not in the least effeminate in manner – you've given the impression you were emotionally involved only with men. Do you have relations with women?'

'I have many women friends.'

'I know you have. But do you bed them, man? That's the essence of it. Do you bed them like a red-blooded man?'

Brophy almost cracked up. He pressed the napkin to his brow and fought back his tears.

'Fred,' his voice quivered, 'tell me: is there anything you resent in me – you must hate me to ask these questions in this way. I feel I'm in the dock! I'm already accused. But what's the charge? I don't know. You can't have the slightest real respect for me or you couldn't ask these questions? I can't tell you about my private life. I refuse to, and I refuse to allow you to pry. If you think I'm a homosexual, you must say so, and say it in the presence of a third person, so that I can at least get legal redress.'

Armstrong knew he had gone as far as he could. He poured some wine into his own half-empty glass. Every item on the table seemed aghast at the things being said while the Mediterranean's blue and white expanses danced in the clear light beside them.

Armstrong had been impressed by Brophy's retort. He had half-expected him to crumple up – so far was Armstrong sure that the rumours had substance – but Brophy denied everything.

'Well, for everyone's sake, I'm glad to hear it. These rumours have got to be scotched. How do you suppose they began?'

'Could it be envy? But who could be envious of me? I don't have an enemy in the world. My only troubles are in the office. Do you mean Dot and Michel have been saying these things?'

Dr Armstrong's denial was not convincing.

'They must have.'

'I know they dislike me.' He spoke as much to the sea making contact with the rocks below. 'I never thought they'd go to such lengths.'

'Of course, they didn't say all these things in so many words. Clearly there's a failure of communication, and they ask themselves why it should be. They think your interests lie elsewhere.'

'Is there anything they *don't* impute to me?'

'They've said a good deal, and I mean to administer rebukes this week which will leave them scorching. There will be no need for you to say anything to them, I'll obviously go straight to Dot and Michel – together or apart. I don't care – and tell them that I've flung the book at you and you've come up smiling.' Armstrong extended his hand. 'So far as I'm concerned the matter is over. So eat up your chicken.'

A rush of gratitude, joy, thankfulness, overwhelmed Brophy. He had a surprising reserve of what is commonly called charity. 'I knew there was a cloud between us – I could feel it in your letters. I'm grateful to you for speaking to me. I'm not just talking. I'm really grateful. It means a lot to me that we can be so frank with one another.'

He lifted his glass: 'To our continued success.'

Dr Armstrong laughed sheepishly: 'Yes. Good thing.' He avoided Brophy's eyes.

Brophy suddenly ate ravenously, ramming huge pieces of bread dipped in the garlic sauce down his throat, so much energy had been burned up in the tension of the past few minutes.

They went on, over crêpes Suzette, to talk about office affairs, and Armstrong hinted that now 'the shadows' were behind them, he had plans for Brophy. 'I shall probably want you to run the London end for about four months from the middle of March. Do you think you could manage that?'

Brophy pulled up abruptly. 'Why? You aren't retiring are you?'

Armstrong snickered grittily: 'No. Despite what people say I'll still give the Institute some more years. No. The reason is that I'm helping to organise a Whitsun conference on problems in developing countries at Durham University and I want my head and hands free. I'd want you home about mid-March to get the hang of things and be my personal assistant in other ways. I'm not as young as I was. Sometime or other I'll have to draw in the reins.'

This was taken by Brophy as a clear hint of retirement; his smile was unforced. 'I'd hate to miss this chance to prove myself.' Armstrong noted the fulsomeness and gave a flash of his smile, but it was impossible to say what it conveyed. Then Brophy's suspicions arose: 'But who will keep the flag flying here? Michel?'

'Of course not.' Armstrong looked at Brophy as though he were mad. 'How can he? No. I'll have to get a confidential, discreet sort of person to stand in. Point of fact, I've approached two or three already. Now I've got your approval for the plan I'll go ahead. It's not easy to find a sound man on a temporary basis.'

Brophy had not, of course, approved any plan. He had not objected to Armstrong's accomplished facts – which was very different – and, besides, what man could question motives when his boss talked vaguely of future prospects as though they were of the most golden variety?

Armstrong knew he had treated Brophy shamefully, with barbaric ferocity, but he had seen the measure of the man in the way he came crawling back like a dog. A man, Armstrong thought, would have socked him on the jaw or, at least, threatened to. There was something lacking in the man. His inability to bed women was a symptom of something more dubious: he lacked dignity, self-respect, a clear sense of himself.

Brophy suggested – to let bygones be bygones – that he should organise an evening at his new flat. Mrs Parslow and Shamseddine would come. 'You'll see how well my servant can cook,' he added lushly. Armstrong made a note in his diary, and Brophy noticed that he was seeing Mrs Parslow that evening, Michel Shamseddine the next day and Neville in the evening and he suspected that Armstrong would be checking up. He would discuss the Tunisian with everyone.

Once the relief of getting back again into his boss's favour had established itself, Brophy felt anxious: how was he to carry off the evening at his flat – especially if Pierre was in a difficult mood? He was chained to his obligation and the only way to get out of it would be to have a fall and go to hospital; and for a moment he considered such a possibility, but realised he lacked the courage to carry it through.

After the crêpes Suzette, Armstrong ordered Turkish coffee and liqueurs, and then, about four o'clock, said he had a longing for Arab sweetmeats, so dragged the broken Brophy to a cake-shop, where he ate *baklava* and *kul ushkour* with glasses of iced water.

Brophy watched him mournfully and realised his time with MEDOC was running out.

7

Dr Armstrong told Doris Parslow, when they were at dinner later that day, what he had told Brophy. 'He's complaining that people don't respect him. I told him respect has to be gained. It doesn't go with the job.'

'You did?' Mrs Parslow's eyes glinted dangerously.

'And in view of all your letters, I asked him point-blank whether he and that Tunisian were up to something they shouldn't be. He said No. And he's invited us all there for a meal to show us how above-board it is.'

'I'm not going.'

'I think you'd better. So far as I'm concerned you've been no better than Paul in the matter of human relations. You've been subversive and a trouble-maker. Yes, Dot, I'm sorry to have to speak so frankly – but you're the worst kind of trouble-maker, and I'm getting tired of it. I can't have you going around saying things about my deputy here without cause. You just can't get away with it.'

'You'd rather *his* word than mine?'

'Well, I went straight to the point. I asked him what he was up to, and he said if people wanted to suggest dirty things about it, they should say so openly, so that he could go to law.'

'Then you'd better ask Michel for all he knows.'

'What does he know?'

'Ah, well, you ask him. He doesn't tell me everything.'

'I'm lunching with Michel tomorrow. I can ask him.'

The waiter came up with Mrs Parslow's slightly underdone steak and Dr Armstrong's shashlik, which was served in an opened round of Arab bread. They went on to talk of Mrs Parslow's poor health and lingered long over their liqueurs. As she anticipated, they went on to a night club, where the poverty of the floor show made it more essential to drink whisky, and by two a.m. Mrs Parslow was drunk, lachrymose and self-pitying. She cried a lot and said Armstrong no longer trusted her, and there was a barrier between them.

'It's all changed since that man Brophy came here. He's poisoned you against me.'

'Paul has been restraint itself.' It was a stilted thing to say, but Armstrong was also getting fuddled. 'Look, Dot, you've got to be serious. You can't go about saying we've got a queer in the organisation. It doesn't do. People don't like it. The Embassy don't like it. It exposes us to pressures.'

'Well, what about me? You think I like having a boss who despises me because I'm a woman and keeps all his smiles for his boy-friends?'

'Really! Really! If I thought you believed that I'd recall you to London at this moment.'

'Well, I do. I can't help it. It's my opinion.'

'You don't really. It's the drink talking. You don't really believe that. If I thought you did I'd recall you to London.'

'But I'm telling you I do. Why make me out to be a fool? I know what I'm looking at.'

'No. No. It's no good. You're feeling sorry for yourself.' Armstrong had just sufficient wit to stop repeating his phrase about sending Mrs Parslow back to London. After all, she did her job efficiently, and his main problem was to get Brophy home.

'I know what he is, Fred. You can't pull the wool over my eyes.'

In the morning, she forgot how stupidly she had behaved, but remembered Fred's attitude and briefed Shamseddine carefully before his lunchtime meeting with the great man.

8

SHAMSEDDINE was determined to be awkward. 'Why are we going to the Copacabana again? It's over-rated. The Palmyra Palace is far better. Rorgis is the only chef who counts.' Armstrong agreed and foresaw a hard time; Shamseddine was wearing dark glasses: a bad sign.

At his private lunches with his boss, Shamseddine always brought up the rising cost of living and usually remarked that it became more and more difficult for a man in his position to keep up appearances. Armstrong wondered whether this referred to the black-and-white shoes and prayed that *their* cost would rise astronomically. Once the cost-of-living issue had been fully ventilated and Shamseddine imagined Armstrong had taken the hint, the talk turned to office personalities. Armstrong liked to know what was going on, but disliked the way Shamseddine presented the report; Armstrong was always dismayed by Shamseddine's viciousness. No one could do anything worthy of praise, no one had ever achieved anything unless, somewhere, somehow, Shamseddine had been in the background. Dr Armstrong recognised his own empire-building in Brophy; in Shamseddine he recognised his own vanity; and he liked neither of his subordinates the better because of this. In fact, had he been honest, he would have said that these were precisely the qualities he most disliked, and he expected that one day, Brophy would edge him out of his job and Shamseddine would claim he had built up MEDOC.

Shamseddine broke the silence: 'It's a bad business, Fred!'

Dr Armstrong removed his pipe. 'What is?'

'This trouble with Paul Brophy. It's destroying me, and it will destroy the academic reputation of the Institute.'

'You really think so!'

'I do, Fred, I really do.'

Dr Armstrong stirred uneasily in his corner. 'We can talk about that later.'

'We most certainly will. I've been saving this up for weeks. Fred, I want to ask you a question: why have you put a queer in charge of us?'

Dr Armstrong looked up over the menu carefully. 'Have I? That's the first I've heard of it.'

'Don't play with me, Fred. You know Paul Brophy is a queer, and I want to know what I have done that you should put such a man to sit on my head?'

Dr Armstrong laid the menu down. 'In the first place, I don't accept that Paul Brophy is a queer. In the second, I don't think it has anything to do with the case. A man's private life is his own.'

'Are you mad? When he goes out of his way to show favouritism to the boys who'll let him pinch their arses.'

'Michel! I shall be very offended if you talk to me like this—'

'And how do I feel, Fred? I am a human being. I am a man. I am an Arab, and you insult me with this half-made thing as my boss – a person one does not know if it is woman or man!'

'All right! All right! But keep calm. Keep your voice down.' (This was not the way to rule by consensus; Dr Armstrong had lost his calm.) He assured Shamseddine that he knew of the difficulties at the Institute; he knew Brophy had never gained the confidence of his staff; he knew something would have to be done; but he saw no justification for Shamseddine's vile language.

'I'll meet you more than half-way by saying that he's been a big disappointment to me, and I've already more or less told him everything I have against him. What's more, unless he's a fool, he'll realise that his contract will not be renewed. But, until we can sort things out – after all, it's the first time such a situation has arisen – it would be far better to say fewer vicious things and keep calm.'

'You say it's the first time. Have you forgotten? We've never had a decent manager and never will. It's deliberate policy on your part to send us rubbish, so that we can never feel happy in our work.'

'Good God, man! What are you saying?'

'Fred, there are over fifty million British people, and of these millions you can only find the Brophies to send out to us. How many managers here have had some sort of cloud over their careers? Nobody really fitted the bill.'

'I agree; we've had unfortunate experiences.'

'Unfortunate for whom? For *them*; for *us*; but fortunate for *you*, Fred. It's kept you from ever having a skilled person ready to take over from you when you reach retiring age.'

'Go on!'

'And so long as there's doubt about your successor, you'll go on being the centre of the picture. I marvel you don't get an attack of conscience, sending out such people and making everyone unhappy.'

'If we were in England I'd sack you for that.'

'All balls, Fred. You're too compromised. You couldn't do a thing. I know too much about you and your precious Paul Brophy. You're a lot of muddlers and meddlers living off our backs. Enjoying your whiskies and water while your senior men have to think twice before they offer a colleague a twenty-five-piastre lemonade.'

Dr Armstrong began to bite a thumbnail. 'You'd like a bottle of something, Michel?' he asked brightly.

'Don't care what I have.' Shamseddine turned to the waiter and said, 'This bloody old fool is paying, so bring me a half bottle of whisky with water and ice.'

The waiter, taken aback, made no move.

'Go on, man! Bring me whisky. Fred, I'm telling him to bring me whisky.' Dr Armstrong, who knew everything about the Arabs but their language, nodded energetically. 'Yes, yes, yes. Bring half a bottle of whisky!'

Armstrong asked Shamseddine what was biting him, and Shamseddine said he was furious because he was being kept out of Brophy's job. 'That job is mine, by all the rules of the game, and you're keeping it from me.'

Dr Armstrong tried to be reasonable and soothing, but Shamseddine refused to be soothed: 'Fred, don't make me your enemy. You don't know what we Arabs can do when we hate. Listen. I'm reading Fathy Ghanem's novel, *The Man Who Lost his Shadow*. I've nearly finished it. A masterpiece. There's this man who rises to great power as a journalist in Cairo, who is open to attack because his father's second wife – a peasant servant girl – works in a brothel. Why should such a man allow his father's own wife to work as a prostitute? Why should such a man allow his half-brother to be reared in a brothel? You ask yourself, and only at the end do you find out why: this woman hates her stepson so much that she refuses his offer of a monthly cheque and prefers to work in a brothel in order to shame him. What a permanent disgrace for him! A hairshirt for him at the tables of the mighty! That's a profound, psychological truth about us Arabs. I admired her. I admired the way she hurt her stepson's career in the only way that would be permanent. I am a good hater – like her. I understood her.'

Armstrong found Shamseddine ludicrous when he played the professional Arab and asked sharply whether Shamseddine meant to go down to work in the Mina – the closed quarter – in order to disgrace MEDOC. Shamseddine pointed a gross finger at his boss. 'Don't mock me, Fred. I can take offence very easily.'

Armstrong still could not stop smiling; the idea was so absurd.

Shamseddine's gross finger prodded Armstrong in the chest. 'Fred, I'm disgusted with you. You don't know how a man of feeling behaves. You disgust me. Fred, you're not a serious person. You and that *manyuk* Paul Brophy are two of the reasons for the decadence of what was once Great Britain. You're shocked, Fred. You ought to be. You don't believe in anything. You don't mean anything to yourself. We believe in something. We Arabs are fighting for our rights, and you British come here with your muddle and arrogance and plot against us all day long. Fuck off and leave us alone!'

'You'd have a shock if the British took your advice and closed MEDOC.'

'Close it! Close it! I don't depend on your dirty money. In fact, I'd be glad if you did close it. I'm dishonoured by your money. It's tainted.'

'Michel, if I didn't know you better, and if I didn't know that you were drunk, I'd fire you on the spot.'

Shamseddine laughed without strain. 'Do you hear that? Oh, my God!' – he muttered something to himself in Arabic – 'How many more years will I have to live before I hear anything so good as that? Very well, Dr Frederick Armstrong, fire me. I beg you to fire me, and then I can get about ten thousand pounds in indemnity. Enough to open a little café in Mina, where I'll get my money more honestly directing customers to the fuck-shops than I do drawing your British money.'

Armstrong chewed the end of his pipe and looked at

Shamseddine in the beady way of a man watching a time-bomb. There were other uncomfortable truths which he could have trotted out, but Shamseddine had his own standards of elegance.

'Well, Michel, have you said enough or will I have to ring your wife and ask her to cool you off with an ice bucket?'

Shamseddine leaned across, his teeth bared, his mouthful of half-chewed chicken barely hidden: 'Don't laugh at me, Fred, or you'll make me your enemy. A man who can appoint that gentlewoman, Brophy, over my head, is no true friend of mine. Don't make me your enemy. What have I done that after fifteen years you still treat me as your inferior – an underling to the genius of Paul Brophy, the man who imports a Tunisian for the purposes of perversion.'

'I'd leave off that if I were you. It's untrue.'

'Who said so? You mean Paul Brophy's denied it.' Shamseddine closed his eyes in scorn.

Armstrong called for the waiter. 'Our bill, please!'

'You're going?' Shamseddine stopped wolfing in surprise.

'There's no point in sitting here with a Sawt-al-Arab I can't shut off.'

'I thought we were going to the Casino tonight. Don't be childish, Uncle Fred, you like the Casino and the pretty girls.'

'Sure, but I don't like Sawt-al-Arab!'

'Come on, Fred. You're cutting off your nose to spite your face.' Shamseddine winked. 'And maybe I'll be able to find you one of those pretty little seventeen-year-olds you like so much.'

Shamseddine's joke fell flat. 'I'll thank you to be quiet. You're stepping outside the known and permitted limits.' Dr Armstrong got up and then sat down again. 'Look, Michel. We've worked quite well together for about fifteen years. If there's anyone I can call brother in this city it's yourself. For years we've had no secrets from one another. O.K.? Isn't that so? I talk everything over with you. You are the man who counts. And don't forget it. I've made mistakes, but I hope we can do something about this one. Let me put you in the picture: Paul Brophy will have gone before next Easter.'

'Thank God.'

'He'll have gone. That's what you want, I take it.'

'That's *one* of the things I want. Sure.'

145

'God is giving you one thing, so be grateful. I won't ask what the other things are.'

'You aren't God, Fred. And so I can ask you a blunt question: when Paul Brophy goes, why don't you give me his job? I can do it better than anyone else in this city.'

'You know well enough that for policy reasons the manager has to be British.'

'Fuck that for a policy! What is there so special that only an Englishman can hold the job?'

'It's a British concern.'

'And Arabs do all the hard work.'

'That's the employers' prerogative.'

'If I were British I could have the job.'

'Yes. Like a shot.'

'Then give me British nationality, damn you!'

'How can I? I'm not the Home Secretary.'

'But you have influence. There must be someone who can work as your *wasta*.'

'That's not the way we run things at home. A *wasta* is a Middle Eastern institution.'

'You don't expect me to believe that, do you?'

'Believe what you like. It's the only reason why you can't become a British citizen without living in Britain for a certain number of years – and a person of your sense ought to know it.'

'Come on, Fred. Get me a British passport, and then I can have the post when Paul Brophy goes.'

'It's impossible.'

'Nothing's impossible.'

'Well, this is. In any case, aren't you humiliated by the thought of becoming British?'

'It's a means to an end.'

Armstrong saw a hint of embarrassment and pressed his point. 'But you, the great professional Arab, accepting British nationality for the sake of a job . . . what is the world coming to? What would you do with the chip on your shoulder?'

Shamseddine would have liked to upend the table in Armstrong's face but thought better of it. 'If it's one way of making the British give me my rights I'd even accept a passport from them. But, believe me, the first thing I'd do with it would be to make water on the Queen's face.'

'There aren't any photos of the Queen on the passport. What a damned silly thing to say.'

'Well, then, I'd shit on it.'

'Which gives me a good let-out for not pursuing the conversation any further.' Dr Armstrong rose, picked up his hat, briefcase and scarf. He looked down at Shamseddine and shook his head. 'You're your own worst enemy, you know. You don't realise the damage you do yourself.'

Shamseddine laughed like a reproved child, sheepishly, but with a tinge of defiance. 'Don't worry about me, Uncle Fred. I'll survive, if only to spite you.'

Armstrong opened his wallet and took out two tickets for the Casino. 'Here. You take your wife. I don't feel up to it.'

'I don't want them.'

'Don't be a fool. You know you like a show.'

'But not when you've paid for the tickets. I'll do the same with them as I'll do with my British passport.' He held up the tickets. 'You give them to me?'

'They're for you and your wife.'

'Good.' Shamseddine called the waiter. 'Here. Take these two tickets for the Casino. I can't go.'

The waiter was unable to speak for a moment; so was Armstrong.

'You can thank this gentleman,' – Shamseddine indicated Armstrong – 'who is the great friend of all the Arabs.'

Dr Armstrong's change had arrived, and he left without another word. The waiter ran after him, but Armstrong was too hurt, too insulted, to answer him.

9

'Bloody Aden pimp!' Dr Armstrong kept repeating to himself as he walked up and down in the wind waiting for a taxi to come. He drove back to his hotel, ordered a double whisky and went to bed. His legs hurt, and he had a nervous rash on his arms; altogether he was in a poor way. He fell asleep and woke up in time to see the sun going down across the bay and turning to old rose, purple and gold the snow crown on Mount Atthis.

Mrs Parslow rang. Would he like to go round for dinner?

'I'll have an early night. Thanks all the same.'

'You've seen Michel?'

'I have.' He cleared his throat. 'And I've taken more from him in an hour than I've taken from most people in a lifetime. Tell him so when you see him. I don't think we'll meet again this visit.'

This was meant to sound grand and crushing; as if Shamseddine, or anyone for that matter, cared whether they saw Armstrong again!

'Your lunch couldn't have been a great success?'

'That's about it. Thanks for ringing.'

'See you!' As she spoke, the line went dead on her, and she was left with Shamseddine, who had already given her a blow-by-blow report of the meeting. 'What did you do to our poor Freddie, Michel?' She sat down opposite him.

Shamseddine lifted his glass of whisky derisively. 'Any man who puts that bloody Paul Brophy to sit on my head deserves everything he gets.'

Mrs Parslow looked old-fashioned. 'Well, Master Fred won't like that. That won't suit his little book.' She was longing to know the Armstrong version of the lunch.

10

IN moments of stress, Dr Armstrong turned to poetry. Sometimes he thumbed through *The Oxford Book of English Verse*, which accompanied him most places, and sometimes he tried his own hand at writing. With Mount Atthis stained with sunset, and the wonderful evening luminosity on land, houses and waves, the Muse began to twang her strings, but not for long. He had to talk to someone, and he suddenly rang Neville to ask him to come round for dinner. Neville accepted, although he had been expected at his sister's.

Neville was going through one of his monkish periods. He was polishing his *magnum opus* and destroying old notes. Although he had just taken his own flat, some instinct told him that his time in Baida might be running out. Since moving into his own place, he had taken to spending his evenings alone, working or catching up with his reading. His only regular visitors were his sister and Katherine Thomson; and Iskander had come occasionally. Neville was fulfilling to its utmost the new experience; it was a period of complete realisation before boredom and dissatisfaction. The way he looked forward to his next trip for MEDOC showed he was already committed to some new idea. It was a form of fickleness, in a way: but it was more a fear of being too committed, too involved. The flat was a commitment, but it gave him the long, fruitful hours by himself during those days when he was completely satisfied in mind and body.

He had set up a table opposite the window, and here he enjoyed the rose-red skywracks which flowered briefly over the descending perspective of roofs between him and the sea. When it was too dark to read, he lit his lamp – the one with the cherry-red shade handed out by his sister – and enjoyed the sensation of his books and papers, and the five hundred or so volumes on the shelves at his side came into his life again – the five hundred books he had carefully chosen from his father's library.

His work-table had the neatness, the tidiness, of an Egyptologist's desk: everything was in careful piles, each one held down by some object which had taken his fancy.

The remainder of the room was taken up by a group of chairs grouped around a rust-red Afghan carpet and facing a television set. Sometimes he looked in as he ate his supper. The plays by local TV playwrights, with their infantile motivation and absence of any real relation with the life around, fascinated him: they were worse than the comparable product in England – and more fascinating for that reason.

He dressed and left his room with regret. As he walked down the stairs – it was an old building without a lift – he had the happiness of one who knows he has more ability than the task in hand demands. It was not far from his building to the Maximilian, and he walked through one of those mysteriously windy evenings when the shadows of trees danced on the streets. In the warm evening, the usual crowds were going into cinemas, the great local diversion. Walking past open-fronted vegetable stores, in front of café terraces, before hotel entrances, with their knots of pimps, shoeshine boys, before cheap cafés where meat and *kafta* broiled on charcoal burners in the street, Neville had a tremendous sense of his own power. He saw things very clearly, as though his coming down into the street after long hours of study enabled him to see the world with purified eyes. The shape of his life was as firm in his hands as a piece of stone; his mind was still formed and shapely, with work successfully achieved.

11

DR ARMSTRONG was refreshed – newly shaved, newly talcumed, newly shirted – his lustrous old man's curls gleamed over his collar, his beard glistened. As he chewed potato crisps he turned over the more successful of his replies to Shamseddine; he had more or less forgotten the dreadful things he had been told. As soon as Neville arrived he wanted to know whether he had heard anything on the office grapevine about his having had to read the Riot Act to Neville's seniors. 'I bet they've been complaining.'

'Oh, so that accounts for all the gloomy faces!'

Ah, Dr Armstrong was pleased at that. 'They look as though they've been told off, do they?'

'Paul and Mrs Parslow are pretty down in the mouth.'

That was what Dr Armstrong wanted to hear. 'Oh, believe me, they'd gone too far. I had to read the Riot Act. Don't think they're not a good team, but they've got to get on together. They've become really childish. Michel and Doris write me long letters of intrigue and complaint every week. It's got to stop. The fact is, Neville, I need the advice of a dispassionate observer.'

'About what?'

'The Institute, of course.'

'I'm not the person to tell you. I'm too new and spend too much time away.'

'It's a human problem, really.'

'You mean the clash of personalities?'

'It worries me sick.'

'I suppose so.'

'Where does the fault lie?'

Neville played for time: 'In the battle between Paul and the other two?'

'Yes.'

'I can't say. I don't know enough; but so far as I have any opinion it's this: Paul Brophy hasn't a chance.'

This was not what Armstrong had expected to hear. 'Tell me more.'

'He's fighting a losing battle with an office Mafia, which doesn't care what it throws at him.'

'You think that, do you?'

'I do. Unless some solution is found very shortly a good number of people will be hurt. Paul's a fool, but he's a good fool. He's too much a gentleman to deal with people like Mrs Parslow and Michel in the way they ought to be treated.'

Neville surprised himself by being such a Brophyite; it was as though Armstrong's questions had helped to mature his half-formed opinions.

'But, to be frank, you oughtn't to ask me about these things. I'm a temporary worker, and Paul Brophy was kind enough to get me the job. Those are two good reasons for my being the wrong person to appeal to. The solution is simple, I suppose: Paul must learn to understand human nature more, and his opponents must accept that he is here to stay as their boss.'

'How do you mean "Here to stay". He only has a short contract.'

'I assume it will be renewed.'

'Most unlikely.'

'Then it's unfair to tell me. That's between you and Paul.'

'As the boss, I think I can tell who I like. I was even going to go further. I was going to ask you how you'd feel about taking the job on temporarily, when Paul comes back to London for a few months to help me out.'

Neville held the offer in his hand, as it were, a moment, turned it over and handed it back. 'I don't think that would be right. I haven't the necessary experience, and I don't think Paul would like it. It's creeping up on him from the rear.'

Armstrong was furious. 'But it's all above-board, man. I've more or less told Paul that he's coming back to London this summer, and I gathered he had no objection to your standing in for him.'

Neville shook his head. Every alarm bell in his head warned him to steer clear.

12

December 15: 'And so you refused his offer?' Rhoda was drinking coffee in Neville's flat at eleven o'clock the next morning – a Saturday, a day when Neville did not go to work. 'I'm glad. It would have been dreadful to have taken over even temporarily from Paul. He came over yesterday, and he obviously knows nothing about the whole thing.'

'But imagine a man who can make such an offer! He went on hinting that the job, under certain circumstances, could become permanent, that I could move into Paul's flat . . .'

'With the boy?!'

'Presumably. I didn't ask.'

'Professor Armstrong must be the most tasteless man in the world – and a villain. My God, I should have been appalled if you'd accepted.'

'There was never any question.'

Neville lit a cigarette for them both and handed her one. 'I've been wondering whether I would have accepted had Paul not been involved. The salary's terrific, so are the perks; but the work is mechanical. What's the point of all that money if your life has no meaning.'

'You feel that?'

'Absolutely. Don't you?'

'Money's very important.'

'But not *all* that important.' The scholar was still dominant in Neville that day. Those were the times when a cell, a good view from the window, a strong light for work after nightfall, and an engrossing subject for study, would have been enough.

Rhoda considered a moment: 'I couldn't live dimly.' 'Dimly' was a family word, and summed up the lives of their relations in London, the relations they hardly ever wrote to and couldn't talk to when they met. He was not much given to *things* but understood her objections. He would have liked a car; he would have liked more books; but there were limits to the price he would have paid at that moment to get them.

'Anyway – go on with the evening . . .'

'Oh, yes . . .' Neville said he and Armstrong had dinner at the Maximilian – all on MEDOC, of course, including lobster – and then Armstrong suggested they go on a bar-crawl, one of his favourite occupations. As they were travelling in a taxi, Armstrong asked Neville, 'You formed any attachments here?' and Neville replied: 'It's like an emotional Clapham Junction.' (Rhoda guffawed.) It was definitely understood that Dr Armstrong would have liked an address – so Neville took him to the Red and Gold Bar to see 'the best shag in town'.

This was not exactly what he told his sister, but he repeated to her Armstrong's amazement when he saw Marjorie, whom he thought 'spectacular, really spectacular'.

He offered to buy her music from the juke-box, and she said her favourite number was 'Hello, Dolly!', so Armstrong bought this for her about three times, and then something else which Neville could not remember, and as the bar was empty but for themselves, Armstrong and the girl danced cheek to cheek. Afterwards, Marjorie danced with Neville and said, 'Your boss is a very lively chicken.'

'What did that mean?'

'What do you think?'

'She sounds such fun. I long to meet her.' Rhoda had an inspiration: why didn't the girl help Neville with his coming flat-warming party? Rhoda was hoping to have a 'supah' affair. Neville agreed without thinking, so caught up in his account of the night out and the way Dr Armstrong had tried to worm facts about Brophy's private life from him.

'Pretending to be worried and in the dark, and showing plainly that he'd been told everything by Parslow. He kept saying, "I know this part of the world attracts such people. I've got no prejudice, but I feel on safer ground with a man who beds women." It was farcical – turned the whole thing into a folk-custom, like wassailing and harvest home. Of course, I didn't say a word. That wasn't my duty, but clearly Paul's sunk.'

'Poor Paul: And he's got so many good qualities. I'm devoted.'

'It's not "poor Paul" at all. He asks for all he gets. If he were to turn on his tormentors they'd all shut up – from Parslow to the Tunisian.'

'Yes, poor thing, he was telling me how much he worries about the Tunisian. He feels responsible for him because he's no longer at home in his own world and not accepted by the western one. It seems complicated.'

'Because he wants it to be.' Neville thought Brophy was suffering from bad conscience because he was holding back on getting the right residence and work permits for the Tunisian. This, he thought, showed Brophy had outgrown the man and wanted to be rid of him. Rhoda had been told something of the kind by Brophy, who was unsure whether it was best for the Tunisian to stay. 'You know, Neville, he's very, very worried. The Tunisian is quite a menace – ungrateful, resentful, jealous and altogether out of control. He has told Paul he wants to go out the night Paul's giving the party for Dr Armstrong, and Paul's at a loss to know what to do.'

'I thought the idea was to show Armstrong how normal and bourgeois the whole set-up was.'

Neville made it sound an essay in the absurd, and they both laughed heartlessly.

Rhoda had good news: The Consort was going to London for urgent consultations and had been given permission to stay on for Christmas, which he would spend in a traditional way with His Dear Old Dad. 'The Duchess thought it was a sweet gesture. "When a person reaches your father's age, you must always think of his life in terms of months, not years. You'd never forgive yourself if you had the chance and didn't take it and your father were to die." The Consort was quite upset. "Christ, Duchess, he's not as old as all that!" But when he saw how The Duchess respected him for his gesture he curled up with pi-ness, and it was all more than I could bear. I've decided our marriage will last for ever if I only see The Consort for three months in six. Otherwise, his silly opinions will drive me dotty.' She got up. 'And now I've got to get back to some dreary people from the Ministry of Defence. I hope I don't fall asleep. These official dinners on which we make claims are nauseating. People think we're frightfully generous, and all the time it's another entry for the expenses list. So bogus.'

And so they parted for that day, and both knew that their life in Baida had begun to drag. Despite the ecstasy of their return, something had gone wrong. They knew life should hold more than the pleasures of exile, superabundant though they once might have been. It was the winter mood, when outdoor life has been severely curtailed, and the inner resources of the city are shown to be inadequate. The way the international community moved *en masse* from concerts organised by the German Institute to lectures at the British Council, and on to poetry readings at the Maison Française, showed up Baida as an exotic suburb of Europe, without any real cultural identity or substance. Arab cultural life was, so far as the resident foreigners were concerned, non-existent, and even to the local people themselves it seemed second-hand, imitative, as though all Arab creativity went into the kaleidoscopic political life.

13

THAT day, a magazine called *La Vie Mondaine* came out with an article on Paul Brophy and his work for Anglo-Arab understanding. Dr Armstrong, shown the article by Mrs Parslow, read it, pushed it aside and asked whether people paid to have such material published about them. The word spread through MEDOC that the old man was displeased, as displeased that is as Shamseddine. No one said a word to Brophy, but they laughed at him and, among themselves, spat at the article, the author and the subject.

That evening, Brophy's arriving guests all referred to the article – except the MEDOC people. Mrs Shamseddine held him at arm's length. 'I really must get this brilliant young person into perspective. When I read about this man, with his impressive presence, his great height, his good looks, his distinction and his devotion to Arab causes, I wondered whether I should be allowed to sit at the table with him.'

Brophy, already distracted by the problem of getting through the evening, hardly laughed, so that people formed the impression he had taken the luscious over-ripe phrases of the magazine seriously and resented being teased.

'We won't hold the article against him,' was Dr Armstrong's only contribution, as he walked up and down the Brophy apartment looking at the luxury on which MEDOC funds had been spent; the elegance and good taste were added irritants. Armstrong had a hard colonial core; he hated the effortlessness of the whole thing; he hated the abstract paintings, the *objets trouvés*; he resented the drinks, the plates of nuts and appetisers, as though Brophy had squandered a legacy which Armstrong hoped to inherit intact. He eventually sat down near The Duchess and Mrs Shamseddine and looked grumpy, almost vicious. He would not respond to Mrs Shamseddine's vivacity, but pretended to be picking out the titles of the books arranged behind him.

Shamseddine, gaping around for a glimpse of the so-far-absent-Tunisian, was reminded how differently MEDOC treated its Arab staff compared with the expatriates. His own flat was about half the size of Brophy's, and the furnishings were nowhere as luxurious. In fact, after about two whiskies – for Shamseddine was like a child, and alcohol went to his head at once – he began to tell The Duchess what a hard fate it was to be himself. Mrs Shamseddine had heard the record before and turned away to talk to someone else leaving The Duchess to catch her husband's tears. He told her he was cheated of his rights as man, an Arab and a human being, and how he was obliged to watch every penny. But the worst was to come: 'How would you like it, Mrs de Vries, if someone came up to you and said, "Fred Armstrong says he made you!"?'

'I should think it was perfectly horrid!' The Duchess replied, mildly surprised. 'Did he actually say that?' She sipped her drink and watched him sideways.

'I regret to say he did. I like Fred as though he were my brother, but he had no right to tell a friend of mine, "I made Michel Shamseddine." I was very hurt. I said: "The only

156

person who made me is myself. I have worked for this position, and if I had my rights I would be higher. What is more," I said, "if everyone had his rights I now ought to have a British passport, because I've worked for a British organisation more than ten years."'

'Does that apply?'

'Of course it does. If it applies to the embassy, it applies to us, too. This is a British concern.' He sighed mournfully. 'And now Paul Brophy has come I'll never get my rights, because he hates me.'

'Hates you?'

'He hates me worse than the devil. I know it, Mrs de Vries, and I've tried everything possible to win his friendship. I say to him, "We two could work marvels together if we trusted one another . . ." but he won't make any gesture towards me, and now I won't make any towards *him*. Don't you think I have my pride? That's how it is. Fred telling my best friend he made me, as though I had licked his boots for seven weeks to gain recognition, and there's Paul Brophy ignoring all the friendship and love I offer him. Yes, Mrs de Vries, I would be prepared to love him like a brother.'

'What a shame it is to turn down goodwill.' The Duchess believed him utterly. 'I think friendship and esteem are far too rare to be turned down.'

'Of course.'

He smoked mournfully, feeling ill-used and misunderstood. 'You know the reason for all this?'

She shook her head.

'It's partly jealousy because I'm so good at my job, and partly racial prejudice because I'm not English. They won't accept me. There are things they say among themselves that they won't say to me. They have to put up a front with me. I hear Mr Brophy, when he gets an English visitor, speaking freely about the British Government, speaking frankly among friends, criticising, openly discussing; but as soon as he starts talking to me he puts up his British front and defends everything and makes the whole thing insincere and false, because I'm an Arab and he's a Britisher. If I were English, he would say to me sometimes, "Don't you think the Foreign Minister is a bloody fool?" – you must excuse my language – or, "don't you think their policy is ten years out of date?" Mr Brophy has opinions of his own, and he expresses them with Mr de Vries, but he won't leave the official line with me, even when I can overhear his thoughts inside his head saying, "That's not what you believe at all." '

He stubbed the cigarette out in a bowl. 'I know what it must feel like to be an American Negro. Yes, Mrs de Vries, I'm not a Negro and never will be one, but I feel I know what it's like to be treated as a second-rate citizen. You know everything you do, no matter how good it is, is not considered anything because of your race. Can you imagine what it's like to be treated like this month after month, year after year? It never changes, and it never will so long as I'm in this skin, and so long as the Armstrongs and the Brophys are in theirs. In their heart of hearts, although they pretend to be friends of the Arabs, they don't believe in us. They never will. It's blood guilt. Nothing that we can do will ever make the case different, because we were judged before we were born. Yes, before we were born.'

'Michel, you're exaggerating and being perfectly self-pitying!'

'Just like the bloody Americans, Mrs de Vries, only the British pretend they haven't any colour bar. Well, they treat everyone the same. I'll say that. French, Arabs, Indians, Jamaicans, they're all the same. All foreigners. All inferior to the British.'

'But Dr Armstrong is a forward-looking liberal-minded person.'

'By British standards he is, but not by mine – because he believes in a double standard. There are pensions and bonuses for the British staff, but what is there for the local people? Nothing. Nothing at all. Our only protection is the employment law. And the Institute tries to worm its way out, and spends more on Maître Germanos than it would if it properly compensated the poor person they sack.'

'You make it all sound most unfair.'

'It is unfair, Mrs de Vries. Believe me, you don't know what it's like to be a second-class person. And in your own country. That's the worst thing. And how would you like it if you were in your own country and you met a foreigner one day – a cheap fellow, someone who has worked up from the ranks – and he refused to shake hands with you?'

'Oh, I don't suppose I'd like it at all.'

'That's what happened to me only the other day when an embassy man' – he was thinking of Macrae – 'came into the office and nodded at me, as though I were an object and he saying, "I'll give you three cents for that."'

'Well, it ill behoves me to criticise my own countrymen, Michel, but I must say I've been shocked by the poor quality I've seen here. Very, very poor quality. In the old days such people would have been kept firmly in their places at home.'

'Do you think so?'

'I don't think so, I *know*.'

Shamseddine nodded his head sombrely as The Duchess continued: 'Why, I ask myself what possible sort of homes these people can have come from. Really ignorant uncouth people seem to hold down the most tremendous jobs . . . money's no object . . . everything laid on from cars to servants, but in the old days we wouldn't have touched such people with barge-poles.'

Shamseddine heard an idiom he had never heard before. 'How did you say that? "Touch them with barge-poles"? That's very good. That fits the case perfectly. I sympathise with you. You are a lady, a well brought-up lady, you must feel the changes very much.'

'I don't know that I feel anything any more. But sometimes the awfulness of it gives me a jolt.'

14

NEVILLE, passing with a plate of savouries, lingered long enough to get the flavour of The Duchess's self-dramatisation. He whispered in Katherine's ear, 'If you want to hear the last of the *ancien régime* talking to the last of the Raj, go over there.'

Katherine looked discreetly towards the sofa, where The Duchess and Shamseddine were tête-à-tête.

'And the beauty of it all is to hear Shamseddine talking

about the good old days as though he had a vested interest in them.'

Neville passed to where Dr Armstrong and The Consort were arguing with a couple of guests, notably Albert Hijjazi, about the so-called affair between the Arabs and the English.

Hijjazi, immaculate in Italian suiting and shirt, thought the affair had never existed. The Consort, in his eternal *Prince de Galles*, with a white handkerchief flowing over his breast pocket like the bougainvillaea in his wife's garden, thought it had. Armstrong, discreetly popping olive-stones into an ash-tray, suspended judgement.

'Come,' said Hijjazi, picking up a salted peanut from the tray someone offered him. 'Did the English ever like the Arabs?'

The Consort brought up the usual rosary of names: Burton, Doughty, Bell, Thesiger, Ingrams – he might even have mentioned Lawrence of Arabia, in his enthusiasm – but Hijjazi was unimpressed.

'Apart from Ingrams, are these real people? Are they real, concrete human beings? I think not. They have invented themselves. And almost everything they write is based on a fundamental unreality and fantasy. The Arabia they are looking for is a thing of the mind.

'You ask the local people: "Do you want to go out into the desert to feel free?" What would they say? *"Ente majnoun?"* Are you mad? The desert is for *Bedw* and foolish Englishmen who think there's something to be found in the desert. It's nothing. The desert is privation, disease, cruelty, primitive morality, primitive taboos and the curse of Islam over all until early death. The romance about it is rubbish.'

This could well be, The Consort said, but people had fallen for this romance and had come to like the Arabs because of it. Dr Armstrong dismissed this out of hand. He doubted whether Doughty had liked the Arabs.

Hijjazi, holding his salted peanut aloft like a philosopher's stone, said Europeans found relief in the desert from their own problems. It came as a relief after the pressures of their own civilisation; but it cured nothing.

Albaciel, a television producer, said he had accompanied some English people to Leptis Magna. Their ecstatic reaction to the desert had amazed him – everything was superb. They felt free; they felt larger than life. The changing colours; the huge sky. Albaciel listed their enthusiasms in quotes. He felt nothing of all this himself.

'I tell you,' – Hijjazi dabbed the salted nut up and down – 'it's because they aren't free.' He held the nut aloft. 'I've been on an educational mission to Saudi Arabia, and, believe me, there's nothing there but boredom, meanness, primitive suspicions. Gehenna. Hell. What did the people do? Nothing. There was nothing to do. Nothing. The rich men sat around drinking fruit juices and repeating the same things they had heard night after night for twenty years, and there were paid poets to make songs of praise for the rich men – using all the conventional epithets. Dull, poor stuff. Mechanical inspiration. It was enough to drive a man mad. Then there was some hunting – but they wiped out all their gazelles and bustards by hunting them in cars. And when there was nothing to hunt, they decided to come here, and now there is a whole class which has got rich here by acting as pimps to the rich men from Saudi Arabia and the Gulf states. But, for the visitor to Saudi Arabia, there isn't even a woman to talk to. And no alcohol. Everything scorched up. Baking heat. Boredom. Flies. It's hell, I tell you.'

Fresh drinks came round.

Hijjazi looked doubtfully at the uneaten nut between his thumb and first finger and described how he had first picked up Doughty's *Arabia Deserta* in Khayat's bookshop in Kuwait. 'I took it back to my room and I tried to read it. I failed. I put it aside and lay wondering why a man like Doughty had voluntarily agreed to go to live with such people, and it was then that I realised it was self-deception. And this self-deception ran through everything concerning the British in the Middle East. They imagined they had some sacred duty, but it was all play-acting. Self-dramatisation. All their efforts were directed towards hiding the hard fact of a power relationship behind the façade of mutual self-esteem or altruism. As though anyone had asked these ridiculous people to wreck their health in the East!

'The fact remains you wouldn't bother with us – from the days of the Aleppo factory to the present oil corporations – except that we have something you want. In the nineteenth century it was control of the land route to India; in this it's oil; but if you found an oilfield in England tomorrow as rich as ours, your troops would fly home on the next plane. The Europeans are masters at clothing their material ends in high-sounding purposes. It deceives nobody but themselves. There's one book I read recently which talks about the immortal image of mystery which Arabia represented in the European or British mind. It's very hard for us to take this seriously, you know. We know and fear the desert, and the Islamic world, too much to be taken in by that sort of talk.'

Dr Armstrong pointed out that it was a case of distance lending enchantment to the view.

'Maybe,' Hijjazi replied, 'and the differences between us are enough for us to be exotic; but we don't find you exotic, or your works. Oil is not exotic; nor is Israel.' He almost put the nut in his mouth, but thought better.

The Consort had never suggested they were, but he believed there had been a fruitful interchange of ideas.

Hijjazi shook his head. 'What did the Arabs get from the English? Well, you listen to the old Egyptian ruling class or the Syrian merchants who did well in Egypt, and what did they talk about? They had some vague notions about English gentlemen and English education – but especially the *gén-tilmen*.' – He imitated the Baidani accent, with the stress on the first syllable – 'But it means nothing. They think it consists of standing about on the racecourse in smart tweeds looking distinguished and cold. All those vulgar Egyptian people missed the whole point of the *gén-tilmen*, which was to have such a sound opinion of their own worth and the rightness of their position in society that they never needed to do a mean, underhand or unscrupulous thing. The true English gentleman is a phenomenon which only a country that has never been invaded for a thousand years could produce.' He looked at the nut pensively – it was his stooge. 'It is something which was so extraordinary that when I was working at our embassy in London I could not accept it. Then I saw that it was true, that these people, with this *formation*, as the French say, really existed, but were a dying race. They were being wiped out by the commercial rat-race in their own country. I thought to myself: How would the *gén-tilmen* have survived four hundred years of Turkish occupation? We don't know. I'm glad for the sake of the English that they were never put to the test. We cannot be gentlemen because we cannot be detached. We have lived too near to disaster to be detached. Every Arab Christian is a fortress; we are all on the look-out; we are all dominated by the idea that we must get in first or we will be pushed aside. So the main thing which the upper classes got from you was a misconception, and the rest of you is rather hard to understand. We don't understand you. You're sentimental, and we are hard, like diamonds; you blur the issue about yourselves, you romanticise yourselves while we go to the other extreme. "We are very poor," we say. "We are poor people." Yes, we stand on our two feet and we say, "We are poor." Wait a minute . . . let me finish . . . You are whimsical and tender. We are never whimsical, never tender in the way you are. We are too fatalistic to waste time on things which fall by the way. We think that must be what God intended and that's it. Too bad for them, but that's life. Too bad for me, too, if I fell into the gutter. Yet my instinctive reaction would be, "That's God's will." '

'I doubt that,' said Armstrong. 'I'm speaking as a person who has Arab Christians, Moslems and two Turks on the staff. They don't accept everything.'

The irrepressible Hijjazi waved his salted nut about mockingly.

'These people know what Europeans are like. They probably send you their tears by post to get more money, more privileges. Good for them. But among themselves, rather among ourselves, we are hard, self-sufficient, disciplined. We don't understand your softness. The Egyptians *do*. They have your humour, your love of the fantastic, but I don't believe you admire them much.'

As he said this Hijjazi threw back his head and popped the nut, now warm and greasy, into his mouth.

Dr Armstrong clapped. 'I thought you were going to nurse that nut until dinner-time. I never saw one nut go such a long way.'

'It takes discipline to balance a nut in one's fingers for half an hour doesn't it?' Hijjazi smiled and acknowledged their applause. 'I could now do with another drink.'

He looked around, and, as they turned to call a hired servant, there was a hubbub from the direction of the kitchen.

15

THE hubbub had been building up all day. The Tunisian refused to do anything towards the party, and Brophy tried to do what he could until Rhoda arrived. She changed the menu – sent out for a huge amount of fruit and cheeses – so that they could concentrate on the main dish – a couscous.

The Tunisian came forward, extended his hand, asked whether she was the Madame Rhoda who had spoken to him on the telephone. Rhoda was startled by the man's cultivated appearance and beautifully modulated voice and said she was. *'Vous êtes beaucoup plus jeune et belle que je vous ai imaginé.'*

The Tunisian smiled at her with flattering wonder, as though she were a birthday present he had been allowed to look at before time. He turned to Brophy who stood nearby, looking apprehensive: a long, sheepish misfit.

'Pourquoi vous m'avez caché de madame?' He looked at Rhoda, and smilingly said: *'Il me semble qu'il a honte de moi. Il me cache dans cet appartement. Il m'a présenté à personne.'*

'That's ridiculous,' Brophy said to Rhoda. 'Of course it's not true. Why should I be ashamed of him?'

Both Rhoda and Brophy were flushed, uncomfortable. The Tunisian was without any reticence or reserve. He looked at Brophy.

'Comme tu es hypocrite. On dit "hypocrite comme un anglais".'

'Why?' asked Brophy.

'Parce que tu n'avais aucune intention de me presenter à tes amis ce soir. Tu m'as demandé de rester dans la cuisine pour surveiller la bouffetance! Je suis le pauvre esclave.'

Rhoda tried not to encourage the man, but he decided to help her, and as she worked by his side – they were about the same height – he kept referring to the fact that Brophy had kept them apart. *'Vous êtes si gentille, madame. Pourquoi Paul ne veut pas que nous nous recontrions. Vous parlez un si agréable français – beaucoup mieux que Paul – ça aurait été un plaisir pour moi de parler un peu avec vous.'*

What was Rhoda to say? She was obliged to retort, *'Vous me flattez. Je parle comme une cloche.'*

Rhoda held her breath as she kept her balance between – there was no doubt of this in her mind – two quarrelling friends. No servant would have spoken as the Tunisian spoke; no master, who was not in some way compromised, could have tolerated such a conversation, such an address. All the same, the Tunisian charmed Rhoda by his appearance, his amiability and his witty French. He spoke of Brophy as one speaks of a great, overgrown child who has to be corrected frequently. He seemed to discount him as a human being, and, allowing for differences of vocabulary and language, used the same tone of exasperated contempt as her brother.

A few minutes before serving the couscous they clinked glasses together, and the Tunisian invited her to his home town, which, in the nature of home towns, had more charms and attractions per square inch than any other place on the Mediterranean.

The couscous was to be served in a special earthenware dish with a conical lid; and everything was ready when, in being transferred from the serving table to a large tray, the dish – and food for fifteen people – slopped over the floor. Neither the Tunisian nor Rhoda knew how it happened, but Rhoda said afterwards the accident had been fated from the beginning of the day – it was an expression of the tension and ill-will in the air. For a moment, Rhoda thought of scraping the dish up again, but just as she and the Tunisian were staring at the broken dish and the spoiled meal, someone shrieked at the door and the whole party knew.

The Tunisian, seeing Brophy's face, said, 'You think I did this on purpose, don't you?' and cried, 'Answer me!' Brophy answered: 'You are happy. *Ente mansour.* You've won.' Rhoda tried to take the blame, but the Tunisian, looking distraught, dashed away into his room and locked his door. The cries, the slams, the turning of the key, were heard by everyone and gave rise to ill-informed chat of a scuffle. Brophy's enemies said the Tunisian had knocked the dish off the table. He had made Brophy cry. He had gone mad.

Brophy had not cried. He had been too stunned to do more than murmur to himself. He had no idea what to do. Seen from the kitchen, it was a dilemma: fifteen people waiting to be fed and their food on the floor. Rhoda said mournfully: 'And it was one of the best I ever tasted.'

Hijjazi came into the kitchen and won Rhoda's goodwill by saying: 'Let me take you all to the restaurant downstairs.' She marvelled at the delicacy and good taste of the man – whom she had always under-estimated and ignored. Brophy refused: 'I'll take you. It's the only way.'

Rhoda suggested they go to a nearby supermarket for steaks, but Hijjazi repeated his offer. Brophy – laid on his back, figuratively speaking, by the cost and his loss of face, and the thought of Dr Armstrong waiting for his food – shook his head like a metronome. He asked Neville to telephone the Italian restaurant downstairs and to tell the guests there would be a change of plan. He went away into his bathroom while Rhoda and Mrs Shamseddine cleaned up the mess.

Mrs Shamseddine screeched out, 'Michel, the best couscous I ever saw!'

There was so much of it: so many vegetables, so many pieces of meat, so much juice – but Mrs Shamseddine had something to compensate: 'I'm crazy about Italian food – especially those veal and cheese dishes.'

People collected their belongings and filed out to the lifts and descended in groups into the Italian restaurant. Paul Brophy was at the bottom, trying to smile, trying to turn the mess into a joke, but unable to do so because his upper lip let him down. All the lines of his mournful face ran to his chin.

Dr Armstrong, not quite sure of the sequence of events, patted Brophy's arm as he passed. Now that the man had kicked away the chair from under his own feet he could afford to be magnanimous.

The restaurant received them with open arms. The red-and-white linen tablecloths gleamed, and the Muzak played 'Come Back to Sorrento'. Brophy tried to concentrate on the menu but was thinking of the Tunisian upstairs and knowing that every mouthful of the meal had to be endured like a punishment. His face had the lines of disdain and ambiguity which the defeated assume in their moments of anguish: everything that had happened was a joke, of no importance, a little mishap; but it was also everything. His private world had come to pieces at the first contact with the public one, and instead of being upstairs comforting the person who most needed his comfort, the one who stood most in need of his protection, Brophy was at the head of a table seating a group of people he had assembled out of bravado. He was in two halves; each one suffered. After about ten minutes the party grew gay on Chianti and forgot their host. Rhoda knew what he suffered. It was both clear and understandable to her.

16

THE party broke up about one o'clock. Everyone was satisfied and happy. Dr Armstrong, who was leaving to join his wife the next day, pressed Brophy's arm. 'Sorry I shan't be able to meet Pierre on this occasion. Most enjoyable evening. Never knew Hijjazi in better form.'

Hijjazi had impressed Rhoda more than usual, too. She thanked him again for his kind gesture when the couscous fell.

'I knew how you must have felt. I guessed it was a tense evening,' he said.

'Yes,' Rhoda said to Neville over The Consort's head, as they returned home, 'that was the gesture of a real gentleman. I must get him round again.'

For Dr Armstrong, the evening did not end until some hours later, for his senior men, bundling their wives home, went back to the Maximilian and sat, drinking whisky and reviling Brophy, until Armstrong fell asleep. They left, just after three, with promises to see him off at the airport the next day. Armstrong tried to dissuade them, but failed, and the three men turned up the next morning. Armstrong felt dreadful – over-tired, over-exposed to wicked people – and was grudging in his conversation. They pretended to share his interest in the morning papers until Shamseddine took an envelope out of his pocket containing a formal petition, signed by the three men, begging Armstrong to remove Brophy on the grounds that his conduct, his character and his inability to give real leadership, were all damaging office morale. The cheek of it – the inopportune timing – enraged Dr Armstrong. His eyes were all rage, all humiliation as he pocketed the letter, only half read. 'I shall think about it.' He stroked his beard rapidly;

167

he hummed tunelessly. 'You seem to think you are the only people who suffer.'

He put on dark glasses and looked around. His employees, all in freshly pressed suits, faultlessly fresh and correct, sat on the edges of the leather chairs, expectant and assured. These were the people Armstrong had himself hired, but they might have been his warders: their hour of mastery had come. If they looked at the floor and chatted in undertones among themselves, they did so out of clemency. After all, Dr Armstrong was old enough to be their father, and they noted that after a heavy night he seemed to have difficulty in holding his pipe between his teeth.

The plane was announced, and Dr Armstrong gratefully picked up his briefcase, which one of the men offered to carry. The old man laughed sheepishly. 'Well, be good.' He took Shamseddine's hand: 'No more treble whiskies. I'll be writing to you.'

Shamseddine handed over a small package, and his boss looked down, perplexed. 'A farewell gift?'

Shamseddine laughed: 'You could call it that.' A moment's pause. 'Go on, Fred, open it. It can't kill *you.*'

Dr Armstrong had an idea the parcel contained something in dubious taste; but, challenged, he was obliged to set down his briefcase and opened the package, which contained a thin dagger, incrusted with blue, red and gilt decorations. 'I'll use it as a paper-knife,' he said blandly. 'Thank you all.'

Shamseddine looked at the other two. 'Shall we tell him what it's for? Use it for a paper-knife if you like, Uncle Fred, but use it on Brophy's back first. Get rid of him.'

Dr Armstrong received the blow like a stoic. 'You've made your point clear, I think,' and slipped the dagger into the open pocket of his briefcase alongside his newspapers. He betrayed his dismay by forgetting to shake hands with the other two, and they were obliged to follow him with outstretched hands. Their eyes, at the last moment, could not meet his, and there was a demureness in their farewell which made the situation even more bizarre.

RHODA was at the airport bidding The Consort farewell. With the insincerity of departure she was clinging tightly to his arm and walking at his side with big, self-important strides. Under a Medusa-like hairstyle, her eyes were appeased and clear, like agates: everything was going very well. Not only had she sent off The Consort to London in a pleasant state of satiation, but she was being allowed her liberty over the holiday period. The agate eyes were brilliant with wishes come true. If only, she thought, one could get rid of The Duchess as easily.

They saw Dr Armstrong half-escorted, half-pursued, towards the plane by his henchmen, and The Consort sniggered: 'There goes Paul Brophy's last hopes of success.'

'How put out he looks.' They dismissed the whole charade. The plane was announced, and Rhoda handed over The Consort's Christmas present. He had forgotten hers, so she parted on a note of moral superiority. 'Don't worry, darling. It's nothing.' The Consort's splendid moustaches drooped; he felt mean.

To celebrate her liberation, Rhoda went to the university bookshop to pick up the books she had ordered as Christmas presents: for Katherine Thomson, a catalogue of furniture styles; for The Duchess, Kathleen Kenyon's *Archaeology of the Holy Land*; Runciman's *History of the Crusades* for Neville. She added the Skira *Dufy* for herself and spent a long time turning over the pages and enjoying the colours like sweetmeats; she felt she could never have enough colour and gaiety. She took a bus to the meat market where, in preparation for Christmas, there were huge displays of poultry and wild birds, shot in the Helissonic Plain, geese from Holland, hams from Prague and Germany, venison from Austria: the choice was overwhelming. She wandered up and down the street for some time wondering what would make the most amusing display for the party. Then she went to the Swiss cakeshop for a fruit tart and wandered around in a daze of pleasure.

Christmas in Baida: the same profoundly blue sky, the same golden, equable heat, the same sensation of well-being coming out of the walls and the windows of houses.

THAT afternoon, Neville brought Hello Dolly! for tea. The girl was not taken in by the invitation or by the engagement to serve drinks at the party. She was flattered, in a way, to be taken up by the brother and sister ('Naturally, any girl would be') but she knew the score: she was a novelty, a gimmick for a party – something out of the ordinary. She accepted this for the pleasure of seeing how the other half lived and to see new faces. She had imagined Rhoda would have been more beautiful and found her rather dumpy, sallow-skinned and foreign-looking.

Rhoda sat on a couch with her legs drawn up under her, and as she had surprisingly thick and stalwart legs for a little woman – rather like a Japanese – she was not at her best. Her clothes were cut very tight. But the effects were of the best – the black patent shoes with a buckle, the art rings.

'What a gorgeous place you've got!' The girl looked around with pleasure. Rhoda pointed out the painted ceiling of the old house and explained the basic rule of Turkish domestic building – the big centre room to allow for a through current of air – and the details of the Moorish-style windows, where the setting sun lit up the details of the coloured glass. The setting sun also made the decorations on the Christmas tree glitter and wink.

The girl said she was disappointed by the Christmas atmosphere. 'There's nothing to get excited about, is there? You know, the decorations fall sort of flat here. We decorated the bar last night and it felt all wrong – not a bit like Christmas, really.'

Rhoda supposed it was the climate. The girl agreed. 'And I sent me flippin' cards off last summer! You know, to get home in time.'

Rhoda had to say that, on the whole, she was happy the local people had not fallen entirely for the westernised, commercial Christmas. She herself preferred the Orthodox festivities in January: 'So much less crowded than the December twenty-fifth celebrations and so much more elegant at the Russian Church.'

Marjorie had no idea different sects celebrated Christmas at different times and was impressed by Rhoda's knowledge. And when do the Moslems have theirs? was the next question. It was the sort of remark Rhoda wished to frame, 'it was so sweet'; but Neville replied gravely that although the Moslems accepted Jesus as a prophet, they did not especially venerate his birthday.

At this point, the girl lost interest: 'It's all a lot of hooey. Well, I think so. I never could see the point of it all myself. At Easter sermons the vicar used to talk of God sending his only son to save the world, and it didn't make sense to me. I believe God made the world, you know, but I don't see any point in letting his son die for it. If he made it he could save it by hisself.'

Rhoda thought it sounded interesting to say she was positively anti-Christian and disliked the assumption of some Arab Christians that one was automatically on their side against the Muslims. In many respects, she thought, Islam was superior to Christianity. 'In a curious way I find the objections of Islam to Christianity far harder to overcome than vice versa. Islam is very down-to-earth, where Christianity is all airy-fairy and disembodiedness. I owe my comparative knowledge to Paul Brophy who has taught me a lot – he's shown me how to appreciate Islamic architecture. He feels very guilty about the way the west has corrupted the old Islamic world.'

The tea came in – the Swiss pastries, the apple tart and a selection of *karabish* with cream, Neville's favourites. The girl said she had to watch her figure, especially as she had fallen for Arab cakes. At first she had not liked the taste of the fat they were made with. Rhoda explained that the basis of all Arabic cookery is *samneh*, a specially reduced butter, which gives all Arab cookery its special flavour.

The girl had once eaten *croissants* made with mutton fat, which left a film on the palate. Rhoda explained that Arabs used the special grease, called *liyyeh*, from the tails of the local sheep.

The girl's face contorted with disgust: '*Oaw*! Those disgusting carcasses hanging outside the shops, with their big bloated tail and their whatnots and innards removed!'

She vowed she would never eat anything made with mutton fat again. Rhoda was not perturbed: 'I don't know, you can get used to everything, I suppose. It's just a question of taste. I mean, think of those tasteless jellies and jams we eat at home, which hardly have a pinhead of fruit in them and get all their flavour from chemicals. Whatever you say about Arab food it's pungent and genuine, which is more than you can say for the average British meal.'

'Oh, I dare say.'

'It's just a question of habit.'

'You're telling me. The things I can now take in my stride. You wouldn't think it was possible to learn so much in six months.'

'Such as what?'

'Well, everything. I mean, take the place where I work. When I started there the boss was very particular about how I behaved. Everything had to be just so. He said the police were very particular, and they could run me out of the country like a shot if I started anything fishy. He said, "You be good girl and you O.K." But what do you think I've just found out? The girl who works with me isn't a girl at all: she's a boy.' She screamed with amusement.

Rhoda thought this reaction a bit odd. 'Doesn't it make you feel spooky?'

'Doesn't worry me. It explains why the boss was giving her all the attention. He was getting it fried on both sides, just like the Americans like their eggs.'

At that point the visit really warmed up, and from then on Neville hardly knew which he found the more amusing – his sister trying to understand the red-haired girl's allusions or the red-haired girl living it up for Rhoda's sake.

Rhoda remembered that the girl could read hands: 'I was always sceptical until you told Neville he would get a job, almost at the same time as he received the offer. That's fabulous.'

'It doesn't always work, you know. Sometimes, you can misinterpret things; and then people's destinies change. It's written for them but something stronger intervenes. I never know how to explain these things.'

'I'd love you to read mine,' Rhoda held out her hand. The girl looked doubtful. 'I can't get results with everyone. I can't seem to see yours clearly, at all. I'd rather not try.' There was a moment of embarrassment, and she let the hand go free.

'Oh, I'm so disappointed. Do try again.'

The girl tried again as though making a last effort. Why, she asked herself, should the hand be full of tears? No. She refused, and Rhoda sighed with a pleasure missed.

As the time ran out, Rhoda explained what she was planning for the party. 'You'll be in charge of the drinks, and the servants will be in charge of the food.'

Before the girl went away, Rhoda went into her room and brought out a small sketch in ink and wash of old Turkish houses in Aleppo, with exquisite detail of windows and *mashrabiyahs*. While the girl was in the cloakroom, Rhoda told Neville she approved of his choice. 'She's a Habitat girl. I can see her a few years from now, a bit plumper and wearing a PVC apron, chopping up beef and onions on a bare pine table. She's got real style. Whatever is she wasting herself here for?'

'I've told her she's mad.'

Neville was to drive her home, and followed her down the graceful stairs to the street. He drove her home, pinned up her new drawing, went to bed with her and then, after driving her to work, went to a cinema to recover.

19

THE fine weather continued; only the hood of snow on Mount Atthis reminded people on the coast that it was winter and the turn of the year. The day before the party, Katherine Thomson drove The Duchess and Rhoda over the mountains to a village where a friend had a small farm. They sat in the farm kitchen as the late afternoon changed into early twilight and watched the valley become twice as large as life under the departing sunlight. The sky from ridge to ridge was a golden saffron colour, a magnitude of light. The poplars lining the avenue to the farm had become long filigree effects in the clear air, in that golden antique light.

On every point of the plain, clearly visible from the vineyard behind the farmhouse, the sunlight was making its vivid statements on white walls, irrigation canals, windows, metal roofs of garages and tractor sheds; but for the cold it might have been a long summer evening in western Europe.

All the way back to Baida they caught the last statements of the sunset over the sea, before the night came down like a cat.

The Duchess said she would be pleased to have Christmas done with: it would mean that half her stay was over.

'Don't you like it here?' Both Katherine and Rhoda were startled by the tone.

'I think it's an acquired taste. I'd hate to spend all my life talking to other women about the servant problem.' This was a backhander at the hostess they had just left.

'You've never heard me talk about servants,' Rhoda said.

'Or me,' said Katherine.

'Not you. You're not typical. But imagine your friend's life in that isolated farm with only that silly little round.'

'Surely it's no worse than Herefordshire!'

Katherine drew in her breath at Rhoda's audacity. The Duchess seemed not to have heard and went on: 'This is such an unjust country. Too much wealth in too few hands and so much grinding poverty underneath. It's unjust the way we Europeans come here and live off the fat of the land and never bother for a moment about the natives.'

Katherine Thomson was shocked. 'But we daren't interfere. We'd be put out on our necks like a shot if we interfered. We're here for business, and we're told plainly that this is the only thing that matters.'

'Well, I don't like business people's mentality! I'm a disciple of G. K. Chesterton.'

Rhoda whistled. 'You're a true blue Conservative, Duchess. Just like my father.'

'There are many things I don't agree with the Conservatives about.'

'Well, don't blame us for everything.'

'But I do. I think the Europeans ought to do more. We oughtn't to come here, turn this city into an international racket, take everything and give nothing.'

Katherine was furious: 'But they batten on us. As soon as they see us coming, prices go up by a quarter to a half. We're their milch cows.'

174

The Duchess's face brimmed over with spite and resentment: 'I mean, the way people come here and live like lords when you know they're nobodies at all.'

'That's another matter.'

'And the money people spend on pleasures. We went to that sale of work for a children's home in the mountains – under some princess's patronage – and people complained that the goods were dear, and yet they'd think nothing of spending ten times that amount on a dinner-party. People spend far too much on pleasure. It's immoral when there's so much suffering in the world and all those awful shanty-towns on the road to the airport.'

'We all go through that phase,' Katherine retorted, 'but I came to the conclusion that the best way to help this country is to spend freely and create employment. You can give until you're blue in the face and nothing improves. So long as you have nine crooks in the government, who probably buy their way into Parliament in the first place, you won't get very much social justice for the people in the shanty-towns. If you ask the rich why they don't start huge housing projects – the same as we saw in Hong Kong – they just laugh. They say the Armenians were glad to get here to escape the Turks; and the Palestinians were glad enough to get here to escape the Jews; and the Spanish were glad to escape Franco; and all have made more than their fair share since they've come here. There the matter ends. Believe me, I've asked all the questions and got all the answers. You can't budge the middle classes – and the Christians are the worst. They simply don't have a social conscience, as we know the meaning of the term. Family ties, yes; tribal ties, perhaps; but social ties? never heard of them.'

'Then it's for the Europeans to set the standard.'

'In that case, start the new Puritanism by not coming to Neville's party tomorrow.'

'I don't intend to go, in any case. I don't think Neville's parties are intended for people like me.'

Katherine Thomson was deeply shocked. 'You can't say that, Mrs de Vries. It would be dreadful if you didn't go.'

'The Duchess can make up her own mind. I'm sure Neville wouldn't want anyone to attend his party as a penance.'

The Duchess controlled herself and retrieved the situation.

'Oh, I express myself badly, as usual. I don't mean anything against Neville's party. I only feel it's an awful pity that we Europeans have one standard and the others have another.'

'Nobody will be a piastre better off if you sit at home in sackcloth and ashes.'

'What a sobersides you are, Rhoda! How seriously you take me.' The Duchess trying to chaff her way back into favour was an unpleasant sight; and the younger women were ashamed for her. 'I'm far from a sobersides. But if you dislike vulgar displays of wealth, or frivolity, your duty is to stay away. You can't have the best of both worlds.' This was exactly what The Duchess did want; she wanted to hit at her stepchildren for the way they spent their money; but, because she was fascinated by them, she wanted to be in on their social life – especially since Neville's glamorous girl-friend was to be there as presiding spirit.

'But, Duchess, what do you expect? Katherine gets you this invitation to tea at that lovely farm and you make fun of it all. Some people are never satisfied.'

'You've entirely misunderstood. Mrs Caylan is delightful.'

Rhoda said, 'Uh-huh,' and kept quiet for the rest of the journey.

Certainly, The Duchess was growing more difficult to please. She was receiving all that her stepchildren offered her and went away to slander them to the Ghanem sisters in return. Every stupid piece of MEDOC tittle-tattle came to The Duchess via Mrs Shamseddine. Rhoda would catch the sisters looking at her speculatively, trying to square her with the things they heard from The Duchess. Only Rhoda's contempt for the opinions of other people prevented her tackling The Duchess about this.

20

WHEN Rhoda and Neville drew up the list for the flat-warming party, their only constant was fear of holding what Rhoda called a 'Burns Night Rout', the sort of get-together where people do and say predictable things. What emerged was a cross-section of the dispossessed, of those wanderers in no-man's-land who were the type of person most sympathetic to the brother and sister: Europeans happy in exile and Arabs unsettled by European life and contact. In their desire to amaze – for both Neville and Rhoda played to packed imaginary houses every day – they invited too many people, and the arrangements were threatened through lack of space. So Rhoda took the thing in hand, took down her own tableware and furniture, and decorated the one large room with a fresco of stylised Christmas trees created from green ribbon and Sellotape. She placed the bar at the far end, using Neville's partly cleared bookshelves for the bottles. On the eve of the party Rhoda lost faith in the affair. She knew it had a fatal flaw: it lacked simplicity. She thought of transferring the whole thing to her place but this would have killed its purpose.

Seven o'clock on the evening of the party: Rhoda opened the doors on to the terrace and hoped the right spirit would come in from the warm evening outside, and took it to be a bad omen that the first guest to arrive was The Duchess. They gave her the most comfortable armchair and a big tumbler of whisky and she sat back and refused to be propitiated. Then Hello Dolly! arrived and they knew she was a mistake. So did the guests. Somehow or other, even those who never drank in dubious bars knew who she was, and the position was reached where everyone whispered about her but nobody talked to her; and a psychic moat around the bar grew harder to cross, until drink removed reservations. It was novel, like having a geisha at a party, and no one was sure whether it was the done thing. At first, Rhoda was put out by her guests' embarrassment, and then pleased. She knew the arrangement would irritate those she would most have wished to be irritated. Who had thought of such a thing before? Like Madame Vigée-Lebrun's Greek 'orgy', which cost fifteen francs, Rhoda would get new cachet from a red-haired *Kellnerin*. At least, Rhoda thought so.

What made the party one of the most talked about in the no-man's-land was a scene between Charles Ghassem, a writer home for Christmas from Paris, and a Syrian woman painter Rhoda cultivated. Ghassem arrived unexpectedly with Albert Hijjazi – friends from their Jesuit College days – and was soon the centre of a group who wanted to know his version of a local literary controversy. Ghassem had an irritating way of dismissing anything concerning Baida as small beer; he liked to give the impression that after Paris everything else seemed potty – which did not please his listeners. He then went on to talk about the Palestine Liberation Organisation in Cairo and claimed to know scandalous and unworthy secrets about some of its personnel – about bribes, numbered accounts in Switzerland and disloyalty.

It was the sort of conversation common at such gatherings, but, coming after Ghassem's lordly disdain for all things not French, it vexed people, especially the Syrian artist, Corinne al Sharqawi. Why, she asked, did people laugh at such a state of affairs when they knew the hopes pinned on the P.L.O. by the Palestine refugees living in the shanty-towns and filthy camps she had seen on her last visit to Lebanon? Ghassem agreed. What surprised him was to find such plotters and turn-coats in the P.L.O. praised as patriots.

His tone infuriated the woman. 'I suppose all this will give you and your cynical French friends plenty of matter for amusement. But you've lost touch with us here. There are certain things which are no longer laughing matters. We hate people who become strangers to their own kind and return to sniff and sneer and demoralise us more than we are already.' Ghassem denied that his friends were cynical. Why did she say so? 'If the truth were known, my dear, they feel sorry for us. They pity us because we are angels whose wings are tied down with chains to the trees.'

'And you can accept this pity from foreigners! Ya, Charles, you should be ashamed of yourself. Paris does not suit you, my dear.' She made a self-important gesture with her shoulders, which covered a good deal of nervous intensity. She was a refugee in every sense – from Damascene politics, Damascene conventions, from lack of sympathy and understanding, lack of any milieu – and terrified of being misunderstood (as a woman, a Damascene and a member of an old Syrian family). There was a narrow strip of territory in which she could operate and patronise Charles Ghassem in the way she would have addressed her younger brothers. Because of the intensities and hatreds under the surface in any such gathering, Ghassem felt himself threatened and despite his achievement and reputation saw

The Enemy in the young woman. He denounced her self-deceiving shrillness and went into a childish defence of Paris and its free life, as though the rest of the company had to be won over. 'And here – here, people are bored. They yawn their heads off with boredom. The newspapers are filled with lies and scandals, which shock nobody because the truth is worse than the filth printed. It's only when a man such as myself gets outside this milieu that he can breathe.'

The argument moved into the political events of the day: 'Look at this morning's paper. The headlines are the same as they were twenty years ago. One has big red letters: "Plots hatched by imperialism, reaction and Zionism!" another says: "Collusion between Jordan's traitor king and Zionist gangs."'

Miss Sharqawi was not put down: 'The tragedy, my dear Charles, is that the *facts* are the same as they were twenty years ago.' She insisted that there was a plot, financed by the United States and Britain and carried out by the Jews, against the Arab world. And who plots against the monarchies and Tunisia? Ghassem asked.

'Nobody wants the truth, and those who speak it get their curls shaved off like poor old Girgez al-Asali over the *samneh* scandal in the Syrian Army.'

Miss Sharqawi said she knew nothing of this.

'You ought to. Your family was up to its eyes in it.'

'That's untrue!'

'As you've never heard of the affair, how can you say?'

Rhoda arrived and asked Miss Sharqawi to come to meet her stepmother. She pretended there was no tension and led the angry and insulted young woman to the old lady as to a special treat. The Duchess wanted to visit Miss Sharqawi's studio. An arrangement was made and then: 'Rhoda, my dear, forgive me. I shall have to go. My family has been insulted.'

Rhoda and Neville begged her to stay, but it was out of the question. Would she stay if Ghassem apologised? Never. She never wanted to hear his name again. Everyone was lost as to what to do, largely because such treatment of a woman was unheard of. She went away, and a furious argument developed around Ghassem, who was reminded by Hijjazi that he was no longer in Paris where it was permissible to speak sharply in argument with women. Ghassem was thoroughly put out. He knew he had made an error, so generalised his attack. 'We take too much from the Syrians. They come here and take the bread from our mouths and feel free to lecture us. She said she knew nothing of the *samneh* scandal. She's living here on the proceeds; the family stinks of rancid *samneh.*'

'God, how these people tear themselves and one another to pieces!' George Ringsett shook his head at Paul Brophy, who blinked. Ringsett was devoted to Arab nationalism in principle – he was said to be the local University's only Marxist – but found it politically naïve in practice. The guests suspected he was a C.I.A. agent in political disguise; and his tendency to stare at people fishily, as if half-expecting to be found out, did him no good. 'Their politics are all mixed up with Islam; and they don't mix.'

Brophy wanted to know why. Ringsett thought Islam an empty room, full of inconsistencies and, for a religion, poverty-stricken in invention. 'You ought to meet my students to get an idea of their ignorance. One of them told me – I swear – that Christianity was invented by Americans.'

This led into a discussion of the merits of Christianity and Islam, and Brophy gave his lecture on the defects of Christianity. Muslims found Christ's teachings too sublime to be put into practice. At the same time, Christianity was too materialistic. There was the dichotomy between too much blue sky and mysticism on one side and too much concern with the fruits of the earth on the other. 'God had been brought into contact with man and lost his infinity. The churches are filled with blasphemous objects and bric-à-brac and the communion service is the greatest blasphemy of all. The wafer turned into the body of Christ and then eaten. Was it cannibalism or theophagy? The Muslims think it as bad as eating pork.'

Ringsett was ill-placed to defend any religion and dismissed both as serious subjects for discussion. 'I can't judge. I know I like the emptiness and silence of the average mosque with its carpets, and people sitting in groups, and the pigeons flying in, and the grandfather clocks.'

Brophy could not be deflected and, waving his glass over their heads, went on to attack the formulas of demand and supplication in Christian prayers. 'They're like shopping lists. The Muslims think them blasphemous because they ignore the simple fact that all depends on the will of God and all is known to Him.'

Ringsett's Turkish wife was amazed to hear an Englishman hold such opinions: 'Islam is a man's religion. It has been *terribell* for us women. We are denied our full rights as *humin bein's*.' As usual, when stopped dead in his tracks by an irrelevance, Brophy blinked. 'That's changing.' He spoke as one who had just given out fresh orders.

Mrs Ringsett was sceptical. 'In Turkey, perhaps . . .'

Rhoda came along. 'Valia, come to meet my stepmother.' So Mrs Ringsett was pushed towards The Duchess, who invited her to sit on the arm of her chair. George Ringsett joined them and, having complained that he'd had his pants lectured off him on Islam, went on to bore The Duchess with a learned exposition in the shallows of Arabic grammar, about European use of bastard plurals. The Duchess knew how to deal with such monologues. 'Languages are full of impurities, my dear sir. *Souks* may be an abominable hybrid, but it suits the general public very well.' She turned to the wife: 'And tell me more about your adorable children.'

Neville heard The Duchess at her most Johnsonian as he crossed the room to the bar to draw some corks. Hello Dolly! was curious about the beautiful girl who had just left. Neville grimaced. 'That was the touch of sulphur without which any party lacks atmosphere.' The girl was curious. She clearly wondered whether she and Neville were lovers. Neville drew the corks and went away without explanations. He bumped into Richard Thomson, who had just opened the door to a Mr Nabulsi, who was asking for Neville. The name at first meant nothing, and Neville's heart did not sink until he saw Iskander standing at the door. He had not been invited, but accepted that Neville should have a roomful of people drinking, chewing nuts and talking; and as half of them were standing, like Jews at the Passover, he felt it was a very European occasion. None of the guests seemed to take his arrival amiss; he was smartly dressed and might have been a businessman – the sort of contact Neville would have made through MEDOC. Neville at once led him to his sister, who spoke to him in Arabic and gave him a brilliant display of 1932 charm.

'What did you say Mr Nabulsi did?' Neville had no idea. Iskander smiled sublimely and said he worked with his brother. The brother, it seemed, had an import and export business. The conversation went on merrily, and Iskander had mixed in with the guests when Hijjazi came in off the terrace for another drink and had to stop in order to believe his eyes.

He touched Neville on the shoulder. 'Is he a friend of yours?' Neville trod carefully. 'One of those odd acquaintances one meets.' Hijjazi raised his eyebrows. 'There isn't another place in this town where I could meet that man as an equal, except in the kitchens of the Egyptian Embassy, where the Egyptians feed their scraps to their hatchet-men. The charm of European parties is that everybody is treated as equally amusing.'

Hijjazi took it amiss that such a person was present, but Neville pretended he was being facetious. 'I wouldn't trust him further than I can see him, would you? But he is amusing.'

'Do you know who he is? He's one of the strong-arm men of the attempted coup in 1960 – unscrupulous, cruel, a black-mailer, a pimp, involved in everything from narcotics to violence. Had he not got the backing of the Egyptian ambassador he would be dead, with the blood of half a dozen men on his hands.'

'You aren't joking?'

'Joking? With that black Muslim in the room? A man who used to torture his prisoners himself and strangled one with his bare hands, up in the gardens beyond the Alcazar. Be very careful, ya Neville, I know you find danger interesting . . . be sure your friend doesn't harm those who are close to you. Your sister and her husband are especially vulnerable. Listen to me, my friend, please don't accuse me of interfering. Pick your friends where you want to – you have the freedom of your thoughts and your body, and no one can take this away from you – I am concerned to prevent your mistaking the small change of experience for the pounds. I know friendship with dangerous animals is attractive. You feel you live more fully so that safe, day-to-day people seem hardly worth knowing, and so you do, until the moment comes, and it must come, when you find yourself at the mercy of the animal. *C'est un abruti.*'

Neville understood Hijjazi in the same way that Hijjazi understood him. He nodded and nodded again. What else could he do? Hijjazi went away, glancing back sorrowfully at the group around Iskander and then at Neville, and shrugged. More people arrived, and Neville moved towards the door again, and it was another ten minutes before he could move across to Iskander again, or, rather, Iskander looked for him. Reared on stories of the immorality and availability of European and American women, Iskander believed Neville would, in the normal course of events, have pleasured every woman in the room. He wanted to know which one he could reasonably make himself. 'Only her,' Neville said, pointing to the *Kellnerin*. Iskander preferred Katherine Thomson and a French girl. Neville shook his head. Iskander then asked Neville to get Hello Dolly! for him. 'Never. I am not your pimp.' And then, 'Ask her yourself.'

Iskander put on his professional Arab act; he was afraid of European women and spoke hardly any English. Neville gave him an obscene gesture for answer and walked off. Hijjazi – watching carefully – thought: 'Neville is the keg of gunpowder which cannot keep away from the fire.'

Later Neville suggested Iskander should go to bed with The Duchess. 'You want me to sleep with your grandmother? By the name of God, she will kill me. I would be ill for days.' Neville was pleased by his joke and repeated it to Hello Dolly! 'He's just the man for you, too.'

'You kidding! He's undressed me three times already.'

'He wants to sleep with you. Will you stay on afterwards?'

'Realleh! Darling boy! You're not quaite naice to know. You wanting a cut?'

The extent of her anger was clear from the way she stubbed out her cigarette.

'I was joking.'

'You certainly have a funny sense of humour.'

Neville and the girl were both crestfallen: he because he had insulted her, and she because he had felt free to do so. Despite herself, she had imagined Neville respected her and that he would know the rules of the game, as she alone saw them. He tried to butter her up, but she pushed him away! 'You make me feel icky.'

Rhoda, meantime, had taken Iskander to meet Richard and Katherine Thomson. 'I've just been told Mr Nabulsi comes from your favourite village, Ain-al-Nabi.' She turned to Iskander: 'My friends wanted a house in your village. They like it so much.'

Iskander beamed with welcome: 'My uncle has a house which he wants to rent. He lived in Hong Kong and wants English tenants before any other nation.' Rhoda faithfully translated, and the Thomsons agreed to think about it. Iskander pushed the matter. Why did they not visit him and look at the house? Katherine agreed: 'I'm destined to have a place there.'

Rhoda translated: 'My friend thinks God has led her to your village.'

Iskander's emotion at Katherine's acceptance made him glow even more. *'Insha-allah!'* Katherine, who had been finding the evening heavy going, now found the event justified. 'Your friend must come to see us,' she said to Rhoda. Iskander had understood. 'Thank you. Thank you. I will arrange with Mr Neville.'

'Madame!' Umm Mansour stood at the door of the kitchen. 'We are ready!' It was a call to eat the delicious things prepared in Rhoda's kitchen and carefully reheated and served by the old cook. Umm Mansour's chocolate cake was as good as ever, and the company toasted Neville's happy life with the champagne which accompanied it. Then Neville and Katherine did a Charleston, Charles Ghassem and the French girl did an Apache dance; everyone clapped and shouted, and the whole thing was over.

Neville, Hello Dolly! and Iskander were left alone and sat drinking whisky and improving Iskander's English. Like most local people he had a smattering of half a dozen languages, and Hello Dolly! was impressed. 'You-would-soon-speak-English-very-well-you-know.'

'I try. I always willing I try. I want I try.'

Hello Dolly! found this richly amusing, and Iskander looked puzzled. *'Shu al ghalat?'* he asked Neville. He had made no mistake; his childish air of precocity had appealed to the girl. 'Don't forget, ya Iskander,' Neville said in Arabic, 'that she is simple.' Iskander looked at her meatily. 'She is a woman. Get her to lie with me.'

'Ask her yourself.' Neville left the room to give Iskander an opportunity to press his case – the idea of these two sensualists savaging one another promised a rich spectacle – but Iskander went on talking demurely. Neville called out: 'What a fool you are, ya Iskander. Take her into my room.'

When Neville returned, he sat down abruptly. He felt sick; he had been feeling queasy all the evening.

'I saw you tucking into that chocolate cake, you glutton.'

Hello Dolly! had found Neville's half-moon glasses and had put them on. 'Neville de Vries, I order you to write out fifty lines in your best flippin' handwriting: "I will not gorge myself with rich chocolate cake after eating thirty shashliks!" ' Quick. Show a leg there, my man.'

'She is wittier than I imagined,' Iskander said. Neville merely replied, 'Don't break those glasses. You can't get that kind here.' Hello Dolly! put them back in their case and suggested they go for a drive in Iskander's much-vaunted American car. Iskander was always ready for a new adventure, and they set off, all three sitting in the front, the girl in the middle. Where to go? The girl wanted to go to the Spanish Club, so they drove south along the coast. Beyond Hyga, under the floodlit battlements of the old Turkish fortress, Neville felt sick. He suggested they stop. 'You've been drinking too much,' was the girl's unhelpful comment as Neville vomited on the pebble ridge below the road. 'Get it all out,' was Iskander's advice. 'Hurry, Mr Neville. Get it up!' He took the girl's hand and kissed it on both sides. 'I love you very much. You understand?'

'Are you all right, Neville?' she called out, falling into Iskander's arms for their first kiss. More sounds of retching came from below. She pushed Iskander away. 'He's very ill,' she said wildly. 'Oh yes, he will die!' His voice was mocking. '*Ya charmoutah al inglesiyah!*' he called mockingly from the car. 'Ya Neville, *ente marid?*' He laughed and began pinching and kneading the girl's thighs.

Neville eventually got into the back of the car and knew that his puppets had escaped him. He sat forlornly, all shrunken and pinched, against the door. He was willing to go to the club but Iskander refused to continue. They returned to Neville's flat, and Neville went into his bedroom for a tablet and came back to lie down on the divan in his living-room. With his eyes closed, his lips pinched, his face drawn, Neville looked like his own death-mask. Iskander kept touching his watch and indicating that he and the girl should go. Hello Dolly! was torn between duty to Neville and pleasure with his friend. She put her hand on Neville's forehead and looked professional.

Neville saw his sickness as a visitation; but he was not quite sure what the message was. Another effort to retch sent him into the bathroom.

Iskander was vexed. 'What is it? It is nothing. Like baby.

Come. Come with me. I want I fuck you very much. Why you wait? Mr Neville will be better.'

'We can't leave him.'

'What?' He frowned with impatience.

Neville came back and took up his Byron-cum-Chatterton pose on the divan. Then it was Iskander's turn to go into the bathroom and he returned smoothing down his hair with his hands.

'You've got marvellous hair, you conceited thing.'

'You like my hair?' Iskander accepted the girl's compliment as a right. 'Better than his.' He touched Neville's head in passing. 'Five years . . . poor Mr Neville. No hair. Finish. Too much boys and girls.'

'Boys? What are you saying?' She forgot Neville was ill. 'Is that true, Neville?'

Iskander nodded. 'Believe me. I fuck him. Many, many times.'

Neville's eyes were closed; he disguised his horror. 'He's likely to want to, I dare say.'

Hello Dolly! was thrilled. 'I wouldn't put anything past you men. Especially him.' – She nodded towards Neville – 'Never met a Britisher like him. He's not nice to know.'

Iskander had not understood. He merely tapped his watch.

Iskander shook Neville's shoulder. In Arabic, he said he wanted to have pleasure with the girl. Without opening his eyes, Neville told Iskander to take the girl into his room. Iskander went back to the girl. 'O.K. In that bed.' He pointed to the bedroom.

'Never! Neville, if you're all right now, we'll leave you.'

'O.K. Thanks for everything.'

He did not open his eyes so that neither of them should see the extent of his humiliation. After they had gone he undressed, washed his face and hands; and then went to bed.

In the morning, the girl returned and made Neville tea and toast. He was much better but still felt unwell. His eyes ached, his stomach hurt, his mouth tasted of old glue. Worse than the body's discomfort was the sensation of having reached a nadir of bad taste. She plumped pillows behind him and he sat up like a distinguished invalid, the poet who has burned his manuscripts and is waiting for the laudanum to take effect. He sipped the tea gratefully.

'You know, my lad, you ought to choose your friends more carefully.'

'Why?'

'Well, I think your friend's got hisself involved in something.'

'What do you mean?'

'He carries a gun.'

'Does he?'

'Doesn't that surprise you?'

'Not here.'

'It gave me the creeps. As we set off for the club he took the gun out of his pocket and slipped it under a duster in the glovebox – you know, just behind the steering-wheel.'

'Oh, I understand.'

'I bet he's capable of anything.'

'Will you see him again?'

'He's not the kind. He's a strange person, isn't he? If he was your pal he didn't ought to have said what he did, did he?'

'What did he say?'

'About you and him.'

'Oh, that's typical Arab humour. Did you take him at his word?'

'He was only joking?'

'What do you think?'

'Well, it shook me. I didn't know.'

'It shook me, too.'

'Not that it matters, really.'

'It *does* matter.' Neville meant: bad faith was disagreeable; probity was important. She misunderstood him and stroked his hand.

'In the end, you're just like other people, aren't you? You don't mind how much you hurt other folks, but you hate to be hurt yourself.' She was offering a sort of sympathy, and Neville, suspecting he was understood, drew away from her like a reptile that does not know what feeling is. He was afraid of her knowledge of him – the direct intuition of simple people – and thought of a way to propitiate her. Would she like to meet him that afternoon in the goldsmiths' market so that he could offer her a present for all she'd done? She laughed: 'You trying to keep up with your mate? He promised me a gold watch. Swiss, of course. And eighteen-carat.'

'We're thanking you for different things.'

She gave the laugh which so upset him. 'Thanks, darling. I like Platonic friendship. It suits me.'

All the same, she was pleased, and they made a date. When she left him, he took a bath and went back to bed, nursing his sickness like a warning. His sickness was a protest at the shock of being found out as an animal among animals; and one who was open to blackmail and compromise. So long as he had these people around him, his freedom was threatened. It was this which hurt Neville the most: the idea that people had power over him; and it made him ask himself what he was trying to do with his life. He grew pensive, almost soulful, and it took a telephone call from his sister to restore the balance. She was thrilled because 'it's all over town' about Ghassem's extraordinary outburst against Corinne al Sharqawi. People were saying what an exciting party it must have been, with so many fireworks. Neville laughed, but thought the evening had been dull. 'We've shot our bolt.' Rhoda agreed.

She had thought Neville looked bored, put off his stroke. Neville also agreed the evening had been a waste of time . . . 'and, do you know, I was as sick afterwards as I've ever been. I felt it was the judgement.'

An astonished silence. 'Judgement on what?'

'On us.'

'What for?'

'Insincerity. Double-dealing. A waste of our lives.'

'Who are we cheating?'

'Ourselves. Who else?' Another astonished silence.

'You're joking, aren't you?'

'Of course. But there's an element of truth.'

21

KATHERINE THOMSON pressed hard for the visit to Ain-al-Nabi, and, when it was arranged in the New Year, Neville could not refuse to go with them. Rhoda and The Duchess made up the little excursion party, which set out in the early afternoon on a clear day of the sub-tropical winter season. Up at Ain-al-Nabi, on its escarpment facing east, the villagers were swathed in wool and heavy coats; fires had been lit, breath rose visibly from the donkeys and their drivers. All the balconies of the village looked towards the mountains, whose colours in the clear, mountain air were blazing and only slightly off-zenith. Because there was no heat haze, no shimmer on the horizon, the hills looked shapelier, stiller, and every rise and fall of the limestone outcrops had a bare, winter look. Those sharply defined mountains, with their dividing chasms, had the African-brown leonine surface of typical hermits' country. Those rocks, that blue sky, that lack of compromise, formed the background to the village which lived from its miraculous spring. This had come into being when a holy man, in flight from his persecutors, was dying of thirst and was saved by water which suddenly came out of the soil at his feet. The spring never dried, never slackened, and its waters fed a network of irrigation channels. At the mouth of the spring, the figtrees are covered with the strips of cloth which countrywomen have tied there that their firstborn be males. Thanks to the abundant water, the village orchards were the best in the district, with terraces of tobacco, maize, tomatoes and aubergines in season. Higher up the slopes, away from the road and gendarmerie, the villagers grew hashish for export – the village's main source of income. From this, as well as from remittances from émigrés in Brazil, France and Kuwait, came the village's spruce appearance – the well-kept houses, the prosperous and jocose old gentlemen by the tric-trac board outside the inn on the main square.

Iskander's house, built on a rocky eminence, was approached by a winding flight of concrete steps. The English visitors were shown into the large, central room and seated on cretonne-covered sofas. Everything was ready for guests except the host and hostess, who had been called away, the little maid explained, offering coffee and oranges, by the death of a cousin. This pause gave the visitors a chance to take in the room – the Persian carpets, the hideous family portraits, the even more hideous ornaments, the Blaupunkt television and the low tables holding plastic flowers and souvenirs from Italy and Gibraltar.

Madame Nabulsi's voice was heard in the garden, and then

Iskander burst in, full of apologies, sweating slightly from the speed with which he had returned from his cousin's house. Then his wife was introduced, and everyone looked with pleasure at a striking woman of about thirty, tall for an Arab woman and with what The Duchess would have called 'an air'. She spoke no English, but careful convent French. She told them that although she was not a Christian she had been educated *'chez les bonnes sœurs'.*

She sat down and supervised the serving of coffee and little cakes. Then the girl came in and said the baby had woken up, and Madame Nabulsi went away, and this gave The Duchess a chance to hand out a compliment. 'Mr Nabulsi, you're a lucky man to have such a lovely wife.'

Iskander smiled and looked bashful. 'You have beautiful women in England, too.'

'But those eyes. That exquisite femininity.'

Madame Nabulsi returned holding the baby, a child of less than a year but with all the father's pugnacity and ruthlessness as he stared about him at the visitors. 'A born boxer,' was Richard Thomson's comment.

The father took the child, swung him to the ceiling, put smacking kisses on chubby cheeks: a wholehearted response to the baby in no way diminished by the presence of visitors. Madame Nabulsi was happiness itself. *'Mon mari adore ses enfants. Il est très bon père.'* When the elder children arrived from school, the father showed the same spontaneous affection, and the four-year-old child Nadia, named after her mother, sat on her father's knee, drank out of his cup and stared at the guests with eyes as complete and all-knowing as an adult's.

Then there was a further explosion of goodwill and pleasure as Madame Nabulsi, Iskander's mother, came. She, too, had come from the house of bereavement and wore a black silk veil over her head, which gave her the appearance of an old-fashioned district nurse. She was the youngest, most attractive grandmother they had seen: white-skinned, clear-eyed, hardly any grey hairs, and, at the same time, polished and *grande dame.* She enjoyed the way the visitors gaped at her; she appreciated their admiration; it was her climate. She took a coffee with them, then put on her veil and led them through back lanes to the uncle's house, the villagers crying welcome at every turn.

The uncle's house was less spacious than Iskander's but provided a big surprise: having lived in Hong Kong, the family had furnished the place in lacquer and wicker furniture, as well as with Chinese carpets and vases. The uncle spoke softly, in good English, and said he would rather let his house to English people than any others.

His wife produced more coffee and served orange conserve on Chinese plates, while Richard Thomson weighed up the old man in preparation for any bargaining. Afterwards, they were taken to the vacant house which stood a little way along the escarpment, and situated in such a way that it had a clear view of the descending roofs and the confessional division of the village: church at one end, mosque at the other. The views made the house; Katherine Thomson said it was what she wanted, so they went back to the uncle's house to talk business. The old man gave an idea of the sum he had in mind and Richard Thomson said he would consider it. The others walked about the garden – Neville bored, disgruntled, Rhoda a little envious of the Thomsons' luck, The Duchess astonished that the Thomsons wanted to take on more responsibilities.

They eventually went back to Iskander's house, where Madame had prepared a 'five o'clock': lemon tea and biscuits. By this time, bereavement or not, other relations had come down to stare, to be stared at and to enjoy the five objects 'Made in England'. Rhoda and Katherine were admired by the women of the family, and no one could believe Katherine had a boy just turned fourteen. Iskander's mother, as one regal being praising another, thought English people must be very beautiful: there was Katherine blonde like a German, and Rhoda dark like an Italian. And children? Did Rhoda have any children, too?

'Ma fi.'

There was a certain defiance in Rhoda's admission in such a room, with babies being kissed and petted on every side, and a wholehearted, human warmth going out every hour of the day to the young; and the reply caused consternation. Someone suggested the saint's spring as a cure for ... it was not said, but barrenness was in the air.

'Never mind! Children will come. One. Two. Three. Maybe four!'

Madame Nabulsi, senior, with her usual tact saved an awkward situation.

They were still being fêted at sunset and heard the local muezzin calling the faithful to evening prayer. For a short time, the tops of the mountains glowed pink and golden and then turned purple, and the village was profiled against the saffron west. The first stars. The first lights in the distant convents and monasteries, the hilltop villages, the last light on the clouds in the east and a mysterious flight of birds wheeling about in the empty sky. The Thomsons' first nightfall in Ain-al-Nabi.

When they came to leave there seemed to be about forty people assembled in the village street, some carrying hurricane and Tilley lamps, which hissed and created dramatic chiaroscuro effects. All the way home they discussed the fascinating glimpse they had had of local life. 'What gorgeous people you know, Neville.'

Neville said nothing; this was a performance he had not enjoyed – he knew the record by heart. Richard Thomson had the last word.

'What gets me is the distant echo of something akin to barbarity under the everyday surface; they look at us out of the seventeenth century.'

'You can bet they felt superior to us in every possible way,' was Neville's comment.

The Duchess disagreed. 'The women are longing to escape into something like our freedom.'

They thought a while. Neville was delighted when Richard Thomson made the reply for him. 'We put our hopes and fears into their hearts. I thought I never saw a happier household of women. It was in every line of their faces.'

A pause. 'What was?' Katherine Thomson asked.

'Fulfilment as women,' was the surprising reply.

'I think you see what you want to see,' said Rhoda.

Part Four

1

DR ARMSTRONG found his fall-guy, in the end – in the court-yard of the British Museum. He had just left the Reading Room and almost bumped into Byrd, accompanied by two of his teenage children. 'Reggie Byrd, of all people!' The two men had first met in Teheran in 1942; it was natural they should greet one another like long-lost friends and stand chatting under the portico. As soon as Armstrong had recovered from the physical encounter he recalled that Byrd had recently resigned as diplomatic correspondent of a crumbling news-paper, *The Age*. He wanted to know what had happened. Byrd gave a bright smile. 'My face didn't fit any more.' He filled in the details of the case – nothing especially uncommon in it – and hinted that a legal suit was pending. 'Journalism is the dirtiest trade in the world. I'll see that my kids don't make my mistake.'

Byrd, used to people's indifference, was touched by Arm-strong's interest. Did he have anything else in mind? Byrd gave a vague reply; clearly he had nothing definite in view. 'Then let's meet for lunch tomorrow. I may have something to interest you.' Byrd agreed willingly. Armstrong could not loiter – he had an engagement – and so Byrd followed his child-ren into the museum.

The next day, he was waiting in Armstrong's club – a slight, sub-military figure with a regimental tie, immaculately brushed shoes, well-tapered trousers, well-brushed grey-white hair. Over whiskies Byrd talked freely of his chagrins and difficulties. 'I know I'm my own worst enemy. I know I've never known how to suck up to the right people, and, quite frankly, with the way things are going, there's nothing that would make me feel more cheap. The new lot at *The Age* are absolutely the end of the road so far as I'm concerned. They hinted that I was too conventional and old-school-tie, whatever that means. Well, that's that. I can't change. They gave me some compensation – and my lawyer is fighting to get more – but with children at an expensive stage it's not funny, old boy. Freelancing's no fun, either, especially since half the people I knew have lost out in office politics, and I can't get in tune with the new ones. They're all so provincial, nowadays. Get away with bad manners, appalling taste, worse judgement. *Bref*, as the French say, I'm pretty cornered, and it would be worse if I hadn't sold a couple of my whodunits to an American TV company. They pay well, thank God.'

He drank his whisky gratefully and looked at Armstrong, who was trying to assess just what made a failed man-about-the-world like Byrd tick. He had never registered as a personality for Dr Armstrong – something always eluded him. 'Writing for TV is a flimsy sort of career, isn't it?'

'But what else? I don't mind telling you, Fred, that I've reached the age when I ought to be able to relax, but I can't. Just got too much water on the wheel. I don't mind telling you that some days I'm really shagged out. I've played my cards badly and I can see no way out of my difficulties.'

Somewhere, at the back of Dr Armstrong's mind, stirred an earlier impression of Reggie Byrd as an essentially mindless person, and, nodding in that indeterminate state between boredom and sympathy, Armstrong saw that this was the ideal person for MEDOC. Byrd went on discussing his financial difficulties in the slaphappy would-be upper-middle-class way which makes a virtue of refusing to live honestly and within one's means.

'Oh, you bet we've always lived right up to my income. We never put anything away, and last year I only cleared a four-figure overdraft by recourse to the oldest standby in the world: I got an old aunt to give me an advance on a legacy!' Byrd laughed madly, sure Dr Armstrong would appreciate the uproarious novelty of it all, and the great man gave a ghostly acknowledgement, almost as fatuous as Byrd's laughter.

'I know we make fools of ourselves, sending our children to schools we can't afford, living in a way that's too expensive – upper-middle-class tastes on a middle-class income.' He smiled vaguely. 'There it is.'

Any other person talking like this would have bored Dr

Armstrong to the grave, but he had decided Byrd was the only person possible and at a suitable pause in the Byrd confessions he put in his offer. 'Don't you think a three-month break would do you good? Set you up, man! Bring back the old sparkle.'

What was more, Dr Armstrong offered to introduce Byrd to 'new, worthwhile contacts' when he returned and hinted at a post in a Government-subsidised agency. Byrd was so enmeshed in his professional griefs and domestic responsibilities that he could not at first appreciate what was being offered to him. The MEDOC-Armstrong gravy-train was before him – a first-class carriage door open. The message got through, and in seconds Byrd had jumped aboard and, as the train got under way, never once asked himself whether there might be any unforeseen difficulties.

Of course, in due time, Dr Armstrong sketched in the difficult situation at the Institute. Byrd listened, but in view of his financial burdens nothing seemed of grave importance except the salary and expenses. 'I'll be discretion itself,' he said. Armstrong thought Byrd need not get involved, but hoped he would keep his eyes open. 'We're always trying to improve our service to subscribers, so an outside viewpoint on the whole operation would be most welcome.'

Byrd was taken in by Dr Armstrong's majestic and empty phrases and forgot any doubts about the old man when he was put 'on a retainer' until he had read in the MEDOC files and completed the preparations for his departure. Byrd, in due time, made his declaration of secrecy – 'a matter of no importance, a mere formality' – and was given a hazy account of MEDOC's relationship with H.M.G. The money offered, the conditions of travel and service, convinced Byrd that the job was on his level – 'right up his street' – and when MEDOC gave him a tropical kit allowance to dress up for his jaunt, he began to believe that leaving *The Age* had been a matter of good fortune.

Byrd's wife, a rather impractical, poetic woman, given to comparative religion and reviewing novels for a weekly magazine, pointed out that never before, in all their married life, had Byrd left his home and parental duties for so long a period. All the same, such a break was what he needed after the unpleasantness of *The Age*, and the teenage Byrds, thrilled by their Pa's good luck, rejoiced to see him walk indoors with his Airey and Wheeler parcels and a new lease of life. The whole family soon saw Byrd's coming trip in simplified, brochure terms. He was going 'to live in the lap of luxury', be 'waited on hand and foot by a houseboy', would be allowed 'almost limitless expenses' and the use of the office car, and would lead the life to which all Englishmen of Byrd's background and class believe is theirs by natural right. Byrd, too familiar with the cheeseparing and economies of gentility, hoped that by being careful he would also make enough on expenses to offer his wife a holiday in Rome.

Although it was agreed that Byrd was to live in Paul Brophy's flat, the two men were not to meet. Dr Armstrong so arranged things that there was no overlap, no chance to exchange ideas and check up on their boss's intentions. Both men were puzzled by this, but neither made an issue of it. Brophy, for his part, sent Byrd a number of chilly memos with instructions how to operate, live in the flat and, most surprising of all, how to deal with the Tunisian. Byrd read them lightly and left London in the same mood people go on holiday. He lost years in the flight between London and Paris, shed some more in the huge cloud-banks over France and, looking down on the islands of the Mediterranean in the amber evening atmosphere, returned once more to some long-lost youthful impulse. Altogether, he lost about twenty years by the time he reached Baida and walked through the opulent, velvet evening from the plane to the airport building carrying a dispatch case and a violin.

Mrs Parslow, waiting outside the customs hall, recognised Byrd at once. She waved. Byrd would not have known Mrs Parslow. She had aged, and, apart from her good legs, had grown ungainly and comfortless, everything Byrd disliked in a woman.

2

THE customs men ignored Byrd's cases and gathered, charmed, about the violin. They examined it for hidden caches of drugs and then stared at it and at Byrd. The men who could accept the gaudy, flower-painted trunks from Algeria and Persia, and the whizz-kid portmanteaux of American executives, could not ignore the violin.

'*Vous jouez, monsieur?*'

Byrd lifted a benign and well-manicured hand. '*Je regrette ... Non.* I'm taking it to a friend who lives here.'

'He works here?'

Byrd nodded.

'Ah!' A pause for thought. '*Mais vouz jouez?*'

'If you knew how badly.'

'What?' No one had understood. '*Jouez pour nous.*'

There was nothing to do but oblige, and, in the fast-emptying customs hall, Byrd gave a wavering version of a Boccherini minuet. The incident delighted the crowd outside, including Mrs Parslow, and she was still laughing when he emerged. 'Never saw such a thing before.'

Byrd was all suavity: 'A little trick to get by the customs learned from Leopold Mozart.'

She had no idea what he meant but shouted, 'Good for you, old boy!' and gave the randy, vulgar laugh Byrd remembered.

On the whole, he was not pleased to see her. He would have preferred to have driven into Baida alone. It was a place where he had been very happy in his Eighth Army days and was full of memories for him. It was a bore having that crass loud woman coming between him and his new impressions of the quick vivid life around him.

Even in his short time in the airport queues, Byrd had responded to the Byzantine faces in the crowd: the subtlety, the antique beauty, the complexity of the human mass. After the hooded British face, enclosed in its private world of doubt, suffering and Protestant double-think, here were open faces with eyes: elegant almond eyes; round black eyes; with occasional blue eyes, going back to some crusader ancestor, which startled by their being set in the classical Mediterranean face. The eyes of the crowd lived in a way it was impossible to ignore after London; they were in rapport sensually with other eyes, other objects, living in a world of endless possibilities. They were the eyes of free people – that was the astonishing thing. People moved as though they had no cares, as though tomorrow had been cared for. Even the tribal women – in long, billowing dresses, had this splendid unself-consciousness. Byrd could hardly keep back a cry of pleasure.

It was just his luck – he thought – to be driving along the Corniche with a woman who looked like an ex-barmaid and couldn't keep her mouth shut, and who seemed indifferent to everything about her. Byrd could remember when that part of the city had been all market gardens. 'Oh, it's all changed, old boy. We've expanded since those days.' They were driving down the Avenue Lyautey, through double lines of tamarisk and palm, towards Mrs Parslow's flat, and to their left the sunset's whirls of gold and scarlet cirrus streaked the sky over the Mediterranean and profiled in sombre purple the fishermen still casting their lines from the stone groynes.

While waiting for dinner, Mrs Parslow and Byrd sat on the balcony, drinking whisky and enjoying the soft evening and the sparkling mountains across the bay. Conversation was hard going. Byrd did not mean to get matey with Mrs Parslow – he thought her in every way an inferior person – and Mrs Parslow, with her hysterical obsession with office affairs, wanted to line him up at once in the anti-Armstrong brigade and find out all he knew.

'And what do you make of Paul Brophy?'

Never having met him, Byrd relied on other people's opinions and what impressions he had formed of him from his memos. He imagined he was a person of drive and ability. Byrd, the graceful amateur, found the number of memos from Brophy 'quite alarming'. Byrd, the former hobnobber with ministers and ambassadors, found their content 'often trifling and silly: written for the sake of writing'. He supposed this was an essential part of empire-building.

Mrs Parslow laughed. 'You've noticed that already!'

'It stands out a mile – but it's a common failing in people who feel they are being groomed for stardom.'

'Who's being groomed for what stardom?'

Byrd made his point clear and assumed Brophy would take over MEDOC one day. Mrs Parslow gave the Turkish negative. 'Never. Never on your nelly! I dare say he'd like to think he is, but he's been called home while Fred decides whether it wouldn't be better to keep him there altogether.'

Byrd failed to grasp her point and, still taking the conversation lightly, thought this meant Brophy would take over from Armstrong in London.

'You misunderstand me, old boy. He's gone back to London with his tail between his legs. He's got the skids under him and knows it. It's just a question of time before Fred can shake him off.'

Byrd had 'seen nothing to suggest this on the files', and had again assumed from the tone of Brophy's memos that he was the young pretender waiting to take power and get even with all those who had bitched him on the way up.

'In this organisation, things that matter never reach the files. They all happen in Doctor Fred's upstairs. He likes it that way – and no one's got any hold on him.'

The 'Doctor Fred' implied a doubtful loyalty to their boss which made Byrd look at her in a fishy sort of silence. He hoped she did not expect him to start stabbing his patron in the back. He looked at his hands thoughtfully and Mrs Parslow, misinterpreting his silence, lifted her glass. 'Cheer up, old boy. Cheers. Here's to a happy stay! Don't look so gloomy. The worst never happens here – but it nearly does.'

She then launched into a long, circumstantial account of Brophy's plan to push out 'Doctor Fred' – the memos, the meetings with directors, including a certain 'Dowdy Dymphna', a creature out of folklore, but concluded that Dr Armstrong was 'up to his tricks'. She reported on Brophy's moves to fill the organisation with people of his choice. 'There's that little social climber, Neville de Vries, hired as a freelance subscriber at not far less than the highest paid local staff; and just a couple of weeks ago Brophy installed a painted dolly as his personal secretary – with orders to send on his mail.'

'Why does Fred tolerate this?'

'Because he's weak and muddled. He doesn't know what he wants! That's why.'

'It seems rather a muddle.'

'Well, believe me, it would be if we didn't have good local staff who keep the place going. First-class people.'

She refilled their glasses and sat down next to him. To change the subject a little, Byrd asked if the Neville de Vries was the son of the one who'd lived in Cairo.

'That's him. He won't stay long, I suppose. He doesn't stick at anything. When he joined us he was busy spending his old man's money.'

Byrd failed to be shocked. 'Lucky devil! That's the sort

of break I'd have liked at his age. If he's like his father, I bet he's as bright as a button. Never misses a trick.'

'You like that sort of person?'

'I'm not here to form likes or dislikes. All I know is that Fred thinks highly of him, and says he's never met a better Arabist.'

'Fred should know! He can hardly say "Thank you" in Arabic! All that's not important. Everybody speaks French, Spanish or English here.'

Byrd couldn't help exclaiming at her odd attitude. 'Looked at like that, almost any accomplishment becomes nugatory!'

'Oh, I'm not belittling him. I'm just saying he's not the sort of person we like in MEDOC – too lightweight.' She had not been saying this at all, and he looked at her fishily. 'Reggie, if I were asked to give an opinion about Neville de Vries I'd say he was a dilettante.'

Byrd was outraged. 'His reports are the best in the MEDOC file: without exception. The best written, the most accessible.'

'You think so?' She was plainly put out.

'His supplement on North Africa was quite splendid.'

'Always interesting to hear another opinion. It's not the general one. All the same, we get on. We're quite pally.'

Byrd disbelieved her. He did not see how any person of cultivation could be 'pally' with Mrs Parslow. He loathed the woman's hardbitten bitchiness. There was an uncomfortable silence in which they gulped their drinks.

She asked him whose idea it was that he should live in Brophy's flat. Byrd could not say; the arrangement had been handed to him on a salver, and two pounds sterling was being docked from his daily living allowance because of it.

'I suppose you know Paul Brophy's Tunisian is still there?'

'I hope he is. He's supposed to look after me.'

'Who said so?'

Byrd was baffled. 'Nobody said so. Well, not in so many words . . . but it was part of the arrangement for my stay here.'

'Well, let me tell you, old boy, that you won't get much comfort there unless you're queer.'

Byrd, utterly scandalised, asked what she meant.

'Just that. Watch out how you go. Don't be surprised by anything. I'd rather you were going there than me.' She went into lurid detail about the reputation Brophy had acquired and about the difficulties in the office. Why, he asked, had she let the arrangement go through? 'I'd hate to get involved in a mucky situation. It's hardly right for me to stay in a place with a bad reputation, is it?'

She modified her tone a little and said the matter was of limited knowledge; and this gave Byrd the idea that she had been lying and was backing down. What could have possessed the woman to make such a statement?

'I still don't understand why you've never said anything about this to Fred. It's no joke for an organisation of this kind, if Brophy is the chappie you say he is.'

'Doctor Fred has known from the beginning.'

'Known from the beginning? My dear lady, are you suggesting he allowed me to walk into this sodomites' love-nest? You must be mistaken! Or did he think I wouldn't notice?'

'Look, Reggie, when you've been in this organisation as long as I have, you know it's useless doing anything that's obvious. I've learned my lesson now, and I never interfere. If arrangements are made over my head, I let them stand. You've got to thank London for this.'

'But it's most disagreeable. How could you sit back and let it go ahead? Fred can't have known.'

She merely smiled knowingly – he had the impression she was enjoying his discomfiture – 'I shall be retiring to my little house near Melbourne in four years' time. My days of fighting are over. My suggestion to you is that if you don't like the way things are run in the flat, you leave and tell Fred why.'

'You are asking me to send in a report that would practically brand Brophy for ever.'

'It's got to come sooner or later. I wouldn't have too many scruples. You're dealing with twisters of the worst kind.'

'But what you're saying is quite dreadful – intolerable. Look,' – Byrd opened his wallet – 'I have a memo here from Brophy asking me to continue his efforts to get his Tunisian a work permit and a *permis de séjour*. It surprised me; but I gathered Brophy's recall had upset his plans.'

Mrs Parslow looked at the memo and handed it back. 'Means nothing. Nothing at all. Brophy never intended helping the man. Even before Brophy left for London the bloke used to come into the office and ask anyone he could find to help him legalise his position. His tourist visa expired God knows how long ago, and he's more or less a prisoner in the flat. He's scared of getting picked up as an illegal immigrant. I know you don't believe me, but Michel Shamseddine will tell you. He told the poor devil to pack up and go back to Tunis, but he stays on for the pickings.' The servant announced dinner, and she stood up. 'Oh, believe me, it's a mess. Brophy's a mess, the bloke's a mess. No one knows whether he's Bahige or Pierre. Neither one thing nor the other. Rubbish!'

Bemused and suspicious, Byrd sat down at Mrs Parslow's glass-topped dining-table, and while they ate thick slices of cold roast beef and mayonnaise, she gave him more and more murky details about MEDOC, and about Brophy and his Tunisian. Byrd, who was hungry, ate well, belched discreetly, and wondered in God's name what sort of organisation he had fallen into. He was aware of his own awkward position and the possibility that he had been duped by Armstrong into it; but he could not understand why Doris Parslow, as an old servant of the Institute, should take such delight in smashing its image. There was nothing left in human terms: the head of the office named a pervert and a moral twister, whose career was ending in disarray, and the grand old man in London dismissed as a muddler and a deceiver. Byrd did not know what to think; he was sure he would have a hard job to keep his feet clean in such a bog of despair.

Over Arab ice-cream, Mrs Parslow, her already thin good sense weakened by wine, said it was so easy to get a bad reputation in the Arab world that Brophy's behaviour had been suicidal. 'You've been here before; you know how it is: two people in a house together with a dark room and a bed in it – well, you've had it!' Her laughter was more randy than ever. Byrd was not amused. 'When I was first out here after my husband died they said the most dreadful things about me – said I paid taxi-drivers to make love to me – Imagine it! – if you get what I mean – It nearly drove me off my head. Now I don't care. They can say what they like. I'm so indifferent to them' – she evidently meant the Arabs – 'that I can walk into a crowded room and feel I'm alone. They don't really exist for me any more. You've got to discount them or you'd go off your head. Honest, you would. Don't look so gloomy, old boy. It gets us all in the end. You bet the servant thinks we're going to hop into bed shortly.'

Byrd, the ex-diplomatic correspondent, was shocked by what he felt to be her vulgar and suggestive way of talking. In his most chilly and distant manner he said it would be a great pity 'if two people of our age can't have a meal together without being misunderstood. Life isn't worth living if one is always under suspicion.'

The remark and tone silenced her – she was even hurt a little – and she rang the bell for the servant in another uncomfortable silence. God knows what she had intended by her remark, but Byrd showed her clearly that he thought she had designs on him; and poor Doris Parslow, who spent half her time talking and acting without thinking, was deeply hurt. In a way, she need not have worried: Byrd had a thing about being pursued. No amount of professional tribulation could shake Byrd's conviction that he was attractive to women and, with his few good teeth and episcopal hair, represented the sort of person certain unscrupulous women would want to catch. In his early days he had had his successes – and enjoyed them; nowadays he was a defender of the sacredness of marriage and, on trips by himself, made a thing about guarding himself against encouraging women like Doris Parslow.

'I'm sorry, if I've hurt your feelings,' he said in his fatuous way, 'but I don't think people of our age can afford to make ourselves ridiculous.'

'That's quite all right, Reggie, old boy. I'm sorry you took my joke the wrong way. I'll be more careful in future.'

It was about as disastrous a gaffe as Byrd could have made on his first evening, and they drank their coffee in a further uncomfortable silence. She was furious at his conceit.

3

THE taxi dropped him in a short cul-de-sac, flanked on one side by eucalyptus and orange trees. The street was unlit, so that distant street-lamps threw the shadows of trees on the white wall of the building; and the shadows moved with the rise and fall of branches shaken by a newly-risen wind. Inside the building, the concierge's office was closed, and the lift which came down from the eleventh floor seemed sleepy.

The door of Brophy's flat was opened by an equally sleepy Tunisian, who smiled politely, and helped Byrd carry his bags into the flat. He was a countrified boy-man of indeterminate age, dressed in English striped pyjamas and with Moroccan slippers on his feet. 'I wait until eleven' – he held up ten inadequate fingers – 'and when you not come, I sleep.'

Byrd excused himself and followed the man into a large bedroom, where a bed was turned down and some fruit arranged on a side-table. 'You want some whisky?' Byrd shook his head, too surprised to find words. 'We got whisky. And London gin!' Byrd still shook his head. 'Then you sleep good.' And the Tunisian went away into the next room and closed the door.

Left standing among his luggage, Byrd caught sight of himself in a long mirror and hardly recognised his face as his own, so weird, so foolish was the expression on his face, so much had Mrs Parslow's warnings and hints prejudiced his first meeting with the Tunisian. Despite himself, Byrd felt ill-at-ease with the man; what dismayed him was the extent to which his face showed it. What sort of relationship could it be when it started so badly? Hardly honest. His thoughts turning pell-mell, Byrd began arranging his possessions in the drawers and cupboards put at his disposal. He took several half-finished manuscripts out of his case – he meant to work hard privately – and placed them in the drawer of his bedside table. Then he examined Brophy's books – a good selection, from Keats to Donald Attwater – and admired the lithographs on the wall. He would have liked to visit the rest of the flat, but felt he had no right to, so, once his unpacking was done, he went out on to the balcony. There was real excitement in the movement of the night, and he was so engrossed in the view that he hardly noticed that the light had gone on in the Tunisian's room. He turned round and saw the man sitting up in bed trying to make out what Byrd was doing. Feeling uncomfortable – like a trespasser – Byrd went back into his own room and got into bed.

Who was he to believe? How much faith was he to put in all Mrs Parslow told him? He wanted to avoid disturbance and scandal during his three months' stay, so what would he gain by believing Mrs Parslow? Just before falling asleep, he recalled with astonishment that she had actually told him to lock his bedroom door against possible assault by the Tunisian. The woman was twisted; it would be a disservice to everyone to listen to her.

4

THE warm wind blew all night, caused shutters to bang and whined in ventilation shafts. About seven o'clock, the Tunisian came into Byrd's room with a small pot of tea and an equally small glass jug filled with undiluted condensed milk. Byrd served himself and lay back in bed trying to assess the tea; it had a strange, sterile taste as though made from dust found in a funeral urn. More of this musty tea was served at breakfast, along with flat bread, butter and goat's milk cheese. It was an unconvincing collation, prepared without love and served without style. Byrd did not feel he had the right to complain; the whole thing resembled the effort of a moth to be a butterfly and so was outside the realms of ordinary criticism.

The Tunisian had changed into what was to be his usual wear: a roll-neck, navy-blue sweater and jeans. He padded about barefoot and, in speaking to Byrd, scratched the top of one foot with the other, and picked his flat nose in an offhand way. Would Byrd be back for lunch? What did he like to eat? Would he hand over some money for groceries? It turned out that there was hardly any food in the flat, and what there was had been obtained on tick. Where was the money Brophy had left him? The Tunisian smiled brightly and without embarrassment: it had gone. He shrugged. 'That's how it is.'

Byrd promised to draw up a list of groceries and get some money. He was vexed; he had not expected to hand out money at once or to start housekeeping. A flash in his eyes, a certain grittiness in his manner did not escape the Tunisian, who saw clearly that Byrd did not like him. To make their relationship more complex, Byrd would not admit to himself how awful he thought the young man was and what a world of difference there was between this rather grubby, depressed person and the 'houseboy' of his imagination. The Tunisian had no idea how to ingratiate; in any case, he was too demoralised to start any new initiative – he was at the mercy of other people and their whims.

A typical Baidani listlessness settled over the flat and over Byrd himself. After his breakfast, he took a shower, dressed and sat down at a desk to write home. As he sat by himself, he looked around the huge room, furnished with so much good taste and in such pleasing colours and wondered what was wrong. It was a little time before he appreciated that there was a film of dust over everything and especially over the Damascene mirrors, so that they gave the impression of having too many times reflected faces at moments of anguish and desolation.

The Tunisian padded about, looking hangdog and unprepossessing, with buckets of water for the plants on the western balcony. Byrd looked at him from time to time, expecting to find something of distinction, of fatal fascination, to have justified Brophy's friendship and patronage, but saw only thirdrateness and ineptness. He was puzzled by the strange, countrified air, the pitiful attempts at domestic arrangements – and the whole underlined by an ultimate indifference and listlessness. The man looked bamboozled and caught out.

Towards ten o'clock, he brought Byrd a Turkish coffee and a glass of water and asked for some airmail paper as he wanted to write home.

He then asked where Mr Paul was. Byrd told him. The Tunisian looked unconvinced. He said 'they' had told him at MEDOC that Mr Paul had gone for ever and that Byrd was taking his place. Byrd shook his head. 'I'm here for three months only.' The Tunisian thought a while, went away and came back looking nonplussed. He clearly thought Byrd was lying and could not understand why. He then produced an envelope, much handled, richly buttered, and took out a document which was his expired Baidani tourist visa. He wanted

Byrd to get him a work card and help him to stay in Baida. He gave an account of his difficulties that tallied with what Mrs Parslow had told Byrd. He needed a letter – Byrd supposed a sort of affidavit – proving that he was gainfully employed. Byrd had no right to sign one. 'I am not your employer. I'm only here as a temporary resident myself.'

The Tunisian went over his griefs, and Byrd sympathised. He saw that life as a virtual prisoner was no fun, but could not understand why the man did not go home.

'There's no work. Here I work.'

What was more, the Tunisian said Mr Paul had suggested he should go to university. He had been to the office, and they had asked for his *Bachot*. He waved a thin, ugly finger, as though Byrd had failed to grasp his point. 'No. *Bachot. Rien!*' He fell into a gloom and picked his nose; then suddenly showed anger: 'Mr Paul is my friend! Why he not write the letter for me? He knows that if I go out police get me and *Khallas! Calabish!* Handcuffs!'

Then, as though offering Byrd a debatable hypothesis, the Tunisian said Brophy must have got tired of him. 'I tell him "Give me letter and then I go", but he will not, and I say bad things to him. Very strong. Very bad. And he come to me and cry and say, "Why are you angry with me? You are my friend. *Ana masuliak.* I am responsible for you."'

Byrd listened fascinated, appalled, and to cut short the importunings and whinings said he would write to Brophy and remind him of his duty. The Tunisian looked pleased, then gloomy. 'He will not answer. He gone to London. He want I go away. I no good for him any more. *Malish.*'

'Mr Paul is coming back. Don't you understand? He is coming back. He must want to keep you as a servant, or he would have sacked you.'

It was not clear what the Tunisian had understood, for he replied, 'I am not his servant. I am his friend.'

So everything Mrs Parslow had said was true. Byrd gasped. 'Yes, I am his friend. I will be with him until he marries.'

To hide his embarrassment, Byrd picked up an envelope and began to address it. The Tunisian thought he had been misunderstood and looked hurt. 'Yes, sir, I am not servant. When people come here – like you – I make meals for them, but I not want they think I am servant. My family does not think

I am here for servant, for cook, for wash floors, to work like woman.'

'I thought you were driver, sort of chappie . . .'

'What you will.'

'What do you mean?'

'For work card I will be driver. I get work like that. But I am Mr Paul's friend.'

From old experience, Byrd detected an endless ambiguity in the Tunisian's replies. Perhaps this was the root of all Paul Brophy's troubles. What did 'friend' mean? According to some it could be boy-friends, bed-friends; to others, it could be old chums who had found a *modus vivendi* together. Any ambiguity arose – and Byrd realised this – because to the Tunisian the distinction had no importance.

The two men looked at one another opaquely. Byrd refused to accept what he had been told, as anyone else would have done, because it did not fit in with his ideas of what was right and proper. Through all the upsets caused by this precarious relationship between himself and the Tunisian he would suffer because he rejected the obvious. It was one of the forms of Byrd's silliness, a kind of British blindness and immaturity in personal relations, at the same level as that of those social workers who fail to take account of pleasure in dealing with prostitution.

How hard Byrd tried to forget what he had been told. After all, it might not be true; the man could be misinterpreting simple things; he could be exaggerating.

The young man remained near the desk, waggling his left leg. He wanted money for the groceries. Byrd set aside his letters and decided to go into the kitchen to see what was there.

He was furious with the Tunisian for interrupting him and for being so frank. It meant Byrd could not pretend he did not know, and that he was face to face with the unknown. Byrd's experience of human relations had not included much contact with homosexual lovers; they were the people Byrd tolerated in the abstract and was embarrassed by in the flesh, largely because he did not know what they themselves regarded as normal. He had the suspicion that while he knew his own limits, they did not know theirs, and that, like any group hemmed in by certain restraints, they were always trying to proselytise and increase their range and number. Without recognising his own absurdity, Byrd felt himself as much menaced and pursued as he had done in Mrs Parslow's flat.

Byrd found a marvellous (and illogical) vent for his disgust and rage in the kitchen, which was covered with stacks of paper in corners, overlapping empty bottles and piles of dirt. He flung open the refrigerator with the fervour of an inquisitor. Inside, were a couple of bottles of Coca-Cola, three eggs, a shapeless lump of butter half wrapped in crinkled silver paper, a vegetable concoction on a dish, a half-empty wax-paper carton of yoghurt and two apples. In a nearby cupboard were scraps of bread and a piece of mildewed cheese. It was all less than appetising, and Byrd ordered the Tunisian to get rid of everything. Symbolically, he was getting rid of all the inconvenient and monstrous things with which he was faced: things which threatened his peace of mind and his holiday. The Tunisian could see no cause for Byrd's rage – the way he suddenly became red and peppery, the way the rather mild, self-satisfied face contorted with anger. 'Get rid of everything. Dirt and filth everywhere.' Byrd made a symbolic journey to the rubbish hatch with a piece of old bread and sent it down. He ordered the Tunisian to throw out all the old newspapers and paperbags; he told him to crate the empty bottles and send them back to the suppliers. The Tunisian protested. The bottles were Mr Paul's and so was the refund.

'I'll settle with him. Take them back. And before you do anything else, please clean this floor. Look!' Two cockroaches scuttled out of a crack in the badly laid tilework, and by the way Byrd pursued and trod on them they might have been the guilty lovers themselves. He had become manic. 'Where is the DDT? Why keep it on the balcony when the cockroaches are here? Why the hell is that stupid man keeping this damned useless customer here? The place is verminous.'

The Tunisian did not understand, although he naturally understood that Byrd was displeased. He thought the old man had gone mad; he had never seen anyone go off the handle so suddenly. 'Mildew. Cockroaches. Filth,' Byrd was saying, and he began jamming bottles into a crate. The Tunisian took up the work and gathered all the empties together. He refused to take them away, since Mr Paul had asked him not to. 'I can't help if Mr Paul is mean. I can't live in this rubbish heap. And now wash everything with hot water and soap. *Beaucoup de savon!'* The Tunisian's eyes rebelled. It seemed to him that Byrd was not so much interested in cleanliness and order as in thrusting him back into livery; it was a deliberate refusal to recognise his rights as a human being and Mr Paul's friend.

'I'm sorry, my friend, but I can't live with a dirty kitchen.'

'Mr Paul never say anything.'

'I'm sure he didn't. He didn't see the cockroaches dancing on his food.'

'I no understand.'

'Just as well.' Byrd the bishop was in charge again, and gave his thin, unfelt smile. To the Tunisian, bowled over by the old man's nastiness, this was pure hypocrisy. He decided Byrd was not a man to be trusted and might even be mad. To prevent a further explosion, the Tunisian began swabbing down the floor, but was sombre-faced as he did it and did not take pleasure in the kitchen's improved appearance; clean or dirty, it was all the same to him: it was the place where he did not want to work.

5

As arranged, the office car came at eleven o'clock to take Byrd to the Institute. Mrs Parslow introduced him to the staff, who rose to a man, hand on heart, and slightly bowed. Byrd was impressed and enjoyed their respects. He then took coffee with Shamseddine, who outlined the week's work, and was presented to Brophy's exotic secretary, who sat in a sort of purdah by herself, filing her nails. She had no work in her typewriter and alongside an empty coffee-cup was a novel by Françoise Sagan, in French. She practised her English a little, and then Byrd went into conference with Mrs Parslow.

That first visit to MEDOC was much more reassuring, much more to Byrd's taste. He enjoyed the smiles of people anxious to please, the deference, the silence which followed his arrival. He did not doubt for a moment that the staff thought he was someone, and his Grand Manner came into play. It was, however, the Grand Manner of a democrat with – to use a Byrd cliché – 'a cheery word for one and all', and he smiled in his most avuncular way on economist and doorman alike. He would have been astonished to know that to the Arabs, he seemed a very old man and pleasantly venerable; more, because one Englishman looked much like another, they thought he resembled Dr Armstrong before he had grown a beard!

A desk had been provided for him in Brophy's room and a telephone extension. Mrs Parslow herself brought him a towel, a piece of soap and a key to the executives' W.C. and wash-room; he had arrived.

Towards the end of the morning, Shamseddine came into his room and invited him to lunch. This was impossible as Byrd was to deliver the violin to his friends in a village six or seven kilometres away, towards the south. Shamseddine at once offered to drive Byrd there, along with the violin, on his way back home.

So they set off together, and Shamseddine asked whether Byrd had any copies of his thrillers with him. Nothing is more pleasing to an author than well-informed interest, and Byrd regretted he had none of his paperbacks with him. Shamseddine said he admired any man who had the energy to write as well as hold down a job. So Byrd explained how he had begun writing, to while away long periods of waiting at air-ports and in hotels as a correspondent sent to international conferences. It sounded very cosmopolitan and worldly; Shamseddine was suitably impressed.

Out in the foothills, away from the suburbs, the spring was under way – peach and apricot trees were in full flower, and the uncultivated stretches in the olive-yards were matted with red and yellow flowers. The impact of the clear, dense light, the effortless way in which forms defined themselves, were overwhelming. This was the sort of day – with spacious cumu-lus clouds appearing over the mountains – that Byrd enjoyed : the sort of day which suggests, however pleasantly, that most of the average man's lifetime is wasted in fruitless pursuits, that the only real activity is contemplation, the only mature reaction, thankfulness. Somewhere, on that road in the foot-hills, happiness descended on Byrd : the kind of happiness he had not known for years. For the first time for months, he could think of all that had happened to him at *The Age* without bitterness, without wanting retribution and vengeance; he lost, for the first time for he could not remember how long, the need to justify and defend himself. Yes, as he stood outside the Exes' walled garden and heard the little French-style *grelot* ringing loud and clear in the house inside, he knew what it was to feel free: a moment, as in the strongest painting, which gives to everyday objects a stunning sufficiency and, at the same time, a magical relevance to the inner life of the observer. The country lanes zigzagging downhill to the distant coast, the ascent of steps through umbrella pines, the Italianate church with its skeletal belfry, the blue-painted garden-gate he was waiting for the servant-girl to open – surely these things were given to him as compensation for years of hard and not especially interesting work and worry on behalf of other people. They were given to him, after years of sharing, as a personal reward for constancy and sobriety. Magical, magical day and moment; the door creaked open on a shady garden.

Inside was Mediterranean domestic charm at its peak. The high walls shut out the village, even the panorama, and the whole private world was centred on a water tank, hexagonal and tiled in Turkish pattern, with a small fountain in the middle. The garden walls were hidden by a profusion of dark-leaved trees, including a lemon, with fruit still hanging, as well as the inevitable jasmines and bougainvillaea. Between the water and the house was an array of geraniums and exotic ferns in art pots and then a table and a group of chairs. Behind the table, let into the wall of the house, was a niche, tiled in sea-green and maroon Turkish faience and completing the marriage of artifice and nature. Because of this balance, there was a suggestion of artificiality in the birds, mostly bulbuls, whistling in their gilt cages hung among the leaves. In all this lyrical profusion and harmony, a couple of Susan Exe's cashmere cardigans, laid out to dry on sheets of paper, did not seem out of place.

6

THE Exes were friends of long standing. The husband worked for an international concern, the wife taught English at a girls' school. Their daughters were at school in England. They were a successful, self-sufficient family, a shade complacent, who had always had the impression that Byrd had missed his vocation, even mismanaged his life. Like a good many academic people they did not consider journalism a serious career and did not take its practitioners seriously. All their friends were academic or from the abstract, highly-paid world of international organisations, and so they knew nothing of MEDOC, except its name, and could not imagine, since it was outside their field, that it could be of great standing. The only thing that impressed them was that Byrd was living in the Blue Dome Building. Who was to look after him? Byrd said there was a man in the flat 'who did'. Susan Exe, as snobbish in Baida as in London, asked, voice breaking with envy, whether the man went with the job? Byrd understood what she meant, but in view of the man's equivocal status could not suppress a laugh.

'Your Documentation Centre does its employees well if they can afford a full-time houseboy,' John Exe said. Both he and his wife were a bit breathless by the apparent, if only temporary, grandeur of their old friend.

'Frankly, it amazes me the way these MEDOC people live. Nothing is too good for them. The flat's enormous – and all for a bachelor! I've plainly wasted my time in London.'

Susan Exe thought it essential for British people to keep up a certain standard in a foreign country.

'Oh, really, Susie! What year do you think it is? Why, look at my own experience: any child of fifteen can do what I'm expected to do. As a job it's an insult to my intelligence – it hardly exists – but I'm paid the sort of money an editor gets at home.'

John Exe smiled vaguely. 'We don't all get money for jam!'

'I'm not saying so. I said *I* am, and so are the other Europeans in the organisation. It's a real mutual benefit society.'

The Exes noted the strange mixture of resentment and awe

in Byrd's voice, and the husband suggested he should be grateful he was getting a taste of honey at last. Susan Exe was far more impressed by the houseboy/major domo. What bothered her was whether he wore a white coat and gloves to serve at table. She had heard this old style had been revived by a number of rich families, especially the Greeks.

Without thinking, Byrd answered: 'But why should he? He's relaxed and free in a polo-neck jumper and jeans.'

Susan Exe thought she had misheard.

'Oh, no. That's the way things are. The man is more like the friend of the man I'm standing in for.'

It took some seconds for the penny to drop. 'You mean, the head of a big organisation is living with his servant? How awful! It's frightfully looked down on here.'

John Exe challenged his wife. 'Nobody cares a damn, Susie.'

'Oh yes, they do, darling. It's O.K. among themselves, but with foreigners it's different. Something always goes wrong. How loathsome for you, Reggie. Do you mind very much?'

Byrd said it was not his affair.

'But the man must be vile!'

Susan Exe's outburst took Byrd by surprise. 'Not so that you'd notice. On the contrary, he's just a sort of peasant caught between two worlds – a most pathetic, inept sort of person. I can't make head or tail of him; he's a sort of clock without hands.'

Byrd then went into the question of the work permit and Brophy's callous and inexplicable behaviour. John Exe gave firm advice: 'Don't get involved. My good chap, leave all that strictly alone. You'll end up by getting yourself disliked – or tarred with the same brush.'

'One can't help feel somewhat responsible for him. He poses some kind of problem . . .'

'Not to people here. Here, we live with unsolved problems for years – look at the local corruption – and would often hate to have them resolved. If this is a homosexual ménage I'd be extremely careful. We had experience of it once, which taught me a lesson for life. The genuine homosexual forms part of a secret world like the Mafia, and they settle their accounts among themselves.'

'Aren't you being over-dramatic?'

'Not a bit. Believe me, Reggie, you'd be a fool to meddle or to think you can do anything. Keep out – and if I were you I'd even leave the flat.'

'Oh, no!' Byrd was appalled by the suggestion. 'It would raise such a stink. It would be tantamount to an open accusation of Brophy.'

'Well, if you feel you must stay on, do so. But I beg you, don't try to interfere. You don't understand. I don't understand. It's another way of life and feeling altogether.'

'Oh, yes, Reggie, listen to John. He knows what he's talking about. Unless you want material for a book!'

Byrd was seriously put out; the Exes' attitude baffled him. How could he become involved? Susan Exe's curiosity got the better of her; she wanted to know what the man did all day?

'Do? Why, reads paperbacks with lurid-lipped women on the cover – and listens to Arabic music on the tape-recorder Paul Brophy gave him.'

Susan Exe's world was no longer solid. All her Scots sense of the fitness of things was outraged. 'But is that right?'

'You haven't understood, Susie. Reggie has explained that the man doesn't look on himself as a servant. He's the boy-friend.'

Byrd said pedantically: 'He said "friend".'

'Oh, what's the odds?'

Byrd felt the water close over his head; he was already out of his depth.

Lunch followed and a short siesta. Then, about five o'clock, the Exes decided to show Byrd their village. They had retained the solid British habit of turning out in heavy shoes and carrying walking-sticks, and looked even more recently arrived than Byrd.

By this time, the magical day had faded. The only poetry was the sighing of the warm wind in the stone pines and in the light grey cloud, which had covered the sky, very high and very austere. A neighbour, tilling his terrace, thought the *khamsin*, the warm, sandy wind from the desert, was approaching and warned the Exes not to walk too far – heavy rain would fall before sunset.

As they walked through the narrow lanes, up hilly inclines and down steps from terrace to terrace, the Exes were greeted like old and valued friends. Everyone, from the man with the donkeys laden with olive-logs to the old lady sitting under a huge white parasol, had something to say. Everyone wished to invite the Exes and their guest indoors, and Byrd was once again back in the Middle East of his youth and appreciating for the first time a tradition of hospitality, whereby a neighbour's guest is everyone's guest. It was a rich village, where each house had its plot of land, its flowering trees, its complement of children, poultry, doves and dogs: a hillside Arcadia, whose inhabitants – at least in Byrd's eyes – were hardly less Virgilian than their setting.

The sudden gusts of wind grew fiercer, and Byrd decided to leave before the storm broke. One of the village taxis was going down with an empty seat, so Byrd broke off his visit and, all the way down, turned over Susan Exe's throw-off about making literary use of the Brophy–Tunisian imbroglio. He turned over themes which could begin with an innocent outsider plunged into a similar situation, but one thing troubled him: he could not see where the dramatic conflict arose. What did it matter if X was in love with Y; what could be more banal? Unless Z, the third person, found the love between the two immoral and morbid and longed to break up the relationship? That could hardly be Byrd's rôle; at least, he did not see himself in it, and he put the matter out of his head. All the material life offers is not susceptible to conversion into books – as Byrd had discovered when he tried to write a political thriller – and yet – he foresaw some first chapter, in which the outsider arrives at his point of destiny in such a way and under such a sky – a dense grey light, which brought out the livid pallor of the skyscrapers of the city down below, offset by a black sea. He would describe, perhaps, how rain suddenly appeared, so that everyone in the cab cried out with the drama of the moment. Within seconds, the rain had advanced up the road towards them, like a phalanx, reducing visibility to a few metres and went on lashing, beating the car all the way into town. By the time Byrd reached Blue Dome Building, some streets were flooded, and the palm-trees were half bent over by the wind. A wild evening had fallen on the coast.

7

INSIDE Brophy's flat all was gaiety and bright eyes. Five of the Tunisian's compatriots and friends had dropped in for cards, Coca-Cola and a glimpse of the elderly Englishman who had gone mad because some empty bottles had been left in the kitchen. The main reception room, dominated by an abstract in red, black and yellow, by the Tangier artist Shibili, was filled with tobacco-smoke and the record-player was going full blast. Everyone stood up, and the Tunisian invited Brophy to take his place at the table while he made coffee.

The game stopped for a drink and a chat, and one of the men said, in good English, that he was glad Byrd was going 'to help' the Tunisian get his papers in order. This was no place to make formal denials, and Byrd's good nature made him say that he would do his best.

'We hope you enjoy your stay in Baida, sir!'

'And when is Madame coming? She's not coming? Then we must find you a local wife. Only for three months? Oh, no, sir, you will be with us for a long time to come.' It was their way of showing disbelief. The 'would' and the 'will' and even the 'is' are hopelessly confused in the ordinary Arab mind, and an honest doubt is as much a part of truth as an item on paper – so Byrd was installed as Brophy's successor and the Tunisian's guardian angel.

Byrd was tired, excused himself and went into his room. Through the open doors he could hear the game begin again and the voice of the Tunisian, louder than all, shouting in excitement and betting more heavily than the others. Byrd supposed he had collected a fair amount of money on the bottles. After a time, Byrd's book dropped, and he fell asleep.

When he awoke it was night; his lamp was still burning, and the rain had stopped. After a short time, he realised that the happy card-players were out on the balcony and were watching his return to life. One called out, 'Whisky, sir?' Byrd shook his head, vaguely irritated at the position he was in – an elderly person of uncertain temper, used to a position of integrity and trust, flung among a collection of unscrupulous carpetbaggers (he included the MEDOC direction) and suddenly bored and on edge.

The card-players could not imagine he wanted to be alone and crowded up to the balcony door, and stared at him as though he had been demonstrating a new mattress in a Fifth Avenue store. Byrd had not felt so ridiculous and embarrassed for years. He pretended to go to sleep again, and his spectators wandered away. He looked at his watch: it was gone eleven o'clock.

The young men went on talking, laughing and chaffing until nearly midnight, when two of them left. Twenty minutes or so later they returned and, by the sound of glasses, plates and cutlery it was clear they had come back with food. Within a few minutes, two emissaries were inviting Byrd to join them. His gall rose like a tide and then subsided. Why should he be vexed? Byrd restrained his anger. They were being courteous and friendly (and, besides, the Exes' luncheon was almost nine hours away).

The dining-table was covered with dishes; there was a jar of ice-cubes, a bowl of salad which someone was tossing, and, in the middle of the table, a bottle of liquor. Wrapped in Arabic bread were slices of grilled mutton and a couple of roast chickens.

'*Vous savez vivre!*' Byrd exclaimed.

The Tunisian crowed with pleasure. 'I take bottles and get money. I win three times as much – so we have food. You are all my friends. *Santé!*'

At the end of the meal, his breath reeking of alcohol, onions and Egyptian beans, Byrd had another glimpse of blue sky. He had not enjoyed a meal so much in years.

The Tunisian made coffee again, and Byrd was asked to show photos of his children. The daughters were especially admired, and Byrd and his wife were complimented on their happy household. To Byrd's great surprise, the Tunisian said: 'I want a baby girl with blonde curls.'

After the guests had gone, the Tunisian went out on to the balcony and ate pistachio nuts and threw the shells into the courtyard below. Some of them littered the balcony in the morning, when Byrd wandered out in pyjamas for a breath of air. The storm of the previous evening had cleared the air, and the yellow, white and ochre buildings around glowed in the sunlight. Byrd felt drained of energy, and this made him disgruntled and dissatisfied.

The people on nearby balconies appeared to suffer from the same inertia and leaned over balustrades, staring at nothing, detached from the town and day around them. They were given over to pure contemplation, like girls in Dutch window-scenes, and took little interest in the vendors shouting in the streets below or in the planes flying low overhead; gathering themselves together for the day was activity enough.

8

BYRD's first day's work began at the same time as everyone else's. At seven-thirty the atmosphere was dour and serious; it was the moment of the day when the disgruntled felt their griefs most deeply. Byrd sat at his desk and read the local French and English press. This took until about eight-fifteen. Then Shamseddine offered him some articles to revise. These were short contributions by local correspondents, mostly in withered academic English. Byrd quickly put them into shape, only to be told by Shamseddine that he had broken about twenty-seven house rules. 'I thought Fred would have told you!'

Byrd cheerfully confessed it was the first time he had known of house rules and asked to see a rule book. There was not one; the rules were in people's heads, and Shamseddine was 'too busy to explain'; so Byrd was left with nothing to do. The other MEDOC seniors looked over Byrd's work sourly and noted where Shamseddine had ringed trifling points of style and presentation. They held up their hands in horror. So this was the creature they were saddled with – a typical English fool; even Paul Brophy could do better.

Byrd was left alone for most of the morning – Mrs Parslow kept to herself, still nursing her rebuff of the first evening.

About one o'clock he asked Shamseddine whether there was anything further he could do. There was not. He asked Mrs Parslow if he was needed. He was not. So he picked up his trilby and left. It was twenty-three minutes before time. The figure was graven on the faces of the senior staff. They looked at one another and smiled.

The next day he told Shamseddine he hoped there would be more work. Shamseddine glowered at his typewriter. 'I can't make work. We have quiet periods. That's how it is.' Byrd had a habit of locking his arms together in front and lightly pinching the base of his upper arms as though testing the strength of his own biceps. He stood like this before Shamseddine. 'You won't be surprised to know that I've brought my own work in. I can't spend another day like yesterday.'

He could hardly have shaken Shamseddine more had he said he was returning to London. Byrd's detached, Olympian approach touched all the senior men on a sensitive point. People whose whole careers were tied to MEDOC could not thole a little man who wandered in and appeared to treat the Institute as a joke. Was there a hint of patronage in Byrd's manner – a suggestion that he had handled bigger issues and regarded MEDOC as a part-time diversion? Shamseddine took umbrage.

'I'd no idea your Reggie Byrd would be such a fool. He behaves as though he were not quite sane.'

'Oh, that's Reggie, old boy. Don't worry. It doesn't mean anything. He's never been really with it, you might say. He's always had this way of putting things out of sight. As my old grandmother used to say, "You can always salt a job of work." Seems to have paid off in Reggie's case. But he's weird.'

They watched him moving about, looking for the London papers, with a vague tra-la-la under his breath, and thought they'd never seen anyone so out of his element.

'He's a nitwit, your Byrd.'

This struck Mrs Parslow as funny. 'Don't laugh at him, Michel. He's one of Doctor Fred's down-and-outs. If he was something or had done something he wouldn't be here on such a footing.'

Shamseddine shook his head, and Mrs Parslow closed the door in order to laugh louder. 'Poor old thing. He's past it, now. You can see he's just hoping to get a nice rest-cure and go back home with a tan. Doctor Fred's latest!'

All the same, Shamseddine felt compelled to make a gesture and again invited Byrd to take a coffee in his room. He offered Turkish cigarettes as well as English ones. He hoped Byrd had settled in comfortably in Brophy's flat. Was he eating well? The voice dropped a couple of tones: had Byrd been troubled by the man there?

'Over his work permit, you mean? I've written to Paul Brophy, but it's essentially a matter for him alone.'

'For the sort of work that Tunisian does, Mr Byrd, no government in the world would issue a permit.'

Like some old grey donkey in a storm, pretending nothing is happening, Byrd merely nodded his head and hoped the matter would pass. Shamseddine blew out a column of smoke. 'He was brought here for the purposes of perversion. That's not a trade registered with the I.L.O.'

'Is it kind to say that?'

'Mr Byrd, you ask me a straight question, and I ask you another: is it kind to us for the head of our organisation to go to his servant for his pleasure, and for his servant to come in here and boast about what he and his master do together?'

Byrd's mouth moved uncertainly. 'I'm not here to look into Mr Brophy's morals. I feel I mustn't get involved. This is a private affair.'

Shamseddine smiled pityingly. 'That is what it is not. Everyone knows everything. We're hoping that as a friend of Dr Armstrong you'll tell him everything you know about Paul Brophy.'

'It's not for me to tell Dr Armstrong. I shall do what little I can for Brophy's chappie . . . and that's the limit of my involvement. I'm really sorry for him.'

'In the Arab world, Mr Byrd – I'm speaking to you frankly – we never feel sorry for a man who cannot help himself. I'm ashamed to say this of a fellow-Arab, but he's merely a bloodsucker, clinging on for all he can persuade that poor, weak, boy Brophy to hand out in return for certain services.'

Byrd tried to make some defence of the Tunisian, based on his vision of him as a poor corrupted provincial, a strayed peasant or lost mechanic; Shamseddine made mock of him as a failed careerist. Brophy had outsmarted him in the end.

'Mr Byrd, I could admire a man in that position if he sold all Brophy's treasures and went off home with the money he made. To sit down under misfortune is to ask for more. Believe me, that man is not the person you think he is, Mr Byrd.'

Coffee over, Byrd went back to his typewriter, and Shamseddine went in to Mrs Parslow. The door closed.

'He's a madman, your Byrd. He doesn't want to open his eyes. What sort of man is it who shuts his eyes to the facts before him? He seems to think Bahige is a poor little innocent.'

'Perhaps he's fallen for him, Michel. He's making up for Mr Paul.'

Shamseddine laughed. 'He's beyond it, now. You can see that. But I wouldn't put it past that Bahige to try his tricks on him.'

'Might be good for him. What do you say, Michel? Wake him up a bit.'

They laughed together and, refreshed by his little joke, Shamseddine went back to work. They were in league against Byrd and soon made him feel excluded. Byrd fell back on his grand manner. He moved about in a nimbus of carefully achieved benevolence, eternally humming or whistling under his breath. He was detached, cool and deliberately underplayed everything. He did not actually call into question the work of the Institute, but his casual manner, his coming a little later each day and his going early, his indifference to the general disapproval, insulted, by implication, everyone else's involvement.

There were other errors of judgement which further alienated his critics. He never learned anyone's name and actually told Mrs Parslow that it was hardly worth the effort since he was leaving so soon. Then, when Mrs Parslow showed him her subscription list – a triumph of careful planning and perseverance on her part – he observed airily that it seemed incredible so many people wanted documentation on the region, a hint that such an interest was a sign of poor judgement. In the day-to-day work, too, he was unco-operative. After his early experience, he consulted Shamseddine, but went too far, quibbling over small points, irritating people to death. With his unsuccessful man's conceit, he felt free to criticise an arid style and the too frequent use of jargon and would infer that his own Augustan periods would show up the rest.

He seemed to think ignorance was *bon ton*. He knew 'next to nothing' about oil and made a joke about the various organisations exploiting them. 'I know I.P.C. but' – he paused like an after-dinner speaker – 'what in heaven's name is INOC? and ERAP? or ENI, AGIP, or SNAM?' The whole battery of entities – UNEAC, ASLOOP, ARAMCO, TAPLINE and UNDP – had to be explained to him; and they felt he forgot the next minute.

The MEDOC staff were embarrassed for him, because they thought he was making a fool of himself and contributed nothing. They discounted him as a congenital idiot and incorrigible bungler. Someone was put to re-read the proofs after no less than seven mistakes filtered through Byrd's first attempt and he had, without consultation, actually altered 'barrels' to 'tons' in an article 'in the interests of consistency'. He opened his second week with his minor duties even further curtailed (as they say, by popular request) and spent the rest of his time in the Institute as a signer of cheques and a flag-waver at official receptions.

These he enjoyed greatly. He felt at ease and at his own level with officials and got on well with people from the British Embassy, to whom he complained bitterly about human relations at MEDOC. He got some good laughs by describing the senior men as 'over-educated bores, obsessed by syntax and anti-imperialism'; who, while hating the British, were hooked on P.W.E. – Protestant Work Ethic. Other adjectives he used were 'humourless', 'puritanical' and 'bolshy-minded'.

9

DURING the second week, Neville de Vries returned from one of his long tours, looking bronzed and wicked. He and Byrd got friendly at once. Now Byrd had known Neville's father and knew him to be a gentleman – the sort of person who offends every potentate in sight (a man after Byrd's own heart) – and so the glow of breeding and good taste played around Neville.

Byrd saw a resemblance to the father; even down to the fine hair beginning to thin at the temples.

From their first meeting, the two men spoke the same language, and all those things in Neville which irritated people – his self-confidence, his trenchant opinions, his devastating accuracy – appealed to Byrd, since they were the products of breeding rather than education. Byrd still believed strongly in the distinction between Players and Gentlemen. Neville was a gentleman; all the others in MEDOC, humourlessly striving over common ground, with mean attention to detail and a sense of injustice, were players. They filled Byrd with alarm in the same way that careerists depressed him. In Byrd's private mythology, things had to be done effortlessly and through the instinct or not at all. Knowledge had to be acquired as a natural thing – his own passion for painting and church music, for example – so that they became part of the man in the way that leaves are part of a tree. This amounted to an appeal to the law of natural genius and hereditary ability, those mysterious agents which produce the 'right sort of man'. Neville's capacity for work, his clear style and his ability to carry his authority elegantly were natural things, which Byrd could admire.

Neville pumped Byrd mercilessly for news of Brophy and kept shaking his head. 'I'm afraid he's finished.' The fact that Byrd had been so badly informed about the state of play in MEDOC astonished him. He advised Byrd on no account to be drawn into the Parslow set. Byrd said he was on holiday, since nobody in his right mind would take MEDOC seriously.

Neville thought it perceptive of a man so much in the Bertie Wooster tradition to have seen through MEDOC so soon and laughed with him over it. Byrd, increasingly puzzled by the loathing Brophy inspired, asked Neville why. Neville's answer was short: 'Because he's the boss. The Arabs always hate the man above them, even while they fawn on him. They always feel they can do the job better.'

'Does this explain Doris Parslow?'

'Oh, she's different. She's probably been in love with Michel Shamseddine for years and, although I swear he's never laid hands on her, he's vampirised her to such an extent that she no longer has her own thoughts.'

'You astonish me! Are you sure?'

'He's possessed her. She's his creature. She tells him everything.'

This explanation was so obvious that Byrd rejected it. There was no real proof, was there? People jumped to wrong conclusions so easily. Neville had moved on: 'Where are you living? Good God! So Brophy put you in his flat with his incubus.'

'You mean Bahige?'

'Who else? He's got himself wrapped around Brophy like the old man of the sea. Brophy will never get rid of him so long as he has a thimbleful of whisky left.'

'I feel rather sorry for him.'

'He's not the sweet, wild child of nature you think he is. At one time, Brophy had some plan of social reclamation, but the man's as stupid as a rock, and now poor Paul can't get rid of him. He's got a bad conscience about him. If those two were married they'd be seeing their solicitors.'

'But the man is fond of Brophy.'

'You bet. He's tortured the life out of the poor devil – ruined his standing – told lies about him – blackened him – done everything but slit his throat.'

'He doesn't give me that impression.'

'I dare say not. He doesn't really appear like that to Brophy. Paul's a curious man – in some ways I'm very glad I've known him: he lacks the vision of evil. He can't believe anyone can do him harm; on the contrary, it's always he who is sending out little notes of apology. He seems to feel he's got to live out the idea of the holy fool. He can't do the necessary harsh thing to save himself – can't sack Bahige, can't put Mrs Parslow in her place. What he ought to do now is send a cable with fifty quid saying "BAHIGE FUCK OFF HOME AND LEAVE ME IN PEACE!"'

'You feel as strongly as that?'

'And more. I would like to send Brophy a cable – "Paul, keep your hands off young men unless you can grow up and learn the rules of the game."'

'It's very shocking!'

'Let me tell you something,' – and for at least an hour, closeted in Byrd's little room, Neville gave the low-down on Brophy's mishaps and mistakes. Byrd was at first grateful to be put clearly into the picture by someone he took to be objective; only afterwards, when he recalled a memo on the files from Brophy referring to Neville as an 'old and valued friend whose judgement one can trust', did he suspect unkindness and duplicity.

The next day Neville's greeting was: 'I hope Bahige has been picked up and deported!' But he was taken up with himself. 'You know, Reggie, one gets tired of people here quickly. The silly little social round, this forcing-house of attitudes – very few people survive the test. My sister and I were saying last night that this is a bad place for second-raters: they get seen through too quickly. It pleases me no end to think I'll be home in a year's time.'

'I love it here.' Despite MEDOC, despite the Tunisian, Byrd was saying, the experience was tremendous: ('You can see how it is; every afternoon and evening free, my week-ends my own – why, it's the sort of rest I haven't had for years. Years. It's doing me the world of good') – and Byrd pinched his biceps in his enthusiasm.

'If you play your cards well you could stay out here for a long time. I'm sure Brophy's post is going begging.'

Byrd shook his head. 'Never. I couldn't demean myself. This office shocks me too much.'

'You'd do all right. You won't make an ass of yourself. After all, what's in the job?'

'Exactly, my dear chap. Exactly. Oh, no' – reconsidering the matter – 'if Brophy can pull himself together he'll get through.'

'Never. He's in deep trouble already. He can't be helped. Don't forget that all these crazily mixed-up people have got a larger than usual death-wish. Brophy has it.'

Byrd bristled. 'I don't accept that sort of thinking. A man can pull himself together. The only really firm complaint I've heard against him is that he didn't know how to cultivate the right people. I'm sympathetic to him. I can't do that – even for my own good. To me it's really loathsome – putting a price on everybody's head, assessing everyone for his or her weak points.'

'It's a game like any other. You play it or you don't.'

Byrd was speaking of something very close to his own experience at *The Age*, where the new executives had seemed to him 'little more than murderous barbarians', whom it was impossible to understand or admire. 'How is one to ingratiate oneself with such people? To me, they represent the new Dark Age. I know it sounds pompous, but the truth is people resent good manners these days. They take them as a personal insult; they feel threatened.'

Neville laughed, but Byrd did not.

'But I mean that. There are times when one has to draw the line – "No-one-ever-taught-you-how-to-behave-so-I-will" kind of thing.'

Neville still laughed. 'You're just the man to tame Dot Parslow.' He said this, but he had had his first doubts about Byrd; he struck Neville as a bit absurd, like a grand duke after a revolution.

10

BYRD continued to renew his acquaintance with the country-side. He felt well and young and enjoyed being a tourist and connoisseur of ruins, in the English style. His free time was divided between his outings with the Exes, excursions on his own and writing.

One day, at the end of the second week, he and the Exes walked to the nearby Roman aqueduct: an enchanting walk through orange groves and pinewoods alongside terraces covered with wild flowers. It was like moving through a landscape by Poussin. There were the quiet woods, the road winding under the shadows of red rocks and the glimpses – between pine-trees – of the cobalt blue sky: a sky of that especial blue depth which Gabriel Fielding calls 'the colour of "is": the secret that's in the distance, what Italians saw when they looked in the mediaeval sky.'

Where the valley narrowed and the pathway wandered through cultivated land – about a kilometre above the aqueduct – they lost their way and wandered into the courtyard of a small country house. A woman, working at a table in the open air, greeted them. '*Tfaddalu!*' There was all the pleasure of receiving unexpected visitors in her voice; she seemed to accept them without a tremor, although it must have been years since anything like them – three middle-aged English walkers, carrying raincoats and sticks – had entered her domain. The Exes talked gardens and weather to her and accepted a glass of water. 'It's our own well. By the name of God, you won't find water like that in Baida.'

She put them on the right track, and on their way back they met a group of children returning to their homes in the orange groves. They were wearing the blue-and-grey smocks of a religious school and carried *cartables*, like French children. John Exe's greeting was met by silence, then giggles; and the group stopped a long time to stare after them, until the walkers had walked around a bluff of rock.

At this point, they dominated the city at skyscraper level. It lay in the full light of the sun under still late afternoon clouds. In the foreground was a stone bridge, leaping in one arch over churning water. It was an entirely classical landscape, where everything has been arranged for maximum pleasure for the eye: bridges over the chasm, mountains crowned with clouds and hermits' chapels, water pouring over the edges of cliffs and craggy recesses flecked with the splashings of high-flying waterfalls. The whole received its patina from the golden light from the west, which came down in prophetic intensity and profiled the arches and ruined arcades of a sanctuary sacred to some divinity since antiquity.

Before they were back in the Exes' home the spring weather had changed and a sharp rainstorm came in off the sea. But once the storm was over, even before the waterspouts from the roofs had stopped trickling, even before the first rain had fallen over in the desert, the mist lifted, and there again were umbrella pines and pink-roofed villas, jovial and intact in the evening sunlight, which was of a sombre, understated rose, as one finds in old quilts, and nostalgic as the first sunset after the Fall must have been.

11

Every day when Mrs Parslow passed with the morning post she made some remark about the fact that Brophy had not yet replied to Byrd's note about the affidavit. This took the place of the mournful and suspect questions which both she and Shamseddine asked about life in the flat. How was the Tunisian? How was he behaving? The simple answer was that Byrd had settled in well. He enjoyed the amenities of the flat, its space and silence and the way he could spread out his papers on a large table near the west balcony; and he had found a way of living there as though the Tunisian did not exist. Byrd told him not to bother with the undrinkable morning tea, used instant coffee for breakfast, lunched out nearly every day, unless he had some engagement, fried up his own evening meal while the Tunisian watched, half fascinated, half vexed. The evenings when the Tunisian had his friends in, Byrd excused himself and typed in his bedroom on a strange old machine he found in the flat. His work advanced well, for the first time for years there was a permanent and delicate thread between himself and his creations undisturbed by personal and professional concerns: a strangely satisfying experience, like going back to college again and starting out on the exploration of one's personality – what psychologists might call a second individuation.

It was about this time that Byrd began to feel he was in a film; instead of growing blasé about his surroundings and his transplanting to Baida, he grew more and more astonished. It was the form his pleasure and gratitude took. If, he appeared to say to himself, this experience had not been possible, if I had not had this time to myself, to set my life in order, to look back and assess what I have done, how much I should have lost. Time and time again, as the days passed, he reminded himself with pleasure that the experience was continuing and would do so for some weeks; he wanted the lovely life in that city, in that flat, to go on for ever.

He had moments of vexation usually over the Tunisian, and especially when he raised the question of the affidavit and spoke as though Byrd had committed himself to solving the problem. Even then, Byrd never once said flatly, 'I can't help you and I don't care what happens to you.'

Byrd was put out too, by the hysterical undertones of the Tunisian's isolation. The man had periods of depression, when he ignored Byrd, or mild drunkenness, when he wept about Brophy and his own uncertain future. 'Mr Paul had a white heart – but he leave me like this!' He would turn on Byrd angrily: 'What is to become of me? I cannot live in poor houses. I like to live like this.' Sometimes he seemed genuinely afraid. 'What if the police catch me? I have no work, no money. Nothing. They will put me in prison or send me home.'

One day, there was an especially bad scene, and Byrd was stupid enough to mention it to Mrs Parslow. She listened attentively, waiting for her moment. 'You've got to tell Uncle Fred. Really, you've got to tell him. You can't let this torture go on.'

Byrd compromised and wrote to Brophy a second time. The letter was sharp and ended: 'Although it's nothing to do with me, I hate to see a fellow-countryman behaving so badly to another. You are the only person who can end this difficulty.'

Shamseddine was told of Byrd's second letter. 'So you're writing to our gentlewoman about her poor boy. You'll never get a reply!'

It took Byrd a long time – in fact, till it was too late – to realise that no one else was bothered about the welfare of the Tunisian. People marvelled that he interfered, marvelled that he had not seen the signs and portents; had not, as the English say, heard the penny drop. No one could decide whether Byrd was naïve, obtuse or was drumming up the Tunisian affair for reasons of his own, mostly self-importance. Even in one of his letters home he said, 'I am doing my best to get the chappie's position put right,' with the suggestion that he was a new Sir Galahad.

By this time, even the junior staff, Brophy's claque, had seen through the Byrd façade and treated him like a joke. They were in a disrespectful atmosphere, where Shamseddine's *bons mots* at Byrd's expense flew around like hail, and they also saw the stubborn, patronising manner he adopted in the office. There were aspects of the old man which amused them in a kinder way – his absent-mindedness, his vague air of hovering a few inches above reality, and his kindly, if avuncular, manner. He mixed up their names, he confounded their duties, he issued instructions which were countermanded by Mrs Parslow or Shamseddine, but they thought kindly of him because he seemed old and *'miskin'* – a poor thing. As the days and weeks passed familiarity led to teasing. One day in the general office he used a wrong word in Arabic – his command had never been strong and had grown weaker – and a little group said they would teach him to speak it properly.

As a first lesson they began with his name – Byrd could be taken as 'bird' and bird in Arabic was *asfour*. Yes, Byrd remembered that. And an *asfour* could only live in one place. Yes, said Byrd. What was it? his teachers asked. You mean a cage? or an aviary? No, they said, *Asfourit*! A huge joke for *Asfourit* is the local women's prison. Byrd understood that he was being ragged and that by normal standards he was allowing them to take liberties with him, but what was the alternative? To show ill-will or resentment, or worse, disapproval, would have been pompous, ludicrous. So he laughed. He passed off the whole thing as an old horse tolerates a cloud of gnats. One of the conveniences of middle age, and one of its weaknesses, is to refuse to recognise anyone under thirty years of age as an entirely serious person. He did not feel he had to put his foot down. All the same, gradually, there were other signs that the younger MEDOC staff were pushing their luck a bit far – there were sly references to the Tunisian. 'He good friend for Mr Broffi. He good friend for you?' Byrd pretended not to know what they were hinting at, and nodded in his most grave, elderly way. 'He's a good servant. He makes good *felafel*.' This was untrue, but it gave them something new to think about.

'You like Arabic food, sir?'

'Certainly, I do.'

'Then you must come to my house and we have good time' – this from an underling whose chief distinction was that he wore sunglasses all the time.

That was the day Dr Armstrong in a routine message to Mrs Parslow, added as an addendum: 'Please tell Reggie Byrd not to lose his head over Paul's servant. Paul is surprised he has got so excited. He is under no obligation to keep the man on, since he has not been very satisfactory. He is writing to Reggie.'

Mrs Parslow, strictly speaking, should not have shown Byrd this note, but she did so with that air of false sympathy which he found intolerable. Byrd did not know what angered him more – Brophy's duplicity or Mrs Parslow's manner and the ineffable way she reminded Byrd of her warnings: 'He's not clean. He'll never clear up the matter.'

'Losing my head! Shoving me into his affairs!'

The usual MEDOC *ronde* began: Shamseddine came in to

offer spurious sympathy ('Fred's gone too far this time') while Byrd worked himself into a fine rage. 'I can't help the man and I only upset myself for nothing. I don't want my stay mucked up with these troubles.' Byrd's querulousness had all the thinness of middle age in it. Mrs Parslow was quick to remind him that he would avoid everything by moving out. 'I think you've been foolish to stay on in that place – getting involved with those disgusting people.'

'What disgusting people?'

'That bunch of queers! And their abominable behaviour.'

Byrd hated her tone. 'I'm not involved – but why talk as though we were in England? Even here, even in this office, people regard the matter as no more serious than a person wearing a funny nose or staggering a bit after too much drink. No one cares; and yet a deliberate attempt has been made to surround Brophy with odium and disrespect – as though he were the first man to be involved with another.'

'But it's disgusting! Think how it reflects on the Institute.'

'Dr Armstrong doesn't think so or he wouldn't have written that note to you. If he doesn't worry, why do you? To my mind, the illegal aspect of the case is the presence of the Tunisian in this country. Living with Brophy is no crime; being here is. No one seems to see that.'

She shook her head obstinately. 'Oh, you're all wrong, Reggie, old boy. It's that simply disgusting thing between them' – she made a mouth as though swallowing vinegar – 'I can't bear to think of it.'

'You astonish me. You've been here for years; you must know how indifferent people are to such things.'

'Oh, no,' – she shook her head – 'you've got it all wrong. It's not so common as you think. Brophy's case stands out for everyone to see.'

'Only because you've insisted on it' – he was about to say 'gossiped about it' but thought better – 'and made an issue of it. It's only remarkable because money and prestige are involved.'

'Brophy's been a fool. Had he wanted this kind of thing he should have gone out and picked up someone off the street and then flung him out!'

Byrd looked at her a long time. 'You see . . . I was right. You know what it's all about. You don't care what happens so long as it's hushed up. You shock me. You really shock me, you know.'

'Well, Reggie, old boy, you shock me. What sort of man is it tries to excuse that kind of behaviour?'

Byrd grew vexed: 'This is not England; we don't have to defend it. We have to accept it. And, in any case, human beings are human beings. They are entitled to their rights.'

'What rights?'

'Individual lives have their claims.'

'Well, in that case, those of us here have the right not to have a boss who behaves as he does. We don't like it, and we won't accept it.'

Their voices had risen; they had not heard a knock on the door: Mr Byrd was wanted on the telephone. Byrd went into his office and found himself being badgered for money by the concierge of the Blue Dome Building.

12

As in many Baida apartment houses, the concierge's lodge contained the switchboard for all the telephones in the building, and the concierge submitted a monthly account of calls out. The first one presented to Byrd covered the last weeks of Brophy's residence, and it was agreed that Brophy should be given the chance to check his own account (which had seemed high to Byrd). Brophy's reply was delayed, and the concierge, a disobliging Palestinian, grumbled. Byrd asked him to be reasonable and was left with the impression he had been given another week's grace before the phone was cut off. But he was wrong; the concierge said no such arrangement had been made and he wanted the money at once. Byrd agreed to pay. It was against his ideas to pay for someone else – caution, in his case, being on the edge of meanness – but it was either this or having the phone cut off – and, in any case, Byrd had caught the mood of the European community: it was fine to spend as much as one liked on pleasure, but it revolted one's sense of fair play to pay a bill to which the poverty-stricken concierge had added his little surplus.

That evening, Byrd tried to ring the Exes. The concierge picked up the phone downstairs and bawled, 'No money! No telephone!' in a barbaric manner.

Byrd went downstairs and was met by the concierge's wife, who said she knew nothing about the telephone. So Byrd barged into the private room off the hall and found the concierge listening to a transistor radio and dipping pieces of bread into a mixture of olive oil and *zaatar*, mixed up on an aluminium plate. A fair amount of oil shone on his unshaven chops. Byrd went up to him. 'If my telephone isn't reconnected at once, I'll tell the police about the prostitutes on the fourth floor!'

This was an old gag with local concierges, and it worked. The man bawled at his wife and blamed her for the incident. 'She is as stupid as a cow. She never understands.'

Byrd was ready, in his own phrase, to 'clip the man over the earhole'. 'Don't lie to me. You shouted at me like a pig!'

'Please, let me explain.' The concierge wiped his mouth with the back of his hand. 'You see, sir, we have much trouble with Mr Broffi. His water bill! His electricity bill! His telephone bill! Every month, something he not wanna pay. He not wanna pay this. He not wanna pay that. He gives me whole *lod* of trouble all the time. His drains go block, his boy throw dirts in the yard. I have much work to clear. No. He just don't wanna help me.' Then, changing his tone, shaking his head and moving closer to Byrd, 'Who is this Mr Broffi? And that Mr Pierre? He says he is Frenchman, but he speaks Arabic. What are they doing? People say bad things about them. They say they are spies.'

'Spies? I never heard such rot. Rubbish. You get your facts right and put me back on the line.' And, just to be unpleasant, Byrd refused to settle the telephone account until the morning.

That evening, he was as exasperated as he had ever been; he felt hemmed in on all sides by unscrupulous people who refused to let him enjoy his holiday. For the first time, he included Brophy and Armstrong in his anger and, for the first time, it no longer seemed possible to live on in the apartment. How he longed to have a place of his own and be free of Mrs Parslow's questions and the Tunisian's whinings and the

muddle created by Brophy. Why should he have to be humiliated by scruffy, semi-Americanised concierges or stay on in a
situation where a sense of fair play, where a refusal to be
shocked, amounted to complicity or worse?

Once the idea had lodged itself in Byrd's mind that he was
doing himself no good by staying on in Brophy's flat, it needed
very little to dislodge him. Three incidents finally influenced
him.

13

NEVILLE had described Byrd to his sister as 'resembling some
old Hegelian at Göttingen, forever walking towards his private
patch of blue sky' and had also described, in terms of comedy,
Byrd's position in the office, his whistling and humming to
himself, his apparent refusal to become a useful member of the
organisation, his refusal to alter his ways or show any interest
in MEDOC, and the way the members of the staff made fun of
him behind his back and to his face; and what a comedown
the whole thing was for a former diplomatic correspondent of
The Age. Neville's wickedly accurate eye had also seen that
Byrd was at great pains to shake off Mrs Parslow and gave the
impression he thought she was after him.

Neville had suggested Byrd should meet his sister, but no
arrangement was fixed, and then, one day, they met in the
city art gallery, where an Armenian woman, the wife of a port
official, was exhibiting. Byrd was presented to Rhoda between a
huge gaudy scene of village life entitled 'Wedding in the
Mountains' and an equally huge and gaudy one entitled
'Funeral in the Mountains'.

'Isn't it all fun?' she asked Byrd, indicating the whole room.
She was tickled to death, she said, by this new evidence of the
sophistication of the local people. At the end of the first world
war, the number of Baidani painters could be counted on one
hand; two generations later, the local middle class were sufficiently educated, they felt, to need, and get, their own primitives

and, what is more, of the same sex as Grandma Moses. Madame Hagopian knew a thing or two; she had more than one style up her sleeve.

Hardly had they arrived in the gallery when a door opened and in she bustled. She introduced herself to Rhoda and offered to paint her portrait from a photograph. Rhoda saw herself like the purple-cheeked abominations outside the Arabic cinemas and cabarets and shook her head. Ah, said Madame Hagopian, many Americans had asked her to paint the view from their balconies, so that they had a souvenir of their stay; she was sure Rhoda had a balcony and a favourite view.

It was a charming, an enchanting idea, Rhoda said, but what was the price? The woman thought a minute, assessed Rhoda's shoes, gloves and handbag and named a figure not far in excess of two hundred pounds sterling. Rhoda flinched. Madame Hagopian looked at her severely. Didn't Madame realise that this was the price? '*Et ce serait encore plus, Madame, si je la faisais à la primitive.*' She nodded eagerly to drive home her point. '*Je sais faire les deux, madame: des tableaux à la primitive et à la classique. C'est comme vous voulez. Comme vous voulez.*'

To stop giggling, Rhoda cupped her face in her gloved hands. '*Je suis sûre que mon mari serait content d'en avoir. Mais il se trouve à Bahrain à ce moment; il faut attendre son retour.*'

Going down to the street, Byrd invited the brother and sister to take tea with him, and as Rhoda had a longing for toast and tea there was only one place to go – the St Andrew's Club.

They wandered through the carpet shops and the dealers in fine porcelain towards the seashore and arrived there just as a startling sunset of purple, black and gold was turning the avenue of palms into cut-outs. The purple-black sea was curled with minute waves.

They looked into Madame Boutaboulo's shop window to see what archaeological loot she was selling and came out on the open pavement in front of the Grand Hotel. This, Rhoda said, was the oldest hostelry in the city, a link with a vanished world, and if Byrd had never seen it he ought to go in. Within a couple of years it would be sold, then pulled down to make way for the sort of hideous development which had gone on a little higher up the hill. The old building with its graceful Ottoman proportions, ogive windows and fine balconies reflected the evening light.

They climbed a steep flight of stairs and came out on a high terrace above the street with a view across the bay. They ordered coffee and walked into the central reception room to drink it. Seated on old-fashioned sofas, they looked round at the sparkling collection of mother-of-pearl inlaid Damascene furniture, the old Moorish lustres, the candle-holders on the wall and the painted wooden ceiling, which was touched by the sunset.

An old lady came forward and recognising Rhoda from some past visit, spoke to them with an exquisite civility about the house, about the people who wanted to buy it and the rooms filled with too many memories and beautiful things to destroy. '*Oui,*' she said, sighing, '*c'est plein de belles choses.*'

The coffee and water were set down on small tables. '*Regardez, madame, regardez ce vieux tableau qui date de l'époque quand les voyageurs venaient directement du bateau dans la rade jusqu'aux limites de notre jardin. Il n'y avait pas ce boulevard. La maison se dressait sur les falaises.*'

'*Ah, c'est beau. C'est spacieux.*'

The old lady drank coffee with them and, holding her cup and saucer as one piece, in the Mediterranean way, looked about her with ancestral pride.

'*Je me demande si vous pouvez faire allumer les chandelles.*'

'*Mais certainement, madame; avec plaisir.*'

A servant moved from candle-sconce to candle-sconce and slowly brought the huge high room to life. As the lights went on and the pieces of lustre, mother-of-pearl and mirror picked up the glow, a whole new world of light was revealed: for a moment they were back in the evenings of the 1860s, in a time which still recalled Lamartine and Alfred de Vigny. The effect was outside Byrd's experience, especially as the golden aura was mingled with the rose-tinted evening light which still lingered on the upper reaches of the walls. When the candles were put out and the electric lights went on, the hotel was once more merely an old hostelry where few people cared to stay for long because of the plumbing and the smells from the drains.

The woman refused to accept payment for the coffee. '*C'est mon plaisir, je vous assure.*' So they tipped the servants generously, before strolling past the fish restaurants and the cabarets to the St Andrew's Club, where, despite their recent coffee, they were ready for toast and tea.

Byrd could not thank Rhoda enough for organising the little festival of lights. As an organiser and a manipulator, this was exactly the kind of thing she enjoyed laying on for friends. She nodded graciously. 'Don't you think your knowledge of a place has to be total? My husband won't see this; he never bothers to read up a place and so misses most of the flavour, since he doesn't know what's new and what's old. Most of the people in this club are like that. They think this is Baida, and miss a whole world of poetic feeling. That's the life here. If the poetic nerve isn't touched it isn't truly itself. That's why I'm so in love with this place.'

She sipped her tea from a white-and-gold cup.

'Hasn't Paul got some lovely things? Those mirrors which he picked up in Damascus, and those sumptuous local materials? He knows a lot about antiques.'

'A most splendid place. It ought to be better looked after.'

This was a fatuous ill-judged remark, and Rhoda asked whether he meant the Tunisian was neglecting things.

'He's so-so.'

'Such a sweet young fellow, like a teddy-bear with a gorgeous, warm voice. But not one of the world's great cooks.'

Byrd reacted rashly: 'But he isn't a cook. He's Paul Brophy's friend.'

Rhoda looked at Byrd. 'So you think his relationship with Paul Brophy is an emotional one, as everyone says?'

'That's the sixty-four million dollar question.'

'I can never make up my mind.'

'Does it matter? Isn't it private? I mean, personal relationships are private.'

'Not in the Arab world, where nothing is private. Every little detail is of interest. The women who work for me know better than I do when my monthly curse is due. It's one of the facts of the household like the bedroom I sleep in.'

'Good God!'

'Surely that's understood? Matters which we glide over or try to hide are of the greatest interest to the Arabs and get discussed openly. Why shouldn't people ask me why I'm childless? At home, they would assume I was taking the pill; here they think the husband is at fault. A good-looking man like Paul Brophy – seen to be alone – never has girl-friends but me, a married woman – brings in this dishy fellow from Tunis to live with him – so what are people to think? They think they are lovers.'

'That could apply to me, as well.' Byrd laughed with a sort of false innocence.

She misunderstood him. 'Of course. People tend to tar with the same brush. Only the other day, my stepmother, who's staying with us, asked whether you were the same kind of person as Paul Brophy, because you were staying in his flat. She thought you were sharing the boy-friend, too.'

'Good God!'

Neville was furious. 'The Duchess is the silliest cow on God's earth. No one takes her questions seriously.'

'Still, it shows you what these silly little minds dwell on. She and Mrs Shamseddine and the abominable Victoria.' Rhoda set down her cup and looked at Byrd coolly, from under her cinema-queen eyelids. 'I'm glad you don't care about all this stupid talk. If you bothered about other people's opinions you'd get nowhere.'

'I'm sorry, but I *do* care. I'd hate to be lumped with Paul Brophy.'

'I thought you didn't care and were openly defying convention by staying at the flat.'

'"Openly defying convention"! Not a bit of it. My dear child, I was put there by our father-figure, Dr Armstrong, and Paul Brophy; and – what's more – I get two pounds a day less for the pleasure of being compromised.'

'Oh, *quelle deception! Je vous ai vu beaucoup plus grand!* – a person after my own style. My husband spends all his time making fun of me or picking me to pieces. Somehow I don't care.'

'Tell me, my dear, Neville's sister – I'm sorry, I never caught your full name – do you think it's a good thing for me to get this reputation?'

She thought a while. 'Oh. . . . You're only here a short time.'

'Granted. Say, on the other hand, something stuck – got back home – what sort of ass would I look to my wife and children?'

'All that's highly unlikely. Aren't you exaggerating?'

'There's a possibility.'

'If I were your wife it would probably amuse me. After all, we've passed beyond blood guilt and guilt by association, haven't we? I'm disappointed you worry so much. I thought your attitude was rather sane. Don't you agree, Neville?'

'I don't think we ought to say anything.' – he kicked her foot under the low table – 'No purpose is served.'

She deliberately ignored him and turned to Byrd: 'I can see your point, all the same, and in some ways I think you're running an unnecessary risk. I wouldn't want anyone of mine to live there for long. Even I, who get a good deal of pleasure from Paul's company, realise there's a real twist in him. He's not really straight. Well,' – seeing Neville's face – '*I* don't think so.'

'I mean,' she went on, 'would a normal person keep that pathetic Tunisian a prisoner? It's like something out of Proust. And a normal person wouldn't put an innocent outsider into the middle of the sort of drama which is going on between himself and the Tunisian. What is more,' – Rhoda looked lucidly at her brother and then at Byrd – 'Bahige told me how much he hated being handed over with the flat like a machine.'

'Well, there's no need to turn the whole thing into a tragedy.'

Rhoda sipped her tea. 'I never said it was tragic. Just a mess.'

'Don't look at me so accusingly, darling. I'm not saying anything. When I suggested the same thing you accused me of disloyalty.'

'Oh, well. Opinions change. Don't you agree?' She gave Byrd a brilliant smile. 'Nothing's more boring than people who never grow on the corpses of their dead selves.'

Neville thought of his sister's marriage: 'It's not true, alas! You don't grow on dead selves. You go round in circles and hold three different opinions in as many hours.'

'That's my charm. It's very feminine to know a thing is true, and to ignore it because it's awkward.'

They laughed, but the men were not happy.

Rhoda, in a sense, corrupted Byrd, and for the first time he felt embarrassed in the Tunisian's company – not because he represented a problem which no one could solve and Byrd felt responsible for, but because he was a figure in a public scandal, whose friendship, whose presence even, compromised. Byrd, becoming self-conscious, thought he was living like a man in a lighted room at night, visible to all outside; and, as such a man, he felt vaguely menaced, vaguely unsure of himself.

14

THE second incident: Another bad night for Byrd with 'Gippy stomach' and vague sense of being ill-at-ease. The next morning, he had a brush with the Americans living in the flat opposite Brophy's.

The Tunisian, in his dumb way, had told him they were missionaries studying Arabic at the university. The women in their big ballooning skirts dangling mid-calf and with their equally big and shapeless shoulder-bags, swinging behind their shapeless posterior, fascinated him. Byrd met the menfolk – tall, stooped, full of vague goodwill to all and sundry – as they hurried in and out of the building with bundles of papers, files and notebooks. There was an earnestness, a paleness, a scrupulousness as to hair-style and spectacles which were intimidating. In a world that saw the United States in a series of clichés ranging through Hollywood flam-flam, Wild West ruggedness, Kinseyesque sexual obsession, Deep South aristocracy, and Manhattan elegance, these people were the visual corrective. As they walked about – the women with hair drawn back tightly showing crisp little ears – the men, crew-cut and dressed in sub-Scottish tweeds and big flat shoes – they represented the American conscience: puritan, nonconformist, naïve, remarkably courageous and self-sacrificing, with wills of steel.

Altogether, three couples shared the apartment, with a local Presbyterian cook. The Tunisian had been approached by this woman, a convert from Islam, and asked to attend prayer meetings in the apartment. Showered with tracts and Arabic equivalents of *The Good News*, the man had grown vexed and unresponsive. Byrd heard the woman sing strange, debased versions of popular hymns and came to the conclusion she was slightly mad. 'They sing before they eat too!' the Tunisian informed him, faintly scandalised. 'They pray the devil fuck off while they eat.'

And what meals! According to the Tunisian, they hardly ever had meat but ate quantities of a paste made of nuts. Nobody drank alcohol or smoked.

'They are drunk with God!' was the best explanation Byrd could give, but the Tunisian had understood all along, since religious exaltation and abstemiousness were commonplace in Islam. To find it among Christians had been unexpected.

Byrd's first encounter with the missionaries was in the lift. 'Good morning, sir! Another wonderful day!' the conversation began and ended with an invitation to drop in 'since we're in the same building'. A second encounter seemed less warm, and Byrd imagined they looked at him disapprovingly.

The American missionaries' view of Brophy's establishment was made clear on the day a workman came to replace the lock on the front door and the Americans, flushed from a breakfast of hymns and peanut butter, stood outside their front door and openly gaped into Brophy's flat, in the same way that the Calvinistic elect – despite themselves – stare over the cloud-banks into hell. Reggie Byrd, late as ever, hurried out and then stopped short at the sight of so many earnest and awe-stricken faces.

'Good morning.' There was no reply. Byrd saw a pale American baby in a Carrycot on the landing floor. 'Can I help you carry the baby?'

The watchers shook themselves with one impulse, gave a collective 'No thank you!' snatched up the baby's Carrycot and retreated indoors. Byrd went down in the lift alone, haunted by the reproving American eyes and the American brush-off. Did they think he would harm or corrupt the baby? Did one laugh? Did one get annoyed? What must have gone on in the flat to arouse such distrust? What could they have heard? Byrd could ignore them – they meant nothing to him – but could not ignore any more that living in Brophy's flat was a perilous undertaking and becoming increasingly dear in terms of peace of mind. Yet he could not make up his mind to leave. He enjoyed the luxury of the place and the freedom. He was in a cat's-cradle of other people's hysteria over the scandal, and his own preoccupation with putting away enough cash for his wife's holiday. There was no way of resolving the tangle with his prestige intact.

15

THEN came the third incident. At the end of the week Brophy himself wrote a cold resentful letter, of inordinate length, accusing Byrd of making a fuss about nothing 'for no good reason I can see' and telling him to stop bothering about the Tunisian, pay the telephone account ('You make hard work of everything, I'm sorry to say'), more instructions for the Tunisian's welfare, but no mention of an affidavit.

Mrs Parslow was, of course, scandalised by the letter and said Brophy must have had Armstrong's backing before he'd have written it. Byrd was sick with resentment and bad temper.

The Exes, to whom he gave the latest developments, were firm: he had no alternative but to leave the flat.

'I'm sorry, Reggie, to tell you this: you should have gone away a long time ago. You tried to do the impossible.'

He had to explain his fears that if he started creating a fuss Dr Armstrong would recall him. 'I'm enjoying it so much. Apart from this, everything's fine.' The Exes knew Byrd was revelling in his second spring; they also knew a matter of principle was involved, and his behaviour could not be weighed indefinitely against his comfort, his money or even his stay in Baida.

All Byrd's instincts were to say nothing, to let things work themselves out, not to upset his own pleasures, but he knew the Exes were right: he was in a dreadful predicament; he was heartbroken at having to make a decision which could end his stay before time – money, pleasure, vanity were all involved.

That Saturday, returning with the Exes and some of their friends from an excursion, Byrd made up his mind to leave Brophy's flat and tell Armstrong why and demand his extra two pounds a day expenses as a right. He would write a hard, brutal letter; the kind that had to be listened to.

The day had been perfect. They had taken their meal among the olive-yards with long perspectives over the southern hills, over the Mediterranean and over the Zeivar roads, where the giant oil-tankers were anchored off the terminal. Susan Exe had put up a good meal with white wine cooled in a portable ice-box. Everyone was happy, agreeable; and as they lay on rugs at the edge of the wilderness, smoking, talking about their children back in England, there had been an ease, an absence of uncertainty, which took Byrd back God knows how many years to the sort of excursions he had taken as an undergraduate, when people had been sure of themselves, when everything in the future had seemed cut and dried – the laurels, the cheers, the acclamations a matter of form, the form of success dependent entirely on choice, as between several different cheeses on a board.

That spring evening the light was Delian: it was the light Claude Lorrain had mastered; its disappearance into the gaudiness of the sunset was a matter for profound regret. The memory of it and the day that preceded it would leave a certain stillness. The western sky, in all its richness, seemed like a message, a letter to the world.

Little people, it seemed to say, you are wasting your lives on trivialities and in pursuing small ends, while the truth of existence, the things that give meaning to it, are these evening skies, the kindness of your friends, the beauty of the day.

It was a brief message, a letter on one side of the paper only, for within minutes the Mediterranean sunset was over, the night had come down like a cat, and the Pharos twinkled like a dogstar across the sea.

16

THE moment the letter to Armstrong was written, the trap sprung and Brophy finished, Mrs Parslow changed at once. 'I shall cable London for authorisation for your extra allowances. Salima will phone round the hotels. I'll tell Michel.'

Shamseddine disguised his triumph under the long, mournful face of condolence. 'You're right, Reggie. You're right. You can't live on in a brothel like that. Paul Brophy is a sick boy, and it's time Fred knew the full facts. We've had to live here month after month knowing all the filth and not feeling able to say a word. We've sat here many times, haven't we Dot, and Dot has been crying and wondering how in God's name we were to save the Institute from the scandal, and I haven't known what to do. Many times I thought of resigning. I've been on the point of signing the letter – but Dot has begged me to stay on.'

'Fred can do what he likes. It can't go on like this.'

'Honesty is the best policy.'

Mrs Parslow sighed and looked cosily at Byrd; she could not have loved him more at that moment had she made him herself.

Ignoring, for the moment, the implications of her warmth towards him, Byrd said he would have to write to Brophy as well.

'Never!' Mrs Parslow jumped up in horror. 'It will make Fred's task twice as difficult.'

So, only one letter was written. Despite his majestic rationalisations about individual lives having their claims, Byrd could not tell the truth to the Tunisian; despite his apparent concern for his position, he walked out on him with a lie. He had been called away and would later live with friends. No, Mr Paul had not sent a letter.

The Tunisian began to drivel about money. He had none left. Where had it gone to? The Tunisian shrugged. It had gone; it was like a magical substance, he implied; it disappeared while he was enjoying himself. In essence, it was a repetition of their very first chat about money, only now Byrd knew it had gone on gambling and whisky, on foolish spendthrift living.

Anyone else but Byrd would have laughed, but Byrd the thorough, Byrd the stylist, had to make a long face and repeat, 'I haven't anything to spare, I'm afraid.'

The Tunisian looked hangdog, empty. No one could pretend he was an intellectual, satisfied with books from the British Council library; he was a small-town waster, no more, no less, who was out of his depth, who, in his own eyes, had done only one wrong thing – trusted Paul Brophy.

He made a Turkish coffee, and he and Byrd sat on the balcony staring at one another in a defeated, perplexed way.

'I think all day. I think, I think. I try to think why Mr Paul leave me here like this. He no more good for me. He tired of me. He wants I go away. I say to him one time, two time, many time, I go from him but I stay here. I want study, learn *Bachot*, earn money and get rich. He want I go away to Lebanon. I want to stay in Baida. I have a friend I want to marry and have home and children.'

For the first time, Byrd did not believe him. He saw no sign of any particular talent waiting for a *permis de séjour* to be released. There was nothing in the man; he was emptiness itself; and rotten with self-pity. He had added another tic to his repertoire, which already included nose-picking, foot-rubbing and scratching his head: he began to fiddle with his teeth and rub his gums mournfully.

Byrd had lost patience with the Englishman; now he lost patience with the Tunisian: 'My dear chap, you're best bet is to go home.'

'I think so, too. Mr Paul is not coming back any more. His enemies in his office say he is finished. That is what that boy Mounir, who is Mr Shamseddine's friend, tells me.'

'What boy, Mounir?'

It was beyond the Tunisian's power to describe him – his visual imagination being almost nil – and he kept repeating, 'He is Mr Shamseddine's friend.'

'I didn't know Mr Shamseddine had a friend.'

'Yes, he tells him all the secrets about Mr Paul when he was here with Mr Paul one evening, when he was drunk.'

'Who was drunk?'

'Mr Paul was drunk. He drink too much all the time. He sit in his chair and drink until he slip to the ground, and I find him in the morning. He worry because nobody like him in the office.'

Very cautiously, Byrd tried to find out what 'secrets' Mounir could have told Shamseddine; but no rational account of the evening was forthcoming. The Tunisian went on massaging his gums and looking dreary. Then he lit a cigarette and stared moodily at the package. 'Mr Paul very happy in Tunis. Always he laugh; always he make ready we do things. Here he sit and look sad and drink. He always very sad in Baida. I say to him,

"Is it me that make you sad?" And he say, "How? You are my friend." He kiss me on my face. You cannot make me sad, he say. So I think if we go back to Tunis we be happy again.'

It might have been true – stranger things had been true in the past – but Byrd began to wonder how much was wishful thinking. Could it be that something grave had happened between the two before he arrived? He wondered, while the Tunisian praised Tunis. The people there were different from the local ones, not like the Baidanis at all. 'In Tunis, we speak from here,' – he touched his chest.

It was the old rigmarole about the sincerity of the people in the home town, and it struck Byrd as hollow.

'Once I speak to Madame Rhoda about him.'

'And what did she say?'

'She say Mr Paul drink to forget. He has many worries. I say to Madame Rhoda why she not ask him about his worries because he loves her like a sister. She shook her head; she could never ask such questions.'

Suddenly Byrd was as bored with the whole affair as he was resentful. Why should he sit there with the man feeling the guilt, suffering from the scruples which Brophy so clearly did not feel? It was not Byrd who had falsely promised anyone a place in some university and a life of ease. Byrd could have damned them all for upsetting his stay, 'and more fool me for trying to help.'

On Monday he told Neville he was leaving the flat for a 'small residential hotel'. Neville had misgivings; he hoped Byrd had not been swayed by his sister. Byrd shook his head. Everything had closed in on him at once. 'Truth is, I've lost sympathy with all of them. That Tunisian chappie played on my soft spot – he's a bad lot. I sometimes wonder whether anything he says is true.'

Byrd smiled self-indulgently. 'I know I shall be criticised for leaving him in the lurch. I've done my best for him, and got nothing but bullets in return. I haven't the authority to deal with the *imbroglio*. Come to think of it, don't think I should be expected to. Not as a temp.'

Neville had slowly learned to dislike the tedious quality in Byrd, a seeping greyness, like a pile of wet wood-shavings. His determination not to be involved, not to take responsibility, was the essence of middle-aged selfishness grasping at the good things of life too tardily offered. This selfishness and the real wish to get the best of all worlds, were half-masked by an obstinate fatuousness: a capacity to turn everything he refused to do into a breach of decorum; people 'should have known better than to ask'. Neville put it down to hypocrisy; Byrd himself was nervously aware that all this was a cloak for inadequacy: he no longer knew how to handle such a situation. In any case, no doubt, he argued he was not an active participant in the events in MEDOC, and in the interests of his own comfort he abandoned all thought of leadership; and he wanted this to be known. He made a public issue of his own helplessness.

Sensing confusion and dismay in Byrd, Neville could not resist taking the opportunity to get in a dig at Bethlehem Lodge, a strange half-missionary establishment. Did Byrd know it 'catered exclusively for the evangelical trade?' Its food was lousy and its standards of comfort worse. Byrd was not shaken. He was not going there to enjoy himself, he said; he was out to save money so that he could give his wife a decent holiday. 'All very well for you carefree bachelors to make the bright spots. Wait till you get a teenage family and you'll appreciate the chance to put a little aside.' Byrd claimed he and his wife had not had a decent holiday together for years, and although he insisted he was not complaining, the fact that he made the remark at all was plainly meant as a commentary on the injustice of things. Neville hated people talking poverty and asked Byrd what he had done with his money, briskly, like a police inspector.

Everything, apparently, had gone on schools, on fees, on schools, on more fees. Too many children, too few family trusts and legacies, too few scholarships available. It all came back to the familiar theme of shiny suits and no poetry – Byrd's well-tried monologue. Why did he talk in such a way, Neville wondered, so deficient in ordinary pride? Armstrong had listened to him because he had wanted to use his services, Neville was not obliged to be tolerant and dismissed the Byrd sacrifice with a toss of a phrase. 'Blessed if I'd sacrifice myself to send *my* kids to expensive schools unless I could afford it. If I were such a kid I'd resent my parents' efforts until the day I died. Imagine hearing your parents discussing making ends meet for the sake of school fees.'

Byrd resented this deeply. 'We never discuss such things in front of the children.'

'Well, what's wrong with State schools?'

'Wouldn't look at them. Not the same thing at all.'

'Why not? Some marvellous schools in London.'

'I don't feel I can deprive my children of the benefits I enjoyed myself. I'm surprised you feel you could.'

'Why not? These things had value in 1910. No longer.'

Byrd made a strange sound in his throat and nostrils, like a strangled laugh. 'You must be living in some cloud-cuckoo-land if you think it's not important where people went to school. People still like the type.'

Byrd became vexed and lost the balance needed for dealing with a Neville. He thought Neville was 'at the bolshy-minded stage'. He thought he and Susan Exe should get together. Mrs Exe, it seemed, was a 'leveller'. She was teaching at one of the most expensive private schools in the Arab world but wanted everyone in Britain 'to go comprehensive'; it seemed she blamed all Britain's deficiencies on the public schools and the class system. Neville could not make out how much the lady really believed this and how much had been ideas pulled out of a drawer to fling at Byrd; it sounded more like the latter. Neville would have postulated the most absurd things in order to vex Reggie Byrd, in the same way as his sister had jabbed at him for staying on in the Brophy flat.

'I'd like to meet your Mrs Exe, Reggie; I'm sure we'd agree there's no point in going to the stake in the interests of snobbery.'

Byrd was vexation itself. 'Rubbish. You'll think very differently when you're my age. Everything's justified if it helps your kids get on. I hope by the time you reach this stage you'll have a little more security and comfort than *I* have. Take a few tips from me about how not to play your hand.'

'You've done well enough; you've tried to do too much. Too much sacrifice is bad for you.'

'That's the difference between us. At my age, sacrifice is second nature.'

Byrd thought Neville's silence meant he had been crushed by this glorious remark; he had merely lost interest in the subject and allowed Byrd the last word. This did not lessen

Byrd's vexation. He considered Neville ill-bred to make fun of him – the last reaction he had expected.

Byrd was a great one for his loyalties and severe about bad faith and failure to serve; what was there to see in Neville de Vries but a traitor to school, class and family? This was a come-down; and he never thought the same of Neville again; more, he was suspicious of him.

17

THE Tunisian watched him gather his cases together resentfully. Byrd avoided his eye. As he was leaving he was challenged: 'They say you are not going to Cairo, but to a hotel. Why do you leave me here?'

'Oh, do they? Whoever "they" are know more than I do.'

The Tunisian was baffled by Byrd's departure and his show of two consciences; he would never understand Europeans.

If Byrd had imagined there was anything of special virtue in his behaviour, nobody had noticed. The next day, he was waylaid by his 'teachers' in the general office with special lessons for him. Mrs Parslow saved him from them; she wanted to know how he had found his new accommodation, and Byrd gave her a report on the pleasures of Bethlehem Lodge. The 'teachers' tried again, and this time Shamseddine intervened. 'Leave the old man alone. He's had to leave Paul Brophy's flat because the Tunisian was on his tail. By God, they say he is thinking of going to Israel to beg Ben Gurion on his knees to put the army between him and that bastard son of Bourguiba.' Shamseddine had turned Byrd into a figure of fun. The point of the jokes was always the same: Byrd thought he was somebody and was *sifr*; Byrd considered himself an Englishman *d'un serieux compassé*, but was an ass. While the jokes flew over his head Byrd went on with his thriller.

About eleven he called for a coffee, and as Shamseddine was ingratiating himself with the censor, there was nobody to hold the 'teachers' in check.

'By God, Mr Byrd, in my village, *asfour* mean a prick!'

'A what?'

'A prick! Do you see,' – embarrassing gesture.

'Really?' A pause. 'Well, why not?'

Those who had not grasped, asked what had been said. *'Laysh la?'* They looked at one another. Was the old man joking? 'Yes, sir, why not? In my village they say to you in the morning *'Kif sayed asfour?'* You known what that mean?'

'I'm not going to your village, if I can help it.'

'Shu? Shu? What? What did he say?' Another translation and Mr Byrd was in great demand; everyone appeared to clamour for him at once. One pushed himself forward. 'Say after me, *"Futu fawki!"* '

'I'm busy.'

They refused to let him pass. They said it was his lesson for the day. They begged him and so, to get rid of them, Byrd repeated the phrase. At the same time, Shamseddine, startled by the noise, came to his door, and heard the 'lesson'.

'Reggie, you must change your teachers. They're teaching you bad things. You have just asked someone to "do" you.'

What hurt Byrd most was the triumph in Shamseddine's face, his pleasure at the Byrd discomfort. 'I suppose you think that's funny, Michel! I don't. It shows the standard of discipline here and the respect for the European staff.'

Still bland with amusement, Shamseddine said Byrd was taking matters too seriously. No harm was meant. Byrd had his hand on his door. 'By your standards it's good clean fun, no doubt.' He slammed the door, and Shamseddine sat down to wipe away the tears gathered in his eyes; as an Arab, he could not stop laughing at the Englishman's humiliation. 'Now, listen, boys. Don't go too far with the old man. I'm serious. I know I'm laughing, but I mean it. He's too old for these excitements. Leave him in peace with his crosswords and his mystery novels.'

Byrd left an hour before time, without saying good-bye to anyone. Shamseddine sent Neville after him to explain that no harm had been meant and to offer to drive him home. Byrd suspected Neville, but accepted Shamseddine's kind thought and got into the car.

'Am I wrong to let these things get under my skin? I feel at a disadvantage, having no authority and no real job of any kind. Those beggars seem to know I'm in an awkward position and play me up. I've never liked the Arabs. I'd forgotten how vile they are.'

'It's a different approach,' said Neville. 'By their own standards, they aren't being especially scabrous.'

'I'd been thinking of complaining to Dr Armstrong.'

'You feel so strongly?'

'There are limits. I've reached mine – between Brophy and the general slackness. I've had to impose myself more than once on that Aussie woman and rebuked her for a loose tongue. Since then, I've studiously refrained from going to her parties. I've ticked Brophy off by letter, and if I had authority here I'd now be going over Michel Shamseddine. I'm sorry to seem stuffy. One doesn't expect people in a British concern to behave in that way. I'd sack the whole boiling, sprinkle the office with D.D.T. and begin again. Degenerate, hateful people.'

Neville, producing vapours of sympathy in order to make Byrd go on, said human relations in MEDOC were bad because there was a struggle for money and prestige.

'What prestige?' Byrd turned to stare at Neville. 'You've got "off" values, if you think there's any prestige here.'

'I don't. *They* do.'

'It's all Armstrong's fault. He's let the place slip out of his control. You can be sure of one thing, that if I hadn't given him my word to see him through this period, I'd go home tomorrow.' The self-importance and show of loyalty disguised an abject wish to stay and, despite his words and brave condemnation of the 'damnable den of intrigue', he felt better. 'The joke's on me, I've no doubt. I said I knew the Arab world and hadn't realised how much things have changed since I lived here. Anyway, let me buy you a drink.'

They stopped at a restaurant in Azurah and took a table in the open air. The first drink, the prospect of the southern coast, the fishing-boats on the horizon with their antique-shaped sails: this was what his stay was all about. Byrd pinched his biceps in his enthusiasm.

'I've been made to seem an unbelievable greenhorn over the Tunisian affair. Everyone but yours truly got the message months ago. There was I with my ideas of English fair play trying to get a square deal for him – and the man was a sponger and rogue of the first water. I jolly well cleared off as soon as I got the score. One of the disadvantages of a classical education is that you imagine *paederastia* must always be something noble and uplifting – as it was, perhaps, in ancient Greece. One takes it far too seriously, because one doesn't understand what is involved. The joke's really on me.'

Byrd was making another confession which disguised his real discomfort. 'I must have looked an absolute prune.' He suggested – all the same – that it was *bon ton* to be a prune in the circumstances; only a rotter would have been alerted.

Neville listened and watched bemused; he could not believe such a person existed. He held his breath, listening. Once or twice he touched his cuffs.

'Of course, it helped when I tumbled on the rivalry between Brophy's chappie and Shamseddine's minion – the one in the dark glasses.' Byrd threw back his head in pleasure, hardly able to speak for laughter. 'I mean, my dear chap, supper with the Borgias must have been dull compared with MEDOC. Ahahahhaaa! And poor Dot Parslow thinks everything would run like silk if Brophy were to go. Ahaahhhahah!'

Byrd ordered a second round. He said he knew exactly where Armstrong had gone wrong: he had abdicated, and in the Arab world 'that's fatal. You've got to be seen to rule; you've got to be merciless.'

A faint irony touched Neville's 'You really think that?'

'My dear boy, in the Arab world no one can rule and show pity. The Arabs like to feel the snaffle and reins. They're a feminine people and have to be treated as such.'

These were the accents of outer suburbia for Neville, the voice of the wandering salesman back from foreign parts in time for a Sunday morning beer at the local and his moment of omniscience.

'I think that's all balls.'

Byrd cocked his head. 'I didn't realise you were one of those waffly, liberal types, but I bet your father would have agreed with me. I know what I'm saying – an organisation that has a Shamseddine in charge must be run by an idiot.'

Neville pointed out how difficult it was to find a man almost equally fluent in English and Arabic, with a knowledge of French, economics and business methods as well. Byrd swung round at once. 'Michel's a formidable brain. Fantastic command of English. I've never heard a non-Englishman speak

better English.' Byrd only recalled two mistakes; once Shamseddine had said 'nature-scene' when he meant a 'landscape
painting'; the other time he used 'gossips' – in the plural –
instead of 'gossip'.

Byrd's drinks had put fresh heart into him. He went on
and on about what he would do with MEDOC if he had
authority, and his purge made Neville forget the time. Byrd
seized the chits. 'They're on me.' He was like a man who has
backed a good horse.

18

NEVILLE was lunching with his sister. She had set the table out
on the terrace and was drinking white wine and reading the
airmail *Times* when he arrived. Although The Consort was
still away, Rhoda kept to the usual late lunch-hour and was
hungry.

Neville drew up the white chair to the table and unfolded a
napkin. 'I've been having a drink with Mr Pooter, alias Reggie
Byrd. I misjudged him. I thought he was P. G. Wodehouse and
I find he's Grossmith. He has this unnerving capacity for producing banalities out of a hat like white rabbits.'

'Such as?'

'He claims he's now woken up to the score between Paul
and his Tunisian. He calls him "his chappie"! God! He's so
absurd, such a well-bred, genteel goon! Nobody tells him anything, he never grasps anything because of his good taste.
He's a sort of caricature of English hypocrisy disguising itself
as obtuseness.'

'Is that especially English? Don't you remember that unspeakable Baptist homespun girl, pretending she didn't know
why the place near the Plaza Cinema was known as the closed
quarter? That was *American* hypocrisy disguising itself as
innocence.' She passed a roll. 'By the way, somebody told me
Fay's going to marry a Belgian businessman.'

'Well, you know what my sentiments are.'

255

'God keep her happy but away?'

'Exactly.'

Rhoda giggled happily and then sighed. 'But as for Paul Brophy, he must be feeling pretty miserable back in London. The *Times* says they've had nothing but winds and storms.'

Seen from the sunlit terrace, London weather was like another way of life. Neville was unmoved and, between taking a fishbone out of his mouth, said, 'Wagnerian effects for the end of his career.' He drank some wine. 'It's curtains for him.'

'Poor boy. I do so miss our little chats. He was such a comfort to me – I always felt I could do no wrong in his eyes. I must write to him.'

'Why not? But don't get involved.'

'I've got to write to The Consort, too. You know, ever since he's been in Bahrain I've neglected him shamefully. There's nothing to tell him. I haven't been going to any of the parties – well, hardly any, and the winter's been the flattest I can remember, especially since Katherine has been spending every spare moment in the new house. I don't know what it is.' She rang the little bell for the servant. 'The Consort went away; you went away; Paul was under strain – everyone was busy doing things – travelling, grumbling about this and that. Even Albert's been in a gloom for months and saying this town will drive him mad. The old happy life seems to have gone for ever. I feel life is passing us by – a bit like a boat that's missed the tide.'

'And then' – she looked instinctively towards the house – 'to have The Bloody Duchess all to myself for weeks on end. That was never my plan. Thank God, she's going off on April the seventh. She said so today just before she went out with the Abominable Victoria for lunch.'

'You mean, she's booked.'

'That's it. Her tenants are leaving, and she wants to put her place in order before her summer guests start arriving.'

'I feel rather guilty about her. I've dropped her, more or less. She's such a bore. As soon as I hear her start on that Cairo-in-the-old-days grind I shut my ears.'

Rhoda waited until the servant had cleared away the plates and put new ones.

'I wouldn't bother about her. She's had a great kick from her old chums, as she calls them, and they've introduced her to oodles of people. She knows far more of the old Montazah set than I do.'

'She's welcome.'

'Oh, I don't complain. I'm glad for her sake. And then she's always sending off little notes to The Consort. She's trying to inspire me, I suppose, or show me up. I really couldn't care.' Rhoda sighed again. 'I'm thoroughly bored with her. The other day Katherine was trying, very kindly, to hint that The Duchess was critical of me for neglecting my husband and doing nothing but read. She was furious because I don't get any fatter! That's how things are. Everything bores me. It's funny how one changes. I enjoyed helping Paul set up his apartment, but Katherine's house bores me. It all seems empty, perfectly empty.'

'Isn't Katherine happy?'

'Madly so. But she seems to realise that once the house is ready, the garden arranged, the furniture installed, there's nothing else to do. The village is deadly dull. You have nothing before you but the limestone outcrops across the valley and a view over a thousand miles of African desert. It's a setting for a life of perfect emptiness, and when the children come out at Easter they'll want to go down to the beaches and not moon about up there with nothing to do. So what's the point?'

But Rhoda had a deeper, graver objection to the way Katherine was arranging the new place: she had misjudged its possibilities. 'I see it as a poet's house, an artist's house. The sort of place you go to after years of being busy – where you start a new friendship with yourself and get to know yourself again.'

'What a sweet way of putting it.'

Rhoda helped herself to vegetables. 'I can't bear them to turn it into something banal and suburban.'

'You think they will?'

Rhoda pulled a mouth. 'It's touch and go. The trouble is, neither of them know how to sit still in a place and meet its mood half-way.'

Neville looked at his sister in surprise and said very softly. 'It sounds as though they've begun to bore you.'

'It's the Baida syndrome. One knows people too well. There's nothing left to know now, because the only things that can really nourish us must come from our own kind of climate, our own country, I suppose.'

'There never was much to know.'
'Oh, they had charm.'
'Katherine did.'
'Richard was always good company.'
'He never understood us.'
It was practically the Thomsons' obituary.

19

DOT PARSLOW telephoned Bethlehem House a couple of days later, at about eight in the evening. She had had a cable from Armstrong approving the payment of the docked living allowance to Byrd and approving the move from the flat.

A letter arrived in due course.

Dear Reggie, Your letter gravely disturbed me, but I do not doubt the truth of it. You did wisely to move out. I have now got the key to the unrest in the office and am recalling Paul Brophy permanently. Thank you for your courage in breaking the silence. I have instructed Mrs Parslow to pay you the full allowance and hope you will be comfortable.
P.S.   Is Bethlehem Lodge quite your cup of tea?

As Byrd read the letter his heart sank: he was shocked because Armstrong clearly understood the connection between his report on Brophy with the forfeited allowance money. Were they so closely tied up together? Byrd made a nervous movement of his thinning lips.

That afternoon, swimming at the Beach Club, he marvelled at the calm way Armstrong had accepted everything he had said – almost as though the letter had been expected. Byrd thought he would have behaved rather differently had he been Armstrong; exactly how, he could not say. As he turned over these thoughts, the afternoon clouds moved placidly over the golden-blue sky, the white sunlight was reflected from the fronts of the seafront skyscrapers; the water refreshed him, and he thought he knew the magic would continue.

Part Five

1

THE CONSORT's winter-long journeys hurrying backwards and forwards from Baida to Beirut and from Beirut to Bahrain and back again to London, ended shortly before the end of March – just in time, The Duchess said, for them to have a last get-together before her sailing. He came home in a strange, prickly mood. He was distant with everyone, unnervingly polite but anxious to show he was not involved. 'How were things?' 'So-so!' He was shorter than usual with the servants and went about the house humming to himself. Something was in the air; they could see he was boiling with resentment.

That first evening back, dining alone with Rhoda, he found fault with the meal. 'You can do better than this!' The tone was nettling, patronising; it implied that where he had come from people had taken more care. Rhoda was quick to take him up. 'Anyone would think Bahrain was a gastronomes' paradise.'

'There's a lot you don't know about Bahrain – or me!'

They exchanged more harsh words until Rhoda picked up her plate and napkin. 'It might be better if we ate apart.'

He looked at her contemptuously. 'You think that would worry me? You silly, opinionated bitch.'

She knew he was deliberately picking a quarrel, hoping she would say something to make his anger against her – at that moment a generalised, abstract thing – a real force, a lethal weapon. 'What have I done? Have the guts to say what I've done.'

He wiped his moustache with a napkin. 'You've been snubbing our friends.'

'Didn't know you had any.'

He ignored her. 'I'm told you've not been seen at a single embassy do since I went away. People have noticed. They're resentful at the way you ignored their invitations. What the hell were you thinking of?'

'They bore me to the roots of my hair – that's what.'

'You prefer Neville's mucky little birds, I suppose.'

'What birds?'

He flung a few basic details of the party in Neville's flat three months before at her.

'But that was ages ago. I've never seen her since.'

'You had that broken-down barmaid as a showpiece. How could you? Everybody's been talking about it. I shan't ever forgive you.'

'It was Neville's party. He knows her. He employed her for the drinks. What was wrong with that?'

'But that kind of girl!'

'She behaved very pleasantly. She was a great success.'

'For you, perhaps. But who, in God's name, would mix up a nightclub hostess with decent people? That's real decadence, when the lower depths come up the drains and flood people's drawing-rooms.'

'What a fuss about nothing.'

'If you weren't so dumb you'd see that one can't mix up the two worlds like that. It's not done and never will be done.'

'What two worlds?'

'You silly bitch! What two worlds? People don't want to be compromised when they go to respectable parties.'

Hazarding a guess, Rhoda said, 'The Duchess didn't tell me she'd been compromised.'

'What has she got to do with it?'

'She's been keeping you in the picture.'

'Of course she hasn't.'

'Do you think I didn't know she was writing to you?'

'That's unimportant compared to the enormity of what you've done.'

'The girl came because she's Neville's friend. What's to be ashamed about? I loathe hypocrisy.'

He laughed hysterically. 'Friend! You say I haven't got any friends – well, what about him? He has people he uses.'

'You're jealous of him. Jealous! That's the trouble.'

'Jealous of a little snit like him? You must be off your top. Dirty little guttersnipe like him – parading his improprieties brazenly to cover up something worse.'

261

She stopped dead in her tracks. 'What do you mean?'

'Never you mind. I could say a lot if I wanted to.'

'About Neville?'

'Never you mind.'

'Crying wolf. No one's taken in but yourself.'

'Anyway, he's not important. Leave him out and let him have who the devil he likes at his parties, so long as the lurid reflection doesn't fall on me. As for you: I find your role in the matter incomprehensible. Didn't it ever occur to you, my darling Rhoda, my silly little bitch, that you can't go dabbling with people like that when you're married to me? I mean, are you an embassy wife or aren't you? People in our position have got to watch our p's and q's. People talk – and I don't just mean gossip. Reports get sent back to London.'

She was too intelligent not to appreciate his point, and she would have agreed, had she loved the man, that she had made an error of judgement; she might even have burst into tears and asked him to forgive her – but because of her contempt for him she refused to make any concession.

'I'm sorry, darling, but I don't take things as seriously as you do. I suggest you tell people who complain to you that I'm not impressed by their opinions. They touch me not. They don't exist for me.'

'Just as well because you won't have to bother with them much longer.' Everything he had said was the long, pleasurable way to saying: 'As a matter of fact, you'll be able to have Neville's birds here indefinitely. I'm going home.'

'You're being sent back to London?' For a moment, she thought he was being reprimanded because of her behaviour.

'Oh, no, nothing so dramatic as that, although I have been gravely embarrassed. No, I'm going home from choice. I've resigned.'

'For God's sake! You're joking.'

'Aha, I thought that would shake you, madame.'

'Are you mad? What are we going to do? We haven't got a penny behind us.'

'Why should you worry? You've got what's left of your father's money. As for me, I wouldn't care if I had to walk home across the Alps; in a few weeks I shall be free of all this – the Arabs, Baida, the Foreign Office, the lot. I refuse to be treated like an office-boy or glorified messenger.'

'But what's gone wrong?' Had there been more than a little local difficulty? Had he been raked over the coals for neglecting his duties? He refused to be explicit. 'Never you mind. I hate everything. It's the only way to keep my self-respect.' He suddenly blazed at his wife. 'Do you think it's my idea of a career – competing with the Macraes of this world – having those uncouth bastards breathing down one's neck.'

She suggested his career was something more than that. He disagreed. 'Besides, I'm not in sympathy with anything that's being done. My only hope is to find somewhere to farm in a decent bit of country. The Duchess has rather fired me with the idea of getting a place in her part of the world.'

'Oh God, that woman crops up everywhere!'

He ignored her again. 'I can't pretend any more. All these clever people. All this empty talk. Means nothing. Most of it was never meant to mean anything. The truth is: I'm not at home in my own house.'

'And what will you do? We've got nothing behind us.' She looked round for cigarettes, a sure sign she was upset. 'To bury ourselves at our age in some sort of provincial Ultima Thule – growing peas or hops or something. It's not possible. You must be mad.'

'Sorry. I've resigned. It's too late to change. I've told them why – that this endless running about for no good purpose means nothing to me. What I want – and it may be news to you – is to settle down in a proper house – not a sort of eastern bazaar, and have a family.'

'I've never stopped you having a family.'

He ignored her: 'I miss my real life. I loathe all this.' And then, a sure sign he was deeply moved by his own position, he began to quote with a grim, dramatic expression: ' "What breaks me, young friend, is tasteless desire, dead iambics, boring dinners!" Too many boring dinners for me.'

The Consort in his tragi-poetic mood was more than Rhoda could stomach; she cut through his clouds of false rhetoric with a cry of rage and rebellion: 'I shall *hate* it! How can you think of turning us into hedgers and ditchers at our age. It's a life for people over seventy.'

This was the wide-open, positive wail of protest he had been waiting for. 'I don't expect you to like it. I'm not even expecting you to come. In fact, I wouldn't want you to come back with me. I'll go even further: I'll protect you from it all by asking you to divorce me.'

The cigarette she was trying to light fell out of her mouth. 'Why should I divorce you? On what grounds? What have I done.'

'Nothing . . . so far as I know. But I have. Look. Here I am in bed with an air-hostess in Bahrain.' He handed her a Polaroid photo. 'It's all the evidence you want.'

She picked up a water-glass, half-filled, and threw it at him. 'You swine! You bloody swine!'

The impact of the glass made him flinch, but he did not bother to get up as the water ran down his coat; he merely removed the snapshot from the damp to the dry side of the table. 'I might add that I'm not going to marry her. I'm marrying another woman who's as cheesed off in Bahrain as I am here.'

2

AT the Maximilian, Katherine Thomson and Neville discussed the disaster. Katherine thought Rhoda was right to refuse to divorce at The Consort's request. 'What woman would? Why should she? For all she knows, the photo may have been posed, you know?'

'It's horrible and unprincipled!' Neville was as shaken as his sister and their friends; all the same, he had known the marriage was doomed and so, while it lasted, had an element of charade in it. 'They don't speak the same language. For that reason there's no real point in refusing him.'

'That's easy. And what is she to live on? He's got no money.'

'Would you take money from such a man?'

'Why ever not? Hasn't a woman got rights?'

Neville shrugged; he was amazed that Katherine should raise the issue of money; it seemed the least important aspect of the affair. He was equally amazed when Katherine burst into tears and nearly spoiled her make-up. She hid her face quickly but need not have bothered. The few customers on the terrace seemed listless, vacant, unobservant, in need of strong sensations to come alive – victims of the tiring, spring day.

'Don't you think this is a cruel place?'

He thought a moment. 'No worse than anywhere else. Do you?'

'Awful. Deep down, I hate it. Really I do.'

'I thought you were so much at home here.'

She sighed naïvely, enjoying an interesting emotion. 'I should be. I've got my perfect little place in the hills. We're doing everything we want to do. But I still hate the place. It makes people cruel and malicious. Could you see a man behaving at home as your sister's husband has? It's the behaviour – you know – of people who have no tomorrows. Like the Arabs. They never think things out. The way the servants cheat and steal – then cry and play on your sympathies when you sack them. Why didn't they think of these things when they robbed you left, right and centre? At home, people move forward cautiously; they don't make friends easily, they judge you and weigh you because they know they've got to live with their choice a long time. Here it's all or nothing. I get tired of it. We go round and round in circles, and it's always the same: all and nothing. I'm not expressing myself well . . . but you know what I mean.'

'I understand all right. I'd never looked at it that way.'

'Richard and I came to that conclusion a long time ago. It's the only explanation of their politics. Everything is done to satisfy the needs of the day. I know some foreigners enjoy this. They say it makes life spontaneous and exciting – you do, rather, I think.'

'Well . . .' he was thinking of his sister's life. 'It's full of shocks. Not always pleasant. I still can't take it in. I've known my stay here was coming to an end – I can't grow in the way I want to – and I've never been able to see Rhoda stuck here indefinitely – or to see her married to The Consort for the rest of her life. Then it happens! *Blonk!* It's disturbing when the clock moves on suddenly.' He ordered two more coffees. 'He must have hated her very much before he'd have done what he did.'

Katherine shook her head. 'He must regret it. The thing done in white-hot anger you regret for the rest of your life. It's Baida. It's this climate. People become vindictive and violent

. . . like Dot Parslow about Paul Brophy. Now his career's in ruins she's probably sorry. But until she'd broken him she couldn't stop sticking the knife in, you know?'

3

WHILE Neville was drinking coffee with Katherine Thomson, Paul Brophy, back in town to settle his affairs, visited Rhoda. He went for sympathy and found her as prickly as a cactus: the first shock modifying into anger and resentment. Katherine Thomson may have wept for her, but Rhoda had not wept for herself. The only water which had flowed was the glassful thrown at her husband.

She was sitting very upright in a chair going through her mother's jewel-box. 'How was London?'

'Quite pleasant.'

'I hear you're leaving MEDOC.' She held up a necklace.

'I've been booted out. I didn't realise how much I was hated.'

'Oh?' She examined the clasp minutely. 'Mrs Parslow, I suppose?'

'Of course.'

'A frustrated bitch, if ever there was one. And she found a ready listener in that fatuous Ronnie Byrd.'

'You mean Reggie?'

'It's all the same.' She locked and unlocked the clasp.

'His letter finished me off.'

'Oh. Does he want your job?'

'I don't think so. Why should he?'

'He hasn't made much of his life, has he? Yours was the sort of job he'd have jumped at.'

'I never thought of it.'

'You're so gullible.' There was real contempt in her voice, real disdain. Brophy sat up and asked why.

'You've never seen people as they really are. You think everyone wishes you well. A person in your position was bound to be surrounded by envious people: Shamseddine, Mrs Parslow. They'd be bound to try to score off you. And it would be a nice little touch if Reggie Byrd came in and took the prize.'

Brophy shook his head. 'I think you're wrong.'

She laid the necklace down and picked up another. 'It's as clear as day to me.'

'Tell me, have you heard people saying things about me and the servant?'

'You mean Bahige?'

'Yes.'

'What sort of things?'

'Well . . . suggesting we were lovers.'

'I never gave it a second thought.' She lied without thinking. 'Reggie Byrd must have got the idea put into his head by Mrs Parslow.'

'Oh!' A pause. 'Then he mentioned it to you?'

'He was obsessed by it. He couldn't think of anything else.'

'Why?'

'I don't know. Really, Paul, why should I know what goes on in the head of a man like that? He's not interesting. He was bothered because you asked him to get a work permit for the Tunisian – and then refused to send a signed affidavit.'

'I don't know why he says that. He must have misunderstood me.'

'Very likely. But Bahige needed a permit, didn't he?'

'He should have got one now. I sent the letter.'

'That should keep Byrd quiet.'

He suddenly blushed. 'You don't believe me, do you?'

'It doesn't concern me. It never did. I like Bahige. I never gave a second thought as to what your relationship was. It's nothing to me whether you are lovers.'

He blushed again; his face fell apart. 'We never were.'

'Then I'd take Mrs Parslow and Shamseddine to court for the things they've said.'

'Why should I?'

'Why should you? Because they've destroyed your career. That's why. What a silly thing to say. Really, Paul, you talk like *le ravi du village*. They've had their knives out for you, and they got you; and they got you on *this*. That's a matter for redress. Don't you agree?'

'I couldn't prove anything.'

'I'd give evidence for you. I'll tell any court what they said and what Reggie Byrd said. According to Neville he tried to get him to add his signature to the letter denouncing you.'

'How can I?' He shied at the idea. 'It would cause such a stink.'

'Then you're giving yourself away. They must have been saying the truth.'

She picked up the necklaces and slid them back into the box. 'I must get dressed. I'm going out this evening. Make an appointment with Neville to see us. We'll have dinner before you go.'

They were both under the influence of shock; too shocked, even, to see that the other was not normal. He whimpered under his breath but could say nothing in self-defence. As he was leaving the house, The Consort drew up in his car, and remained in it until Brophy got into his. Was this further proof of his isolation and condemnation? Brophy panicked. To whom could he talk, explain, ask questions? There was no one but Neville.

4

NEVILLE's hair was still on end from his recent shower when Paul Brophy called. Wrapped in a large black-and-white towel, Neville served him a whisky and returned to his bedroom. When he came back to the living-room, the sight of Paul Brophy, sitting hunched-up and woebegone in a chair, stripped of office, recalled to London, was more than he could take: the resurrection of the man was uncomfortable and dismaying.

He assured Neville he was fighting Dr Armstrong's decision and was trying to get the directors to hold a special meeting to discuss his case. He blamed Dr Armstrong entirely. Had Armstrong given him backing he could have resisted all the Shamseddine–Parslow assaults.

He sighed: 'That's the position: I've been stabbed in the back by the man I trusted. Sacrificed.'

Neville listened with the neutral silence which served as a substitute for sympathy. He refilled Brophy's glass and Brophy, holding his glass in his large hands between his knees, went on to talk of Armstrong's own approaching nemesis. 'More and more it's a paper power he has. Shamseddine and Parslow are taking over from him *de facto* if not *de jure*. In his own way, he's fighting to survive, and, after recent events, it's hard to see Fred has any backers left at all. There's been a mass defection to the Parslow–Shamseddine camp.'

Neville thought such talk was academic; who was there to defect? Most of the MEDOC staff had never had a personal relationship with Dr Armstrong.

'He believed everything Shamseddine and Mrs Parslow said about me because he wants to buy time. Even Rhoda obviously believes the things they say about me!'

'My sister's judgement is a bit lopsided these days. She's in no fit state to talk to anyone.'

'She seemed all right to me.' Rhoda unwell? Brophy reacted resentfully.

'Didn't she tell you . . . ?'

'Tell me what?'

'You mean she didn't say anything about her marriage breaking up?'

'Not a word.' For a minute Paul Brophy forgot his own miseries. 'Would she have expected me to know?'

'Hardly. She hasn't realised it herself.'

'Was that why her husband avoided me?'

'Could well be. The damned Foreign Office pimp.'

Brophy wanted to know what had gone wrong, and Neville, not quite sure himself what was involved, tried to explain. Brophy was all attention, all pain. 'I thought I'd touched the depths of human treachery. Rhoda's gone one circle deeper. Your brother-in-law is not gentlemanly. I can say so now.'

'And you're surprised?'

Brophy was back in Jaufa several months before, when The Consort had made his cruel joke about queers. 'I suppose not, in a way.' He began blinking again, as he usually did when perplexed or cornered.

Neville offered him another drink. Brophy put up his hand.

'Grapefruit?' Neville recorked the whisky and sat down. 'I'm afraid it's our *débâcle*. Rhoda's marriage going pop and your career at MEDOC ending in flames. Extraordinary. Everything had seemed so secure.'

Brophy's face broke up again. 'That's what I felt. You can

imagine what it means to me. I'd thought of spending my life here.'

'Good God!' This was something Neville had never realised. 'Did you really?'

'Is it so abnormal? I was going to get down to some serious research and writing. I had lots of projects in mind.'

'You never mentioned them to me.' It was as much a statement of disbelief as Rhoda's 'They must have been saying the truth.' Neville sipped his whisky, and then, to hide his embarrassment, got up. 'You'd better have one.'

Brophy stared into the tumbler before drinking, and it could have been he saw his friendships sinking to the bottom; at any rate, when he lifted his eyes, he was older, more bitter, his sallow face even more pouched.

'You believe everything people say about me and Bahige.'

Neville felt sorry for him. 'People haven't said anything about you and Bahige.'

'Rhoda says they have – and so has Reggie Byrd.'

'Reggie Byrd's a nincompoop. He's put everyone's back up with his Mr Pooter mind and manners. He's the most mindless person I've met in years.'

'I've never met him; that's my next step. Fred showed me the letter he sent and pointed out that Byrd was really acting in my own interests. I wish he'd told me first so that I could have fought back; but Fred pointed out that so far as H.M.G. is concerned I'm no more use – even though he doesn't necessarily believe everything that's been said about me.'

'You mean, Fred doesn't believe there was anything to create about between you and Bahige.'

'I don't know.' Brophy's inability to lie convincingly obliged him to reflect the neutral tone of Armstrong's reaction. What he had actually said was more equivocal: 'In these matters it isn't always important what your friends think, but what your enemies can make use of. That's why you've got to be withdrawn at once.'

Neville's instinctive contempt for Dr Armstrong overflowed: 'He'd believe anything if he wanted to get rid of a person. Like those fortunate theorists who go out on an intuition and then find the right formula, he is always able to find a justification for something he had decided a long way back. This is only an excuse; he'd decided to get rid of you months ago.'

Brophy refused to believe this and refused to take up the weapons available to him to clear himself. The reaction was unlike anything Neville could have thought possible, expecting more passion, a deeper sense of outrage; Brophy merely suggested someone let down by a fellow accomplice.

'If you feel you've been wronged, you must state a case. All people of goodwill will come to your side.'

'They've all been poisoned.'

'By whom? By what?'

'By lies about me. It's impossible to answer every lie.'

'You don't think your own behaviour might be at fault? Let me be honest: I'd always assumed you were – well, that you didn't find what you wanted in women.'

'That's a lie. A dastardly lie.' Brophy glowered ferociously. 'You have no right to say that.'

'But, Paul, why don't you know yourself better? You've never had a girl-friend in your life.'

'That's a lie. I've had lots of them.'

'Name me one.'

'There's your sister.'

'She's not what I mean, and you know it.'

'Of course not. I respect her too much.'

'All right. Then out of respect for women you haven't any girl-friends. Neither have you got a wife. There we are!'

The doorbell rang. 'Let's leave this for the moment. It's Richard Thomson come to pick me up. He wants to talk about Rhoda's affairs.'

Brophy's anguish was sharpened by alarm. 'I suppose he's heard.'

'It's better to assume so.'

When Richard Thomson came into the room he shook hands with Brophy. 'Glad you're back again.'

Brophy made his unfrocked-priest *moue*. 'I'm merely back to wind up my affairs. My life out here has come to an abrupt end.'

The note of self-importance suggested that Brophy had been promoted. 'Do I congratulate you?'

'I wish you could. No. I've been stabbed in the back by my boss.'

'Hard Cheshire! That's business life.' Thomson looked helplessly at Neville, but Brophy got in first. 'Do you know Dr Armstrong?'

'Sure. I've met him once or twice.'

'He's the author of my misfortunes.'

Neville came bustling forward. 'I'm afraid we'll have to get going. Look, Paul, I'll see you in the office tomorrow.'

'You think I'll be allowed in?'

'Why not?'

Brophy stood up, and it was clear he wanted an invitation – but Neville was holding the door and Richard Thomson held out his hand. 'Better luck next time.' Brophy went away, and the two others sat down. Thomson made a gesture with his head towards the departing Brophy: 'Anyone'd think he'd brought off a coup. As self-important as ever; still longing to cut a dash.'

Neville laughed. 'He ought never to have come out here; people like that are their own worst enemies.'

'I suppose he's been got rid of in case of blackmail?'

'There'll always be blackmail until the Brophies go up to the people torturing them and say, "Leave off dabbling in my affairs." You only get blackmail where there's spinelessness. But . . .' Neville waved the Brophy case away and handed Thomson a cigar he'd been given and never smoked.

5

Richard Thomson said: 'Listen, Neville, I want to try to stop this business of your sister's going from bad to worse. Do you think it would do any good if I went to see your brother-in-law? Try to speak to him like a reasonable man?'

'That's a big order.'

'Oh, no. Come on, be fair. I know you never liked him, but he never behaved badly. Something's gone badly wrong; he may even have been affected by the heat in Bahrain. The Persian Gulf climate has a dreadful effect on people. Terribly lowering. I mean . . . a man doesn't behave as he did; he must have been out of his reason.'

'It's happened.'

'Come on. Do you think it's normal behaviour? I know you disliked him, but in my opinion he was a good scout to you. He was never mean or ungenerous. There's nothing in the past to lead anyone to think he'd do this revolting thing. Hallelujah! It's a sick man who does that.'

'That's what I've always thought he was. His kind of person *is* sick. They're everywhere at home, poisoning the atmosphere: the people from the privileged classes who can no longer fall back on their connections to get by. If he's mad it's not because of the Bahrain climate – it's because he's had to spend a couple of months there. It's clear he's been given a talking-to by someone. He may even have been asked to resign. Who knows? We'll never know.'

Thomson saw Neville's ruthlessness; he would cede nothing in his brother-in-law's favour. All the same, he thought it was worth making an effort to save the crumbling marriage. Neville did not understand how anyone who had been as close to the household as the Thomsons could seriously imagine there was anything to save, and he was as baffled by their goodwill and sympathy as was Rhoda herself.

Katherine Thomson had proposed to her, too, that Richard should approach The Consort. Rhoda refused.

'The break was *maktoub*. It came sooner than I expected.'

Katherine was stunned by Rhoda's detachment: 'You're saying this because you're shocked.'

'If I've been shocked, I've been shocked into the truth of the matter. I despise his opinions, his way of living, the kind of person he is. There was only sex in common.' – Thomson winced – 'Yes, believe me. That's the truth. Of course, I used to be vexed when people' – she meant Neville – 'talked of my marriage as a mistake which everyone accepted, but I had only myself to blame. After all, I didn't show any respect for him, did I? I made it clear I married him on the rebound after something better, which couldn't go on.' Her lips trembled with real emotion. 'Nothing essential in me is touched by the way he's behaved. I married to get away from intolerable circumstances. There wasn't even the attraction of the uniform.'

Katherine Thomson had not even heard this phrase and had to be told what Rhoda meant; she was vaguely shocked. Both husband and wife disapproved of the way Rhoda was carrying on and discounted it. They still believed that when Rhoda had got over her shock she would be pleased to have Richard intervene on her behalf. In the meantime, once Rhoda rejected sympathy and help, there was nothing more the Thomsons could do, and they welcomed the departure of the brother and sister. The Thomsons were disappointed because, it seemed to them, neither Rhoda nor Neville knew how to accept sympathy. They were not hard enough to understand the way the brother and sister 'ticked'. Neville and Rhoda were only rarely compassionate, and they did not know how to assess compassion in others; to press sympathy and pity on them was to misinterpret the high-wire act they were performing. Like hard talkers, interrupted in mid-conversation, they stared around uncomprehendingly, waiting for the interruption to cease.

6

Thus Rhoda's true reaction was only known to her brother.

Sitting in Neville's flat, drinking coffee and smoking, they were shaken and afraid. They stared at books, papers, drawings on the wall; they talked aimlessly until Rhoda flung her tumbler at the wall. 'I could kill him! Kill him! I wish he'd drop dead. Dead. I'll get Umm Mansour to curse him. I'll get her to stick pins in his heart. Imagine that officers' mess bag he's picked up. Not a bit better than she should be – with a tongue always hanging out for gin or whisky – smoking like a chimney – coughing in that disgusting way. . . .'

'She's probably worthy of him. A marriage made in purgatory.'

She burst out laughing. 'Oh, darling, you are funny. You say such sweet things.'

Neville's phrase worked like a charm. At once, The Consort and The Lady from Bahrain had become one more of their private Tarot cards. They had The Duchess, The Consort, The Tunisian, and now they added The Purgatorial Pair. Everything was put into perspective. They astonished themselves by the ease with which they had classified the disaster.

As Rhoda said, it was amazing 'how quickly one got used to a new situation, but what wore one out was the complexity of one's reactions'. She and Neville knew they had been unfair to The Consort, they knew the marriage was a mockery, but they were vexed that The Consort should have called their bluff first. Much more elegant to have dished *him*, since the role of victim, of the one pitied, had never suited either the brother or sister. Their vanity was hurt.

Rhoda was also enraged by The Duchess's duplicity and, threatened to 'spoil her Pompadour hair by pulling it out in handfuls!'

They became hungry and set out for Jamshid's Restaurant. It was gone midnight, but Jamshid's, refuge of all Baidanis whose dinner had failed to touch the spot, was crowded. They attacked the plates of hors d'œuvre set before them – little white onions, *roca*, fool, *homos*, raw liver – and went on to grilled chicken.

By the end of the meal, Rhoda had recovered her tone. 'I asked for this. It's not lucky to marry on the rebound and for advantage. It always backfires. It wasn't fair to him. I suppose he was fond of me.'

'He was enthralled by you. He'd never met anyone like you. Well, that's what he said at one time.'

She wiped her lips before colouring them. 'Fatal.'

'What is?'

She applied the lipstick and rubbed her lips together. 'Fatal to charm a man who couldn't understand you or move you even if he lived to be a hundred.' She put her vanity case away. 'And next we'll have to get back to London. That really makes me ill. It looms up like a kind of prison.' She sighed. 'Tell me, did we always feel like this about England? There must have been a time when it seemed just one's home, one's little shell. Now, I feel as though I'm being exiled. Back to some sort of Ultima Thule' – this was her new phrase – 'where we'll wither up and grow the kind of faces you see in Harrods banking hall.'

'Oh, you'll think of something else to do.'

'What? There's no real escape. It's there waiting for you like a big black spider. However happy one is abroad, England is waiting to tarnish and spoil your life. Everybody we know here is whirling around trying to forget that they've got to return. The black box and coffin complex. Pleasures have to be paid for triply. The ethos of pain and duty seeping out of the very rocks. It's in all the faces, in the blood. They don't believe in happiness or good times. They're not really happy unless they're hedged in with prohibitions.'

As they were being driven up to her house, she said she was not going to divorce The Consort. 'I'll get a legal separation at my own convenience. I see no reason why I should play his game.'

7

MORE or less thrust out of Neville's place, Paul Brophy was at a loose end. To whom could he talk about the crash of his world? There was nothing to do but go home. He and Bahige were hardly speaking. The flat was in disorder and had the air of what Americans call a major disaster area. Brophy's cases were still unpacked; and the kitchen had begun to fill up again with empty bottles, ashtrays full of cigarette-ends, and old flaps of Arabic bread.

The Tunisian was in his room playing his tape-recorder. He had become mindless with forebodings and lay on the bed, sometimes smoking, sometimes reading his paperback novels. From time to time he lifted a hand to keep a fly off his face, or rubbed his feet together or scratched his stomach. He was a person who had no memories, no interest in his own past, and no especial present or future. Brophy tapped on the bedroom door but was ignored. When the tapping went on, the Tunisian called out, *'Foutez-moi la paix!'* Brophy withdrew into the salon and began drinking.

He sat down with a glass of whisky and wrote a note to Rhoda: 'My dear, you must have thought me obtuse and stupid. Please forgive me. I do not know what to say or to advise. If help is needed don't hesitate to ask.' He folded his note into an envelope and then sat staring at nothing.

With every whisky his resentment grew, and he decided that Reggie Byrd was the Judas responsible for his fall. He wrote a second note:

276

Dear Byrd,

I am back to wind up my affairs and would like to see you, before I go into the office tomorrow, about the scandalous rumours you are putting out about me. I want you to know I resent them very much and most emphatically and strenuously deny all the things imputed to me. I am not *and* never have been *a homosexual and cannot imagine how you formed such an impression.*

Brophy's note to Byrd was delivered to him the next morning in Bethlehem Lodge, as he sat in the dining-room eating an omelette and observing the new influx of evangelicals. Byrd was very relaxed and amiable having had a slow, satisfactory morning. He had been woken early by the bells of Our Lady of Africa, by the cries of a fruit-seller and the efforts of a young pianist across the street to master a couple of waltzes by Ravel. He opened his shutters and looked down the street, down the long perspective of tall apartment houses which framed the snow-covered heights of Mount Atthis at the far end. Like Munich or Geneva, the city overflowed with spring warmth, growth and luminosity, while its environs kept their winter dressing; the juxtaposition was a never-ending source of pleasure. He took a shower, cleaned his teeth, ate an orange, counted his small change before going down to breakfast in a grey suit with an open shirt and a foulard: every inch the English week-ender and gentleman. Brophy's note brought him once again to the MEDOC morass.

8

A crestfallen Tunisian showed Byrd into the flat, in a weird echo of Byrd's first arrival at night several weeks before. Both men were stiff; there was nothing left but mutual suspicion, and Byrd did not need to contort his face to hide what he really thought. The Tunisian had 'deceived' Byrd, imposed on him, in some way, and Byrd was enjoying his sensation of power. The Tunisian was still in his roll-neck sweater, still

277

aimless, timeless, hopeless, futureless; and it was refreshing not to have to feel sorry for him – because he was a cheat. He was, of course, one and the same person; it was Byrd who had decided to change. An unfelt conversation was going on when Brophy appeared, very tall and upright, very pompous, freshly shaved, freshly laundered, wearing a white shirt and an old school tie.

He turned to the Tunisian and ordered him to leave. As he turned his head, Byrd saw that Brophy had a broken nose, which gave him an impression of brutishness and self-indulgence. Byrd had so little expected this that he was vaguely grieved; a piece of information had been held back from him deliberately.

Brophy waved Byrd to a sofa and sat down himself. 'Well, and what have you got to say for yourself?' The tone was princely, episcopal: the very accents of the young pretender to power and authority, not at all the manner of a person on the way out.

'You've taken the words out of my mouth. I've been expecting an explanation from you for some time.'

Brophy crossed his long legs. 'Is there anything to explain? It seemed to me that you had the freedom of my home – and you abused it by imputing things to me, which – well, to say the least, were a bit hard to take.'

Byrd leaned back and held his biceps. 'You asked me, if you remember, to help your chappie get a work permit. Tell me, first of all, why did you involve me and then refuse to help?'

'Oh, that?' The tone implied a matter of no importance. 'Fred and I' – the tone was papal – 'thought you took that business rather hysterically. People out here don't worry so much about pieces of paper and formalities; that's a very European obsession. If you'd lived here longer you'd know how few things depend on the written word.'

'My dear fellow,' Byrd gave his diplomatic smile, 'I knew this part of the world before you'd left knee-pants. I can't pretend to understand all I see and hear, but basically I took it that human beings are human beings everywhere, and I thought your man worried as much about his position as any European would have done in the circumstances. He hardly ever left this place for fear of being picked up in a police raid. He depended entirely on the written word – as you so grandly put it – you never told him at any time that his papers were of no import-ance.'

Brophy half-rose to flick his cigarette-ash into a bowl and arrayed his tousled curls with a heavy hand. 'I presumed that as an Arab he would understand.'

'He understood nothing of the kind. He actually cried with fright on one occasion. He blubbered because you'd grown tired of him and had abandoned him.'

Brophy was unmoved. 'He acts well. He's full of illusions about himself.' Brophy smiled pityingly. 'For instance, as part of his self-dramatisation, he's taken to telling people he's not my servant. He's got a mild attack of *folie de grandeur*.'

Byrd gave no sign of believing or disbelieving the statement. Brophy looked anxious. 'I hope he didn't give you any other impression.'

'Who am I to believe? I don't believe him entirely, and I don't believe you. You behaved fraudulently. I've got your typed instructions to help your man, and I want to know why you asked me to get involved in the affair if it was of no importance.'

'I thought you could help him.'

'*I* help him? A person passing through. You don't expect me to believe that, do you?'

Brophy made a spinsterish *moue*. 'You are at liberty to believe exactly what you like; that's your affair.' He lit another cigarette.

'It's not my affair. That's precisely what I've objected to. You got me involved for no serious purpose. It was window-dressing. Hazing. You didn't want the man to stay with you at all; you were praying he'd go away and leave you.'

'I wanted no such thing.'

'You say so, but I know better. You're a humbug, Brophy. You were ready to abandon the man, and you didn't know how to do it. Your recall to London came inopportunely. Eventually, I suppose, you'd have had the courage to tell the man the truth. You don't care a damn what happens to him.'

Brophy half-closed his eyes and tried to assess Byrd. 'What are you trying to say?' He flicked ash sideways. 'This has nothing to do with the rumours you've been putting out about me.'

'What rumours?'

279

'That I was a homosexual.' Brophy recanted, 'I mean, you picked up these rumours and put them out; you recounted them.'

'We'll come to that. What I want to say about your chappie is this: the next time you want to ditch somebody, do it in an open way and don't involve third parties in a meaningless exercise. I was completely taken in by you; believe me, old chap, I don't like that one bit. Not a bit. Everybody had got the lie of the land but me. I'm too old to be made a sucker.'

'Well, I've written the letter for him.'

'Good luck to you. Now, to your note. You say—' Here Byrd put on his glasses and read the note at arm's length. 'Where is it? Yes . . . "about the scandalous rumours you are putting out about me". Who have I spoken to?'

'I'm not prepared to mention names.'

'That's a pity. We could have gone along to see them and sieved the matter.'

'I was told you'd been recounting scandal.'

'I think I know who put that idea in your head. You may also like to know that I left this place after a conversation with Neville de Vries and his sister. She thought I was foolish to stay on and get a bad name.'

'She would never say that. You're bluffing.'

'Well, we can go to see her, too. That's the extent of the faith *she* had in you.'

Byrd's self-assurance rattled Brophy, who suddenly flashed: 'You made it your business to undermine everything I had here. You're really a disgraceful person, Byrd. If I'd known what sort of man you were I'd never have opened my home to you.'

'Do you think I'd have gone into it had I known everything?'

Brophy looked startled, as though he had never realised what Byrd might have objected to. 'But there's nothing to know. There's nothing to object to. You suggested in your letter to Fred that Bahige didn't look after you very well, but that's not enough to make you so vindictive against me. It's pure vindictiveness. You were after my place. That's what it is. Everything else means nothing until that fact is put right in the middle; it's the most telling and significant thing. You wrote that letter to Fred with a view to getting me recalled to London and made it seem high-minded. You said you were saving me from a series of rumours which you yourself had started. You wrote this underhand letter, and Fred swallowed every word. And here I am with no right of appeal and out of a job. Of course, when I get back to London I shall fight for compensation, but I won't get this job back.' Brophy worked himself up into a splendid state of rage. 'You've ruined me on a tissue of lies. You and that Australian witch and Michel Shamseddine – you ganged up on me.'

Byrd took his glasses off and looked at Brophy coldly. 'For God's sake, man, pull yourself together. Shouting hysterically won't get you anywhere. Your story doesn't hold water for a moment. Now, listen to me.' They were both talking at once. 'I'm going to shut you up once for all. Now this is between us. Let me tell you that you've been taken for a ride, and the person you have to thank is Michel Shamseddine – you know he's got his own little spy-system in the office, and the chief spy is a vicious-looking youth who wears dark glasses.'

Brophy knew him; he drew in his breath, waiting for more.

'The precise relationship between him and Shamseddine is their affair, but I don't think there's much doubt but that they had a big influence in your life. I think that if you'd been able to get rid of the Tunisian you'd have had young Mounir to take his place.'

'That's a most monstrous lie.' Even as he said this, Brophy began to shake. 'I don't know how you can have imagined such a thing.'

'Mounir told me.' Byrd laughed. 'There's no such thing as a secret in this place, as I hardly need to remind you; and I asked the right question. I was puzzled by his always inviting me to go home with him to drink coffee, or go to the cinema with him. I said one day, "How often do you go to the cinema?" He said, "Nearly every night." Then he began to treat me to coffees, which surprised me, because there wasn't any special relationship. Then one day, in the general office, I was looking through the files when Mounir came up and asked me to go to his house for a whisky. I refused. He went away and then came back. He wanted to know why I wouldn't come. I was too busy, had too much to do. He looked towards Shamseddine's room, and, as I looked up, I saw what I can only call a wink of complicity between the two; Shamseddine had been watching everything from afar; the lad was under his instructions. There was no risk to me, but I understood then how you'd been caught.'

Brophy blinked: 'In what way?'

'Mounir came into my room. I asked him whether he was going to the cinema. He laughed, looked coy. "You're going there with your girl-friend?" He laughed like mad. "No girl-friend for me. I like men." Just like that, as though I should have understood all the time. I asked him whether he went to the cinema to pick up men. "Of course. What else? I like men. When I go with a man I'm happy in my mind." I made some vague remark, and he thought I was impugning him. "Arabs like men, but so do Englishmen. Mr Brophy likes men a lot. He and me are very big friends. I sleep with him, and if that Bahige goes back to Tunis, I go to live with him." '

Brophy breathed out smoke like a collapsing balloon. 'I've been a fool. I trusted too many people. You're quite right, Byrd, it's better for me to go home.'

'You see what you're up against?'

The younger man nodded, in complete disarray. 'I under-estimated their cruelty. I've been a fool.' He got up and looked around like someone in a daze. 'I'm sorry, Byrd, I should have offered you something. A coffee?'

'Not now. I'll push along.'

Brophy had disintegrated. 'What can I do now? I feel I can't face anyone.'

'Come, come. No one will kill you. Everybody knows every-thing, but nobody will say anything. That's not the way of the world. The damage has been done. You've got to pick up the pieces and go elsewhere. I'm sorry for you, Brophy, I think you've had a raw deal.'

'I've been a fool.'

Brophy fell back in his chair, sprawled out, his mouth pouched.

Byrd stood up; he had the bearing of a mourner come to give condolences. 'You fell into a nest of vipers. I can say this: that, if it's any consolation to you, you're well out of such a place. You were heading for destruction.'

'What will I do, I wonder. What would you do?'

'Go home. Start all over again, I suppose.' Byrd spoke com-fortingly but let it be conveyed that he saw no easy way for Brophy; after all, his weakness was inborn, essentially self-destructive. 'I'd go for the quiet life: a nice little academic backwater. Some research.'

Byrd's advice rolled off his tongue glibly. 'One thing: you've got to keep your nose clean in this world. If I didn't have to go, I'd tell you how I was let down myself on my newspaper. Not quite the same circumstances, of course,' he added hastily, 'but the destructive element was there.'

'Really?' Brophy hardly focused him. His eyes were dreary and opaque, the iris had merged, it seemed, with the whites. He accompanied Byrd to the lift and was already biting a thumbnail as the lift shot down. Byrd was feeling immensely pleased with himself at the neat way he had deflated Brophy and at the way he had 'kept his own nose clean'. He felt the affair had been handled with that effortless superiority which was always his highest ideal: no raised voices, no harsh language – just the truth marshalled with deadly accuracy, with enough goodwill left over to offer paternal advice.

As the lift door opened, the dirty-looking concierge, alerted by spiritual radar, leapt out of his den and began to wail about 'Mr Broffi don't wanna . . .'

Byrd raised a self-satisfied and episcopal hand and put on his most Napoleonic smile: '*Malish. Malish.* God will provide!'

It was an exit line with the right note for a Sunday morning. Byrd had not felt so much in control of himself for months; he had worked out on Brophy all the passive suffering of his experience on *The Age.* In some mysterious way, Byrd stood well in his own eyes; he was again sufficiently pleased with himself to start tra-la-la-ing under his breath – the first time for weeks.

9

LATER, at the Exes, Byrd was able to finish off the story which he had begun several weeks earlier, but the Exes were not satisfied. To them the whole MEDOC scandal was mysterious: a state of hatred and viciousness for no apparent reason, a sort of game or ceremony in which someone had said, quite arbitrarily, 'We are going to hate *him*. We are going to harry him. We will find out something about him that we claim we don't like. We will worry at this one point until others cease to ask whether the criticism is valid or even just. We will create so much tension around this one point that no one coming within earshot of us will be able to think dispassionately.'

The Exes had seen the affair at second-hand through Reggie Byrd's visits; they had seen his indifference undermined, his detachment modulated through vexation to a kind of puritanical self-righteousness. They knew Brophy had vexed him and had done much to exhaust his patience and sympathy – and they had themselves warned Byrd about getting involved – but they could not understand why Byrd took so much pleasure in despatching the fallen man. What was he justifying?

Susan Exe was sorry for Brophy; Byrd was not: 'He got everything that was coming to him. He didn't care who he involved in the mess.'

She wondered how many dragons Byrd was exorcising – the dragons born out of a faulty sense of vocation, a muffed career, a private *débâcle* and resentment at having his stay in Baida upset.

Byrd had come to the conclusion that Brophy, having had too much too soon, had lost his head. It was very bad to have this, according to Byrd; people needed to work hard to appreciate things. 'He lost his head because he didn't know how to carry high office. Until you know how to serve you can't command.'

The Exes did not see any connection but did not say anything; they were so bemused by Byrd's changes of heart. At that moment, Byrd seemed to them really lightweight: a trivial little Tartuffe.

'I had recourse to the oldest technique possible: that of the police inspector. I just wormed my way into that young man's confidence and got him to spill the beans. I was able to lay the facts before Brophy and he couldn't say a word.' He smiled radiantly. 'And now for Dr Armstrong. I'll teach him to show my confidential letters to the man concerned.'

The Exes agreed that this was wrong, that Brophy had been treated badly, that it was abominable to have trapped him in his own vices; and yet they hankered after generosity; they wanted some gesture of sympathy towards the fallen man. 'He must be very much alone at this moment,' was the way Susan Exe expressed herself. 'A man like that is best alone,' the husband said. 'He should never have been exposed to temptation.'

'This is probably the last generation where such things will count. I look forward to the time when people's sexual aberrations and tastes will be their own business.'

Byrd laughed. 'That's a long way off, I'm afraid. When people take public office their whole personality is on trial.'

'Unfortunately. It's only because people have the keyhole complex that it matters even in public figures; unhappy, unfulfilled people forever raging outside other people's bedrooms. They give me the creeps.' Susan Exe threw back her hair. 'I don't know why I defend your man. He belongs to the kind of world I abhor – that businessmen's world with its tortuous ambitions and its Inner Wheel scale of values. And it's all mixed up with public school muckiness and loyalties. These people are bound to come unstuck as soon as they come in contact with a world where their scale of values is unknown. In their own eyes, the Arabs are engaged in a life-and-death struggle with us – with our oil monopolies, our patronage, our contempt. They don't care about our individual victims, the Paul Brophys; they only stand for the great hated symbol of domineering, interfering, commercial, essentially heartless interests based in London and elsewhere. Until that lesson sinks home all the muddled triflers like Paul Brophy will get shown up for the empty people they are. I'm sorry for him as a man – he must be very lonely and unhappy – but for what he represents he doesn't move me at all.'

Byrd resented deeply the way she spoke about the public school 'muckiness'; she was at her most 'levelsome', and he stared ahead without agreeing or disagreeing. John Exe took up one or two points and objected. She refused to accept.

'Look, both of you, I don't know much about Anglo-Arab politics, yet one thing is clear: we're not in this part of the world for our health. We like being here because it gives us a sense of importance and fulfilment we couldn't get at home. People aren't yet ready to help themselves – right? We have that extra know-how – right? We're here on very favourable terms to help them. The business interests are here for precisely the same reasons. They want to make the profits out of Arab oil; they've got the marketing network, the contacts; so they milk the stuff out of the ground and sell it and give a percentage back to the people in whose land the thing began. Brophy seemed to have all the sympathy in the world with the Arabs when it came to religion and sex, but he failed to see what was the most important thing from the Arab point of view: he represented the western business interests, who wanted more and more information in order to exploit the Arab world commercially even better than they do at present. And probably more. If we knew it, Brophy's probably a spook, too. They destroyed him for some reason, and London abandoned him for some reason, too. There's more to the story than meets the eye.'

Byrd was damned if he was going to get involved with her when she was in her bolshy mood. 'Could be; but I doubt it.'

10

AIN-AL-NABI: a peaceful Sunday afternoon on the Thomsons' little terrace, looking towards the hermit country. Rhoda and Neville were there like refugees. They had been debating the duplicity of The Duchess, and Rhoda had heard for the first time of earlier conversations with Katherine. These were an unpleasant surprise which called for a balancing of accounts at the first opportunity.

About half-past four, Albert Hijjazi drove up in his new Swedish car and leaned against the wall of the terrace, drinking, looking down at them, feeling unencumbered and well. He had a wide straw hat, and this, combined with his Gauguin moustache, gave him the air of a French intellectual. He kept looking at Rhoda appreciatively; he had rarely seen her look so well, so distinguished. Would she and her husband be renting a place in the mountains, or would she stay in town? Rhoda lifted her eyes in amusement. 'It's not at all sure I shall be here a month from now. My plans have changed – well, let's be honest: they've been changed for me. My husband has found

286

a lady in the English community in Bahrain and wants to bring her into his life. So, as we are British, and British laws forbid polygamy, I've got to make way.'

'You're joking.'

'I'm not. You know me. I never tease.'

'How can you say these things? You would be crying if they were true.'

He was eventually persuaded that she was speaking the truth and was suitably shocked by her levity. 'I shall never understand you Europeans. Never. I love your literature. I love your life. For me, Paris is a second home-town; I could spend the rest of my life in Rome; but I shall never understand you.' He became quite excited, supercharged. 'There is a coldness in you – please forgive me – a hardness which makes us Arabs shiver. Yes, really, *un vrai manque de cœur.*'

The Europeans laughed a little uncomfortably. Richard Thomson asked whether Hijjazi thought all Europeans had it in them to behave like The Consort. '*We* think he's a cold-hearted monster.'

'He is a man apart. I have watched him at your parties. I have never known what to make of him. He lives in a world of his own; his values are of a world that has gone. I can tell you – now that we are speaking frankly – that I think of him in my mind as The Dinosaur. He never says a single thing which seems applicable to the present age. So a Dinosaur must be allowed his prehistoric ways. But it is you' – looking at Rhoda – 'who astound me. You sit here looking young and beautiful, and you say your husband's throwing you out of his life, without a single regret.'

'I've no regrets. What for? I'm angry. Believe me, I'm angry.'

'You don't even look angry.'

'Why should I wear my heart on my sleeve? I'm angry at the way it's happened. But I've always known the marriage would end one day.'

'You amaze me. Really, my dear. I find myself admiring you. This is an English education: to hide your emotions.'

'Oh, you know me, if I really loved my husband I'd be prostrate with shock. For a couple of days I was numb. I can't remember anything after throwing a glass of water at him.'

Hijjazi probed like a doctor. 'You must be shocked now. All this laughter and brightness . . . I mean, it must still be unreal. One day you will break down and cry. You will feel regret. You must do. Anything involving your fellow men takes a part of you away.'

'No. No. I'm sorry.'

'We're fatalists.'

Rhoda took up her brother's phrase. 'Yes, fatalists. We are behaving like orientals, and you want us to behave like emotional westerners. I'm going to disappoint you.'

She was laughing at him provocatively. 'Don't stare at me like that, Albert. I know you're thinking this woman must be mad. Believe me, I'm quite happy about things. All my dark feelings about my husband have been justified.'

Later that evening Hijjazi rang Neville. 'Ya Neville! Keep an eye on your sister. She's suffering from delayed shock. In this mood she can do anything.'

Neville was surprised by Hijjazi's concern. 'She's not. I assure you.'

'For a woman to be spurned by a man is a terrible thing. She has lost face. Her family has lost face. Everybody is upset.'

'Of course, people are upset. Anger, quarrels, separations are all ugly. But nobody's lost face. Remember that we don't have your Arab sense of honour.'

'You mean that when you go home, your sister will sell her memoirs to that disgusting Sunday newspaper everyone reads in London? Neville, you cannot kid me. This is serious. She must be hurt by this other woman from Bahrain. Any woman would be hurt. It's natural.'

'You don't understand my sister.'

'Your sister is a woman. I understand them. I spend half my life with them, whether as mothers, sisters or lovers. I know them. Your sister's reaction is not normal. When it comes it will be something fearful. I know what I'm talking about.'

Hijjazi had always appreciated the double values posed by Neville and his sister: the extraordinary nearness, the physical resemblance, their ability to accept whatever the other cared to reveal, and he believed Neville was blind over this matter. It never struck Hijjazi that Rhoda might have shared his opinion of her own husband; he thought there must be some intimate tissue, as between any man and woman, which could not be violated without pain. For a woman not to be involved in the world's opinion of her as a mother and wife was unreal to him. He boggled; he gasped; and the man who had translated St Jean Perse into Arabic began muttering old Arabic runes against the evil eye.

The next day, Monday, he rang Neville to ask how she was. 'You must help her,' was his advice. 'You must go everywhere with her as support. You must compliment her. Say she looks well and beautiful. And I will send her flowers.' He was as good as his word; the flowers were delivered almost at the same time as the Ghanem chauffeur brought The Duchess back from her long week-end.

11

THE Duchess knew; The Consort had told her by telephone. When she climbed the graceful stairs slowly, under the weight of years, anxiety and curiosity, she found Rhoda arranging Hijjazi's flowers in a bowl. She stood at the open door blinking. 'Well? Is there anything I can do?' Rhoda went on with her arrangement: 'Yes. You can clear out.'

The Consort – who had not gone to work – came into the room through another door. 'You can cut that talk out!' he bawled at Rhoda as he crossed the room to welcome The Duchess.

The old lady, caught between cross-fire, held her slablike cheek towards him. Rhoda finished arranging the flowers and left the room.

The Duchess acted the innocent for Rhoda's benefit. 'I'm all at sea! What have I done? Just when I'm feeling so happy after a perfectly lovely time.'

'Let's take the case up to your room.' The Consort closed the door and sat down on the sofa near the window. 'I want you to help me. I've behaved abominably towards Rhoda. I don't know what came over me. It was quite unforgivable. I want you to tell her that I apologise, although my mind is made up. Just tell her that.'

The Duchess refused. She did not understand the message; she would have to be persuaded to interfere.

'I told you on the phone. Our marriage is over.'

'The way you lived you never gave it a chance. I could have told you this would happen months ago.'

'Oh? I didn't know you found our way of life so strange.'

'You weren't like a married couple at all. You didn't begin to have a normal married life. I mean this isn't a home – it's a beautiful house where you hold parties and meet from time to time. You and Rhoda have never had a chance. There were too many people about, too many parties, too many trips. You never had time to get to know one another. There were no children, no prospects of children.'

'Was that *my* fault?'

The Duchess suspended judgement. 'I can't pretend to know. You and Rhoda were a mystery couple. It worried me a good deal.'

The Consort had imagined The Duchess was on his side; he had yet to realise that The Duchess was nobody's partisan; the pleasures of denunciation were the only real ones for her. He smoothed his moustache aimlessly.

'There's no place for me here any more. I hate domestic upheavals. I can see that you would want me to clear out. I'll go into a hotel until I sail.'

He did not dissuade her.

The Duchess changed and went downstairs to see Rhoda. 'What's all this damned nonsense about your marriage breaking up? You've never tried.'

'It's probably for the best.'

The Duchess took a high moral tone. 'Let me tell you, Rhoda, this attitude won't get you anywhere. Such a silly, self-opinionated girl as you are! You've spoiled yourself. You've believed your own nonsense. There's nothing wrong with your marriage that a good family palaver couldn't put right.'

Rhoda got up. 'I've no wish to be lectured by you, do you hear? All you say is as false as you are.'

'What do you mean?'

Rhoda repeated her remark.

'That's perfectly uncalled for. You really have no right to say that.'

'You've worked against me since the day you arrived. It's only in the last couple of days that I realised what a traitor you are: a vicious person who can't help herself.'

'No one has ever said such things to me before.'

'You did your best to suck up to John.' – The Consort – 'You encouraged him to think the worst of me. You went about spreading scandal and gossip about me to your friends. Everything was turned into tittle-tattle.'

'Somebody's been poisoning you against me. And I always believed I hadn't an enemy in the world! Somebody's been poisoning you. I know who it is, but I won't mention names.'

'Yes, and I was told that you'd even said we weren't my father's children.'

'Oh, I never! Oh, I never!'

'I know quite well you did. Only you could have thought up such a thing. I'm sorry, Duchess, but I think you're dirty. Unclean. And if you don't mind we'll never speak to one another again.'

'I shall go into a hotel until I leave.'

'I couldn't care where you go. In a few weeks this house will probably be rid of us, too. John is going home to England – he's resigned. He thinks the foreign service is no longer an occupation for gentlemen. As you two get on so well, you might well like to keep house for him. You'd make a good couple. And here's a picture for your mantelpiece. John flung it at me as evidence for a divorce. Take it back to him and tell him I'll get a separation – not a divorce – on the grounds of his mental instability.'

The Duchess lost her powers of speech. Her funny little rouged-up lips and wattle cheeks moved before she said with rising shrillness: 'There isn't anything more I want to do with either of you. You're a disgusting pair. A really disgusting pair. I want nothing more to do with you. You're sex-mad. The pair of you. You all are.'

'That's the man you were sucking up to and going around telling my friends was really too good for me. "She married above herself. They're not of the same class at all." '

With this Rhoda slapped her stepmother loudly on the cheek. 'Why don't you drop dead, you sniffling old bitch? Drop dead, I tell you. You mean nothing to anyone.'

12

'SHE looked mad, John. I'm afraid of her!'

The Duchess, whimpering to The Consort, was a ludicrous figure and an embarrassment to him. 'But I blame you, too, John. You ought never to have done such a thing to her. You had so much to put up with from her and her brother, and now you've put yourself firmly in the wrong. It was a most ghastly thing to do. Perfectly abominable, John. I can't ever think the same of you again.'

He was contrition itself. 'I know. I was off my rocker – I was mad with rage and jealousy – that they should have been having such a good time while I was stuck out in that bloody Gulf!'

'Was that all it was?'

'Really. That's all it was.'

'Oh, John! What a mistake. You foolish boy. And you've given up your career.'

'Bother that! I'm sick of it. I'm sick of the people. I'm sick of living this unreal life abroad. I'm sick of everything. I want to get back to the sort of people I understand. These aren't my kind. You can't hold a decent conversation with those people in the Embassy without someone dropping his aitches or speaking with a Cockney accent or bragging about his working-class granny. It doesn't mean the same thing any more. There's nothing left to be proud of. The sort of England I believe in, that I grew up in, has been beaten back to the wall. I'm a sort of historical left-over in this world.'

'At your age! Why you've all your life ahead of you.'

'Not in that sense. I mean, I've become a stranger in my own country. I only hung on to this life because it pleased Rhoda. Now I've lost everything.'

'Apologise to Rhoda. Try again.'

The Consort shook his head. 'That wouldn't help. They' – he meant Rhoda and Neville – 'really despise me. I know how they patronise me. I'm not clever. My only thing is that I loved Rhoda very deeply. Sincerely. I still do.'

'I understand you'd met someone else in Bahrain.'

'I have. She's the wife of a man on attachment from London to the Bahrain Government. She hates the place. You know, bored by uncivilised people and vulgarity – the husband rather a nit – you know the sort of mix-up – and I felt neglected and alone. Rhoda hadn't written for over a week, and I thought I'd be better off if we separated. I got talking to the lady about my life and grew sorry for myself and that was that. We sort of fell sobbing into one another's arms. But whether it means any more than that, only God knows. We've given ourselves a couple of months to think things over. If I thought Rhoda and I could make a go of things I'd take back everything like a shot.'

'Oh dear, oh dear, oh dear, what a mess! I do see your point about her, all the same. It never ceases to amaze me how much women like her think they can get away with. They imagine they've only got to fascinate their menfolk to get away with murder, almost.' Her rich, contralto voice vibrated with sympathy.

'The brother and sister feed one another's vanities. Coming out, they were the talk of the ship – attitudinising, making drama out of everything. She was quite embarrassing. She turns everything into The Play of My Life – and people enter as small-part actors. Neville has exactly the same attitude.'

The Consort nodded. 'I always understood this. It explains why they called me The Consort between themselves.'

They fell silent. 'Do you think she will go ahead with the legal separation?'

The Duchess thought a moment and then shrugged. 'What can she do if she returns to England? I suppose she'll teach, or something. After all she can't have so much of her father's legacy left. All those books and things.' The Duchess looked vicious. 'Unless it was your money.'

The Consort was vexed. 'I wouldn't have wanted my wife not to have the things she was used to. I didn't care whose money she spent so long as she was happy.'

The Duchess had made a false step and the poor Consort was left asking himself why people had never respected his marriage. He showed plainly that he wanted to be alone. He was angry with himself and The Duchess.

He went swimming before lunch and came back just as Neville was leaving. Both started guiltily and would have passed without a word had not The Consort's resentment made him rash. 'Oh, Neville, could I have a word with you?'

Pretending he had not noticed his brother-in-law, Neville stopped with a theatrical, 'Oh, hello, John!' They sat down on one of the white iron benches under the blue jasmine.

'Your sister tells me she'll refuse a divorce. Out of spite, I suppose. Naturally, she's cut up.'

Neville was uncomfortable; for once, he had no idea what to say.

'I'd like you to get her to do the right thing by me. Get her to take that polaroid snap to her solicitor as soon as she gets back to London – or even set the ball rolling from here.'

'I can't interfere, John. That's between you and Rhoda.'

'I don't agree. You've been pretty close to her all along. She listens to you when she wouldn't listen to other people.' He meant 'myself'.

'It's not my place.'

'It could be in your interest. Out of gratitude to me that I stopped a report going through to your boss Armstrong about your relationship with our friend Iskander. You look shaken, dear boy. So was I. I could hardly believe anyone remotely connected with me would get involved with that bully-boy. I don't suppose you ever realised he's got at least three political murders chalked up to his account on behalf of the Egyptians? He's one of their strong-arm men. He helped keep things going in the coup that failed and he's been living since then on the money he picked up at the time. Our lot have naturally had their eyes on him for years, and, as soon as you swam into his orbit, our people took an interest in you, too. It was embarrassing – to say the least – especially as Iskander was making rather extravagant claims about the extent of your relationship and the favours you were granting him. You get me?'

Neville's voice was almost disembodied. 'He was one of those off-beat acquaintances one makes in this part of the world.'

'You never asked yourself where he got all his money? That big house? That car? And no visible means of support. A fine friend. A human rat who'll be the first – I hope – to get done when any new trouble breaks out. I don't think he can do much harm to the Thomsons, but I'd warn them, all the same.'

They noticed Rhoda's head among the jasmine garlands of the upper gallery. 'If you'd like to go to speak to your sister now, I'd be most grateful.'

'I'll speak to her later. I have an appointment.'

He broke away and ran down the steps. The Consort watched him go. He was smiling. 'That makes me quits with the little tick.'

Shaken and afraid, Rhoda telephoned her brother to find out what The Consort had said.

'Oh, nothing much. He wanted me to persuade you to divorce him.'

'So that he can marry that old bag from Bahrain?'

'I suppose so.'

'Why should I clear out to suit him?'

Despite himself, Neville took The Consort's side. 'Oh, come on. You've often said you never really wanted him.'

'Oh, I'll think about it. Actually, the whole situation is bizarre. The Duchess and The Consort are holding hands. If I'd got a gun I'd make them walk out of the house with their hands above their heads.'

Neville was not amused. He wondered whether The Consort would tell The Duchess – or even Rhoda – what he had just told him. He was motivated by an entirely irrational fear of people knowing things and so having power over him. Rhoda went on talking about the merits of marriage and separation in a completely irresponsible way. She was, in fact, looking into a mirror as she spoke. He hardly listened – turning over his own gloomy thoughts – until she rapped at him: 'Don't you think we need a change of décor, darling? We're too big for this potty little place. It was time to go. You know me. I'd get rid of The Consort tomorrow if I could. Bye-bye.' She used the favourite Baida farewell. 'Someone's knocking at my door.'

It was a servant calling her for lunch. She ordered a tray in her room.

The Duchess rang Neville shortly afterwards. 'All this means nothing, Neville. It could be forgiven and forgotten in a matter of hours if only Rhoda would speak to John. Neville, you've got to do something to help. I'd let Rhoda slap my face again if it would do any good. My own feelings don't count when this dreadful thing is over my head.'

Neville was surprised. He understood The Consort wanted a divorce.

'He says that. He's like a child in a tantrum. He'll break his favourite toy to spite his nurse. He loves your sister, Neville. He's broken-hearted by the way things are going.'

Neville listened heavily. 'He's a bastard.'

'He's not, Neville. He's a good-hearted, generous boy, but he thinks he's never had a chance. He knows he's not clever like you. He knows Rhoda prefers your company – you amuse her, you keep her up-to-date – he knows all this, but *he-loves-your-sister*. You're throwing away your sister's happiness.'

Neville was shocked by The Duchess. What was the inference of all this? That he had a noxious and unwholesome influence over his sister? The idea had never struck him. He had taken his domination over her for granted.

'I'll give Rhoda a tinkle. But, before I do so, could you get John to ring me, so that I know what he really wants?'

The Consort refused to speak to Neville. 'If only I could get Rhoda away from him everything would be better. I've never had a chance. I've been sulking ever since we married because no one took me seriously. Everything's suffered – my career – my marriage. I've done everything for them, and yet they laugh at me. No, I won't ring him, and he can go to hell, and so can she. If he puts himself before Rhoda's happiness. . . .'

The Duchess hobbled along the verandah to Rhoda's room. She banged on the door.

'Rhoda, you must be sensible. There's too much to throw away.'

'I'll give him the divorce he asks for. Don't worry.'

'But he loves you, Rhoda. You'll have bad luck if you throw away so much affection. Yes, you will!'

'Tell him from me that affection isn't enough. One needs excitement. Respect. Everything he can't give me.'

All this bawled across the room and through the door.

'Oh dear, oh dear! You'll regret this. You've got nothing, do you hear? Nothing.'

'That's my look-out!'

So where were they? Was The Consort anxious to be divorced or was he merely anxious to get rid of Neville? Was The Duchess right? Did she understand them better than they understood themselves? Was Neville standing in the way of a reconciliation?

The listening house might have asked these questions, had walls a voice, as the situation grew more complex and the four people, with crossed lines and broken-off conversations, drifted together, apart, together and apart.

It was hot. The first day of real heat had blown in from the desert, out of the south, and the harsh light had imposed its silent rule over the quarter. In every house people were stretched out on beds and sofas, enjoying their siesta. The Consort went to lie down; The Duchess went to lie down; Rhoda was spread regally on a divan nodding and reviving over a book. The servants, although acutely aware of tension, were asleep.

The merest whisper of breeze caused the drapes at the windows to billow and re-form and billow again; the tendrils and sprays of jasmine swung slowly against the cobalt blue sky – afternoon blue, tense and still. A telephone rang in a villa across the shuttered street, but there was no one to answer it. The ringing went on for a long time before the caller, losing heart, hung up and allowed the leafy, hilly streets to bake and swelter in the afternoon heat.

13

The MEDOC office: Paul Brophy arrived about half-past nine wearing sun-glasses and carrying a newish despatch-case. He was drawn and solemn. A brief word with the doorman, and he passed into the building. His presence in town was known, his arrival expected. The staff broke off their work to greet him and rose, one by one, to put hand on heart and shake hands with him. There was the stillness and tension of a big church ceremony.

Brophy even shook hands with Shamseddine, who asked how Armstrong was. Brophy replied: 'Well, I think,' and moved on into his room. Byrd was seated at a table in Mrs Parslow's office signing cheques. He, too, shook hands with Brophy as though they had not met before. The stillness and tension continued. People waited for a sign but none came.

Brophy left his room and went to a cupboard for a pencil. Mounir came across and offered a lemonade. Brophy shook his head, smiled inscrutably and returned into his room. Mounir looked at his colleagues, shrugged, and went on typing addresses.

Byrd waited for the explosion, the drama, and he noticed that Mrs Parslow kept looking towards Brophy's door, expecting him to come out. Only Brophy's dollish secretary came out and asked Mrs Parslow for several large envelopes. Mr Brophy – it was understood – was gathering his papers together. Mrs Parslow, as much to herself as anyone, said, 'Jesus! I hope to God he clears out quickly,' but Brophy was still in his room, sorting and ripping up papers at the end of the morning. Everyone trooped out sheepishly, leaving him alone in the building.

That was what Brophy's disgrace entailed; that was the end Mrs Parslow and Shamseddine had worked for; and Brophy had let the morning pass without uttering a word of reproach or explanation. About two-thirty, a taxi came and the driver helped him carry his papers and books out of the building. Still wearing his sun-glasses, Brophy drove back into the city holding the lamp – his own property – which had decorated his desk.

14

ALBERT HIJJAZI continued to take a disproportionate interest in Rhoda's affairs and rang up in the evening to invite her and Neville to lunch the next day. The brother and sister arrived at the restaurant in good form; Neville had outgrown anxiety about his brother-in-law's power over him, and Rhoda was carrying a note slipped under her door that morning by The Duchess: 'Don't be a fool. He's only bluffing about the Bahrayne [sic] woman. He's longing for you to give a sign.'

Rhoda's happiness in her regained power over her husband was complete. She was leaving *him*: a position of strength; he wanted her: a position of weakness.

They sat on the terrace, under a canopy, drinking whisky and threw their pistachio shells over the balustrade into the sea.

'And there's to be no reconciliation between you?'

'None. The Dinosaur and I are drifting apart.'

'Their marriage, as they said of King George's life, "is drawing peacefully to its close".'

They had, they said, booked passages that morning, and Neville had told Mrs Parslow he would leave as soon as possible, his loyalty to MEDOC having ended with Paul Brophy's departure.

Hijjazi smiled indulgently. They were infant prodigies, conducting their affairs like grown-up people. 'Then we shall all be in London together.'

'How?'

'I have decided to go to London for a year. I need a change of horizon. After a few years in this town I cannot breathe. I have walked these streets too often; I'm known; people think they know what to expect from me. A time abroad will give me a kind of mystery – even virginity – again.'

They drank, in excitement and pleasure, to their London life. Yes, Rhoda said, it already appeared less bleak.

Rhoda went away to telephone Katherine Thomson, and Hijjazi expressed his admiration for the way she 'maintained her brave front'. Neville knew Hijjazi was fascinated by Rhoda and wanted to talk about her, so he said non-committally: 'We conduct our affairs with style. After a few days, every event should be in perspective. Rhoda expected nothing from her husband, and so she's not touched.'

'But this Bahrain hostess – she must burn your sister.'

Neville looked out over the sea. 'Yes, perhaps. I don't think so. She *ought* to, but she doesn't.'

When Rhoda returned, Hijjazi said: 'If I were to stay in London could you find me a place near you?'

They both agreed. He then asked how long she would stay there. She was unsure. So much depended on the way things happened. She might go back to London University to finish the course she had broken off to marry The Consort. *'Je ne serai pas en Angleterre pour toujours. Simplement pour respirer un peu, pour rétablir mon calme. Et puis je sauterai ailleurs. La vie anglaise n'est pas pour moi; c'est l'exil.'*

On the other hand, English life demanded very little of people. Somehow, in the soft, rain-besprinkled light, 'one fitted in easily'. She would probably spend the summer in a village on Dartmoor, in a friend's house.

'But you will miss this?'

'Of course, who wouldn't? One feels so well. So oneself. But it couldn't go on.'

Hijjazi spoke with real warmth: 'You will be missed. Really, my dear. You and Neville will be missed. You are so bright, always interested in events; never dull. On the whole, we are very dull people here. We are businessmen. Our human relationships are primitive, fickle. We express too much and mean too little.'

'Do you think so?' Rhoda was genuinely surprised. 'I always imagine your relationships are so easy and uncomplicated. I used to be envious. I can't think anyone would miss us. Not here. I feel we never make our mark, and our relationships are like quicksilver. By the time you've picked them up with a little forceps there's only a small bead left – nothing worth much.'

'Ah, now you are bitter.'

'Not at all.' What did he want her to confess? 'I'm not in the least bitter. It would take more than The Dinosaur to make me bitter.'

Hijjazi's phrase had replaced 'The Consort' in their private vocabulary. It had cheered her on a dark day and put the seal of heroic nonsense on her marriage; now it was a point of departure for further amusement and self-dramatisation. Over coffee, Hijjazi again returned to the broken marriage: 'I can't believe your Dinosaur was not in love with you.'

'I dare say. But he was jealous of Neville. The change came when Neville came back for the second time and The Duchess – my stepmother – fed his resentment. They think Neville has too much influence over me. It could be true.' She looked at Neville speculatively. 'We grew up together. It has always seemed natural for me to tell him everything. Maybe it's wrong.'

Still Hijjazi could not understand how a man could destroy his marriage because of dislike, distrust or even jealousy of the brother. It was Turkish, Hijjazi said, to destroy everything in order to eliminate one hated object.

'Well, that's it. You become western, and we become oriental.'

Hijjazi recalled, for no especial reason, the anti-Greek riots in Istanbul over Cyprus: 'I was on vacation there at the time. I saw the Turks burning Greek property – houses, shops, churches, everything. It was madness. They even burned Turkish buildings. The mob was mad. Mad! Afterwards – hundreds of dead, millions of pounds' worth of damage – the

Turks wept for shame. A friend told me, "The Greeks had no right to drive us to such a point." Yes, people need protecting from themselves.'

15

DR ARMSTRONG flew out, without informing the office, and contacted Neville. They met, like plotters at the twenty-third hour, and Armstrong offered Brophy's place to Neville again. Neville began shaking his head before Armstrong had finished, and Armstrong said brutally, 'Let me finish what I'm saying first.'

Equally brutally: 'What's the use? I'm quitting for home.'

The history of the end of Rhoda's marriage was painful, but Dr Armstrong did not see how it could affect Neville's future. He tried to bully Neville as he had bullied Brophy in the past: 'It's an opportunity of a lifetime – a salary and situation really worth something, and you're not yet thirty.'

Neville shook his head. 'I might have considered it had you got rid of Mrs Parslow and Shamseddine, not otherwise.'

'The two people I most trust in the world. They've stood by me through thick and thin. A real team I can trust.'

'Well, I don't.'

Armstrong glared; he was put out. He had never imagined Neville would refuse his offer. There was only Reggie Byrd left – the last hope to keep one English staffman during the general rout.

16

HE handed Byrd a stiff whisky and sat down. 'I'm ten years older than when I last saw you, Reggie. This sad business about Paul has about killed me. We're of the wrong generation to take these scandals like a dose of salts.' He shook his head, half-theatrically. He really did not know what he was supposed to feel – or how Byrd would react. Byrd nodded primly; he wanted Armstrong to know he disapproved of him. Armstrong thought he looked diminished – or was it because he was sitting in an enormous chair? At all events, his nose seemed sharper, his neck stringier. After hearing about Dr Armstrong's rheumatics and his elder son's wedding he raised the matter of the letter. Armstrong was taken by surprise.

'It was private, Fred. You hadn't any right to show it.'

Armstrong gathered himself together for a bright smile. 'In this sort of affair is anything served by being two-faced? What you said was true, and Paul Brophy had to be told. I'd had my suspicions, and his usefulness to us was at an end. In this world you can't have that sort of reputation and hold a position or responsibility. I've done well by him – compensation for loss of office, some paid leave, the usual.' He sighed. 'There must have been instability in the family. His old man was as nutty as a fruit-cake.'

'He was treated abominably, all the same.'

'Oh, I agree. But would he really mind? Didn't he always have a sort of Christ complex? I used to think so. Oh, I can't explain. . . . Very mysterious and troubling. Yes, that's the word. He was a troubling sort of person.'

He pressed tobacco into the bowl of his pipe. 'Now, don't think I'm getting rid of Paul because he's a queer. I'm doing it because he's not the man for the job. A bad choice. I've got nothing against queers; and I'd have defended Brophy had he been a good man.' Armstrong's pipe-stem jabbed home each word, while he smiled with pleasure at his own lucidity. He got up and led Byrd, still disapproving, still frosty, towards the dining-room, where they took a seat by the window. From afar, they looked like two successful businessmen with their interest wholly engaged by the columns of expensive dishes. 'What will you begin with, Reggie?'

Byrd thought a while, but was unable to concentrate. He was marvelling at Armstrong's casuistry, at his ability to cheat every inch of the way and alter the rules as he went along. Armstrong, while caressing his beard, gave long, detailed instructions how he wanted his veal to the waiter, and, when he turned to Byrd again, it was to offer him Brophy's place. Byrd shook his head.

'You think about it. Your trip here has done you the world of good. Didn't I say it would put new sparkle into you? Your wife won't know you when you get home.'

Byrd was not even momentarily tempted. Everything Armstrong said was false, calculated to other ends. 'I should have to work with Dot Parslow and Shamseddine. They're poison.'

'I've spoken to them – or I'm going to. Don't worry on that score. You'll get on with them. You aren't a Paul Brophy with his entourage of flimsy would-be intellectuals, waffling away about Islam. You've got your feet on the ground: the sort of man we want.'

'But Dot Parslow and Shamseddine . . . their hands aren't clean. How can you ask me to work with them? You must think I've got no taste or finesse.'

'But what's wrong with them?' Armstrong looked him straight in the eye. 'Dot Parslow tells me she's done everything for you, but you kept her at arm's length. You say you don't trust her. How can you say such things? She's a good-hearted person. Longing to be friendly and helpful. A bit rough at the edges, like lots of Australians.'

'How nice for her if she believes that, and for you if you believe it. I don't. I feel I've taken part in a crime. There's no no blood, no one's dead; but there's been a crime, and it will live on in our consciences. I feel I did the same for Brophy as I did for wounded men in the desert: shot them to put them out of their misery. You allowed a weak, vulnerable man to fall into their trap.'

Armstrong sighed deeply. 'In a way, I suppose I'm to blame. Just before Brophy came out I was talking to Shamseddine and happened to hint that he had a reputation for liking boys.'

'You took him on, knowing this?'

'It was never proved, mind you!'

'Yet you told Shamseddine . . .'

'I wanted him to bear it in mind . . .'

'And Shamseddine knew how to please Brophy best.'

'What do you mean?'

'Well, he put one of his creatures up to the job of seducing Brophy.'

'Never. You're mad. Really, Reggie!'

'That's my honest opinion.'

Armstrong stopped sipping his glass and sat back. 'You've

caught the Arab virus – what I call *Bacillus comploticus*. People see plots, stratagems, wickedness everywhere. No, Reggie. Not Michel. You're quite wrong.'

'I insist I'm right.'

'I know Michel has been under pressure – every business house is, to a certain extent – to give the secret police information about how the office worked; and I told him to tell everything. After all, we've nothing to hide. Michel is not a bully and a tyrant. He's not to blame.'

Byrd tried to explain where and how he had formed this impression, but Armstrong would not listen. 'If anyone's to blame it's this chap here.' He tapped the front of his white shirt. 'I'm not afraid to say I made a big mistake.' To Byrd he seemed phoney in the North American way. 'Yes, Reggie, we all make one mistake; that was mine.'

He almost succeeded in making this sound like the fulfilment of a specious rule of life whereby each man is allowed one unholy gaffe and then automatically forgiven. The sad and shaken Byrd, who had looked up to Armstrong, who had been happy to name him as his *patron*, had to ask himself how he could ever have believed in the man. Everything had been misted over by expense-account values; there was nothing to appeal to in the end.

Byrd looked up: 'We're only little pawns you use, I'm afraid. You expect us to swallow the unmentionable and go on from there.'

'I do no such thing. I expect you to be realists; and, in your case, to see which side your bread is buttered. I offer you the best job anyone of your age can get, and you turn it down. You have scruples, I suppose. You don't seem to realise that on this cocktail circuit everything gets forgotten in a couple of years. In three years, there's an almost complete turnover of personnel. Everything would have been forgotten, and you and your wife would have been happy here.'

'It's not what I said at all.'

'I know; but it's in the back of your mind.'

Was it? Byrd hardly knew, and the rest of the meal passed in a daze, an unclear vision of himself. Somewhere, the impression was forming that he had been bought and used and was being returned to Armstrong's chess-box.

Armstrong – still stroking his beard – saw him to the door

in due course. 'Remember, if you change your mind before the end of the month that will be fine by me.'

17

So Armstrong had not believed him; Byrd's scruples had been discounted – in the same way as the seaport itself discounted him. Byrd, for want of anything better to do, went to the Beach Club and fell asleep in the shade of his umbrella. When he woke up he felt he had the whole picture of events in his own mind in detail and order (it was an illusion, but a common one), and the more he knew the more he felt sorry for Brophy. Had he known what he then knew he might have acted otherwise – might not have written that letter at all. The motives leading to that fatal act had been intertwined (concern about his money, concern about the Tunisian, concern about his own reputation); but what were all these in the light of the crime against Brophy?

Recognition of error, revelation of truth; a kind of illumination changed Byrd's attitude entirely, and he saw with what ease he had been influenced by Mrs Parslow and Shamseddine, how he had played their game without being in sympathy with them. He wished he had gone home. He wished he had never come.

What is the value of these moments of illumination if they come too late? Or find people without any means of acting on them? Useless knowledge, useless intuitions, useless sympathy, like Byrd's early gifts as a poet, had come and vanished, leaving him forever haunted.

He went into the water but was too tense, too unhappy, to enjoy himself; he could not give himself to the pleasures he had once had; and this failure summed up all the lost joys, the tarnished innocent pleasures of his visit. Under the Delian, the sublime, sky, he was living out his part in a crime.

In those parts, you take responsibility for your own errors of judgement, no one will help you until you help yourself. All the same, Byrd thought he would like to go to see Brophy and make some sort of gesture. He hardly knew what to do; apology was uncalled for – in any case, he was too proud – but a gesture of some kind was needed to mitigate however oddly and tastelessly the effects of people's barbarity on Paul Brophy's life. He would try to do the decent thing.

He went to Blue Dome Building and was able to reach Brophy's floor without being seen by the concierge. He rang the bell, but there was no answering tinkle from the depths of the flat. So he knocked as loudly as he could – loudly enough to bring the half-crazy evangelical woman to the door of the Americans' flat. She looked out, caught Byrd's hostile eye and withdrew. He knocked again. Still no reply. But Byrd had the curious sense of being close to someone. The other side of the door someone was standing, still peeping through the judas and waiting for him to go away. Eventually Byrd grew uncomfortable and went away. He had not been wrong : the person the other side of the door was Brophy, holding a glass of whisky, blinking at the door, wondering what the hell the man wanted, and determined not to open. It was his last evening in the flat, and most of his goods were packed. The Tunisian had disappeared.

Byrd wandered back through the late-afternoon heat to the Opera House Square and flopped down on the terrace of a restaurant. He felt he owed himself a drink. He leaned back in his wicker chair and crossed his legs. A bootblack came and for twenty-five piastres brought up the Byrd shoes to their usual pitch of perfection. He was watching the man working his velvet cloth and cracking it like a whip when a European girl, greatly affected by the heat, came into Byrd's line of vision. She was a vivid, red-haired girl with the solid hips and arms which Byrd admired in a woman. She wore the usual huge sun-glasses and a green dress, slit about six inches up the thighs. Byrd gathered she had been walking about, because the cloth under her armpits was sweat-stained in an unsightly way.

Byrd was fascinated; something off-key and out of keeping could not be easily explained. It was only when the girl climbed the steps on to the terrace and crossed towards a vacant table that he realised what it was : although bare-armed and hatless, she was white-skinned, untouched by the sun; but more striking that this was her loneliness. She carried her isolation with her in the way a saint carries his aureole; it was a terrifying isolation, like a badge of office. It was not the isolation which could end by a glimpse of someone known, because she gave the impression of someone who had – at least for the time being – ceased expecting anything of other people.

Byrd embarrassed her, so he looked away; but he began looking at her again as she dabbed her face and ate an ice-cream with an exaggerated curl of her deeply pearled lips. The ice-cream went – she clearly enjoyed it – and was followed by a Turkish coffee, which she drank in the local way with iced water. The coffee drunk, she glanced swiftly towards Byrd and then away across the street. She sat for a little time in this dead-alive position before paying her bill, pushing her sun-glasses firmly into place and walking away. She stood at the edge of the pavement, looked up and down and then turned right; it hardly mattered which way she went.

Later, walking towards his evangelical guest-house, Byrd missed his footing on a section of broken pavement – one of the thousands of botched repairs that make Baida's sidewalks a menace – and twisted his ankle. Deltas of sharp pain shot up his leg and forced him to sit on a low wall. In the midst of his nausea he suddenly longed for the pavements he knew and could trust. O Christ, what a place. It promises everything and gives nothing. He had had enough. He would be counting the days until he returned. It was the watershed of his stay.

18

Rhoda and Neville did not contact Brophy. Such a man could bring nothing but bad luck, and they wished him elsewhere. He hung on far longer than anyone expected, and when he eventually telephoned them it was with a justifiable reproach. He was packed up, the flat was dismantled, but he wanted them to have a last drink with him. He did not express himself clearly and they assumed he was having a small get-together. When they arrived he was alone in the ghostly splendours of his apartment, a lonely, self-possessed figure in slacks and a pullover.

'You're doing the same thing as we are,' was all Rhoda could find to say. 'It's the most beastly job.'

'It's all I've got left of my life here.' He indicated the packing-cases. 'I have to ask myself that this has really happened. I can't believe I deserved it.'

Neville and Rhoda looked at one another, said nothing, and waited for Brophy to finish pouring their drinks. He did so, sat down, raised his glass. 'And how are things with you?'

'The Duchess has gone.'

'I'm sorry not to have said good-bye to her.'

'Whatever for? She didn't mean anything to you.'

'She was always kindly to me. I felt she understood me. I had a friend there.'

'You don't know The Duchess.'

Brophy was determined to hold on to something with which to oppose his guests. 'She was a very lonely person. I understood her.'

'Well why not go to see her? She's staying with the Ghanems until she sails, I believe.' Neville's eyes flashed angrily. 'Why not ring the Ghanems now. They'll be glad to invite you over to have a last drink with your dear old friend Shamseddine. I suppose you don't bear him any ill-will, either.'

Brophy blushed and stirred uncomfortably.

The two men looked at their glasses, half-dazed by the outburst of real hostility. Brophy lit a cigarette. With his eyes half-closed because of the smoke he looked at the ceiling and said he had been disappointed by the way Rhoda and Neville had abandoned him in his difficulties.

'Paul, you're unreasonable. What could we do for you?'

'I'm surprised you're still at MEDOC. I know you don't have to leave because I've left, but I'm surprised you found it the friendly thing to stay on, since I was the one who took you on.'

Neville was at a loss for words. 'I'm leaving within a matter of days. We're going home.'

Brophy nodded. 'Oh, I see!' He drained his glass. 'So if you go, Reggie Byrd will take over. He and Fred are old pals.'

'I doubt it, don't you, Neville?' Rhoda dismissed the suspicions she had herself put in Brophy's mind. 'Byrd is much too lightweight to be considered for the job. Why, that senile old Dr Armstrong offered it to Neville.'

Brophy's expression was electric with jealousy and suspicion.

'That alters the case completely. You ought to have told me at the time. A most telling piece of information. It alters my recall completely. I suppose you've accepted?'

Neville was caught between his sister's indiscretion – was it deliberate? – and Brophy's hatred. 'I've said I'm going home with Rhoda. And I'm not coming back. What's suspicious in that? I'd look on the MEDOC job like a sentence of death.'

'You don't. You want to go there, really. You've always wanted my place. I've always suspected you of being jealous of me. I'm not taken in by your bluff.' His heavy lips and cheeks shook with temper.

'Steady on. Steady on. You've lost your head, haven't you?'

'I'm extremely hurt by your duplicity, Neville.' It was one of the few occasions when Brophy had used his name. 'I fault you for not telling me more, and at once. A most telling piece of information in the light of the way Fred treated me. I shall have to remember that and look into it.'

Neville had a foretaste of Brophy's future: a bed-sitter in Clapham or Finsbury Park and an endless search under a bed for vital missing documents in battered suitcases. There was a knock at the door, and while Brophy was away Neville told his sister to finish her drink so that they could leave. They were standing when Brophy returned. 'But you've hardly come . . .' He looked around pathetically; it was clear that at that moment his world was no longer solid. 'Please stay. If you go I'll be alone here with my thoughts, and I can't bear that.'

'We've so much to do.'

'Please stay.'

'Well, fifteen minutes, then.'

He poured another round of drinks and handed round some soggy cheese biscuits. He sat down and buried his head in his large hands. 'I feel so ill, I want to die.'

The brother and sister stared at him expressionlessly. Then Rhoda got up and knelt down at his side. 'What can we do?' She went to put her arm around him, a thing she had never done before, and he squirmed, he drew away in repugnance. It was as though her face had been slapped. He put his hand out in a gesture of vague apology. 'Please. Don't mistake me. It's just that I've always been like that. I can't help myself however much I've tried. I never told you, but I felt you understood.

I don't suppose anyone really understands what it's like.'

'Oh dear.' Rhoda suddenly realised what he was trying to say, and her hands went up to her face in the same gesture she used in the art gallery. 'Please don't say any more.'

'Yes, I'd like to explain. I'm always trying to explain. It's so terrible to be misunderstood. One is always being misunderstood.'

'I'm a woman, Paul. Please don't tell me. I wouldn't understand. I wouldn't know what to say.'

Brophy swallowed. 'You see, I feel I'm always being judged by the rest of the world by my results while they feel secure in the rightness of their intentions. I have my intentions, too. I do want to make the world a better place. I do want to help people. When I did it in the office I was misunderstood and derided, and now nobody sees anything in what I did except wickedness. The intentions were good but because I'm labelled a queer, they don't . . .'

Rhoda cried out. 'Don't. Don't. I can't bear you to say it. I can't bear it.' She picked up her handbag. 'I must go. Neville can stay if he likes.'

Neville indicated by an eyebrow that he would come with her. Suddenly, Brophy was his old apologetic self. 'Have I said anything out of place? If I have I'm sorry. I wanted to tell you. Perhaps one day there won't be any need to do it in this melodramatic and offensive way and perhaps you'll like me in spite of it.'

Rhoda was near to tears. 'It makes no difference to us, Paul. Really. You know us. We're free people. People's lives are their own affair.'

Brophy looked at her quizzically. 'That's a foolish thing to say. They're not at all. I would like to share my heartaches and triumphs just the same as anyone else. Why not? They're the only heartaches I have.'

They were able to tear themselves away; they fled the apartment like rich people fleeing a plague. They were too guilty, too appalled to speak to one another: for a moment someone close to them had been about to fling himself on their affection and goodwill, and they had panicked: they feared involvement.

In the taxi, driving to Neville's flat, Rhoda behaved like a woman who has seen an accident, something unspeakable. All the free discussion of Brophy's case, all the delicious pirouetting around his problem cut short by a glimpse into his Gehenna.

Neville's reaction was more complex because he knew he was letting down a friend and a patron. He stared a long time at the cigarette burning between his fingers, until the telephone rang. He went into his bedroom and closed the door after him, fearing an out-of-place caller. It was Hello Dolly! She wanted to come round as she was 'in dead trouble'. Her employer had sacked her and owed her a month's wages. Could Rhoda's husband do something for her as an embassy man. 'I'm a British subject, don't forget.'

Why had the boss dished her? Oh, he'd been niggly ever since she'd found out her co-worker was a transvestite. The boss had been picking on her for several weeks, and she'd been walking around looking for jobs. She'd found one, but she still wanted her back pay. Neville bit the side of a nail carefully, and looked at his hands. Why didn't she get in touch with the British Consul? His brother-in-law was involved in other matters. The girl had set her heart on Rhoda's husband helping her. For some obscure reason, Neville could not bring himself to tell the girl his sister and her husband had parted; he fobbed her off with some vague excuse. The matter was left – as they say – in mid-air. Rhoda was horrified at getting involved in such an affair. 'What a damned silly person she must be to think The Consort would help her. She was the cause of half the trouble.' Rhoda's enthusiasm for the Habitat girl had gone the way of many others. 'What a stupid bitch she must be. Only imagine: to think we could help her with her greasy boss.'

That evening, it became plain that their good humour with one another, their shared laughter and their mutual indulgence had disappeared. Both vaguely resented the part the other had played in the disaster.

'I suppose,' she suddenly said, 'we could have asked Paul Brophy to travel home with us. I feel guilty about him.'

'Never. He's bad luck personified. It's like asking for things to go wrong to be involved with him. What a damned silly thing to suggest, darling.'

He knew she was talking for the sake of talking, and it irritated him. There had been too much of it in the past and too little thinking. He went on smoking, an unusually intense indulgence for him. The telephone rang again. This time it was Brophy, who was much the worse for wear. His voice was imperious and aggressive, the young pretender reborn. Would Neville explain how he had come to discuss Armstrong's offer of the manager's position and why, he, Neville, as an old friend, had kept this information to himself? 'I take it as an unfriendly, disloyal act to have kept this to yourself.'

Neville threw his cigarette into the empty fireplace – a gesture everyone seemed to be repeating as their insecure relationships came to pieces.

'Listen, Paul. Do you know the old saying that two and two makes five, five equals red and red means apple pie? You don't? Well, you ought to, because it fits your case. I can't tell you what happened because I've forgotten.'

Neville slammed down the receiver and then, after a short pause, lifted it off the rest and cut himself off.

He turned in fury on his sister, who was leaning at the bedroom door with her hair falling half over her face. 'Thank you, for that. That's your work. I hope you're satisfied. You opened your bloody mouth once too often, and now Brophy will dog me with questions for the rest of my life! You never think, do you? Never. And that idiot will be on my tail for ever.' All Neville's horror of involvement was in his voice. She drew back her hair and half swivelled her nineteen-thirties head. 'I'm very sorry. I apologise.' She was deeply shaken by his anger, which was almost on the edge of hatred.

19

ALL the same, they were much together in those last days, and being given to intuitions and attaching importance to signs and portents, they were open to presages about their coming life. Their foreign experience having short-circuited, they were off back to Europe with what they decided to salvage of their books, their trophies, their Hebron and Damascus glass, their Moroccan materials.

Once The Consort cleared out of the house, the brother and

sister were free to receive those intimations of their future life which providence cared to give them.

They talked endlessly about their next move, and it seemed Rhoda's plan to resume her university course would triumph when, seated among the books she was packing away, she picked up her little 'Livre de Poche' Nerval and opened the book at random.

'*Quand* [she read] *le soleil du soir*
parcourt les Tuileries
Et jette l'incendie aux vitres du château;
Je suis la Grande Allée et ses deux pièces d'eau
Tout plongé dans mes rêveries!'

She read on, as one charmed. How absurd to have missed the cue: Western Europe wasn't only London, it was also Paris or Madrid. Within a short time the casual reading of Nerval had changed her life.

'I was overwhelmed by nostalgia, for all that life that's buried in one – after all, one's roots are there.'

People did not know what she meant by this, but eventually it came to be accepted that London would see her long enough to start her divorce, and then she'd go off to Paris. She spoke of a friend there who restored pictures, who would take her as a pupil.

Even people who hated Rhoda's guts, her self-sufficiency and her ability to be in on the big scene, were struck by this capacity to pick up the pieces of her life and go onwards, if not triumphantly, at least with purpose. Of course, all the people who had known themselves excluded from her private universe or zoo, had a gala day of unfelt sympathy for the husband and deeply-felt loathing for Rhoda herself. 'Ah,' they said, on hearing that she and Neville were giving a farewell party on the *Zeus*, 'Ah, no one will want to know them now that they've been cut down to size. They will be ignored as they deserve to be.'

They could not have misjudged more completely the hold the brother and sister had on their Arab friends. They had never been understood entirely or, perhaps, approved of, but to the local intellectuals and artists who had been among their friends Neville and Rhoda had had one inestimable quality: they had got to know them as human beings, not objects, they had tried to know the local life and the way people had been formed and they had responded to the poetic quality in Baidani life. The old Arabic civilisation, in ruins from the hatred of too many conquerors, too many indifferent people, was still real to its own children; and they cherished those who loved what they themselves did.

20

THE first people who came aboard that late spring evening were Mr and Mrs Macrae. They were going to another farewell party, the one given by John Bowman, one of the British Council bores, and his wife, who were returning home for reposting. The parties were in the same bar, a little separated by other travellers. Rhoda and Neville were surprised by John Macrae's approach, and imagined he had made a mistake. Nothing of the kind; he had brought his life along to meet Rhoda. They were offered champagne and sat down. Macrae crossed his legs and showed an elaborate clock on his midnight-blue silk socks. His silk suit had the shimmer and splendour of the brand-new, only equalled by his wife's parma violet trouser-suit, also in silk. They had arrived. From hours on the beach, at one of the smart clubs, they were already bronzed and hale. Macrae had also grown a moustache, which he smoothed from time to time. The most amazing change came from within: he had been appointed, temporarily, to The Consort's position and had lost his angry bluster and the red, bucolic look so despised by Rhoda. The wife was stunning – full of goodwill and simple good nature – and smiled at Rhoda in the ecstatic way of a fan meeting a star. She made Rhoda feel a bit soiled.

Yes, they said, they were settling down fine. Macrae had decided that he liked the place and the people. 'Oh, we've met such charming Baidanis,' his wife put in, implying this was a vision granted only to the few. 'Most agreeable,' Macrae agreed. Success had made him charitable; he over-estimated people's virtues and played down their incompetence, venality and

314

nastiness. Rhoda and Neville realised that these opinions were based on no sort of real involvement – the people excited him like cardboard cut-outs.

Even about the local food he had grown poised and tolerant in a flip way. Yes, he liked the Turkish *mezzé* well enough; he had 'always wanted to live on cocktail snacks.'

'Sad thing about your friend Paul Brophy.' The remark fell into a well of silence and created huge ripples. 'I was told he had to be practically carried on to the plane yesterday. Absolutely blotto.'

Neville had been told otherwise: that Brophy had injured his foot when a packing case fell on him in his flat, and he was taken to the plane in a wheel-chair and half carried up the steps to the plane by an airline official. Even to the end, rumour and misinterpretation pursued him; there would soon be enough half-true stories flying around to serve as the basis for twenty-five cults.

Rhoda and Neville, distracted by the appearance of the Thomsons, heard Macrae say, 'Fancy wrecking your career for the sake of a black boy!'

The remark passed unchallenged – it was the sort one would fume about later – and the Macraes made their exit.

'Katherine darling,' – smacking kiss – 'thank God' – smacking kiss – 'you've come. We had a visit from The New Merito-cracy: the man who drove The Consort back into the arms of Old Mother England and His Dear Old Dad.'

Neville had put his glasses on and was looking pinched and worried. He smiled vaguely as the Thomsons responded to Rhoda's good humour.

'They're dressed in silk from top to toe like a Delhi Durbar. My first working-class neo-colonialists. *Nunc dimittis.* I've seen everything.'

Katherine Thomson wanted to know how the packing up and the closing of the house had gone, and was given the name of the new tenants as people to visit. There was not, apparently, a shade of regret in Rhoda's voice. Only one thing had gone wrong: in embarking, she had lost a small blue flowered Japanese case containing her address book and her reading for the trip; nothing had any great instrinsic value, but, for the immediate future, it would be like walking with a limp.

Albert Hijjazi arrived, as curious about other people as ever. A lost case, he said, was a good omen. It meant Rhoda would return. 'Even a part of you cannot bear to leave us.'

She was glad to hear this for, despite her indifference, she knew she would be homesick, for her house, for its interiors, for the view of the mountains and the flocks of doves from its windows. 'Do you think it means that?' There was real tenderness in her eyes.

Hijjazi was sure she would return. 'There's always a way back to the place you love. But after Paris,' – he had said he would join her there – 'after a period away.'

To each new arrival she told the story of the case that had gone astray and its portent for her return. Salma Khittar hugged her. 'It would be worth losing all your jew-ils to come back here where people love you. Friendship is worth more than pearls.'

'You lose your case but you take our hearts,' someone else said. Everyone said heart-warming things to help her bear up. To her Arab friends she had become a woman who had been put aside because she was barren; The Consort, they believed, had gone to make his heirs elsewhere.

For Rhoda, softened a little by champagne, the case came to represent all the things she was losing, and she was already diminished, less than half her old self, an orphan. After all, she had no mother, no father, no husband, and she was losing her brother.

Rhoda and Neville were so engrossed by their guests that they failed to appreciate what a huge affair the Bowmans' party was. It seemed to have attracted every bore on the local cock-tail circuit – the British Council bores, the Embassy bores, the academic bores: it gave out a smell of Woodford Green on Sunday morning. Out of this royal flush of bores came Doris Parslow. She had been slugging back the whisky and decided to go across to say good-bye to the brother and sister. 'Hello, old boy! Just came along to say *"Au Revoir"*!' She had never seemed to Rhoda more raw-boned, more colonial. She looked at her distantly, at her most Theda Bara, as much as to say. 'Darling, I suppose we have met?' They imagined she would shake hands and go away. On the contrary, Mrs Parslow stayed and made an effort to place a wreath on Brophy's cenotaph. 'What a pity about your friend Paul! What a *shaim*! A chap like that from a good family – well connected – plenty of talent – what a *shaim*! I really feel sorry for people like that.'

She leaned close. 'I thought he would never go. He seemed to stay on for ever. He was trying to pin something on that poor old thing we're saddled with in his place. Paul thought he was after his job – as though such a man would get a job with MEDOC. No sir! Never. We're mighty careful who we have.'

Waving her glass, laughing raucously, grating on everyone's sensibilities, Mrs Parslow might have been giving an imitation of the sort of behaviour she had condemned in Brophy. People turned away from her, and, eventually, John Bowman came across to claim his guest. Their party was closing down, in any case, the guests were joining hands to sing Auld Lang Syne. Mrs Bowman had a pleasing contralto – the sort with the built-in tremolo much loved in English ladies' choirs. She was having a gala day and towered above her guests like one of the singers of the old school – Clara Butt in the Albert Hall or Madame Kirkby Lunn. She ought to have been singing 'Land of Hope and Glory' on the evening war was declared. With James Pegram from the American Embassy holding her right hand and John McMather of the British Bank of North Africa holding her left, she embodied embattled Britannia counting the blessings of friendship.

To a detached observer there might have been a poignance in the gathering – a group of British people, at the edge of the third world, the last of the Merchant Venturers, the representatives of a nation which had been cut down to size, sending home two of their number. It was all there – all the poignance of departure from old friends, but the Arabs watching from the other party were dry-eyed.

'They are even bigger hypocrites than we are,' someone said and got a general laugh.

While the singing drew to a close a steward came up and said Rhoda's case had been taken to another cabin by mistake: it was now in hers. 'Oh! You've found it!' There was disappointment in her voice and people laughed. 'I've been given my cards, like a servant girl.' She meant: I shan't be returning.

Once the guests had gone, the brother and sister walked around the ship. It was a clear night, and the deck passengers were eating supper, smoking, listening to transistors. Sawt-al-Arab broadcasting its anti-British, anti-imperialist comment-

aries, Israel its martial folk-songs, Radio London a talk on
African problems, were intermingled with an advert for
beauty cream from Cyprus, sentimental music from Athens
and Farid al Atrash from Algiers. From Cyprus, too, came the
close-down of the British Forces Network, the last foothold
of the British in the area. It was both a farewell and a hint of
the normality of home.

'So there we are. That's it. That's the end of our programme
for today. We're closing down until six o'clock tomorrow
morning, when we'll be back on the air with a programme of
morning music and the news. So from all of us here to all of you
there – this is Pete Rogers wishing you a very good night. Good-
night.'

There was a short pause before the Last Post brought the day
to a close.

21

In his last weeks in Baida, Reggie Byrd saw far less of the Exes
than before. Their children came out for the Easter vacation
and there was a slight falling off in the Exes' reception. They
had grown bored with Byrd's too frequent visits. Had he been
a single man they would have said, 'Go and get yourself a girl-
friend and leave us alone.' They appreciated his position, but
they resented him – especially his meanness. During all the
weeks he visited them and ate their meals he never once
brought a bottle of wine or a box of chocolates. Susan Exe felt
Byrd had made a convenience of them. When, eventually, his
time to go off to meet his wife in Rome arrived, he realised that
he ought to take the Exes out for an evening and offered dinner
at the Casino.

They appreciated his invitation, but it had come too late –
the spontaneous flow of friendship and generosity had diminished. They said, 'Come and have pot luck with us.' They made
the excuse that the orchards were in flower: the village was at
its most beautiful, and they went out less and less.

Byrd arrived with a huge bouquet of roses and a box of

sweetmeats. 'Oh, you are sweet,' Susan Exe said, but she was unstirred.

They sat out in the garden with the caged birds, and the Exes looked at Byrd for a last summing-up of his stay.

'It's dragged towards the end. I've been homesick, really. I miss my wife and family. We're really very happy, you know.' He said this defensively, as though he had betrayed them in his heart.

'You made a mistake staying at that dreary pentecostal place. It would give me the griefs.'

John Exe listened and observed. 'What about your writing, Reggie? Did you do your thriller on MEDOC and *l'affaire Brophy*?'

Byrd had finished two things – which he had hopes of placing – but as for the MEDOC book – never. 'I want to put that behind me. It was the most sordid thing that ever I saw. Nothing would be gained by digging up the dead bodies. Nobody came well out of the story – and I include myself. The less said about it the better.'

They were curious to know what happened to Brophy. Byrd had no idea.

'That's the extraordinary thing about the foreign community here,' John Exe said. 'People fill your agenda for months, years, and then drop out. Almost all the people involved in the story will have left the scene in a short time. It's like a play.'

'Well, look at ourselves. We seem so fixed, but in five years we'll be thinking of our retirement.'

The husband and wife exchanged glances. 'Unless we decide to stay on here afterwards.' They went out to look at the orchards, which were already past their best – but it was a beautiful late afternoon, limpid, fresh, with distant cloud-banks over the sea. Climbing towards the house where the Exes bought their eggs and poultry, Byrd stumbled and ricked his foot. He hobbled to a wall and sat down. He was tired and irritated by his mishap – he wanted the Exes to go on while he waited for their return. He leaned on an eucalyptus tree and looked down on the coast, on the city, on the mountains to the west.

That was how the nineteenth century saw the east: a foreground figure relaxing and looking down at a domed and mysterious city; oftentimes a horseman galloped away into the middle distance. It would have been very still, with only the cicadas scratching away in the pine-trees and water tinkling into a garden tank.

That was how it was, and the pleasure of it made Byrd close his eyes. He was half exasperated by the necessity of endurance, half grateful to have a pause by himself while the Exes, especially the wife, who increasingly irritated him by her questions, were away.

Byrd was troubled. He was bored by his life – his foreign experience had all turned sour – and full of forebodings about his return to London. What pained him the most was not the prospect of trying to build up a new life in London but the ends to which it was directed. If only we could live more simply, he thought, and have time for ordinary pleasures. He was tired of keeping five balls in the air; he no longer saw the necessity of doing so. He would never have told Susan Exe and Neville as much, but he felt he and his wife had lived in the past and so had not lived at all. What was the point of a fortnight in Rome as compensation for a lifetime of small change?

There he sat – vain, accident-prone, all his ideas of his own integrity in pieces. New currents were moving in – but almost too late; he could no longer transcend his limitations. Like an old seaside donkey, trained to its hundred yards up and its hundred yards down, he was a creature of custom, the victim of his virtues. Had it all been worth while? There was no answer. Everything was divided, dissociated. His experience abroad had been on two levels all along – the lyrical response to the landscape, where he had found the illumination in the Italian pictures he so much enjoyed, and the horror at human behaviour – the humbug of the MEDOC world, a pale echo of the humbug of the larger business world, whose values it lived by, however corruptly.

He reopened his eyes, and there before him was the evening landscape of the coast: it had all the beauty of things seen in the hours before departure. Above it, the serene sky was about to send another letter to the world. In a few moments even, it would be aflame with its message to the people below; but as there would be no one to read it, there would be no one to give a reply. The two things went on side by side, and there was no connection; the dialogue, as they say in diplomatic circles, had not even begun.